CROW WING DEAD

CROW WING DEAD

Midge Bubany

NORTH STAR PRESS OF ST. CLOUD, INC.
St. Cloud, Minnesota

ISBN 978-1-68201-017-4

First Edition: March 2016

Printed in the United States of America.

Published by
North Star Press of St. Cloud, Inc
PO Box 451
St. Cloud, MN 56302
www.northstarpress.com

To my husband, Tim, who has been my most invaluable supporter
and promoter ... yet calls himself my "driver."

And to law-enforcement officers everywhere
who put their lives on the line daily.

1

May 15
Three days missing.

WHEN BARB HAWKINSON called to tell me her son Mike was missing, my stomach threatened to crawl up my throat.

"When was the last time you heard from him?" I asked.

"Monday morning when he left to see you. I wondered if he talked about his plans."

"Barb, he never showed. I thought he blew me off."

"Oh, God."

"What time did he leave Brainerd?"

"Around ten fifteen. You know how he lives for the fishing opener weekend? Well, he wasn't his happy-go-lucky self. He seemed distracted. When he called you, did he give you any indication what was bothering him?"

"No, he just said he had something he wanted to discuss with me. I have no clue what it was—we haven't spoken for a year."

"A *year*?"

"Yes." *Since the funeral.*

"Well, that absolutely shocks me. Did something happen between you two?"

"No, nothing like that. I guess life just gets in the way."

Whack! A sippy cup hit me in the chest. Throwing objects was Lucy's signal she'd had enough of the highchair. Clara, my sixty-something live-in housekeeper/nanny, lifted her out.

"I tried calling him when he didn't show, but he didn't answer," I said.

"Okay, now I'm *really* worried."

Clara hiked Henry from his highchair, and he toddled off toward his twin sister who'd found the remote control to the television. She turned it on and began flipping through channels. Unbelievable. She was fourteen months. Clara took it from her and turned on Mickey Mouse. I moved into the dining room in order to hear Barb over the din.

1

"What about his wife?"

"Oh, Cat's in Mexico on some *girls'* week—*again*—ten days this time."

"Maybe he had some sort of crisis with work."

"But he *always* calls when he gets home to let me know he's made it. And he *always* returns my texts and calls," she said. "No, in my heart, I know something's wrong."

Mike had been "Hawk" to me since junior high when we guys started creating nicknames for each other. He was his mama's boy. In her eyes, he could do no wrong—even though as a kid he was constantly choosing behavior teetering on the brink of immoral, illegal, or dangerous. Sometimes his activities slid smack into one or more of those categories, and yes, I ended up participating in some risky shit without thought—until there was trouble. And on the rare occasions he was caught because something "went wrong," he always managed to charm himself out of any serious consequences.

For example, when he was sixteen he stole a few of his dad's Grain Belt beers and "borrowed" his grandma's Olds, so he and Adam Sparks—Sparky—could go ice fishing on Gull Lake. Because I had to stay home for a family birthday party, I wasn't able to tag along on that frigid mid-December night when his grandma's car broke through thin ice and ended up in ten feet of water. He chose a spot on Gull Lake not far from where our house was located, so I could sneak out and join them after the birthday party.

It was my Grandma Dee who noticed Hawk and Sparky on all fours outside of our patio door. When she opened the door to let them in, they were close to hypothermia, right in the middle of my Grandpa's birthday party. He shouted orders for Grandma to dial 911, and to the rest of us to get blankets and to strip off their clothing—which we ended up cutting off because it was frozen stiff. I remember being mesmerized by the odd purple color of their lips. Adam's teeth were chattering so hard, he chipped his front tooth. They were whisked off to the hospital in an ambulance.

We didn't know what had happened until we saw the car being pulled from the lake the next morning. As I stood on shore with my family, my Grandpa said to me, "If you ever pull a stunt like that, or are ever remotely involved in anything as idiotically stupid, your life as you know it, will be over."

My mother and grandmother gave me dirty looks of agreement, and although it was never verbalized, I was punished for Hawk's antics. I was not allowed to drive for a month, and I had to be home by ten. Not Hawk. His parents and grandparents were so relieved the boys escaped with their lives and limbs, they lied to the sheriff saying he had permission to use the car.

You'd think with that kind of liberal upbringing, Hawk would be a jerk, but he was one of my favorite people. We were college roommates at St. Cloud State and best men at each other's weddings.

AND NOW HIS MOTHER'S VOICE was quavering as she told me he could be in a ditch somewhere, or because he had a headache the night before he left, he could have had a stroke or a brain tumor and was too sick to answer the phone.

"What does Tom say?" Tom was her husband, the family's voice of reason.

"That I worry too much, but this time I think I have a good reason."

"Wish I could help put your mind at ease."

"Well, I was thinking that you being a detective, you could do something on your end. Check his cell phone records or credit cards or something?"

"Not without a warrant I can't—and Mike and Cat live in Eden Prairie—that's a bit out of Birch County Sheriff Department's jurisdiction."

"Well, to tell you the truth, I'm tempted to drive down to the Cities and check for myself, but I shouldn't go inside their place with the *cat* there."

"The cat? Hawk has a cat?"

"It's Cat's cat, and she bought it knowing full well how allergic I am."

It wasn't the sound of *Cat's cat* that made me grin, but her clever method of keeping her mother-in-law away—with cat dander.

"And Hawk doesn't even like cats," she added.

"Yes, I remember."

He hated them. Hawk and his brother Paul used the neighbor's cat, among other creatures, for slingshot practice.

I said, "Look, I'll make a few calls. See what I can find out. Do you have his work number?"

AFTER DISCONNECTING, I punched in Hawk's cell phone number, but the call immediately rolled over into his message center. I waited for the beep then said: "Hey, Hawk, I was a little concerned when you didn't make lunch on Monday, but I just talked to your mom, and she's freaking out because she can't get hold of you. You need to call her, buddy."

Next, I'd tried the work number Barb had given me. Hawk was a salesman for one of his father-in-law's businesses that manufactured pumps. He hated the job but was afraid to quit because it would displease his wife, which in my opinion, wasn't all that difficult to do. Yeah, Hawk handed his balls over to Cat once they were engaged, and she'd slowly molded him into "Michael." She insisted no one refer to him as Hawk, or even Mike—although *she* wanted to be called Cat, not Catherine. But hey—he let it all happen, didn't he?

A female voice answered, "Ames Lyman Pumps. Our business hours are Monday through Friday between eight and five o'clock. Thank you for calling."

I glanced at my watch—7:16. What was I thinking phoning so early? I'd have to try again later at work.

Clara looked up at me as she ran her hand through her copper red hair. "Everything okay?"

"Yeah, probably. I better get moving. You have blueberries on your T-shirt."

"No matter, it's old."

Clara wore either T-shirts or sweatshirts, jeans, and tennis shoes. When we interviewed her, she asked if it was okay. She said when you were chasing toddlers you had to be quick on your feet. I didn't care what she wore. She not only took care of the twins, she shopped for groceries, cooked, and cleaned—and did it all well.

I kissed the Twinks goodbye—Twinkies come in packages of two like our twins. Just as I made my way to the garage, a blue bi-plane buzzed my rooftop, then rose and did a loop-de-loop. I tried to catch the registration number. My next-door neighbor, Doug Nelson, shouted from his deck, "What the heck? That can't be legal."

"No, he shouldn't be flying so low over residential areas."

"That's the third time this week."

"Is it?"

"Yeah. One time he even flew over upside down. I snapped a picture of it on my phone."

"Good. Send it to me. I'll do some checking." I gave him my email address.

"Some people don't use the brains God gave 'em."

"Nope."

I climbed into my red Ford F-150 extended cab and made my way to the

Birch County Sheriff's Department. Once at my desk, I phoned Rex Balcer, the manager of the Birch County Airport located a mile north of town, and asked if he knew anything about the blue bi-plane.

"Nope, we haven't had a bird like that come in, but I've had a few calls on it this morning. I'll check around. Maybe Brainerd knows something."

"That'd be great. I'm told this was the third time this week. Let me know if you find out anything."

"Will do. In residential areas they have to be 1,000 feet above the largest obstacle. If we can get enough information on him, we can file a report with the FAA."

Rex got right back to me. He said Brainerd didn't know about the plane either, but he would keep checking.

WHEN I CALLED HAWK'S work number, a female voice answered, "Ames, Lyman Pumps. How may I direct your call?"

"Michael Hawkinson, please."

She transferred my call, and I got a pre-recorded message that he was either out of the office or on another call. I left a message after the beep.

I called again and asked for his secretary. After I explained the situation to Val and how worried Michael's family was, she said, "I did expect him back at work on Tuesday morning, but I haven't heard from him."

"Is it typical for him to miss two days of work without letting you know he's going to be gone?"

"Definitely not. He arranges his calendar through me, and if he goes out on the road, I make his reservations."

"And you haven't been concerned he hasn't checked in with you?"

"Well, not until now. I just assumed we had a miscommunication about when he was returning from vacation."

"Has he had any problems at work lately?"

"No, he gets along with everybody and always makes our platinum circle of sales."

"Does he talk to you about his personal life?"

There was a slight hesitation before she answered, "Not really."

"How well do you know him, Val?"

"He's my *boss*."

"That's it? Not friends? You don't socialize after work?"

She let out a scoffing sound. "I'm married if you're thinking we had something going."

"I meant maybe you confided in one another over the water cooler or drinks after work . . . with other employees."

"Once in a while a bunch of us go out for drinks but always in a group. He's a fun, charming guy."

"Yes. Look, if he checks in, tell him to call his parents or me. I'll give you my number in case you think of something."

I then asked if she could transfer me to Cat's father, Irving Ames.

"His office isn't located in this building, but I can give you his secretary's number," Val said.

When I asked to speak to Irving Ames, I was put on hold and subjected to loud, annoying, instrumental music repeating the same few stanzas. I had to hold the phone a couple inches from my ear as I waited.

The first time I met Irving Ames was at Hawk and Cat's wedding rehearsal. He was an imposing figure with his barrel-chest, broad-shoulders and a glare that would stop a bullet. He didn't say much at the rehearsal, but later at the dinner held at Hotel Sofital, he approached me as I was in the bar line. He grabbed onto my hand with a vice-grip and leaned in so close I could smell the hair product he'd used to slick back his full head of black hair. He whispered, "There will be no funny business either tonight or tomorrow at the wedding and reception—no bride-stealing or any such shenanigans."

What popped into my brain was, "Who'd want to steal Cat?" But I had the good sense to mutter, "Absolutely not, sir."

"Good then," he said, and released my hand, which was white from the pressure.

After dessert and when everyone was well into the cups, he came up and smacked me on the back and said, "So far, so good."

"The dinner was delicious, sir."

He didn't respond and walked off.

AFTER A COUPLE EXCRUCIATING minutes of listening to the tinny sound masquerading as music, I was grateful when it ended and someone answered: "Elaine Custer."

"Ms. Custer, this is Detective Cal Sheehan with the Birch County Sheriff's department, and I'd like to speak with Mr. Ames." I used my most polite manner of speaking.

"Mr. Ames is unavailable. May I take a message?"

"Yes, please tell him the Birch County Sheriff has questions regarding his son-in-law's whereabouts."

"Please hold, sir."

"Wait! Have you ever listened to your hold music?" I asked.

Click. The music came back on, but it was only a few seconds before a deep voice barked, "*Who* is this?"

I explained to Irving Ames why Michael's family was concerned and asked if he knew where he was.

"How the hell am I supposed to know where he is? Ask his secretary."

"As I just explained, sir, his secretary, Val, thought he was going to be back on Tuesday and also expressed concern he hadn't been in touch. I understand Cat is out of the country, so I thought I'd check to see if you knew something before we get the Eden Prairie Police Department involved."

"Well, Jesus H. Christ. Maybe he grew a pair and didn't consult his *mama* when he went on a vacation."

Consult his mama?

"You know for a fact he went on a vacation?"

"No. I don't know anything of the kind. I'm saying he shouldn't have to report in to his *mother*."

"Well, here's the thing: If he did extend his vacation, Michael certainly would let his secretary know about it—and his family. He's that kind of guy. Considerate."

Big audible sigh. "You were the best man, weren't you? The big cop?"

"Yes, sir. I'm a detective with Birch County Sheriff's Department."

"Yeah . . . and you cop types *always* think there's something sinister going on somewhere."

"There generally is, sir. And in this case, I'm certain Michael wouldn't take off without letting someone know."

Another sigh. "Well, do what you do."

"Okay, then."

Such concern. Such caring. Such a jerk. Shit. Maybe Ames was behind the disappearance. Then again, maybe I've been watching too many shows like *Justified* and *Breaking Bad* where every other character is a stupid person making stupid decisions. Hawk wasn't stupid, but he was easily bored and had the thrill-seeker gene. Maybe life hadn't been thrilling enough for him lately, so he went on a wild ride.

I called Eden Prairie Police and told the story twice before I got Sergeant Scott Halberg to agree to send a unit over to the Hawkinsons. When he called me back thirty minutes later, he said, "My officer reported no one answered the door, and he could see no evidence of anyone inside. He walked around the entire perimeter, and all the doors and windows were secure. He also mentioned they had a security system."

"His mom is worried he's either sick or injured. I'll see if I can get hold of his wife and suggest a neighbor check the house."

"Good idea," Halberg said. "Mrs. Hawkinson can always call or email me if she wants us to go in on a welfare check."

"I'll let her know."

I then called Ames back to ask for Cat's cell phone number. With great annoyance in his voice, he said, "Just a minute." He didn't put me on hold; maybe he doesn't know how. I could hear fumbling and grunting until he finally read off the number.

"Thank you kindly, sir."

He hung up without saying goodbye. What a knob. You'd think he'd be a little concerned for his daughter's husband.

After five rings, Cat answered. I could barely hear her what with music blasting and people talking and laughing in the background.

"Cat, sorry to bother you on vacation," I said.

"Just a minute. I can't hear you because I'm right under the speaker at the pool."

The music faded slightly. "Okay, so what were you saying?"

"Cat, this is Cal Sheehan."

"Oh . . . hi. What's up? "

"I'm calling because no one has heard from Hawk . . . ah, Michael . . . in a few days. He hasn't shown up for work, and I was wondering when you've last heard from him."

"I haven't talked to him since I left Minneapolis. I'm in Playa del Carmen and these *international* calls are *way out* of network, so we agreed not to call each other."

And yet you have your phone by your side?

"Emailing each other?" I asked.

"No."

"When did you leave on vacation?"

"A week ago yesterday. You say he hasn't been at work?"

"He was expected back on Tuesday, and since it's been over seventy-two hours since anyone has heard from him, the Eden Prairie Police Department did a walk around, but couldn't get inside. Do any of your neighbors have a key? They could go check the house."

"I don't trust any of our neighbors with a key."

"Well then, Eden Prairie PD would be willing to enter the house, maybe check his credit cards to see if there's any activity. I'll give you Sergeant Halberg's phone number, so you can call him directly to give him your permission and security code."

"Just a minute."

I heard her ask someone if she could borrow a pen and paper.

"Okay, what is the sergeant's number?"

After I gave her the number, she said, "Wait. Is this Barb's doing? My God that woman pushes me over the edge sometimes!" She then must have put her hand over her phone because I heard a muffled, "Could I have another of these. Thanks."

"You don't seem too concerned, Cat."

"Not really, no. I'll call Michael to let him know he's got Barb's panties in a bunch."

Nice.

"Good idea," I said, "but regardless, you should call Sergeant Halberg."

"I'm worried if I allow the police to go into the house, they'll let Romeo out."

"Romeo?"

"My kitty."

"Tell Halberg about Romeo."

"This is crazy. You know that, right?"

"Maybe so, but it'd make me feel better knowing something bad hasn't happened to my best friend too."

I was hitting below the belt, using the sympathy card.

"Oh . . . oh . . . of course. How are you doing?"

"I'm okay."

I usually say a little more to most people—because most people care.

"Good to hear. It must be almost a year now?"

"Yes."

"Well, you should be getting over it soon then."

Wow. There are times when I think I haven't been fair with Cat, and then she goes and says something thoughtless and proves my original impression correct. After Hawk had first introduced her to me, he asked me what I thought of her. I looked him in the eye and told him to run. He laughed, but I was serious. It was too late. Hawk was in love with a praying mantis.

ABOUT A HALF HOUR LATER, I got a call from Ames. "You upset my daughter for absolutely no reason," he growled.

"Oh. Have you heard from Hawk? I mean Michael?"

"Not exactly. Cat asked me to check on his credit card history, so I made some calls and found out he's having a high old time on the company card in Vegas."

What? "Really? That's great. Thanks. Well, then, I'll notify his parents."

"Yeah, you do that. Did you call the cops?"

"Yes, sir."

"Well, then *you* call them back and let them know *you* sent them out on a wild goose chase. Cat shouldn't have to deal with your mess. By the way, if you talk to Michael, tell him he's going to have some explaining to do about using the business card on a personal vacation."

"So, where's he staying in Vegas?"

"Hold on."

When the shrill hold music came on, I held the phone a couple inches from my ear as I waited, and waited, and waited. I was starting to think he was screwing with me when Elaine came back on.

"Detective?"

"Yes?"

"Sorry it took so long. It took a little time to find out which Las Vegas property the charges were from. Anyway, Michael's at the Flamingo."

I thanked Elaine and promptly notified Halberg with Eden Prairie PD. He understood: In law enforcement, we frequently deal with missing persons reports, and in the great majority of cases, the person shows up unharmed.

When I called Barb Hawkinson, she said, "I'd be relieved except for the fact he didn't mention anything whatsoever about going to Las Vegas."

"Maybe it was a spur of the moment deal."

"Cal, be honest, does this sound like Mike to you? To leave without telling a soul?"

I didn't know what to say to that because he used to lie by omission to them all the time, so I said, "Maybe he just needed to get away from it all, not answering his phone on purpose."

"Well, I doubt that. And remember he wanted to talk to you about something that was bothering him."

"How about I do some more checking?"

THE DESK CLERK at the Flamingo said Michael Hawkinson had checked in early Tuesday morning for an indefinite stay. "Indefinite" didn't sound right. I left messages on his room phone and again on his cell. In Vegas, the chance of finding a guest in his room was slim, so I expected it'd be a while before he called me back.

Oh, Hawk. What are you up to? My imagination went crazy with possible scenarios. My first thought was he was having a fling, or decided to leave his marriage but neglected to tell his wife. Hawk liked to gamble more than I. Maybe he just decided to play while the Cat was away.

2

May 16
Four days missing.

ON FRIDAY MORNING, I was eating breakfast with Henry and Lucy, when Hawk's mom called to tell me she still hadn't heard from him and asked what I found out.

"Nothing," I said. "Like I told you yesterday, I left messages at the hotel, but he hasn't returned my call."

"Mine either. I just don't get it. This isn't like him at all."

"I'll try again and get back to you."

"Who was that?" Clara asked when I ended the call.

"My friend Hawk's mom." I explained the situation.

"Well, if I were her, I'd be worried too. And why don't they vacation together?"

"Good question. I guess it's because he likes to hunt and fish, and she likes to lie by the pool and shop."

"Kids these days."

FIRST THING I DID after signing in, was use the department phone to call the Flamingo, so whoever answered would see it was from Birch County Sheriff's Department. In my mind, I was justified—Hawk was supposedly headed for my county before he disappeared.

After a brief explanation to a clerk, I was immediately transferred to the hotel day manager Fletcher Cook. After hearing me out, Cook said he'd get security to check Mr. Hawkinson's room to make sure he was okay. He returned the call twenty minutes later.

"Mr. Hawkinson was not in his room, but his phone messages have been picked up. Also, I paged the hotel with no response. You do realize he could be anywhere in Vegas."

"Yes, sir, I do. Thanks for your trouble."

"No worries."

This was weird. Hawk might avoid his mother's calls, but why would he avoid mine? Unless—he was doing something for which he was ashamed. It would surprise me if he'd become a raging gambling addict, but then again I hadn't hung out with him in years.

I called Cat back. She sounded sleepy.

"Did I wake you?"

"Um . . . yeah. What time is it?"

"Almost nine o'clock here."

"Well then it's almost nine o'clock here!"

Yeah, get snippy with me.

"Up and at 'em," I said. I couldn't resist. "Have you heard from Michael yet?"

"No."

"Has he ever done this before?" I asked.

"Done what?"

"Gone off somewhere without telling you?"

"Absolutely not."

"Are you two okay? I mean . . . are you having any problems? Is there any reason he'd feel the need to get away?"

"No! We're fine. He's fine. And I'm officially pissed off that he flew off to Vegas without letting me know his change of plans."

I apologized for waking her, then left another message on his phone telling him he was in big trouble, but I believe Cat will do an excellent job of letting her feelings be known.

May 17
Five days missing.

ON SATURDAY, I had the twins by myself. They were a ton of work, so I paid the neighbor girl to come over and help out. Hillary Kohler was twelve and was very good with them.

It wasn't until evening and the babies were finally in bed, that I had time to think about Hawk. *What the hell was he up to all day that he couldn't answer a message?* I refused to leave yet another.

May 18

Six days missing.

SHANNON WAS PROMPT in picking up the Twinks at noon on Sunday. I had them ready and helped her get them in their car seats in the Honda Pilot. Before she got into the driver's seat she said, "Thanks for the Mother's Day flowers. They were beautiful."

"Glad you liked them."

"You don't have to do buy me gifts from the babies."

"I wanted to. You're a good mom, Shannon."

"Well, thanks. Do you remember our couple's counseling appointment next Thursday?"

"I do," I said. I remember we had one, but not the day.

"When I met with Brett last week, he said he was going to suggest you and Luke meet alone again."

I nodded. "Okay. How is Luke?"

"The same. I wish I knew what to do to help him get past this."

"We're doing what we can."

"I don't think forcing him to stay at your place is the answer."

"No, he has to want a relationship with me."

"I'm sorry, Cal. I've tried."

"I understand."

But I didn't. I didn't understand any of it—how our marriage went from being great to so intolerable she had to move out. And she wasn't even wearing her rings anymore.

SUNDAY EVENING, Cat Hawkinson called me. Her voice was different—weak, shaky.

"Cal, I just got home and Michael isn't here. And Romeo hasn't been taken care of at all. Poor baby was starving."

"What did you expect?"

"I expected before he took off to Vegas he would have stopped to feed Romeo and clean out the litter box. I expected he'd get his ass home before I got back from my trip. And his . . . his carry-on is here. So is his shaving kit. He wouldn't just take off to Vegas without his luggage and his lucky shirt."

"Wouldn't he have taken his carry-on and shaving kit to his parents?"

"No, Barb has everything he needs up there, including clothes. By the way, she called to tell me if Michael isn't home by tomorrow morning, she's sending his cousin to Vegas to get him."

"Really? Which cousin?"

"Sydney Dirkson. She and her husband own a private detective agency in Minneapolis. They were at the wedding—a tall good-looking couple? Sydney and Pete?"

"Can't place them. Why don't you go with her and surprise him?"

"I can't leave Romeo again."

"You should check with the airline to see if Michael has a return flight before Sydney flies all the way out there."

"Good idea."

Maybe now Cat would take this seriously. I found it interesting she wouldn't go with Sydney because of Romeo.

3

May 19
Seven days missing

MONDAY MORNING I'd been at my desk only a few minutes, when I received a call from Cat.

"Michael has no return tickets. What the hell does that mean? Is he going to live out there?"

"I'm not sure."

"Well, charges are continuing to mount on the credit cards."

"I suggest if you want your husband to come home, you should shut down the cards."

"Maybe. Sydney is flying out to Vegas this afternoon."

"Okay, can I have her number?"

SYDNEY DIRKSON ANSWERED on the first ring. She said she remembered me from Mike's wedding. "You were the handsome best man," she said.

"I don't know about handsome, but yes, I was his best man."

"As I recall, you and my husband had a lengthy conversation about law enforcement? Pete was MPD before we bought the agency."

"Oh, I do remember you both now—the beautiful woman in the sexy red dress," I said, giving it back to her to see how she handled it.

"Oh, ha-ha. I'm never happy in a dress. I'd rather be in jeans."

I laughed. "Well, you looked pretty fantastic that day. So, Cat told me you were headed to Vegas."

"Yeah, this afternoon. My mom says Aunt Barb will be a basket case until someone sees and talks to Mike in person. She thinks I'll be able to convince him to come home. Hey, maybe you should come with. You know Mike better than I do. Besides, I could use a muscleman in case I run into any trouble."

"You're expecting trouble?"

16

"Never know what I'm going to find. This isn't like Mike not to answer his phone."

"I tend to agree with you. Let me think about it, and I'll give you a call back."

I was tempted. It was Henry and Lucy's week with Shannon, so my leaving wouldn't be a problem, and I needed to use up some vacation days. I gave Clara a call at Shannon's to let her know my tentative plans.

Without hesitation, she said, "You should go and not give it another thought. You haven't taken so much as a long weekend break since I've been working for you. It's time for you to get out and enjoy yourself."

"This isn't a vacation. This is to find my buddy who may have gone off the deep end."

"Oh, I know. I'm just saying it'll be good for you to get away, and don't worry. I'll get Bullet and bring him over here."

"Thanks, Clara."

I CALLED SYDNEY DIRKSON back to tell her I was in. She'd bought an open-ended ticket not knowing how long she would be in Nevada. I did the same and was able to get on the same flight for more money than I wanted to spend, made hotel reservations at the Flamingo, notified personnel I was taking vacation days, then went home to pack.

On my way out of town, I drove by Clifford Emerson's shabby yellow stucco house with green trim. For the first week after Colby's funeral, I watched his every move. He'd been put on leave until the legal issues were sorted out. Then one evening when I was parked a quarter block down the street from the Emerson's house, Sheriff Clinton pulled up behind me. As she walked up to my truck, I rolled down my window.

The sheriff leaned in and said, "More than one resident on this block called with reports of a suspicious man in a red truck parked on their street. I wasn't too surprised when we ran the plate and it was yours. I know what you're doing, Cal. I believe the word is . . . let me think . . . *stalking*. You're scaring Clifford Emerson's neighbors more than him. If you don't knock this off, I'll personally make sure a restraining order is issued. Cal, you need to grieve properly. Get counseling. Take two or three months. I'll grant both you and Shannon paid leaves. These aren't suggestions."

Shannon stayed home for two months after the accident to recover physically and emotionally, but after three weeks, I was back at work with the condition of mandatory counseling. At first, Shannon and I both had individual sessions, but as our marriage began to struggle from the weight of our grief, every other one was marriage counseling. I didn't think it was helping. She moved out of the house right after Christmas, and I still wanted to shoot the bastard who killed Colby. Colby had been only seven at the time of his death and was such a cute little kid. We had a real connection, and before the accident Luke and I had started to bond. Bam! We splintered apart like we'd been disconnected with an axe. Brett, our therapist, says it just takes time after family traumas. I didn't know if it could be fixed.

BULLET WAS ALREADY GONE when I went home to pack, and soon I was sitting at the airport gate in Minneapolis two hours early for our 4:35 flight. As I anticipated Sydney Dirkson's arrival, my head automatically popped up when anyone walked by. I was making myself dizzy, so I focused on an *Outdoors* magazine I'd purchased.

Just after three thirty, Sydney, a tall, stunning blonde, walked up to me. I stood to shake her hand, then she sat in the seat next to mine. She took off her brown leather jacket and laid it on her lap. Her white blouse gaped a little at breast level offering me a view of her lacy bra until she adjusted the front. Probably caught me looking.

Sydney crossed her legs to tuck her jeans leg farther into her knee-high brown boots. With her body type, she'd look good in anything—or nothing. But Sydney and I were both married, so what I was just thinking was not healthy.

"So how are you related to Hawk?"

"Barb's my mom's sister. They've always been close, saw each other every week until my folks moved out to Phoenix three years ago. They still talk every day, and Barb has Mom in a tizzy about Mike. That's why I'm going out there, for my mom."

I nodded.

"Hey, mind if I ask your opinion of Cat?" she asked.

"Let me put it this way: When Hawk asked me what I thought of her, I told him to run."

She slapped her leg and gave out a hardy laugh. "Do you get why they're even together? His other girlfriends were much nicer."

"Cat didn't come with you because of Romeo, her cat."

She lifted her brows. "She told me she was ill from the Mexican water. So what's the detective's best guess on what the hell Mike is up to?"

"I don't know, but it doesn't seem like him to just take off without telling anyone."

"If he's humping some whore, I think I may shoot him in the nuts."

I chuckled. "And I'll be there to witness it."

"As a kid, Mike always had these ideas of fun that would inevitably get us cousins in trouble. We lived on a farm west of Little Falls with a creek running through it, and one hot Sunday afternoon we were throwing rocks into the water off the bridge, and the mosquitoes were biting like crazy. He had the bright idea we should jump off the bridge into the water to get away from the mosquitoes. He talked my little brother Gordy into jumping off first. Well, the water was shallow and the mud was thick, so when Gordy jumped off he got stuck in the mud. Gordy started bawling his head off, and we couldn't pull him out. I made Mike run up to get our folks. My dad was so mad. He marched us back to the house, tails between our mud-covered bodies, and what did Aunt Barb do?"

I shrugged.

"She laughed. She thought it was hilarious. I was grounded for a week. I used to wish Aunt Barb was my mother."

"Me too." I told her about Hawk sinking his Grandma's car in the lake. "I was grounded for a month, and I wasn't even there."

"I remember that incident very clearly because Grandma was just as bad as Barb. She said she'd wanted a new car anyway. Seriously?"

"So, we're going to find him humping a whore, and he'll get his first consequences—getting his balls shot off."

"And believe me, I will tell Aunt Barb the truth."

I smiled. "We'll snap photos for proof."

She giggled.

THE PLANE WASN'T FULL, and I was in a row with an empty middle seat. I had the aisle seat. A kid with long, dirty hair occupied the window seat. He was plugged into an iPad and ignored me. Once we were at cruising altitude the pilot came on to say we were free to move about the cabin. The next thing I knew the flight attendant shook my shoulder and told me to put my seat in the upright position for landing.

Your Las Vegas experience starts in the airport terminal, the air is charged with the energy of vacationers out to drop a lot of money in the casinos. Passengers leaving Vegas, stand before at the slots throughout the terminal trying to hit it big one more time, then another, then another.

As we stepped out into the Nevada air to catch a cab, I sensed the electric charge in the air—also the desert heat. I removed my jacket. The strip was a short drive from the airport; Las Vegas Boulevard traffic was heavy, but it moved.

While we checked into our rooms at the Flamingo, we asked the desk clerk if Michael Hawkinson had checked out—and no, he hadn't. We made our way to our rooms to drop off our luggage, agreeing to meet in the lobby and then find a place for dinner.

My fifth floor room had a view of the strip, which I admired for a few minutes before I washed my face and hands, then went down to meet Sydney. Because we were both tired, we opted for the hotel dining room.

Once we were seated and had a beer placed before us, Sydney said, "So, tell me about yourself. Are you married? Have kids?"

"I adopted my wife's two kids from a former marriage, Luke and Colby. Their dad died six years ago. When Shannon and I got married we wanted to have one of our own, but she got pregnant quicker than we expected, and with twins—Lucy and Henry. They're fourteen months now. Our son Colby died in a car crash about a year ago—Shannon and I were going through a rough patch at the time, and our loss made it worse. We've been separated for four months."

"Oh, my God, I'm so sorry." She was looking at me with pity. She touched my arm.

"He was the cutest, sweetest kid ever, and he's gone, and we tried to hold the family together but . . . it hasn't worked out."

A tear dripped down her cheek. She wiped it with her sleeve.

I blinked away my own tears, cleared my throat and said, "You have kids?"

"We have one daughter, Elle, who's finishing up her second year at Princeton. She'll be home for summer break soon."

I nodded. "Princeton? Wow."

"She loves it."

"So, how long have you been a private investigator?"

"I joined Pete with the firm eight years ago. I'm also an attorney, so I do legal work as well."

She took a sip of beer then steered the conversation to less serious topics. After we finished our dinner, we asked to speak to the manager. We were told Fletcher Cook was on duty, the same man I'd spoken to on the phone. He shuffled us down to one end of the long counter. He was a small, sullen man with a dark complexion.

I showed my badge and said, "I spoke with you earlier this week. I'm a detective for Birch County, Minnesota, Sheriff's Department, and this is Sydney Dirkson, a private investigator. We are looking for Michael Hawkinson, who seems to have gone missing while staying in your hotel. If you can tell us his room number we can go check . . ."

"That's not possible, sir, but I will ring the room again if you like."

Which he did and received no answer.

"Okay, just to let you know we are going to show his photo around and see if any of your employees or guests have seen him."

"Just a second."

He made a phone call, most likely to security. He hung up and said to me, "You may go ahead and show the photos." He hadn't told them anything. He just listened. Vegas security is creepy—omniscient—they see and hear all.

Sydney had copied a professional photo of Hawk and handed me one. The plan was to separate, show the photo to employees and guests as we wandered through the casino floor, while on the lookout for Hawk. I also brought a photo: a smiley, face shot I took of him during a fishing trip we'd taken up in Canada.

As I meandered through the tables and machines, three different good-looking women approached me. At least I thought they were women—one can never tell, especially in Vegas. Each wanted to know if I wanted to party or go on a date. I did not, I told them. I showed them Hawk's picture. They didn't recognize him, which was probably a good thing since they were hookers.

We met in the lobby at nine o'clock and walked out onto the sidewalk on Las Vegas Boulevard. Las Vegas has a smell like no other city. Maybe it's the exhaust systems of the enormous casinos mixed with the stench of cigarettes and stale alcoholic beverages, plus the odors emitted from the river of human bodies as it moves along the sidewalks. I suggested we hit the casinos Hawk preferred during his bachelor party weekend: Caesars Palace, the Mirage, and Treasure Island.

"Was the bachelor weekend like the movie?"

"Huh-uh . . . what happens in Vegas, stays in Vegas."

"No big cats in your room or tattoos you didn't remember getting?"

"Oh, that."

She laughed. We crossed the nearest pedestrian bridge across Las Vegas Boulevard and made our way to Caesar's Palace.

At midnight, we each declared exhaustion and gave it up for the night. Back at the Flamingo, I glanced at the front desk, considered whether to try the only woman clerk at the front desk. It didn't work this time either. She did tell me she was off tomorrow if I wanted to meet up. I politely declined.

4

May 20
Eight days missing

I PUT MY HEAD ON THE PILLOW, and the next thing I knew it was 5:00 a.m., seven my time. I looked out at the strip, quiet this time of day. I decided to go for a run.

I ran up one side of Las Vegas Boulevard, as far as the Stratosphere, crossed the street and ran back on the other, ending at the Bellagio to watch the fountains as I cooled down. The traffic was starting to pick up when I crossed the pedestrian bridge.

As planned, I met Sydney outside the Garden Buffet at eight o'clock. We took trays and went through the line. Sydney selected oatmeal and a fruit cup. She eyed my loaded plate but didn't comment.

"I'm going to get into Mike's room this morning," Sydney said.

"Tried it again last night with a second clerk. No go."

"Did you tell him you were the wife and came to surprise your husband and palm the desk clerk fifty bucks?"

"I did not."

"Well, we'll see how it works. Sometimes it does, and sometimes it doesn't. If we can't get in, we'll go with our plan to split up and hit MGM Grand, New York-New York, Bellagio, Venetian, and Paris. Surely someone would recognize a handsome, charismatic, six-foot-four, two hundred-thirty pound man."

TO MY SURPRISE, Sydney came back with a room key. She used a phony ID she'd had made up in Minneapolis. We went up to the eighth floor and knocked on the door with the Do Not Disturb sign hanging on the knob. There was a room service tray outside the door. I lifted the lid.

"Looks like food for two," she said.

"Well, that dirty dog."

23

When no one answered, Sydney used the key, and I, being the muscle man, or more accurately, the human shield, entered first. I moved in slowly. The light from the hallway illuminated the bed. As I moved closer, I saw it was empty. I flipped on the lamp. Clothes and garbage had been tossed about like a teenager's bedroom. Sydney listened at the bathroom door.

She whispered, "I can't hear a shower running. Look in there."

With a finger I pushed the door open fully expecting someone to be sitting on the john or worse.

"No one's here," I said. "And he hasn't used the towels."

"He's not bathing?"

"Did you see the mess? Hawk wasn't a tidy person when I lived with him, but this is extreme."

Sydney said, "Looks like Mike's partying down." She pointed to the end table and said, "Oh, my God. See the spoons? He's doing dope."

"Shit."

While Sydney searched dresser drawers, I started examining the clothes in the blue duffle bag, which would explain why Cat said his luggage was still home. I picked up a pair of black sweatpants.

"Sydney, look at these. They're way too small for Hawk. He must have company."

She began to kick through the clothes. "There are no clothes his size."

"We could have the wrong room."

"That shit-for-brains desk clerk screwed me over," Sydney said.

We went downstairs and chose a different clerk and asked to speak to Fletcher Cook.

"Mr. Cook is not on duty at the moment. But follow me," the young woman said.

We followed her down a hallway. An assistant manager named Margot greeted us with a smile.

Sydney told Margot the truth about why we entered the eighth-floor room and what we'd discovered.

"I see," she said. She did some quick typing on her computer and said, "All I can tell you is that's Mr. Hawkinson's room."

I said, "I'm hoping you can show us film of him checking in, just to verify it's actually him and not someone fraudulently using his identity and credit cards."

That got her attention. "I'll call security."

A few minutes later, a large African American man wearing a black suit entered the room. The sleeves of his jacket were tight around his biceps. He introduced himself as Mr. Baird. Sydney and I showed him our IDs. He didn't appear impressed.

We repeated the story leaving out how we gained access.

"How do you know he's not the one staying in his room?" Baird said.

"We sorta checked," Sydney said.

"Did you." It wasn't a question.

She nodded.

"By way of the front desk?"

"I don't want to get anyone in trouble," she said.

"It's a bit too late for that," Baird said.

I said, "Is there anyway we could see film footage of who checked into his room?"

"Wait here. I'll see what I can do."

While we waited, Margot served us coffee. She was a chatty one when she found out we were from Minnesota. She was originally from Deer River and had been living in Vegas for six years. She hated Nevada's hot summers, but loved the winters. When Sydney went to the restroom, Margot asked me, "So, are you two together?"

"No."

"Um, if you're free for dinner tonight, I'd love to take you to a few local spots away from the crowds."

"Uh, tempting offer, but no, I best not. And . . . I also need to find the restroom."

She kept her smile as she said, "Down the hall to the left."

I ran into Sydney when I came out of the men's.

"What do we do if it's not him?" Sydney asked.

"If it's not, then we need the police."

We went back to Margot's office to wait for Baird to return. We waited for an uncomfortable thirty minutes, forcing conversation with Margot, who'd grown quiet. Mr. Baird came back with stills of the man who checked in using Hawk's credit card. He was a small, white guy somewhere north of forty.

"That's not Michael Hawkinson."

"Can you find this man for us?"

"We already have. He's being held in one of our offices. We've called Las Vegas Metro Police Department."

I suggested we wait for them to arrive in order to do this right. I didn't want the suspect escaping or getting off on a technicality because we didn't follow proper procedure.

Detectives Fred Nunn and Robin Miller arrived within a few minutes. Nunn was in his forties, of average height and weight. He wore his dark hair buzzed to the scalp, and was stingy with his smiles. Miller was younger, stocky, about five feet eight inches. She wore a short, black blazer with a blue, button-down shirt and jeans. Her hair was slightly longer than Nunn's.

"That was quick," I said, as we flashed our badges and introduced ourselves.

"Mr. Baird alerted us of trouble with illegal credit card activity."

I nodded, then told him the story from the beginning. Nunn, Miller, and I were taken to the second floor; they preferred Sydney wait in the lobby.

I'd been so sure Hawk was having some sort of meltdown. I hadn't expected to find some little piss-ant using his card. My biggest fear was he was now vulture food in the desert.

An armed security guard stood outside the door where they held the individual using Hawk's credit card. He spoke into his radio fastened on his collar as we approached.

"We patted him down," he said. "Nothing on him but a lighter and a joint tucked into a pack of cigarettes."

The security guard's clone was standing just inside the room. I smiled—he didn't. He ducked out.

I could smell the guy from two feet away from. The stench was a combination of booze, smoke, and sour body odor. He wore a wrinkled, long-sleeved Harley-Davidson T-shirt and a pair of black nylon athletic pants with a white stripe up the side.

"I'm Detective Nunn with Las Vegas Metropolitan Police Department. I'd like you to stand up against this wall so I can pat you down."

We never assume pat downs completed by others have been done properly.

The man grimaced and took too long to get up for Nunn's liking. He grabbed his elbow and walked him to the wall. The man assumed the search posture: arms up, hands on the wall, feet spread. It wasn't his first dance. Nunn pulled out a worn, brown wallet and threw it on the table. After Nunn finished patting him down, he asked the man to have a seat, then sat across from him and next to his partner, who'd pulled out a laptop. I remained standing off to the side. This was Metro's party.

"Sitting with us at the table is Detective Miller. Standing to my right is Detective Sheehan with the Birch County Sheriff's Department out of Minnesota."

The man glanced up at me and began jiggling his left leg. His eyes were ice blue and blood-shot. His lower lid was red from lack of sleep or drugs.

"Do you know why you're being detained?" Nunn asked.

He shrugged his shoulders. "No, sure don't." I detected some sort of regional twang in his voice.

"What's your name?"

"Raybern Ginty."

"Well, Raybern Ginty, you are under arrest for using a stolen credit card and identity." He read him his Miranda Rights, Ginty waved them.

Then Nunn picked up his wallet. "Let's have a look-see what's in your wallet," Nunn said.

Nunn pulled out several cards from the wallet and displayed them on the table.

"Let's see. You have driver's licenses and credit cards with three different names: John Adam Pencroft from Huntington Beach, California; Raybern Jerome Ginty, from Kansas City, Kansas; and Michael Thomas Hawkinson of Eden Prairie, Minnesota."

"Huh," he said, like it was the first he knew of it.

I moseyed over to look. They all had this man's picture. I picked up the Minnesota license and changed the angle to see if the loon image seemed to sink before the surface as I moved it. It didn't. Miller handed me a small ultraviolet flashlight, but I didn't really even have to use it to know I wouldn't see the seal of the state of Minnesota under the light. The card bore Ginty's photo with Hawk's information. This man was quite a bit shorter than Hawk's six feet, four inches and 230 pounds.

Nunn picked up Ginty's license. "So you're saying you are Raybern Jerome Ginty from Kansas. You sure? You do not want to supply us with false information and add to your trouble."

"Yeah, that's me. I go by Bernie with an e."

Nunn picked up the Kansas license and handed it to me. If this was his real ID, he was only thirty-eight years old—but he looked a decade older.

"Well, Bernie with an e, what's your birthdate?" I asked.

"February the fifteenth, nineteen hundred, seventy-six."

"How tall are you?"

"Five eight."

"Weight?"

"One forty-nine."

"Not one-fifty?" Nunn asked.

Miller snorted.

"This is a fairly good copy," I lied. "Who does your work?"

Ginty rolled his head and looked off.

"Your Kansas driver's license expired a year ago," I said, as I passed it back to Nunn, who handed it to Miller.

Ginty closed an eye and pulled the same side of his face into a half-grimace. "It did? Huh. Haven't been back there in a while, I guess."

I stood behind Miller who had plugged the name into NCIC, the National Crime Information Center database. She glanced back at me gesturing with her head to look at what was coming up. Ginty was a frequent flyer. Since he was eighteen, he'd been in and out of the correctional systems in Kansas and Oklahoma; his latest conviction was for felony theft in Hennepin County, so we knew he'd been in Minnesota.

"How do you know Michael Hawkinson?" I asked.

"I don't."

Nunn fanned his hand above the licenses.

"You're using other individual's identities and credit cards in order to stay in the hotel and gamble," he said. "Nevada doesn't like that. And you used Michael Hawkinson's credit cards. Deputy Sheehan and Minnesota don't like that."

Ginty laughed nervously and gave his chin whiskers a scratch. "Wasn't me."

Nunn said, "We have you on tape handing over the card. The desk clerk welcomed you as Mr. Hawkinson. So how did you come by Mr. Hawkinson's credit card?"

He cleared his throat. "Okay . . . okay. A dude handed it to me and told me to have fun."

I glanced at Nunn who rolled his eyes. "Where and when?" he asked.

A hesitation then, "In Minneapolis last Monday afternoon."

"What did the guy look like?" I asked.

"He was a big white dude, dark hair."

"Anybody with you at the time to witness this grand gift?"

"Witness? Nah."

Nunn then stood and said to me, "I'm gonna take him in. Come with."

Sydney wasn't waiting in the lobby, so I left a message on her phone. Ginty was placed in the back of a transport van that had pulled around to the rear of the hotel. Ginty joined two other men in the van, also bound for the Clark County Detention Center.

Nunn's unmarked Taurus was in the same lot. Miller sat shotgun. I crawled into the backseat.

Miller turned to look at me. "Tell us about Michael Hawkinson."

After I filled them in, she asked, "Do you think he even made it out of Minnesota?"

"I'm beginning to think whatever happened to him, happened back home. I'll check with Hennepin County," I said.

GINTY WAS BROUGHT to an interview room, and while Nunn was setting up, I called CISA, Criminal Information Sharing and Analysis, Hennepin County's own data center.

I was told Ginty had recently been released from St. Cloud Correctional after a six-month stint, and was in violation of his parole because he'd missed two check-ins, and left the state. The deputy told me they'd contact Clark County to sort things out.

He also shared Ginty's known Minnesota associates: Roseanna Martinez and Nevada Wynn, a lowlife I'd encountered in the past. Wynn's moniker was Snake because of his cobra tattoo running from his cheek, around his neck and down to his junk. A Hennepin County jailor said Wynn's dick was the tail end of the snake. Who in their right mind would inflict that much pain to their penis?

Roseanna had been arrested for prostitution and possession of narcotics (heroin). Her moniker was Little Zanna. Raybern with an e had three: Ray-Ray, Bernie, and Gint the Flint. I can understand Bernie—but Ray-Ray and Gint the Flint?

Regardless of what transpired in Nevada, Ginty would eventually be getting a free ride back to Minnesota courtesy of Hennepin County because he had violated the conditions of his parole.

After I gave Nunn the lowdown on Ginty's record, he nodded and said, "It was obvious it wasn't his first circus parade."

"And it won't be his last."

AT TWO O'CLOCK, Nunn got a call saying Ginty had been processed. He said I could have first crack at him. When we walked into the stark, interrogation room, Ginty looked up and gave us a shit-eating grin. He may be one of those guys who's more comfortable wearing the orange jumpsuit.

"Mr. Ginty, to refresh your memory, I'm Detective Nunn and this is Detective Sheehan from Birch County, Minnesota. Deputy Sheehan has questions for you."

"Mr. Ginty, what have you've been up to since you were released from Minnesota Corrections St. Cloud?" I asked.

"Trying to stay out of trouble," he said, and snickered.

"Hanging with Nevada Wynn? AKA Snake?"

"Once in a while."

"Is he still working at North Cross Warehouse?" I asked.

He made a face. "Far as I know."

"So your story is that some random guy on the street in Minneapolis just hands over his credit card and driver's license for you to use? I find that odd."

"You know that old saying: Don't look a gift horse up the butt," he replied, giving a little grin, thinking he was cute.

"How'd you know the credit card was good?" I asked.

"'Cause I tried it out."

"Where?" I asked.

"Target in Minneapolis, and I thought, hot damn why not use it to go to Vegas like the guy said."

"And did you use the same card to fly to Las Vegas, Mr. Ginty?" Nunn asked.

"You obviously know I did."

"Who came with you?" I asked.

"My old lady, Roseanna."

"You're married to Roseanna?"

He smirked. "Why would I go and do that?"

"What's her last name?"

"Johnson."

It's Martinez, you lying sack.

"Was she with you when you checked in?"

"Nah, she was too anxious to get to the slots."

"Where's Michael Hawkinson?" I said.

He shrugged. "I have no idea."

Sweat stains bloomed under his armpits.

My cell phone vibrated. It was Cat Hawkinson, so I told Nunn I needed to take the call. Nunn nodded. "Detective Sheehan is leaving the interview."

I moved a few yards down the hallway. "Hey, Cat, what's up?"

"Did you find him?"

"Not yet."

I didn't want to tell her anything until I had something more concrete.

"Well, this might help. Michael's also been using his debit card. Three hundred dollars has been taken out every day since Tuesday, and he's used his VISA card at Target, Caribou Coffee, and Sports Minnesota. He used the company American Express for Delta Airlines and the hotel. The airline ticket price seemed pretty high, but at the last minute rates are always highest."

And when you purchase two tickets.

"Do you know when he left Minneapolis?"

"The charges were made on Tuesday, the thirteenth."

"Did you close the cards down as I suggested?"

"Not yet."

"Do it as soon as you hang up. Do you know which machines the cash is being withdrawn from?"

"No."

"Call your bank and find out. Then call me back."

"Okay."

I summoned Nunn to the hall, so I could explain what I'd just found out.

"So how much of Ginty's story do you believe?" he asked.

"Not a lot."

Nunn and Miller waited with me in the observation room until Cat called me back ten minutes later.

"He used his debit card at Frank's Plaza in Prairie Falls and then three hundred was withdrawn from the Wells Fargo in Prairie Falls, and the rest were all from the same ATM in Vegas. Find him, Cal."

"I'm trying. Thanks for the info. I'll get back to you."

Nunn said they'd book Ginty on the fraud charges. He'd get a search warrant for the room Ginty rented and the ATM company.

"I'd like to see if I can get more out of him."

"Go for it."

I went back in and sat down across from Ginty. I restated who I was to identify myself on the recording.

"Before you left for Vegas, were you in northern Minnesota?"

"Nope." He tightened the muscles around his mouth like he had when I asked him what Roseanna's surname was.

"I know you used Michael's American Express card to book a Delta flight to Vegas from Minneapolis and to pay for the hotel. You've been withdrawing cash with his debit card, so that means you know the password. How did you get it?"

He blinked a few times, then said, "The guy who gave me the card told me what it was."

"I find it hard to believe Mr. Hawkinson handed over his credit cards and said, 'Have fun, and by the way you'll need my pin.' Really?"

"Well, he did," Ginty, said grinning at me like a damn fool.

"Are you and Nevada Wynn in the drug business together?"

Ginty's smirk dropped off his face. "Okay, I think I'm done talkin' to ya."

"See you in Minnesota, Ray-Ray."

Hennepin County would handle extradition for Ginty, but I had no idea if he was involved in harming Hawk or if he was just the beneficiary of the spoils.

5

May 21
Nine days missing.

SYDNEY AND I SPENT HOURS showing Hawk's photo to casino employees, and no one remembered seeing him. By Wednesday noon, we were convinced he never made it to Vegas, so late that afternoon we caught a flight home. When we said good-bye at the Minneapolis/St. Paul airport, Sydney hugged me, and she said she'd be in touch.

I called Cat Hawkinson from the terminal and asked if I could drop by on my way back home. They lived in an Eden Prairie golf club community called Bearpath. As a wedding gift, Irving Ames gave them an eight-hundred-thousand-dollar four-bedroom house located on the tenth fairway. I hadn't been there for years, so I needed the GPS to get me through the winding roads in the dark. The light rain didn't help visibility.

It was ten o'clock by the time I arrived. When Cat answered the door, she was holding a longhaired white Persian cat, obviously Romeo. I'd never seen her without eye make-up, or with her chocolate-brown hair pulled into a ponytail. She looked softer, wholesome even.

I said, "I'm sorry, it took me longer to get here than I thought. It's late. I could come back tomorrow morning."

"No, I want to know what you found out. Please, come in. Besides, I don't usually go to bed before midnight anyway."

We proceeded through the expansive house designed with a modern, open concept.

"You've redecorated," I said. "I like the gray and red."

Their house had all the amenities: hardwood floors, large windows, granite counters, up-scale bathrooms, media room, bar, pool table—you name it; they had it.

"Michael actually helped pick out the new furnishings. It was fun. Join me in a glass of wine?" she said.

"Sure."

33

"Okay, Romeo, down you go," she said as she placed the cat at her feet. White cat hair clung to her yoga pants and black top with the plunging neckline. I tried to avoid staring at her cleavage as she bent over. But do women expose their breasts so we don't look?

I followed her to a seating area. As soon as I sat in one of the light-gray leather sofas, Romeo sauntered over to rub up against my legs. Cat went to the kitchen where she poured me a generous glass of red wine and refilled a glass sitting on the counter.

She handed me the glass, then took a seat opposite me.

With worry lines formed on her forehead, Cat put her glass on the coffee table and said, "So tell me what you found out."

With one smooth move, she lifted her legs onto the couch and sat cross-legged. Romeo jumped up and settled in her lap. He looked suspiciously at me.

"Your cat has one gold eye and one blue eye."

"Yes." She petted him in long strokes, and he closed his eyes and purred. As I chronicled what I'd found out in Vegas, Cat listened intently.

When I finished, she said, "My God, and I thought he was having a premature mid-life crisis."

Tears began to stream down her face, and she began to sob. I sat with my elbows on my knees and watched her. Her strong reaction half-surprised me because I was under the impression she didn't give a shit about him.

She went to retrieve a tissue from the counter, dabbed at her eyes, then blew her nose.

"So what happens now?" she said.

"We have to retrace Hawk's steps and find his vehicle. Is he still driving the black Mercedes SUV?"

"Yes."

"I'll put out a BOLO."

"What's that mean?"

"Be on the lookout for."

"In your professional opinion has something really bad happened to *Michael*? Be honest." She emphasized *Michael*, letting me know I'd erred when I referred to him as Hawk.

"The longer he's missing, the worse his odds are."

"Michael's mother said he was on his way to visit you, but never made it."

"No, and he never called to cancel."

"Did you try calling *him*, like right back?" She sounded a little pissy.

"Of course, I did."

"Why didn't you do the BOLO thing that day?"

"People blow people off all the time, and we don't issue BOLOs for that."

She nodded. "Tell me. Was it Michael who used his credit card in Prairie Falls, or was it the guy you talked to in Vegas?"

"I'm not sure. Ginty says a man handed him the card when he was downtown Minneapolis, but in my opinion that's all bullshit."

"So, he could be anywhere between Brainerd, Prairie Falls, and Minneapolis?"

The reality of her statement took me aback. That was a huge area.

"Yeah, that's about the size of it. I called the owner of the gas station where the card was used and asked him to save their security tapes."

She nodded. "You're not going back up north this late, are you?"

"Thought I would."

"I insist you stay in our guest room."

I could feel the wine because I hadn't eaten since breakfast. "All right."

And as if she could read my mind, she asked, "Are you hungry? Do you want a sandwich . . . or cheese and crackers?"

"I am a little hungry. Fix whatever's easy."

"Get your things from your truck, while I fix you a plate."

By the time I came back in she'd placed on the coffee table a royal-blue glass plate loaded with various cuts of cheese, crackers, and small, fancy sandwiches. She'd also refilled my wine glass.

"How did you do all this so fast?"

"My mom brought these things over this evening. I didn't tell them you were stopping by, or they'd have insisted on staying to talk to you. When they left, I felt a little panicked, so I'm glad you're staying over."

The ice princess was showing a side I'd never seen. But ice melts under heat, doesn't it? I wasn't convinced she wasn't involved in his disappearance.

"So, tell me what Michael's been up to these days."

"Work mostly. I never thought I'd say it, but I was happy he was taking time off to go fishing."

"So, what about his relationships with other people. Any conflicts? Even if they seem minor, it could be important."

"You know Michael. He gets along with everybody."

"Have you ever suspected him of having an affair?"

She scowled. "God, no. Why? Do you know something I don't?"

"Just covering the bases. I don't mean to offend you, but have you had anything extracurricular going on?"

She shot me a dirty look. "Of course not!"

"Are you still working?"

"Michael didn't want me to work anymore because I hated my job so much."

"Do Michael and your father get along?"

"Um, sure."

"A while ago Michael told me he didn't think Irving liked him."

"Well, at first maybe. Mom says, in Dad's eyes, no one would be good enough for me, but they love him now."

"How about friends and neighbors?"

"Well, the neighbors to our left are awful, and Michael's called them on it."

"Tell me about it."

"They have these big, vicious dogs who come on our grass to poop. So Michael takes an old pitching wedge and slings it back in their yard—then they get mad at us."

"Sounds justifiable."

"Every summer they have several big backyard parties and blast music. It's just so thoughtless. So the last time we called 911 on them. And their kids? They're so obnoxious—they fight and swear like sailors right out in the front yard in front of everybody. Believe me, everyone wants them to move."

"What are their names?"

"Louis and Demi Cavara. And they were *so nice* when we moved in, but we found out quickly that no one, and I mean no one, on the block likes them."

I pulled a notebook from my pocket and wrote down the neighbors' names. We drank our wine, and I ate all the little sandwiches, and then she began to yawn, so I said I should probably hit the hay.

She showed me to the same room I'd slept in five years ago—with Adriana who'd jokingly called it the Pepto-Bismol room. Thank God, it had been redecorated from shades of pink to black and white. Cat brushed past me to check if there were clean towels in the attached bathroom. As she made her way back out, she said, "Well, I guess you're set then. Do you need anything else?"

"No, I'm good."

She hesitated creating an awkward moment. "Well, I'll . . . just go . . . Cal, thank you for all you're doing."

"Look, Hawk . . . Michael . . . is my best friend. I'll do whatever it takes to find him. And I should have the names and numbers of the women you went to Mexico with and the place where you stayed."

A flicker of something in her eyes. Whether it was fear or anger, I wasn't sure. "Okay. Is tomorrow morning soon enough?"

"Of course."

She scrunched up her face like she was going to cry, then waved her hands in front of her face, and disappeared toward the master bedroom on the opposite side of the house. That was weird. Why did she react so strongly when I told her I wanted to talk to her friends? Maybe she vacationed with a man. And was she just hitting on me?

I closed the door and regarded the room's decor: black-and-white comforter, a zebra print chair and rug, black-and-white photos of Romeo hung on the light-gray walls. I moved the red, decorative pillows from the bed to the chair and turned down the bed covers. The sheets were white with black dots.

Four years ago, when Cat and Hawk had invited us to spend a weekend to celebrate their first year anniversary, Adriana and I had been together for about the same time. And here it was five years later. They were still together, and I wasn't with Adriana or Shannon.

Adriana liked Cat—she thought Cat had refined Hawk. I thought she made him into something he wasn't. Cat seemed genuinely distressed he was missing, but maybe she was that good of an actress.

Maybe Shannon had a right to be jealous of Adriana because I couldn't seem to erase her from my life. Thinking of Shannon used to make me smile. Now it brought me down, and the separation had just made things worse. We needed to make a decision—either make a serious attempt at reconciling—or get a divorce. But in my heart, I knew such an ultimatum would be the quick end of us.

6

May 22
Ten days missing.

I LOOKED AT MY WATCH—6:15 a.m. I tried to go back to sleep but couldn't. I rolled out of bed, showered, dressed, and found Cat sitting at the counter drinking coffee and working at her computer. She was wearing an over-sized gray T-shirt, probably Hawk's. I wondered whether she had on anything underneath.

"Sleep well?" she said.

"Surprisingly, yes."

Without asking, she poured me a mug of coffee and set it on the counter in front of the stool next to hers, although there were four. I put some distance between us by taking the second one from the end.

"Cream or sugar?"

"No, thanks."

I took a sip. She handed me a large pink Post-it note with several names and phone numbers written on it.

"The top three are my traveling companions, the others are friends we socialize with, and that's the resort where we stayed," she said.

"Thanks."

"Cal, if something's happened to Michael, I don't know what I'll do." She blinked away tears. "I thought about you last night—losing a son, even if he was a stepson, it must have been horrible."

"I'd adopted him—he *was* my son."

"Oh, sure, of course. God . . . words just fly out of my mouth like that. I wish I could be more like Adriana. She always says the right thing. She's so together, classy. Have you heard how she's doing?"

"She had a baby with my former partner. They're together."

"Ouch."

"We both moved on. You should know, Michael's disappearance is going to go public today with the BOLO."

"Well, someone has to know something. Maybe they'll come forward."

"Let's hope so. And now you'll have the media camped out on your street, so you may want to stay somewhere else—with your parents or a friend."

Her mouth gaped open. "Oh, I hadn't considered that. I keep hoping he's going to walk through the door. In the middle of the night I found myself thinking he got tired of me and took off somewhere to start a new life. You hear about that happening."

"Is there a reason why he might want a new life?"

She looked down and away, then bit her lower lip. "We had a disagreement before I left on vacation. He told me he wanted me to get pregnant, but I told him I'm not sure I even wanted kids. But I thought a lot about it while I was gone, and I was going to tell him he was right. He should be a dad. He loves kids. He cried when you called to tell him about Colby."

"I know. He cried at the funeral too."

"Cal, I miss Michael so much. What happened to him? Did some druggie kill him for his wallet?"

She began to cry and hopped off her stool and leaned into me pressing her soft breasts into my chest. She wasn't wearing a bra. You can't do that to a guy who hasn't had any in a long while. I gave her a couple pats on the back then pushed to an arm's length.

"Cat, I know it's tempting to imagine the worst, but don't do that to yourself."

"I know."

"Do you think eight o'clock is too early to start talking to your neighbors?"

"No, that should be fine." She put her hand on my arm and said, "Thank you for being such a good friend of Michael's. You mean the world to him."

Is she playing me?

BEFORE I SET OUT to speak with the neighbors, I parked a half block down from the Hawkinsons' driveway. Then as a courtesy to the Eden Prairie Police Department, I called Sergeant Scott Halberg to let him know I would be talking to some of the Hawkinsons' neighbors.

"Sure, that's fine. Keep me updated, will you? And if there's anything you need from us, just call."

I thanked him and decided to approach the Cavaras' home first. Before I even rang the bell, I heard barking.

"Yes?" came a voice through the door.

I put my badge up to the peek hole and said, "Deputy Sheehan. I have a few questions for you, ma'am."

"Just a minute."

A petite brunette with the body mass index of a peanut opened the door a few inches. Three massive English bulldogs wedged their bodies through the crack in the door and forced their way out on the step and surrounded me, snorting and barking as they circled their prey.

"They're harmless," she said.

I've learned not to trust owners who think their dogs are "harmless" after I got bitten in the hand by a "friendly" rat terrier. Four stitches later.

Demi Cavara crossed her arms and said, "Okay, what did we do now?"

"Ma'am?"

I gave her one of my disarming smiles. "Gee, nothing I know of. I just have a few questions about your next door neighbor, Michael Hawkinson. He hasn't been seen for over a week. I'm checking to see if you've seen him coming and going in that time?"

"Is that why the cop car was at their house last week?"

"Yes. So have you seen him or anything suspicious going on next door?"

She cocked her head and looked up to her right. "Oh, gosh, the last time I saw either one of them was the Wednesday before Mother's Day. A limo pulled up to the curb and some women were screaming Cat's name. Yeah, and they complain we're loud?"

"How did you nail down the day that fast?"

"Because the next day I bought petunias and when I was planting them, I saw Michael get his mail. I know it was then because I bought my mother some flowers for Mother's Day at the same time."

"Did you see him after that?"

"No, it didn't look like anyone was home for a week or so, which meant we could relax. I'm always so concerned the kids make too much noise for them."

"Tell me what you know about the Hawkinsons?" Couldn't wait to hear this answer.

She pursed her lips. "We have issues."

"Such as?"

"Here's an example: We had a birthday party for our youngest son, the police show up at our door. They said one of the *neighbors* complained about the noise. Louis was convinced it was the Hawkinsons, so he went over to make peace. Cat shouted at him, called him horrible names. And that woman screeches at my boys if their football goes one inch into their yard. She's not a very nice person. The neighbors call her Cat the Brat. Personally, I like Michael better than her."

She gave me a couple more instances, and I pretended to be interested, but all the bullshit convinced me I should also have a talk with the husband. I asked for his work number.

After canvasing the neighborhood, I came to the following conclusions: Only a few neighbors actually knew Cat and Michael by name, none socialized with the couple, and beside the Cavaras, no one reported any problems with them or saw anything unusual, other than the police car in the Hawkinsons' driveway a week ago.

When I phoned for an appointment with Louis Cavara, a secretary told me he had no openings in his schedule. When I mentioned his neighbor had disappeared, and I only needed ten minutes of his time, she penciled me in for eleven o'clock. I had time to get a coffee and Google Cavara while I waited. He was the Cavara in Douglas, Peterson, and Cavara, attorneys specializing in personal injury law. It brought to mind Shannon's car accident and the twenty-five solicitous letters we received from personal injury lawyers.

Cavara's law practice was located on the second floor of a three-story building off Park Place in St. Louis Park. I showed up at ten fifty and waited the ten minutes before Mr. Cavara came out to greet me. He was small in stature, balding and gray, and appeared to be a good ten to fifteen years older than his wife. He removed his dark-rimmed eyeglasses and let them hang from a chain around his neck. He extended his hand to give me a firm handshake.

"Louis Cavara," he said.

"I'm Detective Cal Sheehan with the Birch County Sheriff's Department. Thank you for fitting me in. I know you're a busy man."

"I have exactly fifteen minutes," he said. "Come on back."

I followed him down to the other end of the hall and into a large but basic office with a view of another building. It wasn't nearly as lush as Phillip Warner's in Prairie Falls.

"Have a seat," he said, and pointed to one of the club chairs placed in front of his desk, then walked around to his gray swivel chair.

"My secretary said this concerns the disappearance of a neighbor of mine?" He folded his hands and appeared interested.

"Yes, no one has seen Michael Hawkinson for over a week."

Cavara leaned forward. "Are you sure he didn't take off to get away from his shrew of a wife? We can hear her screaming all the way to our house. Hell, maybe she killed him for the life insurance."

Yeah, don't hold back your opinions. "I've heard you've had altercations with the Hawkinsons."

"We've had words. We don't particularly like each other."

"Where were you on Monday, May 12?"

"Am I a suspect?"

"You're an attorney. You know everyone's a suspect in these deals. And neighbors not getting along is certainly something we look at."

"Well, now wait a minute. I was being flippant. I really know nothing about Hawkinson's life—other than he takes good care of his property and has a whacko wife whom we steer clear of. Now, if you'll excuse me, I believe we're through here."

He stood. I stood. I walked out.

Well, that was interesting, but I would be surprised if he had anything to do with Hawk's disappearance. And it looked like I wasn't the only one who had an unfavorable opinion of Cat, which validated my original impression. Next up—her friends and former co-workers.

THE FIRST WOMAN on the list was Sarah Rice. She worked at a hair salon in Edina. A young thin receptionist went off into the bowels of the salon to retrieve her.

Sarah was a tall, full-figured woman. Her dark-brown hair was streaked with purple, and she wore enough eye make-up for an entire cheerleading squad. Her purple fingernails were unbelievably long. I had to wonder if they got caught in her scissors. She brought me back to the waiting area where she sat next to me and ran her fingers through my hair, her nails scratching my scalp. She gave a few strands of my hair a tug.

"Now, you're going to have to grow your hair out a few weeks before I can do anything with this."

"How can you even use a scissors with nails that long?"

A smile of amusement crossed her face. "Don't you worry, honey. I manage."

"And I'm not here for a hair appointment. I'm Detective Cal Sheehan, and I'm here to speak with you about Cat Hawkinson." I showed her my ID and badge. She looked bewildered. "I'm told you were with her in Mexico."

"Yes," she said tentatively.

"She was with you then?"

"Uh-huh."

"What can you tell me about Cat and her husband?"

"Well, they love each other and are a super great couple." She tilted her head and blinked her fake eyelashes.

"Did Cat share any information about the fight they had before you all left on vacation?"

"They had a fight? All I know is Cat was beside herself with worry when she was notified he was missing."

My phone rang. I picked up without thinking.

"Cal, where the hell are you?"

It was my boss, Sheriff Patrice Clinton.

"Uh . . . in Minneapolis."

"I'm confused. Are you on vacation or conducting an investigation?"

Uh-oh. "I'm not sure how to answer that. Here's the deal. One of my best friend's mother called me and told me she couldn't get hold of her son. So I looked into it—he's been missing a week, his company credit card was being used in Vegas. I took vacation days, so I could go with his cousin to check it out."

"This friend is Michael Hawkinson?"

"Yes."

"Eden Prairie just issued a BOLO and conducted a press conference asking the public for help in finding him."

"I expected as much. I was going to do it if they hadn't."

"And *how* in your mind is this *Birch County's* case?"

"He was on his way to Prairie Falls to see me."

Long pause. "But he never made it?"

"No, but someone used his debit card in Prairie Falls."

"And someone burglarized Chester Brooks's cabin near Rodgers Lake. Now, I know that's a common thing around here, so I didn't think much of it until Austin Spanney told me about the missing items. Beside a half bottle of Johnny Walker Red and a full bottle of Finlandia vodka, Brooks listed rope, a new roll of duct tape, his Remington 12-gage shotgun, and a box of slugs."

"Shit, that doesn't sound good."

"There's a remote chance they're connected."

"Are Betty and Les working the scene?"

"They're still there. Hold on, Cal. I have something coming in."

I could hear her radio loud and clear. They'd found an abandoned black Mercedes SUV—plate match for Michael Hawkinson.

Shit!

She then repeated the news to me.

"I'm on my way," I said.

By the time I had hung up, Sarah had left. I glanced in the back and saw her cutting a client's hair, moving her hands with a flourish like a pianist at a piano. I ran a hand through my hair where she'd scratched my scalp and left.

I called Scott Halberg and told him Hawk's car had been discovered abandoned in Birch County. He said it now looked like it was Birch County's case, but they would be happy to assist where and when needed.

I put off interviewing the rest of Cat's friends and headed straight up to Prairie Falls. As I slowly made my way on I-94 through the construction traffic, I caught my reflection in the rearview mirror. The grimace on my face mirrored the tightness in every muscle in my body. Finding Hawk's car abandoned was not good—not good at all.

7

BROOKS'S CABIN WAS LOCATED eight miles northwest of Prairie Falls. The rustic cabin, painted brown with dark-green trim, was set in a wooded lot about a quarter mile from the road. Deputy Austin Spanney, who went by Spanky, came out and stood on the back steps of the cabin. He was six-foot-four and 230 pounds of rock-hard muscle. Hawk was his height, but the last time I saw him he was beginning to look doughy.

Spanky was soft-spoken and polite to everyone he encountered, but any suspects who mistook his gentleness for stupidity and gave him trouble found out the hard way when he flipped them to the ground and slapped cuffs on in one fell swoop.

As I approached he said, "How was Vegas?" He was one of the few people I'd told where I was headed and why.

"Tell you later. What have we got here?"

"When Mr. Brooks arrived this morning about seven, he noticed this door lock had been pried open. Looks like a tire iron or crowbar. Come on in for the tour. Won't take long. It's a one-room cabin."

Before I went inside, I put on footies and gloves so as not to compromise the scene.

"Hey, Betty and Les," I said to our crime scene investigators dusting surfaces for prints.

Betty said, "Hi. We're pretty much done here."

She was a fifty-something, no-nonsense woman whose real name was Catherine Elizabeth Abbott, but prefered Betty. I called her Catherine for a long while before she corrected me—sometimes I still forget.

Les Ruper ignored me. I didn't take it personally. He looked and acted like a bulldog—grunted a lot, and what he lacked in social skills he made up in job expertise. Betty thought he was autistic.

"I'd like some DNA samples taken," I said.

"Deputy Spanney already requested it. Got some especially good prints off the fridge door and DNA swabs from various places including the toilet rim. Men give us nice drops of urine with their inability to hit the bowl," Betty said.

"Ha. Good then."

Spanky pointed to the table. "Chester Brooks said they ate some of his food—we bagged an empty potato chip bag, three Pepsi Colas, and two empty cans of Dinty Moore Stew."

"It always amazes me how many burglars stop to eat and drink. Burglary is hard work, I guess," I said.

Betty snickered. "Then they have to pee."

Spanky placed his hands on his hips. "We searched the entire property for evidence but didn't find anything. There are neighbors on each side—both full-time residents."

I surveyed the one-room cabin. It was only big enough to hold an old plaid couch, one small round table, a full-sized bed, an old four-burner stove, a chipped white porcelain sink, a few cupboards, and a wood-burner for heat. The bathroom, which appeared to have been a remodeled closet, held a toilet and sink, but had no room for a tub or shower.

"Does Brooks use this as a hunting shack?" I asked.

"Exactly, and he stores his boat here too. Brooks uses the public landing on Rodgers Lake."

"That's a good walleye lake," Les said, as he continued to dust the kitchen cabinets.

"Must be only a mile away," I said.

"That's about right," Les said. That'd been the most he'd spoken to me in months, and today I found out he was a fisherman.

"Where does he live?"

"Prairie Falls," Spanky said. "Yeah, this place is pretty basic. The shower is outside the garage next to the fish-cleaning table."

"Anything taken from the garage?" I asked.

"Mr. Brooks had it locked up, and it didn't appear to be broken into."

"Let's take a look."

Spanky picked up the key from the table, and we made out way out to the garage that was more spacious than the cabin. It had white exterior vinyl siding, a cement floor, and room enough for one extra-large vehicle, plus the sixteen foot Alumacraft fishing boat on a trailer parked inside.

Fingerprint dust covered the doorknob and window into the garage. Nothing inside seemed disturbed. When we returned to the cabin, Betty and Les were starting to pack up.

She said, "I have three hundred photos for you to look through." She chuckled.

"Thanks. Did you use Fluorscein to detect blood evidence?" I asked.

"Yes, and none showed. Now we are on our way to the county garage to take a look at the abandoned Mercedes SUV we had hauled in," Betty said.

"How did it look?"

Spanky said, "Had a broken taillight is all. Happened somewhere else because the broken pieces weren't where it was found. I had some deputies search the area, and they didn't find as much as a footprint, but it rained recently, so whatever was there was wiped out."

"I'd like to take a look," I said.

HAWK'S MERCEDES HAD BEEN found three miles from the Brooks' cabin on an abandoned farmstead, where only a weathered gray house and barn remained. The grove of trees commonly protecting farm buildings from winter's blast had been removed, and the newly planted field came within ten feet of the structures. We parked along the road and walked in on the gravel driveway so infrequently used weeds were growing in the center. NO TRESPASSING signs had been posted along the drive and on each of the buildings. The windows of the house had been boarded.

"The Mercedes was parked next to the house where it was hidden from the road," Spanky said.

"Who found it?" I asked.

"The owner, Lyle Nissen. He thought someone parked there and went for a walk or bike ride or something. He put a note on it saying it was private property. When he came back two days later the SUV was still there, his note still under the wiper blade, so he called it in."

"Did you search both buildings?"

"Yeah, nothing there."

"Was the Mercedes locked?"

"Nope, and no keys were left in it. And because of the rain, there were no tire tracks."

"Where does Lyle live?"

"Half mile down the road. There was nothing out here—not a cigarette butt, pop can, or even a scrap of paper. I was thorough, Cal, but I have the keys if you want to do a walk through. I know you always say two pairs of eyes are better than one."

I nodded. I did want to see the scene for myself. It was difficult for me to relinquish control of an important case to a part-time investigator, with far less experience than I had.

We put on booties and gloves and walked through the front door and into the dark. The stench hit straightaway—a putrid odor mingled with the dank and dusty smell of the abandoned structure. But the odor indicated a rodent infestation, rather than a corpse. We flipped on our flashlights to illuminate the rooms absent of anything other than dust and rodent droppings. Mice scurried across the linoleum, curling and chipped. The faded, top layers of tattered wallpaper were chipped away as well.

Spanky shined his light on footprints. "Those are mine."

"So no one else was in here or their tracks would show in the dust."

"Exactly. The house has been stripped of any useful materials. He's going to take these two buildings down this summer, but until then he keeps everything locked up tight to keep the kids out."

After we looked through the barn, I said, "You're right about nothing helpful here, Spanky, so let's go have a talk with Brooks's neighbors."

THE DOUBLEWIDE TRAILER was nestled in a small clearing approximately fifty yards in from the road. I quickly ran the plates on the small Toyota pickup parked alongside the residence. It came up as registered to Nathaniel Cook. A very pregnant young woman exited the trailer. Her bellybutton created a bump under her knit shirt stretched tightly over her enlarged belly. We got out of the Explorer and approached the smiley, freckle-faced young woman. After I introduced the two of us she said, "Hi, I'm Tammy Johnson."

"There was a break-in at the Brooks's place next door, and we were checking to see if you saw or heard anything recently?" I asked.

Her eyes widened. "A break-in?"

"Have you heard or seen anything out of the ordinary?"

"It's usually real quiet out here, but one day I heard people talking—I thought Chester had company."

"You wouldn't remember the day and time, would you?" I asked.

"Yep, it was a week ago Monday. I was sitting out on the front step getting some sun on my face while I was waiting for my story to come on TV. The *Bold and the Beautiful*? I was anxious to watch that day to find out what happened. They always leave you hangin' on Fridays."

"What time of day was that?"

"Well, my show comes on at twelve-thirty, so just before that."

"Could you tell how many people you heard?"

"Two or three men."

"Was there anything distinctive about the voices? Were they speaking in regular conversation tones, or did they sound upset or angry?"

"Regular voices, except one of the guys shouted 'Hey' real loud. Then I went inside for my story."

"Anything else you remember?"

She wrinkled her nose while she thought about it. "Nope."

"Does Nathaniel live here with you?" I asked.

"Yep. He's sleeping because he works nights at Estelle's Candies."

Spanky took out his notebook and began writing.

"How long have you lived here?" I asked.

"A year."

"Do you know Chester Brooks next door?"

"Oh, sure, he's our landlord," she said. "Nice old guy. He gives us fish and venison, and vegetables from his garden."

"We should speak with your boyfriend at some point," I said.

"Okay, I'll be right back." She went inside.

I asked Spanky, "How far into the woods did you search?"

"To the property lines. It's approximately a hundred yards from the trailer to the Brooks cabin."

"Okay."

A short, slight man came to the screen door of the trailer.

"Nathaniel Cook?" I asked.

"People call me Nate." He stepped outside.

He was wearing a white T-shirt, pajama pants, and flip-flops. He yawned and ran his fingers through his hair. He was quick to smile like his girlfriend, and appeared to be a few years older than Tammy.

I asked him the same questions.

"This is the first I've heard about Tammy hearing anything."

"I didn't know it was a big deal, otherwise I would have told you," she said.

"So you rent this property from Chester Brooks?" I asked.

"Yes, he owns several acres around here."

"Does he also own the residence on the other side of his cabin?" I asked.

"Yes, sir. He used to live in that house before he moved to town."

"Have you met the folks who live there?"

"We tried on two occasions to welcome them, but no one answered the door. So, we kinda gave up."

"How long have they lived there?"

"Just a couple months."

"Do you know their names?"

"I think they're Mexicans," Tammy said. "I forgot what Chester said their names were. Do you remember, Nate?"

He shook his head. "I feel bad because I'm supposed to keep watch on Chester's place. I walk over there a couple times a week. I didn't notice anything. What did they do to it?"

"Not much really."

I didn't want to give him details. He could be the one responsible.

"Well, he doesn't keep much there," Nate said.

"So you've been in Brooks's cabin then?"

"A few times. He had a fish fry the Saturday night of the opener."

"Then you need to go to the county jail as soon as possible to have your fingerprints taken and give a DNA sample to tell yours apart from the burglar's."

"Cool, I've never done that."

ON THE DRIVE OVER to the other rental property, Spanky said, "Why wouldn't Nate Cook have noticed the back door had been jimmied?"

"Maybe he didn't go over there to check like he was supposed to—or he didn't pay close enough attention. Was the door closed when Chester got there?"

"Yeah, but anyone could see the damaged door lock."

"When was the last time Chester had been there?"

"Last Sunday. He left the place late afternoon about five."

THE WHITE, RANCH-STYLE HOUSE was not visible from the road. Marigolds and purple petunias had been newly planted in front of the house.

I rang the bell, waited a few seconds and rang again. The door opened and a goliath-sized man wearing a black eye patch stuck his head out. A faint scar above the left patched eye ran through his eyebrow and up his forehead.

The strong aroma of meat, garlic, and onions cooking drifted out the open door. My stomach rumbled in protest of the meal I'd missed. I flashed my badge and said in my most friendly manner, "Hi. I'm Detective Sheehan with the Birch County Sheriff's Department, and this is my partner, Deputy Spanney. We have a few questions about your neighbor's property. Might we come in?"

He stared at me with his one good eye—dark as pitch. He let seconds pass while considering my request, then stepped back and opened the door. I'm not used to feeling like the small guy with my six-foot-three, 210-pound frame, but this dude had to be at least six-foot-five. He was wearing a plaid flannel shirt, jeans, and cowboy boots; his long, dark hair was pulled into a ponytail at the base of his neck.

I glanced around the living room as we walked through a short hallway into the kitchen. The furnishings were simple and sparse. He went to the stove and turned down the flame under a large pot.

"Smells good," I said.

"What's this about my neighbor?"

"May I have your name for the record?"

He lifted the undamaged brow. "Bobby Lopez," he said.

"Nice to meet you, Mr. Lopez," I said.

I glanced back at Spanky, who had remained in the kitchen doorway a few yards behind me. He nodded at Lopez who returned the gesture. Lopez's reluctance to let me inside was not unusual, but his demeanor was making my skin prickle.

Lopez picked up a Molson Ice sitting on the gold laminate counter, took a sip, then held it up.

"You boys want to join me?" he asked.

"No thanks, we're on duty. We just stopped by to see if you had any information about the break-in next door."

"Break-in? I wasn't aware there was one."

"Have you seen or heard anything unusual within the last ten days?"

He narrowed his eyes like he was thinking about it. "I may have."

When he didn't elaborate, I said, "And what would that have been?"

"A black Mercedes drove into my yard. I looked out the door, and they backed out."

Oh, whoa. "When was this?"

"Maybe a week ago."

"What did this person look like?"

"Couldn't see because of the glare on the windshield."

"Was there more than one person inside?"

He shook his head. "Don't know."

"I'm told you've been renting for a couple months. What was your previous address?"

His good eye shifted back and forth, like he was trying to decide whether to tell me the truth or not.

"LA."

"What kind of work do you do?"

"Invest wisely," he said, with a smirk. "Only renting this place until I can find something I want to purchase."

"Tell me, Mr. Lopez, have you been in the Brooks's cabin?"

"Why yes, Deputy Sheehan, I have. I was there to sign the rental agreement, and then a while back he asked me over for beer."

Was he mocking me?

"Okay, then we'll need you to go to the county jail to give fingerprints and a DNA sample to eliminate you as the burglar—as soon as possible, please."

"And that's necessary?"

"Yes, sir, I'm afraid it is. Well, we won't keep you. Thanks for your time. And here's my card if you should think of anything that would help us find who broke in to your landlord's property."

He took the card and put it in his shirt pocket. "Not much to steal from that cabin," he asked.

"Enough."

He nodded a couple times.

Spanky was already out the door when I turned to ask Lopez, "Anyone else live here?"

"Just me," he said.

"All right, thanks for your time."

When I crawled in the driver's side, Spanky said, "He is one scary, weird hombre."

"Yes, he is."

"We'll want to check him out?"

"We will. First, I'll drop you at your vehicle back at the Brooks's cabin. Then I'll stop by and see Chester Brooks. You've put in a long day. You can go on home."

"Are you taking over the case?" he asked.

"We'll work it together."

"But you're lead?"

"Yeah, I'm lead."

"Think your buddy could be inside Lopez's house?"

"Oh, man, why did you have to ask that?"

"Sorry. I know there's no just cause to search his residence," Spanky said. "I hate that law."

"Me too, but if I could, I'd run twenty-four/seven surveillance on Lopez."

IT WAS APPROACHING six o'clock when I parked on the street in front of Chester Brook's two-story stucco home on Twelfth Street NE. As I walked around a gray Chevy pickup in the driveway, I could hear shrill barking coming from inside the house. A foo-foo dog popped up in window and carried on something fierce as he defended his house.

A short, plump woman answered the door, behind her, a tall, lean man. He scooped up the little yapper just before he reached my ankles. After I gave them my name, the woman said, "I'm Peg and he's Chester. Please, come in."

The dog continued to bark.

"Muffy, be quiet," Chester said, gently petting the tiny dog's head. "York-shire terriers make the best guard dogs."

Muffy growled at me.

"Yeah, they're real lions."

I smelled tuna hotdish. "Have I interrupted your dinner?" I asked.

"No, no. It's not quite ready."

I was lead to the living room and right into the eighties. The piping on the pink and magenta floral sofa and chairs showed wear, but they faced a flat screen television. The room was tidy and clean. A basket of knitting materials sat on the floor by a wood rocker.

Mrs. Brooks sat in the rocker, and Chester took the stuffed floral chair. They offered me the one chair that appeared new: a brown cloth recliner.

"This is a fantastic chair," I said as I sat in it.

The couple beamed. "It's a rocker too," Mrs. Brook's said. "Our kids gave it to us for our fortieth wedding anniversary. We bought ourselves a new HD TV."

"Wow, nice. Look, I'll try to make this quick, so you can get back to your dinner. You talked to my partner, Deputy Spanney, but I just wanted to touch base with you as well. Have you had any burglaries prior to this one?"

"No, that was a first for me. I know other people who have, so I never keep much worth stealing out there, but my shotgun. Now, it's gone."

"Hopefully, it will be recovered."

"That would be real nice."

"Anything else you can think of that would help us?"

"Golly, can't say as I do."

"Do you remember seeing a black Mercedes in the area?"

"No, I'd remember a Mercedes. You don't see too many 'round these parts."

"That's true. I met your tenants."

"Oh," he said. "Good renters, both of 'em."

"Do you run credit checks before you sign the leases?"

"Yep. Phillip Warner suggested I do that."

Phillip was a local attorney—Adriana's old boss.

"Tell me what you know about Bobby Lopez."

"He had good credit. I'm not sure how long he's gonna be there because he wanted a month-to-month, and that was okay by me."

"Did you ask for a former address?"

"It's on the form. Want me to get it for ya?"

"If you wouldn't mind."

While he was retrieving the paperwork, Peg told me they had four more rental properties in the area. I wondered if all that rent could afford them a new sofa. People are funny with what they choose to spend their money on. I admit I'm tight with mine, but I haven't had frayed furniture since . . . well, since Adriana insisted I buy new furniture four years ago. Okay, not that long ago.

Chester photocopied the lease applications for both his renters. Bobby Lopez had listed his former address in Bel Air, California, and although the form had space for three references, he'd written only one.

"Al Gore?" I said.

"Yeah, well, I'm not sure he really knows him, but he paid for four months in advance and that was all the reference I needed."

"Okay then," I said.

I left Mr. and Mrs. Brooks to their tuna hotdish, then stopped at the department to sign out and turn in my vehicle. Because I hadn't eaten since early morning, I stopped at Save Rite to pick up a prepackaged salad and the biggest steak they had.

While the coals were heating up, I sat on my back deck enjoying a beer when a blonde wearing short shorts appeared on the deck of the house across the alley from me. If binoculars wouldn't be too obvious, I would have retrieved them to get a better look. That house had been vacant for months . . . and presto—now I have something to look at. I grinned and took a pull of my beer.

She was facing me but acted unaware I was there. She took out a phone and made a call. She laughed, then went inside. Jesus, I'm pathetic—a voyeur watching the hot neighbor woman.

I HAD JUST FINISHED cleaning up the dishes when my cell phone rang. I looked at the display—my mother.

"Hey, Mom."

"How are you?"

"Busy."

"Were you gone?"

"Yeah, I was in Vegas and Minneapolis looking for Hawk. No one's heard from him in ten days."

"You didn't find him?"

"Nope. I don't know what to think."

"Barb is beside herself."

"She called you? You knew I was in Vegas?"

"Yes, and she was counting on you bringing him back."

"He wasn't in Vegas."

"Then why did you go out there?"

"Look, Mom, I have to go."

"Oh, okay. Let me know if there's anything I can do for you, sweetie."

"Get a job. Volunteer."

"Oh . . . ha-ha. Bye now."

I TURNED ON MY COMPUTER and Googled Robert Lopez; I got over five million hits. Common name it seems, and I knew he wasn't the songwriter or the golfer.

I checked with the DMV database. He'd had a Minnesota Driver's License since April. That must have been when he moved into Chester's house. I turned to NCIC, the national crime database for law enforcement, to see if Lopez had a record. There were several hits, but none seemed to be the Bobby Lopez I met.

8

May 23
Eleven days missing.

THE EARLY MORNING LIGHT filtered through the slats of the blinds, casting stripes across my bedroom. I rolled over to spoon Shannon, but my body only met the bunched-up comforter. I hated the moments when I realized she was no longer there.

I rolled out of bed. Sunrise—time to run. I put on shorts and a T-shirt and looked for Bullet. Then I remembered he was still at Shannon's, and I'd have to drop by and pick him up. She doesn't get to have him when I'm home.

WHEN I ROUNDED SIXTH STREET, I noticed a tall, blonde woman running a block ahead of me. Could be my neighbor. Her ponytail was swishing back and forth in time with each stride. I increased my speed, but she was really trucking, and I didn't catch up until the Northwoods Coffee Shop parking lot. Must be six o'clock because the front door was just being unlocked by one of the employees. The woman went in. I felt for the emergency five bucks I kept in my pocket. When I entered, I headed directly to the bathroom to rinse the sweat off my face and arms. Then I went to the order station and ordered the coffee. A lemon scone could push it past five bucks.

The blonde and I were the only customers. I sat at a table three away from her and in her line of vision. She ignored me while she read the newspaper for fifteen minutes. I finally asked myself what the hell I was doing and jogged home.

After I got back, I showered and dressed, then flipped on the TV to watch the news as I ate my breakfast—three packets of instant oatmeal. Michael Hawkinson was not yet in the news, but that would change today with the news of his car being found. I had to get hold of Cat before the media did.

She answered on the third ring.

"Sorry if I woke you, but you need to know Hawk's car has been found in Birch County."

"Oh, my God. Oh, my God. Where?"

"On an abandoned farm place."

"What does that mean?"

"I don't know yet."

"It means something. Do you think he's . . . dead?"

"I don't think anything right now. I have a meeting this morning with the sheriff, and we'll discuss how to proceed."

"But it looks bad. Doesn't it?"

"Cat, I'm sorry I don't have more to tell you. I just wanted you to know before you saw it on TV."

"Thank you for that anyway. Will you call me after your meeting?"

"I'll try."

Sheriff Patrice Clinton and Spanky were waiting for me in the large conference room on third floor across from the Investigations Office. Patrice was an attractive, trim, strong, well-spoken woman—the first woman sheriff of Birch County and politely said, a hands-on type of manager.

She wanted to be updated on the particulars of the burglary case. When wrapping up, Spanky said, "I think it's related to Cal's missing friend."

Patrice cradled her head of dark hair with her hands. "Because his vehicle was found three miles away?"

"Yes," he said.

"Cal?" she asked, removing her hands and leaning back in her chair.

"Could be."

"Well, let's give your friend's missing person's case a number."

As I put a case number down on the form, a lump appeared in my throat. This was real. My buddy was really missing.

"Why has this gone on so long before someone took charge?" Patrice asked.

"We didn't know if he'd made it back to the Cities or not," I said.

"And now we know he didn't" she said.

"*Think* is more like it. We don't have . . ."

"A body," she said.

"No," I said.

"I can't afford a massive search party without more information."

I stared at her. "What can you afford?"

"Let's use our new canine unit and our reserve equestrian team out near where his car was found. I'll authorize it this morning. Is your friend into anything illegal?"

"Not that I'm aware of. He has a great job, a big house in Eden Prairie, a pretty wife."

"This pretty wife hasn't noticed any evidence of drug use or hidden financial problems?"

"I will ask again."

"Has she been notified?"

"Yes."

"Is there a big life insurance policy? Affairs?"

"I've thought of all that, plus more."

"More?"

"His father-in-law is a powerful business guy."

She cast me a quizzical look. "How powerful? Mafia powerful?"

"Probably not, but he fashions himself as a tough guy."

Her eyebrows furrowed dismissively. "Well, while we're searching for Mr. Hawkinson, I suggest you ready yourself for Victoria Lewis's trial next week. Oliver Bakken wants to meet with you ASAP."

"Shit."

"Did you forget it was on the docket?"

"No, it just came up fast."

"I should think you'd want to get it over with."

I nodded. The trial meant Troy Kern and my ex-girlfriend, Adriana Valero, would be in town to testify. Just what my struggling marriage didn't need.

Victoria Lewis was the daughter of a mega-rich business tycoon named Adam Lewis. My ex-girlfriend, Adriana Valero, had been married to Lewis for a few months. Not knowing her connection to Adriana, I'd briefly dated Victoria when she first moved to town to work at one of her father's newspapers, *The Birch County Register*.

Victoria was a sociopath who wanted her daddy's attention and admiration—and would do anything to get it—like orchestrate anonymous threats against her own person. She paid some fool kid to shoot a hunting arrow through my apartment window nearly missing us—Victoria and me—so she could get a newspaper story about the incident. Also, she got off on frightening and retaliating against those whom she perceives as having done harm to her or her daddy. My ex, Adriana, was one of those people. Victoria dumped paint on her BMW convertible and burned her house to the ground. We had enough evidence against Victoria to arrest her and bring her to trial.

Since Troy and I investigated all these cases, we would be called in as witnesses. Oliver Bakken could have added filing false police reports to the mix, but he was only prosecuting Victoria on fraud, vandalism, and arson. Because of my "entanglement"with her during the newspaper threat incidents, it was going to be tricky businesses.

I wasn't exaggerating when I said she threw herself at me, and I was hooked by her beauty and sexuality. Our relationship was brief and ended once I saw her for who she was. She had a thing for cops and had duped several of us, including our very own Spanky. While she was in town secretly harassing Adriana, she hung out with him—reeling him in up to his bobber. He didn't know who she really was because she went blond, had some plastic surgery and assumed her roommate's identity—Sadie Jones. He'd be called as a witness in her trial. He'd made the arrest. In hindsight, he was the wrong person to bring her in.

"Oliver thinks it's a shoo-in,"Patrice continued.

"Oh, that's not a good sign," I said. "Oliver does better when he's unsure about a case."

"He doesn't think she will even show up."

"She may not. She could be hiding out in France with her aunt," I said.

"I think it was ballsy to bring her to trial anyway."

Spanky said, "Matt Hauser says the attorneys her father hired are so slick they slide through the courtroom like greased pigs."

Matt was a deputy assigned to courts since he was hired twenty-six years ago. He could pretty much call the jury verdicts.

"It'll be interesting," I said.

MY FIRST ORDER OF BUSINESS was to obtain warrants for Frank's Plaza and Wells Fargo for the film footage of their security cameras. Both businesses said they still had the discs for May 12 and would have just handed them over, but it was always best to follow legal protocol.

After getting Judge Olann's signature, I stopped at Frank's Plaza on First Street and Highway 51. I found Anton Frank in his office. He smiled and shook my hand.

"How's it going," he asked.

"Good, and you?"

"Great, great. I suppose you're here for the discs?"

"Yes. Did you view them?"

"Didn't have time." He handed two over. "One is for the camera behind the cash register, the other is above the pumps," he said.

I smiled. "If one gives us something, I'll have to keep it as evidence," I said.

He nodded. "No problemo. Have some coffee or soda before you leave," he said.

He offered free beverages to all law enforcement officers.

"No, thanks. I have to get back to work."

"Sorry about your friend. Tamika is bummed she's not on the case."

Of course she is.

"She'll be involved."

Tamika was his wife and the other full-time investigator. He was white, she was African American; he was five-foot-seven, she was five-eleven; he was 140 pounds, she was 170; he was forty-eight, she was thirty-eight—and they were happy.

"Tamika said the odds of finding your buddy alive aren't good at this point."

"No . . . well, I better be on my way."

You know how you can complain about a family member, but if someone else does, you get defensive? That was how I felt about hearing Hawk's chances. I wanted to believe he was okay. But after eleven days, I had to face it—the statistics weren't in his favor. But Hawk wasn't a typical victim. Was he into something bad, or was he an innocent victim of a random crime?

I then drove one block to First Street and Wells Fargo Bank and picked up their disc, which showed footage of the ATM. I was thrilled they still had the recording of May 12 on disc.

TAMIKA, SPANKY, AND I each grabbed one of the three discs. Spanky took the ATM, Tamika took the inside camera at Frank's Plaza, I had the gas pumps.

Tamika said, "Anton's looking mighty handsome behind the register."

"Good to know," I said.

I scrolled through the black-and-white recording to May 12, then down from 9:00 a.m. Frank's had two rows of four pumps. The camera was mounted on the top of the middle of the canopy over the pumps for a full view of all vehicles. When I got to May 12, at 11:13, Hawk's Mercedes pulled up to pump number five. I know the number because that's the one I liked to use.

"Here he is getting out of the Mercedes."

Spanky and Tamika came to take a look. He was wearing a baseball cap, jeans, and a long-sleeved dark T-shirt. We watched together as Hawk slid his credit card into the slot, pressed a button, and began pumping gas. A light-colored van pulled up behind Hawk.

A white male with long hair exited the slide door of the van and tried to pump at six without using a credit card. He was wearing a sleeveless light-colored shirt and dark shorts.

Spanky said, "He's going in to pre-pay with cash."

Tamika said, "He's a big dude. Looks like he's a body-builder. Look at those tattoos covering his arms and legs."

"That's a lot of ink," I said.

"That's a lot of man," Tamika said.

Spanky and I frowned at her.

"What?" she said.

When he returned from the store, he moved in close to Hawk and spoke to him. Hawk said something to the guy.

"Wish we could hear what they're saying," Spanky said.

The driver pumped gas while the big guy continued to talk to Hawk.

"Driver is a small guy."

"Driver, turn toward the camera so we can see your face," I said. He wore a hoodie which was obstructing a view of his face.

"That's a Cardinal's hoodie," Spanky said. "See the dark stripe from the shoulder down the arm, two white stripes on the upper sleeve?"

"You know your sportswear," Tamika said.

Just as Hawk replaced the nozzle into the pump, the driver of the van quit pumping gas and looked toward the big guy who was walking back toward the van. I caught my first glimpse of his face.

I said, "The small guy could be Raybern Ginty, the guy I interviewed in Vegas."

Tamika pointed to the screen. "Hey, look, it's Shannon driving up to the pump across from your friend. Does she know him?"

"Yes, of course. They must not see each other."

I backtracked through the tape, so I could see the Pilot rolling in again. It definitely was Shannon, but who the hell was sitting in her front passenger seat? Too big for Luke. She got out to pump gas. I moved my face closer to the screen. Who the hell was that?

"They're following him," Spanky said.

My attention diverted from Shannon's car back to the white van rolling out behind Hawk as he drove out of the station and turned east.

"Tamika, see if you can pick up the tattooed dude inside the station."

She went to her computer and clicked away until she found him. "Here he is," she said.

The man looked to be in his thirties, long thin face, big nose and ears.

"He looks familiar," Tamika said.

"Let's have Samantha Polansky make photos of the men, then enhance the plate on the white van," I said.

Samantha was our IT person.

"Hey, look at this. I think the white van used the ATM at Wells Fargo."

Spanky scrolled the film to the point where the white van pulled up.

"Same hoodie. See the white stripes?" Spanky said.

"Yep, he withdrew cash," I said. "What time does the recording say?" I asked.

"Twelve forty-two," he said.

"That's an hour and a half after their encounter at Frank's. Something happened within that time frame."

"So, if they hurt your friend," Tamika said, putting a finger up, "they did it without anyone seeing."

"His broken taillights indicate they could have rear-ended him to get him out of his vehicle," Spanky said.

I said, "Then forced him into their van where they robbed him. One of the passengers could have driven his Mercedes off, parked it at Nissen's farm. They could have forced his pin number out of him."

"I'll bet his body isn't far from where his car was found," Tamika said. "There's a million places to dump a body around here."

"Tamika! This is Cal's friend we're talking about," Spanky said.

She looked at me with wide eyes. "Oh, sorry. Was I being insensitive? I was, wasn't I?"

"Yes, but I'm thinking the exact thing," I said.

"Why didn't they steal the Mercedes?" Spanky asked.

"Because they're not car thieves. They're something worse," I said.

"When is the canine unit going to be dispatched?" Spanky said.

"I'll check right now. I didn't finish interviewing Cat Hawkinson's friends. Which of you wants to drive down to the Cities tomorrow?"

"I will," Spanky said.

"There's a list with phone numbers on my desk. Tamika, you contact Samantha to make some still copies. You know what we need."

"On it."

I wanted to ask to have the photo of Shannon's passenger enhanced. But shook off the thought. I was being ridiculous—it was probably her dad.

I went into the conference room where we met for larger cases. It was a white board opposite a bank of windows. I drew a line down the middle of the board. On the left I wrote "Brooks's Cabin Burglary" and circled it. Then I drew a web of four lines off the circle to resemble a wheel, and I wrote the neighbors' names on two and made question marks on the others. It was possible the perpetrators were kids or druggies looking for something to pawn for quick cash, like a shotgun. I made a note to check the area shops.

In the middle of the whiteboard I drew another larger web: one circle in the middle with Michael Hawkinson's name in the center. Off it I drew three lines with a circle at the end. In the circles I wrote people, circumstances, motive. Off people I drew six lines for Raybern Ginty, Nevada Wynn, Roseanna Martinez, tattoo guy, Cat Hawkinson, and Irving and Monica Ames. We always look at the family.

For circumstances I made lines for Mercedes found abandoned, gas station interaction, cash card used by someone in white van. For motive I had a question mark. I'd have to add to the web as evidence came in. I wasn't certain if these two cases where related. Hopefully, the DNA tests would tell us.

I filled out a search warrant for Hawk's financials and phone records and went over and had Judge Olann sign it during his lunch hour.

AT ONE O'CLOCK, I met the canine unit out at the Nissen farm site where Hawk's car had been found abandoned. We had one search-and-rescue dog, a Malinois/German shepherd mix named Vito. He was purchased from some

Eastern European country, made possible with a generous donation from anonymous benefactors. They were Silver Rae Dawson's parents. Their daughter's remains had been found fifteen years after she went missing. Memorial donations had poured in from across the nation, and the Dawsons wanted to do something with the money that would help others in their situation. Little did I know when I suggested the fund to the Dawsons, the dog purchased would be deployed to help find my best friend.

Deputy Dan Babcock was the dog's handler. Dan had picked up Hawk's Twins baseball cap from Mrs. Hawkinson. That was the only thing of his his Mom hadn't laundered. I was there to document and record the search.

Dan took the dog off leash to let him track. With nose to the ground, Vito sniffed around and looked up at Dan.

"He's not picking up a scent," Dan said.

"So he wasn't here?"

"Either that or the recent rain washed it away."

I nodded. "Okay. Let's go on over to the Brooks's cabin to see if Vito picks up one there."

Dan followed me over. Chester Brooks agreed to meet us there with the key. Before we entered, Dan gave Vito another smell of Hawk's cap. The dog moved quickly about the room, and Dan said it was clear he caught a scent on the floor, a chair, and in the bathroom.

We tried the garage, no scent there. So, we knew Hawk had been at the cabin and possibly at the farmstead, but neither place had any traces of blood, or shell cartridges, which allowed me to remain optimistic he was still alive.

I thanked Dan and Chester, then headed back to my office where I had a message from Oliver Bakken to see him ASAP. Before I did so, I went into the conference room and drew a line from the burglary case to the missing persons case and wrote M. Hawkinson was at cabin. There were plenty of people between the farmstead and the cabin Hawk could have asked for help, and he wouldn't abandon his car and walk three miles to the cabin and burglarize it. He was forced. But why?

IT WAS A NICE DAY, so instead of taking the tunnel to the courthouse, I walked outside over to the impressive red-brick building built in 1913. I walked past the courtrooms and offices on the ground floor and down the marble staircase to the county attorney's office on the lowest level.

Oliver's clerk said they were waiting for me. John Mertz, assistant county attorney, was half of the "they." Mertz was in his early forties, balding, and had a pleasant disposition. I liked him more than Oliver who reminded me of a rooster, the way he strutted and held his beak of a nose high in the air.

"You wanted to see me?" I said.

Oliver pointed to the empty chair. "Have a seat." I did and he said, "Ready to testify in the Lewis trial?"

"No."

Oliver pursed his lips. "John will prep you. Jury selection will wind up by Monday. Just so you know, the defense will be allowed to bring up your prior relationship with Miss Lewis, and Troy's with Ms. Valero."

"Terrific. I thought you said it wouldn't."

"The judge said the defense's argument that the relationships tainted your arson investigation was valid. Also, defense added a last-minute character witness," Oliver said.

"Who is it?" I asked.

"Brock Snyder," Mertz said. "We're investigating him."

"Did her attorney mention if she's showing up?" I asked.

"Didn't ask. Don't care," Oliver said.

"Good for you," I said.

"We've got her. Now John will brief you."

I followed John into his adjoining office and once we closed the door behind us, I said, "Shouldn't he be more worried than he is?"

"Just between you and me, Oliver's worst enemy is his ego. When he feels intimidated, the posturing begins. Acts like he won and the buzzer hasn't sounded. Do you know he wouldn't have caught that Brock Snyder was added as a witness if I hadn't pointed it out."

"Who is he?"

"At this point, all I know is that he is a pilot. He lives in Minneapolis, divorced, no children."

"A pilot? I wondered if he was the jerk in the biplane who was flying too low over town."

"I'll check to see if he owns a plane. Now, we'd better brief you."

So I spent an hour I didn't have, going over Oliver's questions and likely ones the defense would hit me with. John said to answer the questions truthfully and not give any additional information unless Oliver asked for it, which was nothing new. But this was not an ordinary case. Oliver was up against a defense team skilled at discrediting testimony and rattling prosecutors.

WHEN I GOT BACK to the office, Tamika showed me the photos Samantha Polansky had made up. She was able to print off good images of the two men at Frank's. One was a partial face shot, and it looked like it could be Ginty. The windshield created a glare so we couldn't get a good shot of the front passenger.

"Tamika, may I ask you a question?"

"Ask away," she said.

"Have you spoken to Shannon lately?"

"Sure, we talk most every day."

"Do you know who was with her that day at the station?"

"I think you should ask her."

"But you know?"

"I think so, yes."

"Not her dad, then."

"No."

"Is she *dating*?"

"Cal, I'm not getting in the middle of this."

"But you're listening to her, so you already are."

"Listening. I'm also offering her advice, which she isn't taking."

"Which is?"

"To end it."

"With me or him?"

"Him, of course."

"Jesus Christ, just tell me who it is."

She shook her head.

I drove directly to Shannon's house. Her Pilot was in the open garage along with Clara's Volvo. Clara answered the door.

"Well, hi, Cal, this is a surprise."

"I need to speak with Shannon."

"Come on in."

"No, would you tell her to come outside? I don't want to talk in front of the kids."

"You seem upset."

"I am."

"I'll get her."

Shannon had already changed out of her uniform into a pair of black slacks and a silky white blouse I hadn't seen before. I caught the scent of a new perfume as she stepped out the door. She'd dropped weight; her hair looked lighter in color and cut in a new style.

"What's up?"

"Who are you seeing?"

She straightened her spine and sighed, and then Bullet bounded out the door, which had been left ajar. He wiggled his body up against mine, so I leaned down to pet him. That's when I noticed her polished toenails in new sandals. She rarely bothered to polish her toenails.

I looked up at her from a crouching position. "So, are you?"

She shrugged. "Yes."

My face prickled. I experienced it whenever I was blindsided. A lump formed in my throat, and I felt sick to my stomach.

"For how long?" I asked.

She ran her hand through her hair. "Not very."

"I thought we agreed we'd wait until our counseling sessions were through—and *together* we would decide."

"Well, we aren't making any headway, are we? I told Michael I was through with marriage counseling. I'm taking Luke in for individual counseling and if you wish, we can continue to meet as a family."

"Well, it'd been nice to have been in on this decision making process instead of finding out you were seeing someone while I was examining a frickin' video feed from Frank's Plaza."

As I spoke, she looked around the neighborhood. I may have raised my voice.

Her face had turned crimson. She took a deep breath and blinked several times. "Shit," she said.

"Just tell me who it is."

She hesitated then whispered, "Mac Wallace."

"Mac Wallace? The realtor with his smiley mug on all the billboards?"

"Yes."

I shook my head and said, "Come on, Bullet. We're going home."

Bullet romped across the front lawn and waited at the truck door, his tail wagging a mile a minute. As I pulled away, I looked back to see her still standing on the steps with her arms crossed. She used a fist to wipe her eyes. Good. She *should* feel bad.

THE PHONE WAS RINGING as I walked in the door. The display said it was Shannon's home phone. I fully expected it to be her, contrite and apologetic, but it was Clara.

"I just called to ask how you're doing. You looked so upset."

"Did you know Shannon was seeing another man?"

"She didn't tell me she was, but I figured she was meeting someone going out all dolled up."

"When did it start?"

"Beginning of March."

"So over two months."

"Yes. My daughter said she saw her with a man at Minnesota Fare."

"That's just great. I feel like a gigantic fool."

"Cal, it's not your fault, you know."

"It's never one person's fault, Clara. I had my part in it. Look, I should be talking to Shannon. Is she home?"

"Yes, after you left, she canceled her plans."

"May I speak with her?"

"Sure. Just a second."

A minute passed before Shannon said, "Hi. Look, I'm sorry you found out about Mac before I had a chance to tell you."

"You had the last two months to tell me. I think we need to end our relationship, so you can feel better about the new one. I'll call Phillip Warner and get things started."

Silence.

"Shannon?"

"If that's what you want."

I laughed.

"What's funny?"

"How you turned it around on me. I can't talk to you right now."

I hung up, picked up Shannon's favorite coffee mug and threw it at the fireplace. Bullet barked, then whined.

"Oh, shit. Sorry, boy."

I put him outside and swept up the pieces. Then the front doorbell rang. I looked through the peephole and saw someone I didn't expect to see—Cat Hawkinson.

I opened the door. "Cat?"

"You didn't call me back."

"Oh, sorry. I got busy."

"Well, I need to know what's going on."

"Okay. Come on in."

As we walked the hallway to the kitchen she said, "I was wondering if I might stay with you and Shannon, if you have room, that is. My new credit cards haven't arrived yet. Daddy gave me some cash, but it's not enough to stay in a hotel room for long."

"Um, sure. You can take our third floor efficiency apartment."

Our former nanny, Britt, used it, but Clara chose Colby's old room.

She took a look around the kitchen she said, "This is nice. I like it."

"Thanks."

Her eyebrows knitted. "So, where is everybody?"

"Um . . . Shannon and I are separated, and the kids are with her this week."

She made a flinching motion with her head and neck like she stepped in dog shit.

"Oh . . . why didn't you tell me?"

"You're having your own problems."

"Can I ask what happened?"

"I'd rather not talk about it."

Then came the uncomfortable silence where seconds seem like minutes.

I said, "Are you hungry?"

"Not really, but I suppose I should eat."

"Italian, Chinese, or pizza. They all deliver."

I didn't want to be seen in public with Hawk's wife—or any other woman, for that matter, so I could remain superior.

"Italian."

We both selected a pasta dish, and I called in the order in. She had brought a bottle of wine, so we opened it. She suggested we sit out on the deck and wait for the delivery, and I didn't know how to say I didn't want my neighbors to see her, so I went along with it.

I shared with her most of what we knew and what we could do to find him, which wasn't much without a lead.

"How are you holding up?" I asked.

"I'm not. I can't stand to be in my own skin these days. Look at my hands." She held out her hand. I could see it shake. "I'm so afraid he's dead."

"I don't think . . ."

She got a text and ignored me to read it. Then she glared at me.

"I knew you were questioning my friends, but they're getting the feeling you think I had something to do with Michael's disappearance."

"It's routine to look at the family members in these cases."

Her bottom lip quivered. "I answered all your questions truthfully."

"People lie all the time. I hear many more lies than the truth in my job."

She sat up straight. "So, you think I'm lying and I'm a suspect? Really?"

"*Everyone* and *everything* in his life will be looked at. I've got warrants for your bank statements and phone calls."

"Why didn't you just ask me what you needed? Seems like you're going about this behind my back."

"You think my investigation is bad, wait until the media starts looking at you. Your life, as you know it, will be turned upside down and inside out. Cat, is there anything you haven't told me? Was Hawk into gambling or drugs or in trouble of some kind? Anything that could turn up by asking around?"

She put her hands to her cheeks. "Okay, there was this one time . . . a long time ago. We were invited to a party in downtown Minneapolis by these people we barely knew. They had cocaine. We tried it."

"Okay. Did he seem to like it?"

"Yes and no. It was a terrific high, but we both agreed it made us feel too weird, and we never did it again."

"How do you know he didn't?"

"I just do, okay? You know what? I don't need this. I changed my mind about staying here. You have my cell phone number. Call me when you find out something."

She got up. I don't know why I felt bad she was leaving, but I did.

"Where are you going?"

"Why? So you'll know where to come and *arrest* me?"

"Cat, this isn't personal. I have to do my job to find Hawk and why he's missing."

"Yeah? Well, I'd appreciate it if you'd stop calling him 'Hawk.' It's a god-damn bird of prey."

She picked up her purse she'd set on the counter, stomped off, and slammed my front door. My my.

I texted Spanky and asked how much he'd accomplished interviewing Cat's girlfriends. He texted me back saying he was finishing up tomorrow morning and returning by noon.

I Googled Mac Wallace. His realty company popped up first. Boring stuff. I looked up his address and phone number for future reference. The address looked familiar. He lived in Riverview Estates. The guy had money. I stared at the notebook page and decided the future was now.

IT WASN'T UNTIL I GOT to Wallace's gate that I realized he'd bought the Gage's house. Bet he got a good deal. Dr. Bentley and Mrs. Lillian Gage fled to Duluth after a family scandal. Adriana Valero's old boss, Phillip Warner, lived in this development as well. I needed to call him tomorrow—no tomorrow was Saturday. It'd have to wait until Monday.

Since Wallace's gate was open, I took it as an invitation. There were lights on in the colossal brick home. Before I even exited my truck, he opened the front door and stepped out. I approached him.

"You're Cal Sheehan," he said. He stood on the top step looking down at me.

"And you're the asshole who's banging my wife."

He turned his face away from me and shook his head.

"No? You're not banging my wife?"

"You're being unnecessarily crude. Is this an official call, or are you here to intimidate me?"

I nodded. "Yeah, the latter."

He was better looking in person than his photo on the billboards. I could see why Shannon was attracted to him. He was wearing khaki slacks, a white dress shirt, and a blue tie. Probably what he was going to wear on his date—with my wife. I took a deep breath and told myself to remain calm even though I wanted to punch his face bloody. I stayed at the bottom of the steps to keep my distance, so I wouldn't be tempted.

"I don't want to argue with a man in a sheriff's uniform wearing a gun, so I'm asking you politely to leave. If you don't, I will call 911."

"Have I *threatened* you in any way?"

"You're *being here* is a threat."

"You're being a bit dramatic. It is not my intent to make you feel *threatened*." I put my hands up. "I'm here to politely ask you to stay away from my *wife* and *my kids* until the divorce is final."

"I haven't met your kids . . . and it's Shannon's decision—all of it."

"I'm just asking you to back off for the time being."

"Like I said, it's up to Shannon."

I nodded slowly. "Well, I thought you'd be a man about this, but I guess you're still a boy who wants what he wants when he wants it no matter who gets hurts."

"Wow. Talk about the pot calling the kettle black. I think you need to look in the mirror to reflect on why your wife left you."

What the hell did she tell him? "Yeah? What about *your* wife? Why did she leave your ass?"

"Don't come back here."

"We'll see about that."

Before I climbed in my truck, I gave him the finger like a damn twelve-year-old. I couldn't help myself. Oh, boy. I was crossing the line from a protective husband into a jerk, and I knew I'd be hearing from Shannon very shortly.

As I drove home, my cell phone rang. I glanced at the display and didn't pick up. I was through fighting with her—and for her.

9

May 24
Twelve days missing.

O N SATURDAY MORNING at 7:00 a.m., I met with the sheriff's reserve sergeant, David O'Neil, who was coordinating the equestrian search team. As the six volunteer deputies were heading out on their horses, Tom and Barb Hawkinson drove up and parked in front of the horse trailers and sheriff's vehicles. When I saw Cat get out of the backseat, I knew where she had gone after she left me last night—to her "beloved" in-laws.

"Hello, Cat. Surprised to see you out here."

"I called the sheriff to find out if a search was being conducted. She told me you were out here with the horses."

"It's going to be a long day. I don't know what you can do here."

"You'll see," she said.

"And what does that mean?" I asked.

She pointed to a large vehicle approaching, and then I understood. A WCCO news van drove by us and parked ahead of all the vehicles.

"You called them?"

"Not me," Cat said, looking toward Tom.

I turned to Tom Hawkinson. "This isn't a good idea, Tom."

"What do you expect us to do? Just sit on our hands?"

"No, but calling in a news crew creates a whole lot of circus without the peanuts and popcorn."

"Cal, we need the public's help with this whole deal."

A female reporter approached. "Mr. and Mrs. Hawkinson, can we have you stand by the horse trailers?" she asked.

I held back, watching Barb and Cat give their accounts of how Hawk had been missing for several days before the authorities took his disappearance seriously. Barb mentioned I was the only one interested in finding him, and that Sydney and I flew out to Vegas only to discover someone else had been using his credit cards. Then Barb Hawkinson invited all Minnesotans to join the search. Oh, man.

A light plane flew over, fairly low. Next it would be news helicopters.

After they'd finished questioning Hawk's family, I was sought out. Refusing to make a statement would make me look like a self-serving prick, so I decided to defend our delayed action.

"Until Michael Hawkinson's vehicle was found in Birch County, there was no evidence he'd been in our jurisdiction. When Sheriff Clinton was made aware of this, she ordered a canine and equestrian search at once. If and when we have something to report, the sheriff will convene a press conference. I have no further comments at this time."

As I walked away, the reporter shouted questions about an organized community search effort. I hid in my Explorer and called Patrice. I describe the situation and suggested she send out more squads for crowd control and appoint someone to manage the search effort.

"Why can't you coordinate it?" she asked.

"Because I have too much to do. I need to get back to the office so I can do my job. You do want me to solve Hawk's disappearance and the burglary, right?"

"Okay, okay. I'll take care of it. We have a couple light plane pilots who are searching the open areas from the air."

"When did you decide that?"

"I didn't. Irving Ames called me—your friend's father-in-law?"

"I know who he is."

"Well, he demanded I have my deputies go door to door and search every residence in the county."

"And you said?"

"That we didn't have the resources to pull that off. He said he was hiring planes to do an aerial search and divers to search Rodgers Lake. So, he kind of forced my hand to commit our sheriff's reserve water patrol as well. Why didn't you tell me about Ames?"

"I thought I had. Honestly, I didn't think the prick cared enough to get involved."

"Don't you know powerful pricks like to flex their muscles for the world to see how very powerful they are? Anyway, please stay until someone gets there to take your place."

"My place? I'm one guy, and there'll be one gigantic circus here any minute."

"Damn it. This is just what I need."

By eight thirty, the public was beginning to arrive, along with folks from KSTP, KARE 11, *Star Tribune*, and *St. Paul Pioneer Press* newspapers. It was clear someone did a thorough job of notifying the media.

When newly appointed Chief Deputy Carole Knight and four squad cars arrived to take charge, I waved at her and got the hell out of Dodge. What was supposed to take me a half hour, grabbed almost two hours of my time.

WHEN I ARRIVED AT THE OFFICE, Tamika was waiting for me. Her eyes were lit up as she said, "Remember I said the big dude with the tattoos looked familiar. Well, his name is Glenn Hayes. DOB was 12/25/80. Two years ago I arrested him on possession with intent to sell. He lives here in Prairie Falls. He's been in trouble since he was a kid, mostly small-time burglaries to feed his drug habit. Released from St. Cloud last January."

"Maybe Ginty was in Prairie Falls to see this guy."

I then called the lab to find out if Brooks's tenants, Nate Cook, Tammy Johnson, and Bobby Lopez, had come in yet. Les said he was busy and would get back to me. That man could never give me an answer right away.

I checked my email messages. I had one from Hennepin County Sheriff's Department that Raybern Jerome Ginty was now in their custody. That was quick. He also gave me the Minneapolis address they had for him.

While I was filling out the paperwork for search warrants for my four suspects (Raybern Jerome Ginty, Nevada Wynn, Roseanne Martinez, and Glenn Hayes), Greg Woods stopped by to tell me he arrested Jesse Emerson last night. He was Clifford Emerson's kid.

"Following in his old man's footsteps?"

"Nah, he just had a little weed on him. I wrote him up, gave him a ride home. Clifford was there. He must be drinking at home lately—his car hasn't been at Buzzo's. He's still not back driving for Estelle's. When's that lawsuit going to be settled anyway?"

"Not soon enough for me."

"My Jen's a friend of his wife, Celia. She had to go back to work at the post office. Times are tough. Jesse's acting out, but I guess that's not your problem."

"No, it isn't."

"Celia's worried about losing their house."

"We're not taking their house from them. The lawsuit is against the company for letting him drive with infractions on his record."

"That's what I told Jen. Look, I just thought you'd want to know about the Emerson kid."

"Yeah, okay, thanks."

Folks in town were in two camps: one said the accident was just that, and the most Clifford should get would be community service—the other said he deserved to go to prison for murder. He didn't get either because his attorney proved Shannon had been texting at the time of the accident.

SHANNON AND I HAD a fight the morning of the accident, an extension of the heated argument from the night before when I expressed my concern how we were constantly battling about something, that we needed to end it. I meant the fighting—not the marriage. She retorted that our marriage was a mistake because we only dated a few months before I proposed.

But it wasn't sudden, we'd been flirting friends for eleven years, and she didn't hesitate to say yes when I asked her. The next morning our argument continued. She said she felt like a guest in *my* home, that she couldn't be herself, and she was going to notify Spanky she wanted him to move out of her house she'd been renting to him, so she could move back in. It was the last thing she said to me before I took off for work—and Luke heard it all. When I texted her that morning, I had no idea she was driving the boys to school; they should have taken the bus.

After the accident nothing was mentioned about the move, and we stayed together for several months. At first, we seemed closer than ever, clutching onto to one another as it could mend the hole in our hearts. But as time passed, the distance grew wider than ever.

I WENT TO GET JUDGE OLANN'S signature on the search warrants, then made my way to Glenn Hayes's last known address in South Haven Estates. Sounded fancy, but it was the trailer park on the south side of town. Hayes lived on the eastern edge of the park. A pink Chevy pickup was parked in the gravel drive. Rust had taken its toll on the bottom quarter of the body, the back fender was dented, and the tabs on the plates expired last month.

I knocked on the door. It opened about six inches revealing a plump cheek and one eye defiantly staring at the badge I flashed.

"Good morning. Detective Sheehan with Birch County. I need to speak with Glenn."

She opened the door wide to say, "He doesn't live here anymore."

The top half of her hair was the color of oatmeal, the bottom had been colored the same pink as her truck. Her tight pink flowered tank top emphasized her stomach rolls and fleshy arms, and her leggings were stretched to their limit. Gotta wonder if she owned a mirror.

"And your name is?" I said.

"Shelly Hayes."

"You're married to Glenn?"

She laughed and coughed at the same time. "Eewww, no, he's my brother."

"May I come in?" I asked. "I have a few questions."

She stepped aside to let me in. I entered cautiously. You never know when some whackadoodle will burst out of a room toting a weapon. The smell of the place reminded me of a school lunch box left untended in a locker for a couple weeks. Dirty dishes lay mounded in the sink; trashy magazines were piled high in a corner. A half-eaten box of doughnuts lay in a butt depression on the couch, and the amount of wrappers strewn about indicated she was doing her part to keep Hostess, Nabisco, and Frito Lay in business.

She placed herself so she could keep an eye on the television tuned to *Godzilla Brides*, and I sat on a sticky bench seat opposite her, affording me a view of the back of the trailer, which is preferable for safety reasons.

She lit a cigarette, exhaled upward.

"When was the last time you saw your brother?"

"Been a while."

"What's a while? Days, weeks, months, years?"

"Weeks. Why?"

"Just want to ask him a few questions. Who does he hang out with?"

"Anything living under a rock." She let out a gravely laugh.

"Do you know Raybern Ginty and Nevada Wynn?"

"Those assholes? They're nothin' but trouble."

"Do you know anything about their activities?"

She pointed to her couch with the butt impressions and said, "They sat right there, in my house, and talked about selling dope."

"When was this?"

"Maybe March."

"Does Glenn deal for them?"

"Says he doesn't, but why were they talkin' to him? That's what I have to say about that."

The Joint Drug Task Force assumed the Hackett brothers were Nevada Wynn's Prairie Falls connection. I made a note to pass along Hayes's name to them.

"Do you know where he's living?"

"At Max Becker's. You know where that is?"

"Yep."

"Todd Hackett told me. Otherwise I wouldn't know."

He's been released already? "Where did you see Todd?"

Todd and Chad Hackett and their sperm-donor father, Kent Silva, had been serving time after I caught the trio burglarizing an auto parts store.

"At Buzzo's the other night. He was trying to hit his ma up for money—you know Connie? She's a barmaid there?"

"Yes."

Connie Hackett was a nice lady who had bad taste in men. And although her sons were worthless, she raised an incredible daughter, Britt, who was our nanny for two years while she attending community college.

"Yeah, I was sitting at the bar talking to Connie when he came up and sat next to me."

"What's he up to?"

"Not much. He just got out."

Because she didn't have any more information, I thanked her and got up to leave. When my hand was on the doorknob, she stopped me cold.

"Your little boy was in my son's class."

"Oh?"

"Yeah, Colby and Devon played together at recess. I was gonna take him to the funeral, but it was so packed we couldn't find a seat, so we left and got ice cream."

They got ice cream. That was going straight to the top of the list of top ten clueless remarks I'd heard. It'd take the place of: It was God's will Colby died. I could tolerate when someone said it was a mystery we couldn't understand, but His will?

I nodded. "The church was full," I said.

"Yeah, I had to park and walk three blocks in my heels for nothing."

And now, that's number one.

As I pulled out, I noticed two little boys playing in the dirt behind a unit. One of them could be Shelly's son. How much of a chance did a kid of hers have? And how about Jesse Emerson with Clifford for a father? On my way to Max Becker's, I made my daily drive past Emerson's on Maple and Eighth Street. The garage was closed, no lights on. An old-fashioned Big Wheel sat near the street. A few years back Clifford's wife left him and the two boys, and took off for Oregon with one of her post office co-workers. Celia returned nine months later with a seven-month bun in the oven. Clifford took her back. According to his pals at Buzzo's, that's when he pushed the drinking lever to heavy. He's been punishing somebody.

Clifford registered a 0.06 BAL at eight thirty in the morning when he slammed the Estelle's semi into the side of Shannon's Honda Pilot killing Colby. When I saw the car, I was surprised Shannon and Luke made it out alive. Both spent only a few days in the hospital.

10

WHILE DRIVING TO BECKER'S, Spanky called to tell me he'd returned from Minneapolis. I asked him to meet me in Becker's alley. I arrived first and parked behind Max Becker's Ford Focus, then quickly checked the registration of the gold Dodge Dart parked next to it. Bingo! It belonged to Glenn Hayes.

After Spanky pulled up behind me, we briefly discussed our plan, which was for me to go around to the front door, while Spanky covered the back. My heart skipped a beat when Hayes answered the door. I had to be smart about this. He was big and a wild card. I might not be able to handle him alone. New strategy.

"Hey, there. I'm Detective Sheehan and looking for Max? Is he home?"

He shrugged and opened the door to let me into the living room which reeked of pot, sour socks, and stale beer. Empty beer cans were lined up on the coffee table like the soldiers guarding the small bags of weed and a glass pipe.

"Hey, buddy, mind if I pat you down for my own safety?" I asked him.

"Go 'head. Do I look like I'm carrying?" He was wearing shorts with no shirt.

"Just making sure you don't have any weapons on any kind."

"Okay."

I pulled out an empty baggie that probably once held marijuana.

The guy was a bit shorter than I was, but had spent some serious time in gyms—and tattoo parlors. He was heavily inked on his arms, legs, chest, and back with images of medieval weapons and mythical creatures. *Does all that ink go to the brain?*

Max Becker shuffled into the room in bare feet, Spanky behind him. Max eyed the bags of pot and the color drained from his face. He scratched his stomach through his dingy white T-shirt, then hiked up his jeans before he dropped himself on the couch. He coughed, and when he thought we weren't looking, grabbed the bags and stuffed them between the couch cushions.

I laughed out loud at what he must have thought was a smooth move. I gestured for the big guy to sit as well.

"What's your name?"

"Glenn Hayes."

"Where's your ID?"

"Upstairs."

"Max, go get your pal a shirt and his ID and a pair of shoes for yourself. Deputy Spanney will accompany you. Okay?"

"Why? What's going on?"

"We're going for a ride to the sheriff's department."

Max turned white but turned heel and ran up the steps to the second floor. Spanky kept pace. Above, the floorboards creak with each step they took. Max would be an unlikely threat to us, but we'd never ever assume that.

"Mr. Hayes, you are being arrested for your part in the credit card theft of Michael Hawkinson."

He stared at me, his cheeks blossoming to pink, as I read him his Miranda Rights. I was pleased he waved his rights.

WE KEPT THE TWO MEN apart by transporting them in separate vehicles and placing them in different interview rooms.

While we set up to film interviews, I asked Spanky if he got anything interesting out of Cat's friends.

"You want me to brief you now?"

"No, after we finish with these two All-American boys."

I studied the men through the observation window. Max, in Room Three, had his head down on the table. He was probably worried about what his old man, the dentist, would say about his being involved with the likes of Hayes. Max was the kid Victoria coerced to fire an arrow through my kitchen window. At the time he was arrested, he was going to school and working at the *Birch County Register* on the loading docks, where Victoria also worked as a reporter. She snagged him in like a siren and manipulated him to do her dirty work. After he pled guilty, he was sentenced to six months of community service cleaning ditches along county highways and back roads.

"Did we get the registered owner of the van in the videos at Frank's and Wells Fargo?" I asked Spanky.

"Yeah, Raybern Jerome Ginty."

"Perfect. You question Max. See if he's involved in any way with the burglary and/or Hawk's disappearance."

Spanky was new to investigations and eager to interview, but he hadn't done many. I observed him as he took a seat across from Max Becker. They were polar opposites: Spanky a clean-cut, big guy who didn't smoke, drink, or swear—while Max was a disheveled pot-head kid who gravitated toward the trouble makers and ended up knee-high in shit because of it. I wondered what he was up to these days after the debacle named Victoria. I stayed to find out.

Spanky asked, "What do you do for a living?"

"I'm going to school at Birch County Community, mowing fairways at the golf course."

"And you didn't have to mow today?"

"I work four to one."

"How long have you known Glenn Hayes?"

"He hung out with my older brother during high school. He asked if he could stay with me 'til the end of the month when everybody has to move out. My dad's putting the house up for sale."

"Do you know Raybern Ginty?"

"That the guy they call Ray-Ray?"

"Yes."

"Well, I just met him a couple weeks ago when he and Snake dropped in to see Todd and Chad."

"How long were Snake and Ginty in town?"

"Far as I know, just a day."

"Did they crash at your place?"

"No, I don't know where they stayed."

"Did Glenn seem to know Ray-Ray and Snake?"

"He called 'em by name, so yeah."

Spanky was doing fine, so now it was Glenn Hayes's turn. He startled when I opened the door.

I took the chair across from him. I pulled Hawk's photo from my pocket and laid it on the table.

"What happened to this man?"

Hayes put on a puzzled face. "I wouldn't know."

"We have you on film talking to him at Frank's Plaza."

"Here in town? He works there?"

"Not quite. On May 12, cameras above the gas pumps captured you exiting a light-colored van and talking to Mr. Hawkinson for quite a while. What did you talk about for so long?"

His cheeks blushed a telltale red. "I sure don't remember that."

"Think harder."

He pressed a hand to his temple, and after a few seconds of frowning and showing me how hard he was thinking, he said, "Just shooting the shit, I guess."

"An hour later, Wells Fargo bank cameras caught the same van drive up to the ATM machine, whereupon someone withdrew three hundred dollars using Mr. Hawkinson's debit card. To use the card, he'd have to have the pin number. How do you explain that?"

"Okay, here's the truth. I was with Ginty at the gas station, but then I went home so I wasn't there if he did use that card."

"That's convenient. So who was in the front passenger seat when you were at Frank's Plaza?"

"Snake."

"Snake meaning Nevada Wynn?"

"Yeah, you heard of him?"

"Yes, and now I've heard of you."

His lips twitched.

"Look, you're on film following Michael Hawkinson out of the station."

His breathing quickened and his eyes shifted back and forth as he was scrambling for an explanation.

He clasped his hands together and said, "Okay, this is what I know: Ray-Ray followed the Mercedes out. When we came to a stop sign, he tapped the rear bumper. And I'm like sayin', 'What'd you do that for?' and he tells me to shut up. So, the guy in the Mercedes gets out, mad as hell. I didn't like what was going down, so I told Ray-Ray and Snake I was leaving, so I got out and walked home."

"What was going down that you didn't like?"

"They were gonna take him somewhere to scare him."

"Why?"

"I don't know. They're just mean like that."

"Where did they take him?"

"I have no idea."

"Was Max Becker with?"

"Nah, he was working."

"Okay, let's say you did walk home, what happened when you met up with Ray-Ray and Snake again?"

"I didn't. Far as I know they went back to Minneapolis."

"So you're sticking to your story that you don't know what happened to Mr. Hawkinson after Ginty tapped his bumper."

He gave me an eyebrow lift and said, "Nope . . . I mean yes."

"I don't believe you, but, hey, if you want to go down for something Snake and Ginty did, that's fine by me."

His eyes squeezed shut for an instant. "I do not know what happened after I left."

"Why were Snake and Ginty even at your place?"

"They just stopped in to say hey."

"You doing some business with these guys?"

"No, absolutely not."

"What *are* you doing for work these days?"

"I'm in between."

"Where are you getting your money?"

He looked down and shook his head. He couldn't come up with a good lie.

"You come clean, tell me the whole truth, and the county attorney will go easier on you. You think on that."

I left him sit alone for fifteen minutes, went back in with a Coke and went round and round with this character for another hour, but he held to his story.

We released Max because we believed he knew nothing about Hawk's disappearance. He did tell Spanky that he didn't see Glenn Hayes that evening or the next day. After I took Hayes over to the jail for processing, Spanky and I went back to the Becker house to look for evidence and found nothing incriminating other than weed.

We then went back to the department, grabbed a cup of coffee, and made our way to the conference room to add to our notes on the whiteboard. I finally was able to ask Spanky to share what he'd learned from Cat's friends.

"I interviewed the other two women who vacationed with her: Hadley and Karen. They said Cat and Michael were real tight. They said she was texting someone they assumed was Michael."

"Oh, really? We'll have to run her phone records."

"I've already got it in the works."

"Spanky, you're right on top of things. Anything more?"

"Hadley said Cat told them the night before the trip, she and Michael had a tiff about when to have kids—he wanted then now, she wasn't sure she wanted them at all, but by the end of the trip she changed her mind and was going to tell him she was ready to get pregnant."

"Do women tell each other *everything*?"

"I think so. When I asked if they thought Michael and Cat had been faithful to each other, they said Cat suspected Michael had cheated on her while he was on the road, but she had no proof."

"And she told me the opposite. I know people can change, but he was always faithful to his women when I knew him."

"When was the last time you've seen him or talked to him?"

"Just briefly the night before he went missing, but before that, it had been a year ago . . . at the funeral."

"A lot can happen in a year."

"True. Did you ask if Cat had cheated on him?"

"They said no, but they may have discussed what to say, because they both used the word 'distraught' when describing how she acted when she found out he was missing. I got the sense they were being very careful. See for yourself."

"I'll check it out later. And we are going to have to bring in Nevada Wynn for questioning because Hayes said he was in the front seat of Ginty's van."

"When?"

"I'd go tomorrow but it's my week to have the Twinks. I don't want to give Shannon any ammunition for a custody battle."

"It's that bad, you're talking custody?"

"She has a boyfriend—Mac Wallace. You know him?"

"Oh, shoot. He's my realtor. Want me to get somebody else?"

"No, of course not."

"Because I will."

"Not necessary. I'd like you to go to Minneapolis to pick up Wynn. Take someone experienced like Greg Woods or John Odell with you. I'll give you

Wynn's parole officer's number to get his address. Wynn used to work at North Cross Shipping."

"Okay. If we leave about 5:00 a.m., we'd be there at seven."

"Best time to apprehend. Maybe ask Minneapolis for back up. In any event, give them a courtesy call."

"Will do."

I GAVE A CALL to the lab and asked Betty if the DNA test results had come back from Bemidji yet.

"As a matter of fact, they just came in."

"Terrific. I'll be right down."

I took the stairs two at a time to the second floor. I was panting when I walked into the lab. Les ignored me.

"Hi, Les. Where's Betty?"

"Here," Betty said as she poked her head out from the small fingerprint room. "Come on back, Cal."

We stood at a counter and she said, "Okay, I have prints in the cabin matching one I lifted from the Mercedes. Whoever left a print in the Mercedes was also in Brooks's cabin.

"Okay."

"However, when I ran the prints through the data base I didn't get a hit."

"Ginty, Hayes, and Wynn are all in the system—so they weren't there?"

She lifted her index finger and smiled. "The DNA results say they were. Now, here's where it gets interesting. Michael Hawkinson's DNA was on the toilet lid, but so was Ginty's. Wynn's was on a spoon left in a stew can."

"What about Glenn Hayes?"

"We had Glenn Hayes's prints and DNA all over the cabin—the refrigerator, door knobs, and a kitchen cabinet door."

"Excellent. I've got them for the burglary in any case, and at that point Hawk was still alive."

"The only DNA we got on the Mercedes was from Mr. Hawkinson."

"All right then."

"So what do you think happened to your friend?"

"I wish I knew. I just hope one of the dirtbags will come clean."

She said, "You also put in a request form for prints and DNA for Bobby Lopez?"

"Yes."

"I got a hit on his print. Came back as a Cisco Sanchez."

"What? An alias?"

"Yep."

"I guess I'm not entirely surprised. Well, thank you, Betty."

"You bet. Good luck."

When I got back to my desk, I plugged Sanchez's name in the NCIC system. A message popped up saying his records were classified. Classified? Why would he change his name? I needed to have a little talk with Mr. Sanchez. Let him know I knew who he really was.

Tamika shuffled in carrying a paper bag and soft drink from the Sub Shoppe.

"Come on, we're going out to see Bobby Lopez."

"If I can eat my lunch on the way," she said.

As she whittled her sandwich down to nothing, I filled her in on what I'd learned. When I was through, instead of remarking on what I'd said, she asked what I'd done to upset Shannon.

"I paid Mac Wallace a visit. She didn't like that, I guess."

"Shut the door. Did you hit him? 'Cause if it was me, I'd bitchslap the woman who messed with my man."

"No, I didn't *hit* him. But I am through with this bullshit. She obviously doesn't want to be married to me any longer."

"Well, they have a history."

"What are you talking about?"

"Uh-oh. You didn't know?"

"No."

"It was way before you two got together. She felt guilty, so she called it off."

"Why?"

"Because he was married at the time."

"And now he's not. Okay, this makes a little more sense to me now."

"I thought you knew."

I settled into a funk as we drove in silence the rest of the way to Bobby Lopez's house.

We walked up to the door, and I knocked.

A Hispanic woman opened the door.

"Yes?" she asked.

"I'd like to speak with Bobby," I said.

"He's out of town for a few days."

I showed her my badge. A flicker of fear flashed in her eyes.

"I can speak with you. May we please come in?" I asked.

She slowly opened the door and stopped just inside to the living room. She was a petite woman, pretty, approaching fifty—her dark hair had a few strands of silver.

"And your name is?"

"Nancy," she said.

"Nancy Lopez?" Tamika said, grinning.

"Yes."

Tamika chuckled. I shot her a dirty look.

"There's a famous golfer by the same name," I said. "Are you Bobby's wife?"

"No, sir. I am his sister-in-law." I detected a slight Mexican accent.

"And your husband?"

"Isn't here."

"Do you live here?"

"I'm just visiting."

"Where do you come from?"

"Laredo, Texas."

"Who else is staying here?"

"My mother and daughter."

An older woman appeared and stood in the hallway. Nancy spoke to her in Spanish. The woman left. She turned her attention back to us and smiled faintly.

"What did you tell her?" I asked.

"That it was nothing, and she should go back upstairs. She's a very nervous person."

"We won't keep you. Just tell Cisco I stopped by to chat."

She did a double-take and nodded.

When we were in the Explorer and driving out onto the road, Tamika said, "Oh. My. God. Did you see her face when you said 'Cisco?' And her mother can't speak English? They must be illegals. He could be a big time criminal on the lam. Ooo ooo, maybe he's part of the Cartel."

"Cisco Sanchez's records are sealed, so maybe all or none of the above is true. Maybe he's in witness protection or something, and we just poked a hornet's nest."

I dropped off Tamika so she could head home, then stopped at the house to let Bullet out and feed him and grab a peanut butter sandwich. I spent some time throwing the Frisbee for Bullet, then went back to work for three hours to do paperwork, and didn't get home until ten o'clock. I made myself a bowl of Cheerios while I contemplated the day and Tamika's revelation that Shannon had been with Mac while he was married. She omitted that little fact.

"Shit," I said aloud.

Bullet perked up his ears then walked went to his leash hanging on a hook.

"That wasn't a command, boy."

He stayed put, looked at me with his big brown eyes, and wagged his tail.

"Okay, short walk."

We made a six square block circuit and he'd peed twice, so I headed down Seventh Street so I could walk by the blonde's house across the way from me. It was in her yard Bullet chose to start his pre-circling for a poop. While he was choosing the right spot, I checked out her house. A television flickered inside. Maybe I'd bring her Sportsman's cinnamon rolls as a welcome to the neighborhood gift. But what if she didn't eat carbs or was gluten free like some women these days? I carefully picked up Bullet's droppings and headed around the corner.

As I walked along the sidewalk, Eleanor Kohler and her five kids were getting out of her van. She waved. I waved.

"I want you to taste test something for me!" she said. "I'll send Alicia over with the samples."

She'd been giving me baked goods every week since I moved in. I wasn't sure why. Maybe she still felt beholden to me because I solved her husband's murder. Clara and Shannon believed she was getting to my heart through my stomach, which to be honest, did cross my mind. Well, I liked the goodies, so I wasn't going to tell her to stop.

I tossed the poop bag in the trash, went inside, turned on the television, and then grabbed my laptop to check my messages. As I could have predicted, I had an email message from Shannon. I clicked on it.

Cal, stay the hell away from Mac. This is between you and me. I told him if you ever stepped foot on his property again, to call 911. I'll drop the twins off at noon sharp on Sunday.

I answered: *Mac can have you. I'm done. I'll expect you at noon sharp.*

I had another from Oliver Bakken: *Be at the courthouse ready to testify on Wednesday.*

There was a knock on the door, but it wasn't Alicia, it was Eleanor herself.

"Alicia had a phone call. I think she has a boyfriend."

"Oh-boy. Crazy times."

She gave out a hearty laugh. "Mm-hmm." She handed me a nine-by-twelve pan covered with foil.

"I thought it was a sample. This is a whole pan. Hey, want to come in for a glass of wine?" *And why did I just do that?*

"Well, sure!" she said with more enthusiasm than appropriate. I hoped she didn't read anything into my invitation other than me being neighborly.

"White or red?"

"Anything white."

"Chardonnay?"

"Perfect."

She set the pan on the counter. I lifted the lid and sniffed. "Cinnamon rolls? They smell great!"

"My grandmother's recipe. Tell me what you think. I'm trying to beat the Sportsman's."

I poured two glasses of wine, then found a small plate, took a spatula and lifted a roll onto it. I cut it in two.

"Join me."

She giggled. "Okay."

We sat at the counter and drank wine, and I devoured two more rolls bite by bite. As I'd finish a bite I'd say, "I don't know, I need to taste a little more."

She'd giggle every time.

"So? What's the verdict?" she said, when I finally put the fork down.

"They're definitely better than the Sportsman's."

"Really? Are you just saying that?"

"Nope, they are. They're softer and melt in your mouth."

A smile spread across her face. "Coming from a connoisseur, that's a compliment."

We clinked glasses.

"So Cal, is the rumor true? Are you getting a divorce?"

"Where did you hear that?"

"Nina Wallace came into the bakery this morning. She said her ex is dating Shannon."

"Does everybody know but me?"

"I'm sorry. I shouldn't have brought it up."

"No, it's fine. I just found out—and I guess I have to get used to the idea. So, how's the bakery business?"

"Better than I expected. I've hired someone to do wedding cakes, and I'm thinking of hiring another baker soon."

"That's great."

"I've been meaning to ask how Luke was doing? I haven't seen him in such a long time."

"We're all still struggling, and Luke's successfully avoiding me."

We then talked about the struggles of kids and marriage for another hour until her phone rang. She flushed as she said, "Right now."

When she hung up, she said, "That was Alicia. The kids aren't going to bed so easily for her."

"Always a problem, isn't it?"

"Yes." She put her hand on my arm. "Things will get brighter for you, and you'll find someone more suited for you."

"What do you mean?"

"Well, Ted and I believed a spouse should come first, and Shannon puts the kids first, especially Luke."

"Oh."

"But it's really none of my business. Oh, Cal, I hate to see you feeling so down. You're such a great guy and if I was ten years younger and without a six-pack of kids . . . well, I'd give her a run for her money. I'm lonely. I miss my Ted so much. He loved my baked goods too, so thank you for letting me bake for you."

"Wave some of the cinnamon rolls under the men's noses, and they'll come running," I said.

"I wish it was that easy. Well, it's late and I better get those kids in bed. See you later."

I STOOD ON THE BACK STEP and watched her walk back to her house. She was feeding me because she couldn't feed Ted anymore. I felt sorry for her—losing her husband, raising five kids on her own, and she was a nice lady, easy to talk to. Our talk—or maybe it was the wine—had uplifted me.

But when I went to bed, my mood slowly turned south as my mind began to twirl Shannon's deceit and Bobby Lopez's need for an alias, along with all the players in Hawk's disappearance. But I had to focus on Hawk and the players in his disappearance: Ginty, Hayes, and Wynn. The likely scenario was that they killed Hawk and disposed of his body somewhere in Birch County.

11

May 25

Thirteen days missing.

AT NOON ON SUNDAY, Spanky called to say Wynn had been booked into our jail. I had to cut the call short when Shannon drove up with the Twinks. Luke was not in the car, as he usually was. We transferred the kids from the car to the great room without Shannon speaking to or giving me eye contact. She kissed the babies and walked toward the door.

I said, "Bye, sweetheart." She never hesitated, nor did she glance back.

Within a few minutes Hillary Kohler was at the door to help with the kids. I fed them macaroni and cheese for lunch and then Bullet, Hillary, and I took them to the park for an hour. They fell asleep on the way home. After we put them down for their naps, I handed Hillary five dollars, and she said she would come back when they woke up. But she never did. She probably had a boyfriend too.

Clara arrived around four o'clock to make dinner. She eyed the half-eaten pan of cinnamon rolls, but didn't say a word.

May 26

Fourteen days missing.

ON MONDAY MORNING, I took Bullet for an early run, then went to the department to work out. I was back by seven thirty to eat breakfast with the Twinks. Clara served blueberry/raspberry pancakes in the shape of stars.

"Eleanor Kohler left a message on the phone."

"Oh?"

She pursed her lips then said, "She said she enjoyed having *wine* with you Saturday night."

94

I could feel the heat in my cheeks. "Just a neighborly glass of wine, Clara."

"She also said she shouldn't have made those remarks about Shannon. What on earth did she say?"

"Not important."

"She thought it was."

"Okay, she said Shannon put the kids before me, that she always put Ted first."

"Oh, lordy, that woman wants you bad."

"Don't be ridiculous. She knows she's too old for me."

"Look at Demi Moore."

"And look how that turned out? And why are we even having this conversation?"

"Fine. I'll mind my own business."

"That would be a plan."

"Humph. Anyway, I'm going to take the kids to the Memorial Day Parade this morning."

"Oh, it being a holiday slipped my mind. What time does the parade start?"

"Ten o'clock. I'll be at my friend Char's place. She lives on Hickory and Ninth Avenue if you want to join us."

"If I can. Hey, Clara, would you please use the security alarm?"

"Why?"

"Just until Victoria Lewis is out of the picture."

"Oh, her. Are you concerned she might come around?"

"I'd feel better is all."

"Maybe it'll keep Eleanor Kohler out too."

"Clara."

"What?"

"You know what."

SHORTLY AFTER EIGHT O'CLOCK, I had Wynn brought over from the jail for questioning. I was looking forward to this interview.

"Orange is your color," I said.

"Fuck you." He sat back and crossed his arms. He had a new tattoo on his forearm—a headless frog.

"I have bad news for you," I said.

His eyes slowly rose to meet mine.

"Your DNA was on a spoon sitting in a Dinty Moore Beef Stew can in a burglarized cabin." I tossed him a wide grin. "Yo-ho-ho."

"It was Hayes's uncle's cabin."

"Is that right?"

"Yeah, that's right," he said with a sneer.

I pulled my phone out and called Chester Brooks. "Mr. Brooks, I have a quick question. Is a Glenn Hayes your nephew?"

"Yeah, he's my sister Norma's kid."

"Did he have permission to use your cabin?"

"Not without Peg or me there. Why? Was he the one who broke in?"

"Yes, and he had some friends with him."

"Well, that little shit."

"Still want to press charges?"

"You bet, and I want my shotgun and booze back too."

"I understand, but they may be long gone."

"Well, thanks for letting me know. By the way, when can I use my cabin again?"

"You're good to go anytime."

"Thanks for everything."

"You bet."

Wynn was leaning back, chin jutted forward, a triumphant tough guy, cocksure he'd be released. We stared at each other for a few seconds before I said, "You didn't have permission to be in the cabin, so you will still have to face those burglary charges. But personally, I'm much more concerned about what happened to this man."

I placed Hawk's photo on the table in front of him. He looked at it, then back at me.

"Your DNA was found in the Brooks' cabin, and so was his, and now he's missing."

He wrinkled his nose as he hiked his shoulders and lifted his hands. "So we spent a little time with him."

"Why?"

"Just talkin'."

"About?"

"This and that."

"What did you do with his body?"

"His *body*? What are you talking about?"

"Does playing stupid usually work for you? Your buddy Hayes, who you were with that day, was caught on camera talking to Mr. Hawkinson. Your other pal, Ginty, rear-ended the Mercedes . . . on purpose, which was later found abandoned. You all left DNA all over that cabin, along with Mr. Hawkinson's, and now he's vanished. Two plus two equals four."

He gave out a raucous laugh. "Your arithmetic is a little off. Last I saw him he was driving off in that fancy Mercedes, which he tried to give me."

"Is that how you're playing it?"

"That's how it was. He said I could have it."

"Now why would he do that?"

A shrug. "Exactly. I thought it was part of a sting. You know that show on TV where cops leave the keys in a car and brothers jump in and steal it, then the cops shut it off and arrest 'em?"

"*Bait Car*?"

"Yeah, *Bait Car*."

"Tell me what business you and Ginty had in my county on May 12?"

"I had a delivery."

"What *sort* of delivery?"

"A pump to the candy factory."

"Estelle's?"

"That's right."

"We have you and your pals on two different cameras in the city. One was at Frank's Plaza where you boys got gas for Ginty's van. You couldn't have pumped more than a couple gallons because you took off shortly after Mr. Hawkinson did. Then an hour later, the same van pulls up, and Mr. Hawkinson's debit card and pin number were used to access $300 from his account. Now, how was all that possible if Mr. Hawkinson just drove away?"

"I sure don't know."

"When did Mr. Hawkinson offer you his car? At the gas station? When Ginty rear-ended him? Or later when you held him captive at the cabin?"

He pushed air through his barely parted lips.

"Was Glenn Hayes with you when you went to the cabin?"

"Yes."

"Were all three of you in the van when you used Mr. Hawkinson's debit card."

"I thought it was Ray-Ray's own card."

"Like hell. Answer my question."

"I don't remember who was with, that was a while ago."

After going round and round with no new results, and even more inconsistencies in the stories, I had him returned to the jail. Then I had Hayes brought back over. It wasn't long before he broke down and admitted he and his cohorts had broken into his uncle's cabin, ate his food, stole his shotgun and booze. His version had Snake leaving Monday afternoon and Hawk shortly after, but he and Ginty stayed the night in the cabin. Obviously, the three agreed on what to say if questioned; they would admit to the burglary, but not the murder. Hayes was still my best bet to cave, so I needed to have a conversation with Oliver about offering him a deal.

Which reminded me I had to testify in Victoria's case this week—just what I needed in the middle of a big case. I didn't know what made me more anxious: being on the stand or the high probability of running into Troy Kern and Adriana Valero.

Last time I saw Troy was at Colby's funeral. He'd come alone, but we only exchanged a few words. We had once been partners, and we clashed early on—it was a personality thing. Shortly after I was married to Shannon, he developed a relationship with Adriana, and with her influence, he changed. He tried harder not to be a jackass. She'd given him a son, and they were living together in Minneapolis where he was working for Hennepin County Sheriff's Department. I hated that they were together—and I didn't admit that to anyone but myself.

I left an e-mail message for Oliver suggesting he think about offering Glenn Hayes a plea for testimony. Then I decided to drive over to Brainerd to give the Hawkinsons an update. I was hoping Cat was still there. I had a few more questions for her.

Hawk's parents lived in a gray two-story on Ninth Street a block from the Catholic Church. Four cars were in the driveway when I pulled up. Hawk's brother, Paul, answered the door. The older Paul got, the more he resembled Hawk, especially with the apparent weight gain.

"Nice goatee," I said.

He rubbed his chin. "Thanks." He moved in for a man hug—short duration, strong claps on the back. I detected something screwy with his eyes. His pupils were dilated, jumping around. I wanted to check his arms for needle tracks.

Paul lived in Brainerd and worked as a mechanic in a shop that did custom rebuilds, called Woody's. He had a long-time beanpole girlfriend named Tulia who was a barmaid at a local popular watering hole called The Dive, the kind of place where patrons threw peanut shells on the floor. Tulia and Paul had a history of drug abuse. A year earlier when I spoke to Paul at Colby's funeral, he said he'd been sober for a year. Considering what I was detecting, he was using again.

He looked at me hopefully. "Do you have news?"

"Some."

"Come in to tell the folks."

I touched his arm. "What are you on, Paul?"

"What? ... Oh ... I took a little something to help me relax, sleep at night. Nothing heavy. This situation is rough, you know?"

"You can't be taking narcotics that aren't prescribed, Paul."

He raised a hand. "I know, I know. Don't worry."

"Okay, I'm just gonna ask you this once. Do you know anything about Hawk's disappearance or where he is?"

"What? You think if I did, I wouldn't tell you? What kind of a brother do you think I am? I loved Mike. I mean I *love* him. This is killing me, man."

"Did he ever partake of the *substances* you had available?"

"No, of course not. He's the one who got me to quit that shit."

"Except for whatever shit is making your eyes bounce like ping pong balls. Are you on meth?"

There'd been a resurgence of meth and heroin with the cheap imported products getting across the border.

"Nah, it's just Valium or something. Honest."

"Jesus Christ. You don't even know what you took. That's kinda stupid, don't you think?"

He gave me a shrug.

"You still living on Eighth Street South with Tulia?"

"Yep, I'm fixing it up. I put on a new roof, new siding. Looks good. You'll have to come by some time."

"I will do that." Last time I'd been to Tulia's place, it looked like a crack house.

"Surprised the media isn't camped on your parents' doorstep," I said as I followed him inside.

"They pulled out last night. There was some cop-involved shooting in the Cities."

"Oh? I hadn't heard."

Officer-involved shootings always make the headlines, especially lately. Last year on the first day of testimony in a high-profile case, the defendant was shot as he approached the courthouse. I happened to be there and took down the shooter and, lucky for me, the media caught it all on tape. The Minneapolis/St. Paul news channels replayed the video for three days, but everyday I put on my firearm, I replay it in my mind.

Paul led me into the dining room where several people were seated around the table. Barb and Tom stood as I entered. Others present were Tulia, Cat, and her mother Monica, Sydney Dirkson, and an older woman who resembled Barb. All eyes were on me, their faces filled with the anticipation of the bad news they thought I was going to deliver.

"Hi, everyone. Sorry to interrupt your meal."

"Has he been found?" Tom asked.

I lifted a hand. "No, I just have an update."

Sydney introduced the attractive woman next to her as her mother, Anne Bartes, who'd arrived from Arizona just that morning. Barb invited me to fill a plate, but I declined. After I'd told them what I knew, Tom said, "So how do you get those bastards to tell the truth? Torture them?"

"That's only in movies, Tom. Not that I wouldn't like to punch a few faces, pull off a few fingernails."

A few chuckles, a few nods in agreement.

"Maybe if Tom and I could talk to them. Tell them how important it is we know where he is," Barb said.

"At this point, you need to let us do our work."

"Well, there's gotta be more we can do. They're only so many square miles in your county," Tom Hawkinson said.

"We have boatloads of people willing to help," Cat added.

"Didn't the planes and horses and dogs come up with anything?" Monica Ames snarled.

"If it's money, we can pay more people with better equipment to search the other county lakes," Cat said.

"Well, my God, there are hundreds of lakes in the surrounding lake area, they can't search them all," Tulia said.

I raised my hand. "Folks, you can speak to Deputy Chief Carole Knight with suggestions and questions. But you must recognize these things take time," I said.

"What? Like the fifteen years it took to find that girl in Birch County?" Tom said.

"I still have hopes one of the men involved will cave."

"I could take my sledgehammer and cave the side of their heads in," Tom said, "give them incentive."

"Oh, Tom," Barb said, rolling her eyes.

"Say, Cat, could I talk to you privately?" I asked.

"Sure." She jumped up and followed me to the Hawkinson's front living room. She looked up at me expectantly. "Are you telling us everything?"

"Pretty much."

She started crying. "I hate this."

"I know. Me too."

My instinct was to hug her, comfort her. But I refrained. Instead, I stayed in my detective mode.

"Cat, you told me you and Hawk . . . Michael . . . had no problems, but your friends say you thought he was having an affair. Was that just a hunch or did you have concrete evidence? Emails, texts, etcetera?"

Her mouth dropped open. She hadn't expected to be ratted out. "No evidence. It was just a feeling I had."

"That's it? A feeling?"

"Well, he seemed distant and treated me like something I was doing wrong, but he wouldn't talk to me about it."

"Okay . . . Did you tell your parents about these suspicions?"

"No, I did not. Why would I? They already don't . . ."

"Don't like him?"

She folded her arms across the front of her body and sighed. She looked down then away. "I was going to say they don't think he's good enough for me."

"Cat, I need the absolute truth from you. If the press gets wind of anything you said to anybody, friend or not, you'll get convicted in the media."

"Convicted? You think I had something to do with his disappearance?" She started to blink away the tears welling in her eyes.

I put my hand on her shoulder. "No, I don't." And at that particular moment, I didn't.

Sydney interrupted our conversation asking if she could speak with me when I was through with Cat.

"He's all yours," Cat said, and left for the dining room.

"How are you?" she asked.

"Been better. And you?"

"Extremely worried. Do you know anything you didn't share in there?"

"No."

"I hope you don't mind, but I've interviewed some of his neighbors and friends, and no one seems to know a thing, and if something weird was going on, you'd think people close to him would have picked up on it."

"I agree. What I don't get is why Hawk was singled out. Do you believe he could be into drugs?"

"God no. He was always on Paul's case. By the way, did you notice how screwed-up he looks today? Tom or Barb are in denial—they bury their head in the sand and don't say a word. They're afraid to confront him."

"Maybe so. Are Cat and Monica staying here too?"

"No, they're staying at a vacation home of a friend of theirs. It's on Dexter Lake. Mom and I are staying here though—if you need my help with anything."

"I'll keep that in mind. Well, I better get back to work. I'll say good-by and take off."

"Thanks for coming over. It means a lot to all of us."

I MISSED THE PARADE but decided to stop home and have lunch with the Twinks before they went down for naps. As I drove down Sixth Street, I noticed a black Cadillac Escalade parked in front of my house. I pulled onto the driveway and saw my mother's new car, a white Nissan Cube, the marshmallow on wheels. She wasn't sticking to the agreement she should call before she came over.

When I stepped inside, I stopped in my tracks. Sitting on my couch—with my children at his feet—was Bobby Lopez. Adrenalin pumped through my body.

"Oh, hi, Cal," Mom said, a big smile on her face like nothing was wrong.

I pulled my firearm and aimed it at Bobby. "Get facedown on the floor," I said.

My mother gasped. The jerk had the nerve to grin as he slowly did as I ordered. Lucy went and crawled on his back.

"Mom, grab her."

My mother was frozen in a look of absolute shock I'd pulled my gun.

"Mom!"

She finally got up and lifted Lucy, so I cuffed Bobby's hands behind his back. It was when I was walking this giant out to my vehicle that I realized I'd just put my family in great peril. Thank God the man went willingly. My mother traipsed after us to bring Bobby his black leather jacket.

I grabbed the jacket from her and said, "Get back in the house, Mother."

"Thank you, Hope," he said, as he got into the backseat.

Seeing her smile at him, I had a feeling he now knew all about my family.

"Mom, go! We'll talk later."

When I got in the driver's seat, Bobby said, "Cal, why don't we go to the Northwoods Coffee Shop and get a cup of coffee, have a talk—I promise I will meet you there."

"Not a chance in hell."

I wanted to fucking shoot the man—coming in my house—sitting with my kids.

I CALLED AHEAD and asked Deputy Crosby Green to set up for the interview. Crosby's legs had been crushed in a snowmobile accident, and he could have been on disability for life, but he begged Patrice to let him come back in any capacity. He couldn't assume regular duty, but he was able to do many things in the department and was grateful for the work.

Once Bobby was seated in an interview room with the cameras rolling, I took the cuffs off his wrists. His facial scar popped in the bright lighting. He was one scary-looking dude.

He rubbed his wrists. "That whole scene played out in front of your children was a bit dramatic. Don't you think?"

My left eye twitched. "When I come home, I find you sitting in *my* house with *my* children and mother. A man who is not who he claims to be—a man using the alias of Bobby Lopez—and you think I'm being dramatic?"

"Well, since you came to *my* home and spoke to *my* family like we were good friends, I thought you were desperate to speak with me."

"I ran your fingerprints through the system . . . Cisco Sanchez."

He sighed and then crossed his hands on top of the table. "Yes, okay, I changed my name."

"Legally? What about your brother?"

"Yes, both of us legally changed our names. Look, I'll tell you my story, but the microphone and cameras have to go off."

Using my radio, I informed Crosby to stop the camera. He answered, "That's a 10-4."

I leaned forward, putting my elbows on the table. "All right. What's the big secret?"

He mirrored my movement and spoke softly, "There are people I don't want to know where I am."

"People?"

"Very bad people. My father, for one. His name is Julio Sanchez. He was involved with the drug trade early on and later hooked up with the CDG, the Gulf Cartel, based in Matamoros, Tamaulipas, Mexico. When my mother was pregnant with me, she left my father to live with her aunt in nearby Brownsville, Texas, because she felt she was in danger. Only it wasn't far enough. When I was one, she left my three-year-old brother and me with her aunt while she went out shopping. She was gunned down in the street. My aunt and uncle were convinced Julio killed her and were afraid he would come for me or kill all of us, so they packed up and moved us to California. When I was eighteen I joined the army. I later became a Ranger."

"And your fingerprints got into the system how?"

"Probably the assault charge in Missouri. It was dropped. Look, I served three tours of duty and then was recruited by the government. I can't tell you for what or I'd have to kill you."

"Right."

He lifted his brow. "I'm not kidding."

"When did you change your name to Lopez?"

"When I started working for the government, I expressed my concerns about my father. They set me up with a new identity. My brother, too."

"What are you doing here? Are you retired?"

"Not exactly. Sometimes I'm given a small assignment—a mission impossible." He laughed.

It all sounded like such bullshit . . . right out of a frickin' spy novel. This prick was having fun with me.

"So, why Birch County?"

"It's peaceful."

"I want to warn you. If you bring any shit, legal or not, into this *peaceful* county I will personally kill you and bury you where no one will ever find you."

He lifted a hand. "Okay, I consider myself warned. But it's important to my safety not to draw national attention to myself. I don't want my father, or any his associates . . . or enemies of our country, for that matter, to know where I am."

"You sure your father's still alive?"

"My sources say yes."

"So, what's your story on the eye."

"Let's just say I got too close to a knife—but you should have seen the other guy." He chuckled. "I was fitted for an artificial eye, but they sent the wrong one. Now, how would I look with one blue eye?"

"How long ago did that happen?"

"Going on a year. Had some reconstructive surgery—had to heal."

"Okay, Bobby, or Cisco, or whatever the hell name you go by, here's the deal: You never, ever, come close to my family again, or I'll shoot your good eye out. You do not drive down my street. You do go not near my house."

He laughed. "Tough guy. Okay, Deputy, you have my word . . . if I have your word you will do the same for me and my family."

"What family members are we talking about?"

"My brother Hector, his wife Nancy, her mother Rosarita Vasquez, and my niece Penny."

"Are they legal?"

"Not my sister-in-law's mother. If you hand her over to Homeland Security, she will be deported, and she will die. Her husband was a police officer in Nogales and was killed by the cartel."

"Such dramatic life tales."

"All true."

"Where is your brother?"

"Right now in Texas. He brought his mother-in-law to me and went back home."

What's his story?"

"No story. He has a landscaping company. Rosarita is staying to be my housekeeper. Nancy and Penny will go back to Texas soon. So, Cal, your mother told me your family was in a terrible accident?"

I felt my breath escape my body. "What exactly did she tell you?"

"She said you and your wife are separated. You had four children, but a young adopted son was killed. The older boy survived, but he is not doing well. He lives with his mother who is also a deputy. The twins are shuffled back and forth. And you are testifying in court tomorrow in a case against Victoria Lewis, but you don't think she will show up for her own trial."

Jesus Christ.

"See? Now we know almost everything important there is to know about each other."

"Are you married?"

"I wasn't exactly husband material, and I never stayed in one place long enough to start a family."

I couldn't arrest him. I had nothing on him. So I said, "Well, Bobby Lopez, I'll drop you off at your car, and don't let me see you for a very long time . . . unless you know something about Michael Hawkinson's whereabouts."

He chuckled. "You got it."

As I walked Lopez down the hallway of the interview rooms, Crosby Green came out of the small observation/taping room. He winked letting me know he kept the tape rolling even when I pretended I had wanted it stopped.

I asked the first deputy I saw, Greg Woods, to follow me home.

Bobby turned to look back at Woods and said, "I love a parade, don't you?"

I didn't answer or speak to him the six blocks to my house. When I dropped him at his car, Greg Woods pulled up behind me but stayed in his vehicle.

As I opened the back door of the Explorer to let Lopez out, he said, "Want to be best friends?" Then he tilted his head back to give out a raucous laugh. I could hear him continue to laugh as he drove off. Was he having fun with a small-town cop who he underestimated? Or was he telling the truth about his mysterious lifestyle? I waved Woods off, then went inside where my mother and Clara were waiting for me, both with worried expressions across their faces.

My mother put her hand up and said, "Okay, I want to tell you how stupid I feel."

"Well, that's an appropriate response because you were very stupid for letting a total stranger into my house. Henry and Lucy were right there, for God's sake. Do you have a brain?"

"Cal!" Clara shouted. "Respect your mother."

I pointed at her. "You stay out of this."

It was if my words were a physical force moving her back a couple inches. I had probably just lost my nanny/housekeeper/cook.

Mom sighed. "He said you were *friends*. He said he was supposed to meet you here."

I closed my eyes in frustration. "Mom, we are not *friends*. He is a dangerous man ... dangerous. And you told him *all* about our family and now he knows many personal things about me, my marriage and my kids—things few people should know."

"He seemed very nice."

I hit my forehead with my hand. "The scar and eye patch didn't give you a clue?"

"Uncle Joe had an eye patch. Remember? Farming accident. He ..."

"Stop with the farming accident story."

"Well, I'll guess I'll be on my way."

"Good idea."

She picked up her things and headed out without another word. Clara stood in silent brooding.

"Clara, you're standing there looking all pissed off at me. Do you *approve* of what she did?"

"No, I'm horrified, actually."

"Then why not support me?"

"I had already told her what I thought. She knew she had done something really idiotic."

"Then what's the problem?"

"I'm sorry I let your mother stay alone with Henry and Lucy. I ran into her during the parade and asked her to watch the kids while I went to pick up Save-Rite chicken for lunch. She was going to eat with us. Gosh, she's a bit of a flake, isn't she?"

"Now you're getting it."

"Before I forget, Brett Nickel's office left an automated message reminding you of your counseling appointment on Thursday. Do you want me to cancel it for you with all that you've got going on this week?"

"No, better not." Which reminded me I had to call Phillip Warner to get the divorce started, but he wouldn't be working on Memorial Day.

12

THE FIRST THING I DID back at work was jot a note on my calendar to call Phillip Warner tomorrow. Then as I ate the chicken lunch Clara packed, I thought about all the paperwork I needed to catch up on.

Later in the afternoon, Sheriff Clinton dropped by to ask me for an update before she took off for the Cities for some sheriffs' meeting.

"Did you hear about the reward?" she asked.

"No."

"Irving Ames offered $50,000 to find his son-in-law."

"Huh. I don't know if that's good or bad."

"He's hoping fishermen will scour the lakes with their sonar devices. He said it was cheaper than hiring expert teams."

"Probably true."

"I released a statement to the press informing them of the reward and set up a tip line, which I put Crosby in charge of. Carole Knight is going bonkers with all the volunteers, which, thank God, dropped back this morning as everyone returned to their own lives. I mean I think it's nice people are willing to help, but most just get in the way. She assigned the remaining die-hard volunteers to different areas in the county where they'll go door to door."

"You're doing all you can. Thank you for that."

"It's my job. Crosby told me about this Bobby Lopez character. Do you think he's involved in your friend's disappearance?"

"I doubt it, but I don't know who or what he is."

She looked at her watch. "Well, I have twenty minutes to hear an update on the Hawkinson case."

After we went through the notes on the whiteboard, she said, "Well, you have to dig deeper."

I reminded her of my court appearance Wednesday and possibly Thursday.

"You have Tamika full time, and you can bump up Crosby and Spanky's hours from half to full as you see fit. Delegate. We gotta close this case out. And I need to be on my way. If anything breaks inform me immediately."

"Of course," I said.

As I was sitting at the conference table, making a list of people to interview, Tamika bustled in and sat next to me.

"How's your friend's case coming?"

I explained that I'd have to send someone else to the Cities to interview more of Hawk's associates."

"I'll go."

"You sure you want to be away from your kids?"

"Are you kidding? They're at each other's throats lately. I could use a break."

"Okay then, sure."

After we discussed individuals to question and the strategy, she said, "Are you nervous about testifying at Victoria's trial?"

"Sure."

"Oliver said I won't be on the stand long just having to testify about Victoria dumping paint all over Adriana's car. That broad's a serious lulubird. Hey, I had lunch with Shannon."

"You don't have to report to me when you see her."

"I thought you'd like to know what she said."

"Not really." Thirty seconds later, I threw my pencil down and said, "Okay, what did she say?"

"That Adriana would be in town, and she wondered if you'd see her."

"Oh, see—that's the kind of shit I don't need to hear. Okay?"

"Okay. I don't like being in the middle anyway."

"You're so far in the middle you're sitting on the bull's-eye."

She tipped her head and made a smug face. "Well, I'm moving my butt off it."

"Wise decision."

"Adriana texted me that she'd see me Friday, so she and Troy must be coming up soon."

"Back on the bull's-eye."

"Fine. I'll head out this afternoon."

"Thank you," I said.

Maybe she would get more from his coworkers than I could. She had a chatty way that disarmed people.

I pulled the picture of Shannon out of my wallet and stared at it. Tomorrow, I was starting the process of ending the marriage to my best friend. She was right after all: Getting together was the end of a beautiful friendship.

13

May 27
Fifteen days missing

PHILLIP WARNER HAD A CANCELLATION—he could see me if I could be there in ten minutes. The drive to Warner's office building along the river felt like a funeral march to me. This was the beginning of the dissolution of my short-lived marriage. Warner was the best attorney in town, but he had a cocky edge to him. Adriana had worked for him—twice—and they remained friends despite her pattern of quitting to move back to Minneapolis.

Phillip greeted me at his office door with a smile and a handshake. As he strode to his desk, I noticed he'd grown a slight paunch since I'd last seen him.

He leaned over to punch an intercom button on his phone. "Cal Sheehan is here."

He gestured to the round table in the corner. "Have a seat." He buttoned his dark-gray suit jacket covering his new poundage before he sat on one of the four black leather armchairs. Once seated, he looked over his black-rimmed eyeglasses and said, "Just you today, or is Shannon joining us?"

"Just me." I sniffed the air. "Mmm. Your office smells like crisp new money."

"Ha-ha. I'm sure you mean that in a most positive way."

"You betcha."

We dealt each other a smile.

"I was certainly dismayed to hear you and Shannon are considering divorce. In my experience a tragic loss is often a trigger."

"I suppose so."

A knock, then the door swung open and the blond jogger who I followed to North Woods Coffee entered. She was smartly dressed in a pin-stripped black suit. Her flaxen hair grazed her shoulders.

"Cal, meet our newest addition to the staff, Iris Kellogg. She'll be handling your case."

111

Handling my case? Wait. What?

I stood and shook her hand. Firm grip.

"A pleasure to meet you," she said, not bothering with a smile. She took a chair and put a yellow legal pad on the table.

"You too." I cocked my head to look at Phillip. "No offense, Iris, but I thought Phillip would be handling this."

He said, "Iris is handling all our divorce cases."

"And wills," she said. "We'll update yours in the process."

"You have Adriana's old job," I said.

"Yes," Phillip said. "Actually, Iris has been with us for a few months but just recently bought a home in town."

Perhaps I should have kept my mouth shut, but I hadn't counted on being handed over to the newest employee, so I said, "How much experience do you have with divorce law, Iris?"

"Before Warner, I worked for ten years with Harper, Jones, and Halloran in St. Paul, and all I did there was family law."

"She came highly recommended, and she's doing a wonderful job. You're in good hands, Cal," Warner said.

"Okay," I said.

"Okay," Phillip said. "You found the pre-nuptial agreement, Iris?"

"Yes."

"Then you're good to go." Phillip stood and offered his hand. "You'll be pleased with Iris's work."

I was dismissed. Iris and I made our way down the hallway that smelled like a new car.

She showed me to a room with a rectangular table that would seat eight. As we took places across from one another, I said, "I believe you're my neighbor."

She froze and only her eyes moved to meet mine. "Oh?"

"Do you live on the corner of Seventh and Morris?"

"I do. And you?"

"Behind your house on the corner of Sixth and Morris."

"You're the house with the pool and yellow lab."

"Yes. I have pool parties. You'll have to come."

I didn't have pool parties except for one disastrous kid's birthday party for Luke. Never again. Too many out of control boys. But since he was refusing to see me, it was not an issue.

Not responding to my half-assed pool party invitation, she proceeded to open a brown leather notebook case and pulled out a red-colored file. She handed me the top paper. It was a copy of the pre-nuptial agreement.

"What was yours before the marriage is yours after, and vice versa. Do you both still have sizable separate savings?"

"Hers is from a lawsuit award when her husband was killed by a drunk driver. It's a college fund for the children."

"It doesn't matter how either of you acquired your wealth. Phillip filled me in on your family's tragic accident a year ago. So terribly sorry for your loss. I'm told you haven't settled with Estelle's Candies yet?"

"No."

"We'll include the future settlement in the agreement. Okay, let's get started. By the time we're through, I'll know what your bottom line is, especially with custodial rights of the children."

"I want to be fair. I don't want to screw her over."

"That's the attitude I like to hear."

AFTER AN HOUR, she said, "Okay, that's all I need for now. Fill out this financial disclosure statement and fax it or drop it by. After I have a look at it, I'll run my recommendations by you before we send a copy to Shannon. I don't know what kind of relationship you have with her now, but I suggest you suck up any hostile feelings and play nice. In my experience, amicable divorces are better for everyone, especially the children."

"So, maybe I should tell her I started the process?"

"Yes, but she may have already have done so herself."

"Maybe."

I DECIDED TO GET the conversation over with, so I wouldn't have to think about it. I knew she had the day off, so I took the chance she'd be home.

When she opened the door she said, "What's up?"

"We need to talk."

She gestured for me to enter, and she followed me into her living room. She sat stiffly on a stuffed chair and crossed her arms in battle. I took the couch across from her, sat forward, leaned my arms on my thighs.

She set her mouth in a defiant tight line.

"I met with an attorney today to start the divorce process."

Her mouth went soft as a flash-over emotion crossed her face. I couldn't tell if it was relief or hurt. "Okay," she whispered.

"It's not because of Mac Wallace, although I was certainly hurt when I found out about your relationship with him."

"I know. I'm sorry I didn't tell you before you found out from someone else."

I bit my tongue. I pushed down the anger that bubbled up. It'd been simmering for a while. I didn't like that about myself, but it was the way I am.

I said, "I don't want to fight anymore, and I want our settlement to be fair. Just so you know, I told my attorney I want joint custody, fifty-fifty down the middle like we've been doing."

"Okay," she said, barely audible.

"You're being awfully quiet. What are you thinking?"

"I thought you came to apologize. The reality of divorce makes me so sad." She began to cry.

"Come here," I said. She reached out her arms and fell into mine.

I held and felt her body shudder with sobs. Soon my own tears spilled down my cheeks. When we stopped crying, she said, "I was afraid from the beginning this was going to happen."

"Why? And don't give me the best friend bullshit."

"Maybe it was because I saw you through all your women, and one by one you broke it off, and I don't like waiting for the end."

"It doesn't have to happen. It's not too late."

"Yes, it is. We're not even friends anymore," she said

"Maybe as time passes we can get there again."

"Maybe."

I disengaged my arms from around her and said, "I should go." I stood.

"Cal, I hate to ask this now but . . ."

"Just do it."

"I found out yesterday my family is celebrating my grandmother's birthday on Friday, and I was wondering if I could have Henry and Lucy for just that night?"

"Sure. Does Clara go with or get the night off?"

"She can have the night off."

"Okay then, you'll be hearing from my attorney."

"Mac says it would save money if we use the same one."

"Oh, *Mac* says." I counted to ten. I wasn't any calmer. "Of course, you've already discussed getting a divorce with him. I may have to get used to the idea of Mac being in your life, but I don't need to hear what he says and thinks."

"I shouldn't have phrased it that way."

"No."

I stopped at the door and said, "My attorney is Iris Kellogg with Warner."

"This isn't easy for me, you know."

I remembered Iris's advice to play nice, or I would have said: It was easy enough for you to sleep with Mac Wallace, wasn't it?

I BROODED ALL THE WAY HOME. I stopped to have lunch with Henry and Lucy, but they were already napping. Clara made me a tuna sandwich on rye.

"So, how was your morning?" she asked.

Since my private life affected Clara, I told her pretty much everything, and as I did so, tears slid down my cheeks.

She patted me on the back. "Oh, Cal, things will get better."

"I know."

"I met Mac."

"Yeah, so did I."

"Oh, from the conversation I overheard, 'met' is too tame of a word."

"Hmm. So, what do you think of him?"

"Pleasant enough man. You don't want your wife and kids living with a jerk. Do you?"

"Are they going to live together?"

"No, no. But if they should."

"Right."

"Your mom called. She wants you to drop by before or after work some day soon."

"Not gonna happen. You do remember she let Bobby Lopez in my house?"

"I know. But she is regretful, and you don't do yourself any favors by being unforgiving and angry all time."

I glanced at her.

"Oh, you think you're disguising your emotions, but simmering inside is gonna kill you like it did my husband. Isn't that therapist of yours helping you with letting go?"

"He's trying, but I'm not sure I want to."

"Why not?"

"Because then I'll have to feel something that's worse."

"What's that?"

"Rejection, loss, loneliness."

"Oh, honey." She came to give me a hug. "You'll find someone better suited for you. Someone who's not afraid to lose you and fulfill her own prophecy."

"Is that what Shannon did?"

"In my opinion. Every single one of us operates with fears. We just need to name them before we can handle them. And I think you just did."

"Why am I paying Brett Nickle? I have my own live-in therapist."

She laughed. "I read a lot of self-help books."

"Now, I have to get back to work and dig into the paperwork."

"Oh, and Cal?"

"Yes?"

"You can find someone without five kids."

I shook my head and left.

THAT NIGHT I FILLED out the financial documents Iris needed. I'd drop them by her office the next morning.

14

May 28
Sixteen days missing.

WHEN THE CLOCK READ 5:30, I got up and peeked out the window to see if it was raining as predicted. The street looked wet, but it wasn't currently raining. I saw a light on in what I believed to be Iris's kitchen. I wondered if she was getting ready to take a run. Could attorneys socialize with clients after their case was settled? I was getting ahead of myself. She might be with someone or married, although she wasn't wearing a wedding ring, and I hadn't noticed any male presence around her house.

Bullet watched me dress. He knew if I put my running shoes on, he would get to go along. He'd taken to sleeping in Luke's room when he lived here, now he was back sleeping on the floor alongside me. I didn't mind being second best.

Bullet was confused when I jogged back and forth on Seventh Street waiting for Iris to come out. I was about to give up and take off for the park south of town when she burst out her door and ran straight toward me. I stopped as she got closer. She slowed.

"Oh, it's you," she said.

"Hi, didn't mean to scare you, but I have something to run by you," I said. "Want to run and talk?"

"I do the South Park Loop."

"Just where I was headed."

Her mouth curled in a tiny smile. She didn't believe me because I was running parallel, not toward the park entrance.

We kept a comfortable pace while jogging. She had long legs and a stride that matched mine—better than Shannon's—and what a petty sour-grapes thought to have.

"This speed okay for you?" I asked.

"A little slower than I usually run, but we can probably talk better at this rate."

117

Huh.

"I spoke to Shannon and told her I was starting the divorce process."

"And how did that go?"

"All right, I guess. She wants us to share an attorney to save money, but I have a concern with that."

"Which is?"

"That I get screwed in the deal."

"Look, you came to me first and if we can't reach consensus, she's the one I drop because your demands are reasonable. I'm not one of those attorneys who screws over either party."

"Good. I want her to accept our proposal."

"To expedite the process?"

"Yes, although she moved out only a few months ago, we've been emotionally separated for a year. I need to move on. She already has."

"She has a boyfriend?"

"Yep."

"Who is it?"

"Does this make a difference?"

"Not to me. I'd just like to put her indiscretion on the table if we need to." I smiled.

She smiled back.

"It's Mac Wallace, the realtor."

"The one on all the billboards?"

"Uh-huh. He's the top seller. It says so on the billboards. You didn't use him did you?"

"I bought my house from the owner."

"Good."

She giggled. "If she marries him, it'll be better for your wallet."

"I suppose I should start looking at him as a dollar sign. Hey, can I buy you coffee after our run?"

A hesitation then, "Okay, sure."

Pleased with myself for making a move, I smiled broadly at her. She was beautiful and smart, and just maybe ... and then I stumbled on the uneven sidewalk, my arms and legs flailing about like I was a complete clod. I recovered quickly and handled my embarrassment by saying, "And for my next act ..."

"Are you all right?"

"The ol' jock ego is a bit bruised."

"I fell down on all fours as I walked into my first interview. I was wearing four-inch heels, and one caught on the carpet. I sprained a wrist and bruised my knees as well as my legal ego."

"Did you get the job?"

"No, evidently being a klutz wasn't part of the job description."

"Their loss. So tell me why you moved to Prairie Falls? This is a big change from St. Paul."

"My grandparents live here, and as a kid I always loved this town. I thought it was so cool when my sister and I could walk to the candy store with quarters jingling in our pockets."

"And do you walk to the candy store with your quarters jingling now?"

"I've given up sugar."

"And how are you liking the community as a sugar-free adult?"

"I love it—even though everywhere I go I get stared at like I'm some kind of freak. My lord, don't people know it's impolite?"

"Iris, you're a stranger, a beautiful one. I like to stare at you too."

"Do they stare at you because you're a hunk?"

"I'm a hunk?"

"Pfft. You know you are."

"Well, if you say so, but people generally don't stare at law-enforcement. They ignore us to prove they aren't doing anything wrong."

"You're right. I do that."

"Hey, you should get a T-shirt made that says DON'T STARE AT ME I'M LOCAL."

She let out a laugh. "When I passed the bar a friend of mine gave me one that said LAWYER FOR SALE OR RENT. You know, it was a play on an old Roger Miller song called 'King of the Road.'" She started singing "'Trailer for sale or rent' ... know it?"

"I do. My grandparents loved Roger Miller."

"Must be a generational thing. Where did you live before you bought your house?"

"With my grandparents on South Walnut, and my grandma spoiled me: She cooked for me, did my laundry, but it was time I got my own place, so I could be an adult again ... have a full life."

"Ahh. So you don't have to sneak a man in and out of the bedroom window at night?"

She let out a hearty laugh. "Something like that."

Our non-stop conversation continued over coffee at Northwoods. I wanted to ask her out, but I also didn't want to give her the chance to turn me down because I was her client. I would be patient with this one.

We walked home together and when it was time to split off to our respective homes, I said, "I enjoyed our talk."

"Me too. See you soon."

"I'm dropping the financial documents off today."

"I look forward to seeing you again."

Yee-haw. Things were definitely looking up.

Now, to face the day—testifying against Victoria, the arsonist, Lewis. Her attorneys were sharks circling and ready to attack me in cross-examination because of my short relationship with their client. I had been single at the time, but still, who wanted their personal life part of a court record and plastered all over the local newspapers? Victoria had remained absent though all the pre-trial hearings, and no one expected her to show up for her own trial, so I had to give Oliver credit for taking on the case.

I SHOWERED, SHAVED, and dressed in the dark-gray suit I got married in. As I adjusted my conservative blue tie in the mirror, I decided to give this one to charity and buy a new one.

On the drive over to the courthouse, I had a call from Tamika. She wanted to update me on what she'd learned from Hawk's office staff.

"Michael's company was accommodating. They gave me an empty office to use, and the staff came in one by one. Everybody *loved* your friend, by the way."

Past tense.

"Did you get anything else? Any office rumors?"

"Nothing about him doing anybody, if that's what you mean. I came right out and asked."

"What about his secretary? Val?"

"Valerie? Was he into big girls?"

"Not that I know of."

"You may not have noticed it, but I'm no skinny mini, and that gal's way bigger than me. She's like the super-sized version of Jessica Simpson. She wears the make-up, does the Jessica Simpson hair, polishes her nails, dresses real nice and all, but there ain't no way your friend was on that stuff—unless he was into big girls. Now, my Anton, on the other hand, might find her attractive."

"Okay, I get it. So what about the sales team?"

"Just so happens today is the second of a two-day sales meeting, and I'm gonna interview the sales staff before and after the meeting. In between times, I'm going shopping."

"What? No."

She broke out in a chuckle. "I can just see your face. No, thought I'd question more of Hawk's neighbors, like you asked."

"Would you also talk to Haldis Moore at North Cross Shipping and see if Wynn still works there? I want to know why he was in town on Monday, May 12. He said he was delivering a pump of some kind, but I don't trust a word any of those bozos said, except for a portion of Glenn Hayes's statement."

"I'll do that. Good luck today kicking Snow White's ass."

Tamika had been called to the crash scene when Victoria rear-ended me. She'd made the remark she looked like Snow White. Turned out, she was her evil twin.

"Thank you. Okay, I just pulled up to the courthouse now and have a brief meeting with Bakken before court."

"Catch ya later."

AS USUAL, A SHOCK of Oliver's blond hair hung down over his forehead just below his eyebrow. The more nervous he was, the more frequently he tried to push it back up. He sat back in his chair and crossed his arms and looked at me like he was the principal, and I was the naughty kid. I didn't particularly like being around him.

"You ready for today?"

I sat forward. "You bet."

"You know Judge Susan Patterson is presiding. She's Birch County's Gloria Steinem. A real man-eater."

"I heard. A bit of bad luck there."

He pushed his hair back. "I'm not worried."

Okay then.

AT NINE O'CLOCK I was in the witness room watching the clock inch it's way to ten. I played Battleship on my phone to distract myself. When the door opened, Deputy Matt Hauser poked his head and said, "You're up, Cal."

I turned off my phone.

"The defendant show up?"

"Nope," he said, a wide grin on his face.

Matt Hauser always worked courts. At forty-six he was in better shape than most deputies. Everyone called him "The Howitzer"—like the artillery cannon, because of his size. He looked like a force, but he was a gentle man who'd raised four kids by himself after his wife died from a stroke during childbirth. It happened during my first week of work, and all the deputies stood as honor guards from the hearse to the church when the casket was taken into and out. Matt never remarried.

"Hey, Matt, have you been to Eleanor's Bakery? She makes a mean cinnamon roll."

"Oh, yeah? I'll have to give them a try."

We walked together from the waiting area through the hallway and into the solemn courtroom. After I was sworn in, I glanced at the defense table where two men and a woman, all impeccably dressed, were seated and sizing me up as a witness. They emitted an air of importance and confidence, like they had the case all wrapped up and tied with a bow.

Oliver and Assistant County Attorney John Mertz sat at the prosecutor's table. John smiled and nodded at me. Part of Oliver's strategy was to get my relationship with Victoria on the table, so it wouldn't be the bomb the defense attorneys wanted it to be. He stood and asked me to state my name and position, then asked how long I had been employed by Birch County.

"Twelve years," I said.

"When did you first meet Victoria Lewis?" he asked.

"On October 7, 2012, when she rear-ended my vehicle . . ."

"Objection!"

Bang! The courtroom door swung open. In walked Victoria. Her face was flushed; her hair—once again dark brown—stuck up in odd places. Her red leather jacket was falling off a shoulder. What an entrance! I stifled my urge to laugh. Her attorneys looked back to see what was happening. Their jaws went slack when they saw their client.

But it was the person coming in behind her who gave me pause—Bobby Lopez. He slipped in behind her and took a seat in the back row.

What. The. Hell?

The entire courtroom was still, except for tiny moans coming from Victoria. Oliver waited to speak while one of her male attorneys met her halfway down the aisle to guide her to the table. But there wasn't even a chair for her. Oliver grabbed an extra from the prosecution side and set it down with a thud. He couldn't contain his smirk as he walked directly toward me and stood a few feet in front of me. He raised his eyebrows and mouthed, "Do you believe this?"

"Deputy Sheehan, I'll repeat the question. When and how did you first meet Victoria Lewis?"

"We met when she rear-ended my vehicle."

Oliver took advantage of the fact that Victoria's attorneys were busy whispering to each other and temporarily not paying attention to his line of questioning.

"Did Miss Lewis call you and ask you for a date?"

"Yes, sir."

"You then had a short relationship with her?"

I said, "We dated only a couple weeks."

At that point, Victoria's attorney snapped to attention and began to object to nearly every question Oliver asked, causing Judge Patterson to scowl with annoyance. But when I was asked about Victoria inviting me to her father's wedding in Las Vegas, or how I hadn't been told the bride was Adriana, there were no objections because this was going to come back and bite us in the butt.

Once the relationship was in the open, Oliver moved on to the early nuisance acts of vandalism in and around Adriana's house. As I recounted the facts of the case, Victoria kept her eyes narrowed and her lips pursed like a member of the Temperance Union at Sturgis during a motorcycle rally. I couldn't help but wonder what she would do to retaliate. Pour paint on my truck? Burn *my* house down?

The time dragged as Oliver meticulously questioned me on every factoid of the case, having me point out specific evidence on the slides, slowly building his case.

At eleven o'clock the judge recessed the proceedings for lunch. We were to be back at one o'clock.

As I was making my way down the hall, I heard someone call my name. I turned to see Bobby Lopez scurrying to catch up with me. He had an amused expression on his face.

"You're pleased with yourself for some reason," I said.

"I found Ms. Lewis for you."

"Why on earth would *you* get involved?"

He shrugged.

I lifted my brows and sighed. "How did you find her?"

One side of his mouth curled in a smile. "I have skills," he said.

"Skills?" I waited for two people to pass by before I asked. "Where?"

"In her suite at the Rivers Inn. It wasn't difficult."

"You forced her to come?"

He wagged his head. "*Force* is too strong of a word. Maybe *encouraged* would be more accurate."

"Were there any threats or weapons involved?"

He scowled. "No, of course not."

"Did you mention my name in this encouragement?"

"No. Gee whiz, Joe Friday, I should think you'd be more grateful."

"What did you call me?"

"Kids, these days." He shook his head and sauntered away in the opposite direction.

What the hell? Why would he bring Victoria in? What was he up to? I tried to shake off the creepy-crawly feeling that began in the pit of my stomach and radiated out to all my limbs.

I made my way down the wide marble stairs to the basement of the courthouse to pick up a sandwich at the cafeteria. As I ate a ham and Swiss on rye, I thought about Bobby Lopez doing me a so-called favor, and I shivered in revulsion. I turned on my phone to check for messages. I deleted a text from my mother and opened one from an undisclosed number. It contained a You Tube film called *Dragnet to be a Cop—Joe Friday*. I clicked on it and watched as Joe Friday told what it was like to be a cop. How did Bobby Lopez get my phone number?

After I finished eating, I drove over to Warner Law Office to drop off my financial statement. I asked for Iris. The secretary said she was at lunch, so I handed her the file folder.

I was just walking out of the building when Iris was walking in. She looked stunning in a royal blue sleeveless dress.

"You clean up nicely," she said.

"Court today. I just dropped off the paperwork."

"That was quick turnaround."

"Was it?"

She smiled. "Well, I have an appointment. See you later."

"Okay."

Phillip sure liked to surround himself with beautiful women.

OLIVER BAKKEN AND I met briefly in his office before court.

"Looks like we got enough to convict the three amigos on the Brooks's burglary," he said.

"Good."

"Without a body, there's no murder charge."

"I figured as much. Did you talk to Glenn Hayes?"

"Haven't had time with this trial going on."

"How do you think it went?"

"That asshole objected just to object. This afternoon I'll concentrate on the destruction of Adriana's car with paint and the arson. Then possibly there'll be time for the cross-examination."

"I didn't investigate the fire."

"You don't think I know that? I have other witnesses," he snapped.

Yeah, I don't like him much.

"I should have charged her with fraud and attempted murder two years ago."

"I understand why you didn't. It would cost too much to extradite her from France."

"It wasn't the money."

He shook his head and tapped the desk with his finger. "And I wasn't too concerned about that Mickey-Mouse nuisance shit she pulled at Adriana's house—until she dumped paint on her BMW convertible and torched her house. If I'd have known she was going to come back to pull that, I would have taken the former more seriously. That bitch is a whacko."

"Don't forget she painted Spanky's and my front steps silver as a threat, like we were next."

"Not going there. But Austin will testify about the silver paint cans she dumped in his garbage, her smelling like gasoline after the fire, and how she used Sadie Jones's identity. The real Sadie will be a believable witness. If we can just get Victoria for the arson, she'll be out of commission for a few years."

"Let's hope."

"Hey, do you know the one-eyed guy who brought Ms. Lewis in?"

"Bobby Lopez. He rents Chester Brooks's house out by Rodgers Lake."

"I wanted to go up and kiss him."

"I didn't know he was your type."

"You dickhead, you know what I mean."

It amused me when I rattled him.

"I do. The dude definitely has skills, but I can't quite figure why he got involved."

His eyes narrowed, and he gave his desk a knock with his knuckles. "Well, it was a wonderful surprise to see Victoria enter the courtroom with a bang." He grinned. "Gotta go."

THAT AFTERNOON THE GALLERY was packed with spectators. Judge Patterson wouldn't allow television cameras in her courtroom, and it was clear most of the people assembled were reporters as they were taking copious notes. I also spotted an artist at the end of a row sketching me. Terrific.

When Oliver asked me a few questions about the fire that destroyed Adriana's house, his voice cracked and his hands trembled. He was feeling the effects of the large media presence.

After I was dismissed, to avoid the press, I used the security tunnel between the courthouse and department. Back in my office, I checked my messages, then left for the day. As I pulled out of the parking lot, I couldn't help but notice the many news station vans lining the streets along the courthouse. Not only Minnesota stations, but CNN and CNBC as well. An heiress on trial made for juicy headlines. No wonder Oliver was nervous. In the next few days, Troy, Adriana, Tamika, and Austin Spanney would have their turns testifying, and ordinarily our testimonies would seal the conviction, but the sexual relationships involved muddied this trial. I worried a little about Spanky's ability to handle the defense lawyers' questions.

CLARA AND I HAD just walked downstairs after putting Henry and Lucy to bed that evening, when the landline phone rang.

I didn't recognize the number. Hoping it was about Hawk, I picked up.

"It's me."

Adriana.

"Oh, hi."

"Is it too late to call?"

"Nope. What's up?"

"I just wanted to know how court went."

"Okay, I guess. I'm more worried about tomorrow when the defense gets its turn."

"You'll do fine. I heard Victoria actually showed up. Was Adam there?"

"Lewis? No, come to think of it."

"He'll probably come for my testimony just to intimidate me."

"Don't let him."

"Hard not to. I'll be arriving in town tomorrow, and I thought we could go out for dinner one night."

I was speechless.

"Or lunch, if you're more comfortable with that."

"That's a bad idea."

There was a pause before she said, "Tamika told me you and Shannon separated."

"What does that matter?"

"Why are you being so crabby with me? I don't want to reconcile. I just miss talking to you."

I didn't respond.

"Cal?"

"It's not a good idea. One of the kids is crying. Gotta go."

When I hung up, I realized Clara had been watching me. "Who was that? You acted so secretive."

"I wasn't being *secretive.*"

"You turned your back and spoke softly—that's secretive if you ask me."

I gave her a long stare.

She sighed. "All right. I get it. You have a right to privacy."

"Yes . . . I do."

WHEN I TOOK BULLET out for his last pee, I walked the entire perimeter of the house looking for Victoria lurking in the shadows. Knowing the vindictive sicko Victoria was, made me uneasy. Her behavior had escalated from annoying to criminal in two years. I hoped her lawyers were keeping her in check. Hopefully, the jury would realize how evil she was and convict her before she killed someone.

LATER, WHILE I LAY in bed tossing and turning, my mind spun with everything going on in my life: the divorce, my kids having to deal with split custody, Hawk, the cross-examination, and Adriana. I didn't need or want any more complications in my life. Argh! No wonder I couldn't sleep with all this shit bouncing around in my brain.

15

May 29
Seventeen days missing.

MOST OFTEN IN THE CROSS examination, the defense attorneys ask law enforcement officers to clarify points and/or admit they didn't actually witness the crime. Because of my personal history with other witnesses and the victim in this particular trial, it was a given Victoria's attorneys would attempt to negate my testimony and turn things around, so that Victoria was the so-called victim of poor police work. Yeah, the nausea I was feeling was justified.

Before I walked over to the courthouse, I stopped at the department to sign in. Patrice and I bumped into one another in the squad room.

She took a sip of coffee then said, "You should know Ginty's back in St. Cloud Detention Center, but Nevada Wynn's out on bail."

"Wynn's out? What about Hayes?"

"Still with us. Oh, I meant to tell you Troy called me a few days ago to ask if I had any openings."

"And you said?"

"That I didn't have any."

"That's it? Did you ask him what was going on?"

"I did not."

"I want you to know since he's been with Adriana, he looks at me like I'm the fox in a chicken coop, and he's the farmer with a shotgun."

"You country boys have such a way with words."

I put my hand up. "I'm just saying, if I end up dead, look at Troy . . . or Victoria, for that matter."

"You're exaggerating." She left it at that and walked out.

I found Spanky at his desk in our investigations office. "Hey, how ya doing?" he asked.

"Just dandy. And you?"

"I couldn't sleep at all last night. I'm up to testify after they finish with you."

"All we can do is tell the truth."

"I know, I know, but still."

"You did nothing wrong."

"Besides being a fool?"

"A fool is someone who knows the truth and behaves as if he doesn't. Victoria was very convincing—she uses her feminine charms."

"I'll say. Whew. She knows stuff." He wiggled his eyebrows, which made me laugh—I recalled the hooker moves she used on me.

Victoria was a badge bunny—she liked cops. When she went after Spanky, she deceived him by using her roommate Saddie Jone's identity (not for financial reasons because her father was loaded), but because it was a game to her. When Victoria bleached her hair blond, she and Sadie looked like twins. Sadie would testify they had fun switching identities when she and Victoria had been college roommates.

In hindsight, it was a mistake to let Spanky make the arrest. Victoria's attorneys would try to prove it was personal, and I could understand why a jury would buy it. I pulled up my case notes on the computer. Together Spanky and I reviewed the slides Oliver had chosen to use.

When I left for the courthouse, Spanky wished me luck.

"You too, brother."

TODAY VICTORIA WORE her Lois Lane outfit, including the cosmetic eyeglasses. I turned my attention to the packed gallery. No Bobby Lopez—and that was a relief. Or Adam Lewis, Victoria's father.

After Judge Patterson reminded me I was still under oath, the female attorney stood. Having a woman cross examine me was strategic. She was forty-something with an I-eat-small-town-cops-for-lunch look in her eyes. She ran her hand down the front of her white blouse then gave a quick tug on the lapels of her black suit jacket. She came around the table and pivoted toward the jury to introduce herself as Elizabeth McCall. She moved midway between the jury and me.

"Good morning, Detective Sheehan," she said, smiling slyly at her prey before the pounce.

"Good morning." I gave her an I'm-not-afraid-of-you smile.

"Yesterday, you testified you met Ms. Lewis when she worked as a reporter for *The Birch County Register.*"

"Yes."

"And shortly after you'd met her, you began a sexual relationship with her?"

Getting right to it. "Yes."

"And no one forced you to fly all expenses paid to Las Vegas. Is that correct?"

"No, ma'am."

"While there, you dined, danced, played golf, and gambled all courtesy of the Lewis family. Is that correct?"

"Yes."

"After this all-expenses-paid weekend, you stopped seeing Ms. Lewis. Correct?"

"Yes."

"Deputy, was it because you were very, very angry at seeing Adriana Valero marry Miss Lewis's father?"

"No. And I wouldn't characterize my feelings as *very, very* angry."

"But you were angry with Miss Lewis, were you not? Yes or no?"

"Yes."

"And you remained angry with Ms. Lewis for some time, although you continued to sleep with her. Correct?"

"I object, your honor!" Oliver cried.

Finally! Thank you.

"Sustained. Ms. McCall, keep to the facts and testimony before you."

"And, Deputy Sheehan, to clarify what you said earlier. You also had a sexual relationship with Adriana Valero, the victim of the crime Ms. Lewis is accused of committing?"

Sexual relationship? Oh, for godsake, why wasn't Oliver objecting?

"We were together for over two years, yes."

"And how long after you ended your relationship did she remarry?"

Oliver! Are you awake?

"Objection! Irrelevant!" Oliver shouted. *Finally.*

"Sustained."

"You testified this morning that skeletal remains were found on Ms. Valero's property, where upon random acts of trespassing and vandalism occurred. Yes or no?"

"Yes."

"You testified you had suspicions Ms. Lewis was involved."

"Not in the beginning . . ."

"Please answer yes or no."

"Yes." *When the acts turned more destructive and vindictive.*

"Did you find Ms. Lewis's fingerprints or DNA anywhere on Ms. Valero's property?"

"No."

She faced the jury. "In other words, you had no physical evidence."

I didn't respond.

"Detective?"

"Was there a question?"

Someone in the jury snickered.

"You had no physical evidence? Is that accurate?"

"No, it's not."

She narrowed her eyes but moved on.

"You testified your fellow investigator at the time was Deputy Troy Kern?"

"Yes."

"And Deputy Kern also became sexually involved with Ms. Valero. They had a child together, did they not?"

"Objection! Irrelevant!" Oliver shouted.

"Sustained. Ms. McCall, questions regarding Deputy Sheehan's testimony only please."

McCall turned to face the jury. "You did state you considered Victoria, Ms. Valero's ex-stepdaughter, to be your only suspect in the acts of vandalism and the more serious arson case. Yes or no?"

"We looked at all possibilities."

"But you had no other real suspects on your list, did you?"

"Objection, your honor," Oliver said with irritation.

The judge said calmly, "Overruled. You may answer the question, Deputy."

"Yes or no, did you have other suspects?" Ms. McCall asked.

"No, because the evidence pointed . . ."

"No further questions of this witness at this time," Ms. McCall said. "I reserve the right to recall Detective Sheehan at a later time."

"So noted."

Oliver rose and said, "No further questions of this witness your honor."

Really?

He wasn't going to try to correct the impression we were going after Victoria for some kind of personal vendetta, and that the male deputies in the department were of a bunch of horny bastards trading women like baseball cards?

I passed Spanky on the way out.

"How'd it go?"

"Piece of cake," I said. "You'll do great. Just answer yes or no." No need to alarm him.

WHEN I RETURNED to my desk, I checked texts, email and phone messages. I had a few more from my mother. I called her back hoping she'd stop once I heard her excuses for allowing a deranged individual near my babies.

"Mom, what is it?" I asked, not disguising my annoyance.

"I wanted you to know I was seeing someone."

"You've had many boyfriends, many of whom I never met."

"*He* thought you should know."

"Okay, don't keep me in suspense. Who is *he*?"

"Cisco, I mean Bobby Lopez."

"I'll be right over."

My heart pounded as I flew down the stairs and across the lot to my Ford F-150, then sped to my mom's condo on Fox Drive. I pulled up to the blue vinyl-sided, three-story, eighteen-unit seniors only condos on the eastern edge of Prairie Falls.

It was a security building, so you had to use the phone in the entryway to call up to have the resident let you in. The buzzer continued sounding for at least thirty seconds. Some security—anyone could slip in behind me. I chose to take the stairs to the third floor then fast-walked down to the left corner unit. I rang the doorbell. I could hear music blasting—Rolling Stones's "Wild Horses."

When she let me in, I said, "What the hell do you think you're doing with Bobby Lopez?"

She giggled. It was noon, and she was holding a margarita. Tequila. Great. She almost burned our house down once drinking Tequila with one of her boyfriends.

"Bobby's going to make me a genuine Mexican lunch. He says you should stay and eat with us. He's made plenty."

Bobby rounded the corner out of her kitchen area. He was holding a mug and as he took a sip, he smiled.

I marched over to him and said, "What the hell are you doing, Bobby, Cisco, or whatever the hell your name is?"

"Turns out your mother and I knew each other from before."

"From *before?*"

"When we were kids." He laughed. "We spent a weekend together."

"Jesus H. Christ."

"She was in LA with her friend, Dinah. You know her?"

"Dinah? Yeah, I've met her."

"Well, that night Dinah and Hope were the hottest chicks in Ledbetter's on Westwood Boulevard. They were sitting at the next table, and we kept exchanging glances through John Denver's performance. When he took a break, Steve Martin went up on stage and was doing his tongue through a napkin routine, and your mother leaned over and said to me, 'Is he stupid or what?' And I said, 'He's stupid. Want to go to my place?' I shared an apartment in Manhattan Beach at the time." He sighed wistfully. "Anyway, the girls said yes and off we went. They stayed the whole weekend. It was a wild and crazy time."

"Oh, that's just great." I took a deep breath, so I wouldn't puke.

My mother took the break in the conversation as an opportunity to chime in, "So, when I saw him at your place he looked so familiar. We both said so."

"Later, I figured it out and called her. Asked her over for dinner that night."

"You have got to be kidding me."

"Nope. All true. It's such a small world ... after all. You ever been to Disneyland?" he asked with a smirk plastered on his face.

"Shut the hell up," I said.

I took my hand and ran it through my hair, and glaring at Bobby, I said, "I need to speak with my mother privately. I would like you to leave."

"Don't be ridiculous. You stay, Bobby."

"I'll go for a walk," Bobby said.

When he closed the door behind him I said, "Do you *know* what you're doing?"

"Having fun?"

"You have no idea who that man is."

"He's told me all about himself."

"Want to share?"

She began to give me some sugar-coated version so I just said, "I don't think you get it. He's a dangerous man."

"Don't be silly."

There really was no reasoning with her when she got something in her head. She'd have to find out the hard way. I just hoped she didn't end up dead like Hawk.

"Tell you what, you just go at it. Just keep him the hell away from my house and my kids. And don't say I didn't warn you."

BOBBY WAS WAITING by his Escalade in the parking lot. He walked toward me and said, "Cal, I really like your mother. I won't hurt her. Trust me."

"You do and you're dead. You can *trust me* on that."

He dropped his smile. "I understand. You're being protective of her like I am with my family."

As I reached for my car door handle, he put his hand on the top of the door to stop it from opening. He said, "If you want to find your friend, look at the brother."

"What? What are you doing?"

"His disappearance interests me. The brother is reckless, into illegal substances and such. You were aware of that, right?"

"Back off. Stay away from me and my investigation."

"Whatever you say. Just trying to help."

"Well, don't."

I MUMBLED CURSE WORDS all the way back to the department and walked into Patrice's office without knocking. She appeared startled with my entrance.

"I want Bobby Lopez watched twenty-four/seven and his phone tapped."

She looked up at me with puzzlement. "Brooks's neighbor? You think he had something to do with Michael Hawkinson's disappearance?"

"He's getting himself involved in our investigations." I gave her the whole story.

She tilted her head and said, "Well, you have a lot of nothing there. No judge is going to sign any warrants on that basis."

"Fine," I said and started to make my leave.

"Cal," she called after me, "best leave him alone even if he is with your mother."

Not likely. "He's not *with* my mother. He's the flavor of the month."

Patrice said, "How many times has she been married?"

"Once, to my deadbeat dad."

"But I heard your dad was a millionaire, and you inherited a bundle from your real mom."

"*Hope* is my *real* mom . . . flakey, but she was a good mother. Her sister, Grace, was my *biological* mother. Who told you this anyway?"

"Troy. I think it was around the time of Adriana's fire."

"Figures." *Big mouth Troy.*

BOBBY LOPEZ'S COMMENT about Paul Hawkinson distracted me from my work. I had hoped to figure out a new strategy for finding Hawk, but it wasn't working. About three o'clock I gave up, grabbed my briefcase, and then drove a department Explorer over to Tulia and Paul's place on Eighth Street South in Brainerd.

I pulled up behind a yellow Beetle parked on the street. The house had a new roof and had been repainted a light blue. A few shrubs had been planted under the picture window. Through the screen door, I could see directly into the living room. Heavy metal music was playing somewhere in the back of the house. I rang the bell three times.

Tulia walked through the room and happened to notice me. She came up to the door, but didn't open it. "You looking for Paul?"

"Is he home?"

"No, he's at work."

"Mind if I come in and ask you a few questions?"

"Well, I have to get ready for work in a few minutes."

"It won't take long. I just want to run some photos by you."

"Okay, if it's quick."

"Would you mind turning down the music?"

She went over to the sound system and turned it a few notches lower. I raised a brow, and she turned it off.

When we were seated on the couch, I spread out photos of Nevada Wynn, Raybern Ginty, Roseanna Martinez, and Glenn Hayes over the gossip magazines covering the coffee table.

"You recognize any of these people?"

She shrugged and said, "The men—not the woman."

"Tell me how you know them?"

"They've been here. I think one of them's having a car restored at the shop."

"You saw the car?"

"No, but Paul said they came to talk about a restoration. That's all I know. Why? Who are they?"

"Can you tell me the exact date?"

"Sure, it was the last time we saw Mike right after fishing opener. He stopped to see Paul before he went back to the Cities, or supposedly went back. It's all so wierd."

"How long did he stay?"

"I'm not sure because I was getting ready for work, and by the time I got out of the shower and dressed he was gone."

"What time was that?"

"Umm, I had early shift that day. I traded with Linda, and she starts at eleven, so it was before that. They were kinda creepy lookin', Cal. I told Paul he shouldn't have them over again."

"Did Mike say where he was headed after he left your place?"

"Not to me, he didn't."

I PARKED IN THE CONCRETE drive in front of Woody's Custom Builds. I walked into the office and asked for Paul. The guy behind the counter was obese and wore his greasy, gray hair tied back in a ponytail. From the framed newspaper clippings on the back wall, I deduced he was Woody Nash who had recently celebrated forty years in the auto renovation business.

Woody lifted himself from the chair with a grunt and shuffled to the door into the shop. As soon as he opened it, the whine and whir of power tools became louder. Shortly after, Paul entered the office with hearing-protection earmuffs pulled down around his neck. He was wiping his hands with a rag. When he saw me, his shoulders lowered a couple inches. Woody stood behind Paul, eager to hear what a deputy wanted with his employee.

"Let's take a walk, Paul."

Paul shrugged then handed Woody the rag and the ear gear. We were a few feet out of the door when he said, "Is it about Mike?"

"No. Get in my vehicle."

His eyelids fluttered a few times but climbed inside the front passenger seat of my department vehicle. He stared straight ahead.

"Know these guys?" I watched his face as I showed him the photos of Wynn, Ginty, and Glenn Hayes one by one. His hand came to his mouth, and he rubbed his chin.

After the last photo, he shook his head. "No, I sure don't."

With an open hand I slapped the back of his head.

He ducked and said, "Ow! What'd you do that for?"

"Don't lie to me. I just talked to Tulia. These scum suckers were at your place the morning Mike dropped by your place. You jerk. Why didn't you tell me?"

"I forgot."

"You forgot. Don't give me that shit. So what happened before, during and after he was there?"

"Nothing. Honest," he said, his voice carrying a hint of desperation.

"I don't believe you. You tell me exactly what went down and what was said, or I'll haul your ass to jail for your brother's murder."

He wrinkled his nose. "Murder? You think I murdered my own brother? Jesus, Cal. He just happened to drop by when they were there. I told him it wasn't a good time to talk, so he took off."

"These nimrods were captured on film talking to him at Frank's Plaza in Prairie Falls."

"What? You didn't tell me that."

"What were they doing at your house?"

He let the air out of his lungs. He slumped. "We do a little business with them."

"What kind of business? Drugs?"

"Yeah."

"You're selling drugs for them?"

"Not exactly. We move their product."

"How?"

"In wrecks and old cars up on trailers. It looks like we're transporting the cars to other locations."

"You stupid shit. Does Woody know?"

"Hey, it's his deal, man, not mine."

"Then why were they at *your* place?"

"They just showed up. I owe Snake some money."

"How much?"

"Uh ... maybe ... ten."

"Grand?"

He nodded.

"Jesus H. Christ, Paul. How did you manage that?"

"Ginty brought up some product, but the trailer wasn't back from Chicago yet, and Woody said to get it out of the shop, so I put it in my garage. When I went out to get it the next morning, it was gone."

"When was this?"

"The Thursday before fishing opener."

I checked the calendar on my phone. "May 8th."

"Sounds right. So Snake covered me and brought up some new stuff that day, only he said I owed him ten grand for the stuff that was stolen."

"You fuckup! You should be the one missing, not Hawk. Or was he involved?"

"No, no. He didn't know anything about it."

"Do you know what happened to him?"

He glanced at me. "If I did, you'd be the first person I'd tell."

"Did it occur to you your debt has something to do with Hawk's disappearance?"

His face contorted, and he began to cry. "Yeah."

"What did they say when Hawk left?"

He didn't answer. He was too busy crying.

"Oh, stop your damn bawling and talk to me."

He sniffled a couple times, then wiped his face on his sleeve. "He said it looked like Mike did okay, driving a Mercedes and all. He thought I should ask him for the money."

"Who's he?"

"Snake, but Ray-Ray jumped on it too."

"Why the hell do people call him Ray-Ray? Why not just Ray?"

"I don't know, man. They just do."

"All right. Now I need to get your side of the story on tape, so let's go tell your boss you'll need to take off for a couple hours."

Paul frowned but moved out of the vehicle and toward the office. When we entered, Woody looked up.

"Everything okay?" he asked Paul.

"Fine," he said, and nothing more.

I put my hand on Paul's shoulder and said, "I'm going to borrow Paul here for a short while. It's about his missing brother."

Woody's eyes bounced back and forth from me to Paul. He was trying to size up what was going on. "Oh, sure. Take all the time you need, Paul."

"How many people do you have working for you, Woody?"

"In the shop? I have two guys. One guy to transport. Why? Need a job?" He let out a raspy laugh.

I returned the laugh. "Nah, there's plenty of criminal activity in this area to keep me busy."

Woody held his grin, but his eyes lost their part in it.

When we left, Paul started walking toward his restored 1972 black Camaro. I said, "No, Paul, I'm driving you."

"How am I gonna get back?"

"I'll make sure you get a ride. And, Paul, you better tell the whole truth." He took a deep breath and let out a big sigh.

After we pulled out on Highway 10, he said, "Woody knows."

"What does Woody know?"

"That you're really talking to me about Snake and Ray-Ray."

"Are you afraid of Woody?"

"No. I'll just tell him . . . well, I don't know what I'll tell him."

"Does he know the product was stolen?"

"No, Snake covered for me."

"That's why you owe ten grand?"

He nodded.

"You aren't making the best decisions these days, Paul."

"Things have been a little fucked up, I know. Tulia and I are thinking of moving west."

"West?"

"Yeah, maybe Oregon. Get a fresh start. They're in jail, right? Snake and Ray-Ray?"

"Ginty's back in St. Cloud, but Wynn made bail."

He jerked back. "You let Snake go? You got a spare pistol I could borrow?"

"What do you think?"

"I think I'm gonna get my rifle from Dad's."

"Leave it the fuck there."

AFTER THE INTERVIEW, I arranged for a reserve deputy to drive Paul back to Brainerd. Then I checked my messages. Patrice wanted to see me, so I went down to her office.

I stood in her open doorway and asked, "What's up?"

"Judge Olann's clerk said you could pick up your signed search warrants for Raybern Ginty and Nevada Wynn's residence, employment records, and vehicles. You have forty-eight hours."

"Well, then it looks like I'll be headed to the Cities tomorrow morning."

"I spoke with Oliver. He says Ms. McCall roughed you and Austin up a bit, but believes everything will come together with Tamika and Troy's testimonies. Troy's up tomorrow."

"I hope he's right. Do you have time to see Paul Hawkinson's interview?"

"I'll make time."

After she reviewed the video, she said, "Would have been nice if he'd told you all of that earlier."

"He's scared."

"He should be. Do you believe he knows anything about his brother's disappearance?"

"I think he'd tell me if he did."

"You *think*? Well, he's admitted to participating in criminal activity. I'll contact Sheriff Hudson in Crow Wing County. I'd say he's going to want to look into Woody's operation. I'll also give the task force a heads up."

She was referring to the Joint Drug Enforcement Task Force, JDETF, a multi-jurisdictional special ops group, which Troy used to be on.

"Sounds good."

"Do you think Woody is the area distributor?"

"According to Paul he's using his restoration business to transport drugs in the cars, but since my visit, he may have already gotten rid of any evidence."

"The heat is on."

"I'm a bit worried about Paul's safety."

"Well, he'll have to figure it out, now won't he?"

I ASKED CROSBY GREEN to study and crosscheck phone records for Cat and Michael Hawkinsons, Paul Hawkinson, Wynn, Ginty, and Hayes when they arrived. Crosby immediately went to work at the desk he and Spanky shared. He started with the only ones we had at this point—Cat and Hawk's.

"I especially want to know who Cat was texting while in Mexico."

"Okay."

Tamika entered the office and threw a notebook on her desk.

"Remember the lady in Myrtle who called 911 this morning? She found footprints in the dirt under her bedroom window and thought someone was trying to break in to rape her."

"Yeah," Crosby said.

"Turns out it was her own kid. He got locked out and hers was the only un-locked window. She didn't ask him, so he hadn't told her. When I started taking fingerprints from the window frame he casually mentioned they could be his."

She cocked her head, and said, "Hey what's up with you, Calvin? You look like you lost your best friend."

"I have, remember?"

"Oh . . . sorry, it's just a figure of speech. So what's going on?"

I told her about Paul Hawkinson.

"What a loser," she said. "Who's the huge dude with an eye patch I saw your mother with at the grocery store?"

"That'd be Bobby Lopez."

"Brooks's neighbor?"

"Yep."

"She likes the bad boys?"

"She's never been a conventional mother. She dresses like a hippie, lives in the past—and believe me she has one—and I think she just ran into it with Bobby Lopez."

She said. "Maybe he's good in the sack."

I threw a wadded piece of paper at her.

She laughed.

"I'm going to Minneapolis tomorrow to search Ginty and Wynn's apart-ments. You free?"

"Uh-huh. I'm not due in court until Monday."

"I'll pick you up at 4:00 a.m. We hit Wynn's residence tomorrow at 7:00 a.m."

She made a face. "You should have led with the time I'd have to get up."

"Up to you."

Crosby said, "I'll go. Tamika can do these phone records."

"No way, Bing."

She called him Bing. You know—for Bing Crosby.

A horn sounded on my phone reminding me of my family counseling appointment with Brett Nickles.

"Gotta go," I said.

16

THE FIRST THING YOU NOTICE when you walk into Brett Nickle's office is a poster-sized Charles Schulz cartoon. It's of Lucy van Pelt standing in her box waiting to give out advice to anyone with a nickel. The sign says PSYCHIATRIC HELP 5¢.

Brett was a licensed psychologist specializing in family counseling, not a psychiatrist; he couldn't prescribe medication. Shannon's personal physician prescribed something for her depression. I didn't know if she was still taking it—or if Mac Wallace did the trick.

Donna Benson, Shannon's mom, was sitting alone in the waiting room.

"Hi," she said brightly.

"Hi. Are they in there already?" I asked.

She lifted her shoulders along with a hand. "Just Luke. Shannon had something to take care of so asked me to bring him."

Her tone indicated she didn't approve. I went to give her a hug then told Carole at the desk I was there, as if she couldn't see me.

"It'll just be a few minutes," Carole said.

I sat next to Donna. She patted my hand.

"Okay. Donna, I think it only fair to tell you I've given up fighting to keep the family together."

"I don't blame you, honey. I don't agree with how Shannon's dealing with things, but it must be because she's suffered so much loss. First, Chad, then sweet little Colby. Everybody grieves differently."

"We all do the best we can."

Shannon's first husband died seven years earlier; while out jogging he was hit by a drunk driver. She used to keep Chad's urn on a shelf in her living room—a shiny black model—hard to miss. It may have made the move to my house with her, but I never saw it. When she moved back, it reappeared on the same shelf and now sat alongside Colby's.

We sat in silence for a few seconds before I said, "I don't know how much good these sessions with Luke will do. He seems hell-bent on hating me for trying to replace his dad."

"Don't give up on him. He needs one."

I wondered if Donna knew Shannon was working on getting him one he might like better.

There was a buzz, Carole picked up the phone, then said they were ready for me.

Brett greeted me at the door with a smile and a handshake. He had a kind face and soft-brown eyes that made you think he wouldn't judge you. He always wore khaki pants and dress shirts without a tie. His brown hair was as short as mine, and his mustache and beard were neatly trimmed into a Van Dyke.

Luke looked younger than his ten years sitting in the big chair, with his arms crossed and his hands curled into tight fists. He was staring at the bird feeder tied to a tree branch just outside the window. A male cardinal chirped, looked at us, ate a little seed, chirped again, then flew off. Luke's eyes remained fixed on the feeder.

"Hi, Luke. It's good to see you. I really miss going to your baseball games."

The last one I attended, he took one look at me and walked off the field and made his mom take him home. Later, Shannon called to tell me I shouldn't attend any others, or he wouldn't play. I'm not sure she tried to convince him otherwise.

"I don't want you there," Luke said.

"Why do you think that is, Luke?" Brett said.

"Because I hate him and don't want him watching me."

"We need to talk about this more, Luke. But first, as we discussed, we need to focus on the morning of the accident. Luke, tell Cal what you told me about how you remember it."

He didn't speak for several seconds then said, "Mom and Cal . . ."

"Remember you're speaking to Cal."

"Mom and *you* fought. She said it was a mistake to marry *you*. You got real mad and shouted at her, and it scared us."

"Speak only for yourself, Luke," Brett said.

"You scared *me*."

This conversation was obviously rehearsed.

"Then what?" Brett asked.

"Then you slammed the door and left. Mom cried for a while until Grandma Donna came and asked why me and Colby were still home. We missed the bus, so mom said she'd have to drive us to school."

Donna was babysitting that day because our former nanny, Brittany, had the day off.

"So what happened next?"

"Mom said since we were already late and the coffee shop was on the way, she was stopping at the drive-through."

It wasn't on the way. It was way out of the way. If she had dropped off the boys first . . .

"Then?"

"Then she started driving to school, and that's when she got a text from Cal. She told me to read it to her."

"Do you remember what it said?"

"He asked her if she wanted a divorce."

"Then what happened?"

"We got to the light, and she was crying."

"You were stopped for a red light."

"Yes."

"Then what happened?"

"The light turned green. I told her to go, and she did, and that's when the truck hit us." He turned and shouted at me. "It's his fault!"

His words were a punch in the belly.

"Luke, remember the rules?" Brett said.

Luke pulled his face into a defiant scowl, and his fists were so tight his knuckles were turning white against dark-red hands.

"Okay, now it's Cal's turn. Remember we look at him when he's speaking."

He slowly lifted his eyes to meet mine. My throat felt tight as I swallowed. This was it. I needed to say the right thing—if I only knew what it was.

"That morning before I left for work, yes, your mom and I did have words. And, you're right, she did tell me she thought we made a mistake by getting married so quickly."

"Did you hear her say that Luke?" Brett asked.

Luke nodded.

"Did you also hear me say I disagreed? I said we had four kids now and needed to stick together. My dad wasn't around when I was growing up, and I know how hard that is on a kid."

"You're not my real dad," he said.

"I adopted you. You are my son."

"My dad is dead."

"He is, and now I want to take care of you because I love you," I said.

"Bullshit!" Spittle flew out of his mouth.

"No, it's true."

"Then why did Mom say you didn't act like you wanted us in your house."

I hadn't realized he'd also heard the argument we had the night before.

Fueled by my hesitation, Luke screamed, "I never saw my mom cry before she married you and we moved into your house."

"Your mom and I didn't know you were listening."

"People say things they don't mean when they're upset," Brett said.

Luke's face said he wasn't buying a word of it, but I continued. "That morning after I got to work, I texted her and asked if she really wanted a divorce. When she answered yes, I texted her to say I would fight for our marriage, but you wouldn't have known that, Luke, because I understand that's when the accident happened."

"No, you said, you weren't going to let it happen."

"You're right. That's exactly what I said. I'd forgotten. So you saw the text?"

His face reddened.

Brett leaned forward. "Did you see the text, Luke?"

"Yes."

Then it dawned on me. It was Luke who had the phone and answered my texts—not Shannon. He was the one who said he wanted the divorce. The texting was at the crux of the legal case. Clifford Emerson, the Estelle's Candies truck driver, said the light had just turned yellow when he entered the intersection. Their company attorney argued Shannon was texting on her phone at the time of the crash, that even if the light was red, she could have avoided the crash if she had been attentive and looked before she entered the intersection.

"Luke, do you understand how important it is to admit it was you who was on your mother's phone and answered my text?" I said.

"Why? So she will go back to you?" he said with a snarl.

"It was *you* who texted 'Fuck you.' Wasn't it?"

Tears started forming in his eyes, he pushed his tongue into the side of his cheek as he looked out the window. I didn't know if Shannon wasn't even aware of what he had done, or if she was protecting him from being involved.

"Luke, answer Cal."

"Yeah, I said it because I hate your guts and didn't want to live with you anymore."

Silence filled the room like the aftermath of a storm. Brett lifted his hand to stroke his beard.

I looked to Brett for help. He only nodded. I should say what was on my mind. What I wanted to say was, "You little shit." But instead I chose: "I enjoyed having you live with me because I love you. The house seems empty without you and your mom."

His lip quivered. "Can I go?" he asked.

"Well, we've accomplished a great deal today, so, yes, you can go now, Luke. We'll meet again next week."

Luke got up, stalked out, and slammed the door.

My eyes slowly moved from the door to Brett.

He let out a breathy, "Whoa."

"That went well," I said.

"I think we made great progress today."

"If you say so. Did you know he was the one who texted me back?"

"No. Didn't you and Shannon ever talk about it?"

"What happened before didn't seem to matter after the accident."

"The good thing is his hostility is out in the open, which needs to happen before he can get past it. You do know you have similar feelings towards your own father, so you should get how he feels."

"Only I really didn't do anything to Luke to warrant his hatred, like my father did to me."

"You and I both know that. You're his scapegoat. He can direct all his pain toward you without much consequence. And by being stubborn and refusing to see you, he gets more of his mom's attention. I'll take it up with Shannon. And now, you and I should talk about your decision to divorce."

"*My* decision? You do know Shannon has a boyfriend . . . Mac Wallace? She saw him years ago when he was still married. They split up because of it, and now that he's divorced, they're back together."

"I wasn't aware of any of this."

"Neither was I. A mutual friend, thinking I knew, spilled the beans."

"I appreciate knowing. So, Cal, we've spoken at great length about your father. Are you ready to relieve yourself of your own negative feelings for him?"

"I don't know."

"Why not?"

"Because what he did was reprehensible."

"I want you to pretend to be him for a few minutes, and tell me in his words what happened."

"He impregnated his wife's sister, carried on an affair with her for years, then, when caught, they both split for California where they remained until Grace died. Then he comes crawling back, begging forgiveness for being absent for thirty years, offering me money."

"That's you talking. Change the he to I. Just try."

I took a deep breath. "I fell madly in love with Grace. I didn't mean for it to happen. When everything came down on us, I thought it best to get Grace out of Minnesota and have a fresh start. Her parents disowned her anyway. We lived happily ever after when we had our daughter, Angelica. We made up for our years of neglect by bequeathing a large sum of money to Cal. He should forgive me now."

"Are you being entirely fair?"

"I think so."

The look on his face reminded me of my grandfather's face when I lied to him about putting a dent in his Olds.

"You must realize your anger is hurting you more than him. It affects everything you do and all your relationships—even your friendships and how you get along with co-workers."

I'd heard it all before, but this time the words touched on something. He was right. My life was shit. My pent-up anger was affecting every relationship I had.

"How do I get rid of it?"

"I've been waiting for you to ask. Think about why you want to hold onto the anger."

"It's not because I want to."

"But what does anger prevent you from feeling?"

"You tell me."

He stared at me for a while making me squirm.

"Okay, it may prevent me from feeling other things."

"Folks, we have a bingo. This week think about what those things are and we'll talk about it next time."

"Are you going to recommend the same to Luke?"

He smiled. "It's different with children. I like to fly kites with them. We attach our problems to the tail to lift them away from our bodies."

"Well, you better get flying."

"I think we have more work to do before he's ready."

17

May 30
Eighteen days missing.

AT 4:00 A.M. SHARP, Tamika lumbered her way to the Explorer. She put a small carry-on in the back alongside our equipment I'd pre-packed the night before, then dropped herself into the front seat with a groan. She held her throat. "Coffee."

I drove to the Quick Stop on the way out and bought two coffees that tasted like metallic sludge and two sticky muffins, then made my way to Highway 71 to catch I-94 at Sauk Center.

Yesterday, I had contacted Wynn's parole officer, and he gave me a new Minneapolis address on Queen Avenue North. MPD had four patrol cars stationed on the street down from the stucco house at six thirty when we rolled up. We handled it like a raid, securing the scene before the search. I expected Wynn to be home, and I assumed he had weapons.

A woman who identified herself as Roseanna Martinez answered the door in a dingy white, extra-large men's T-shirt. She had a baby bump of about six months. The officers went through the door first and secured the scene while Tamika and I stayed with Roseanna. The house was covered in a layer of grime and smelled like cigarettes and weed. Ants crawled on Coke cans, and crusted plates lay on the floor in front of the sagging sofa.

They came back down stating the only people present were two women, the other was in a bedroom upstairs. I asked Tamika to go keep on eye on her while I questioned Roseanna, Ginty's girlfriend. Two officers stayed to keep watch while we did our business.

I showed Roseanna pictures of Raybern Ginty and Nevada Wynn and asked if she knew them.

"Yeah, they live here."

"Who's the woman upstairs?"

"Franchon Inman.

151

"Where's Wynn now?"

"Working, I guess."

"Were you in Vegas a couple weeks ago with Raybern?" I asked.

"Yeah, we went there on a little vaycay."

I invited her to sit at the kitchen table. Ketchup stains spotted the formica top. I pulled over a *Hustler* magazine to set my iPad on. I touched the record button.

"Tell me about your Vegas vacation."

"Ray-Ray came home and told me to grab my purse because we were going to Vegas. He bought me the clothes I needed at the airport and in the hotel."

"Sounds like a special time," I said.

"Was—until he got arrested. I had to pay my own way home."

"What a shame. So tell me about yourself. What do you do for work?"

"Franchon and I are escorts."

"Prostitutes?"

"Well, yeah."

"Do you have a pimp?"

"Me and Franchon are independents. We work downtown, mostly Washington or Nicollet. We just work 'til three, get the last-call boys after the bars close."

She said in March, Ray-Ray and Snake moved in—they had once been their johns. A few days after the move, the two men kicked out Vickilee and Topaz, also hookers, because they were always late on their rent—they put all their money up their noses. The change in roommates was fine with Roseanna and Franchon because the men currently paid all the rent and utilities. It was all head-shaking stuff.

She knew Ginty was a drug dealer.

"It don't bother me," she said.

"Do you keep the product here on the premises?"

"No, just a little bit for us to use rec-crea-ationally. I'm no junkie."

"How does Snake make a living?"

"He drives a delivery truck."

"For North Cross?"

"Don't know."

How could an ex-felon like Snake get a promotion from the loading dock to truck driver, then get away with using the truck to transport his drugs?

He was either that good, or someone at the company knew what he was up to and was in on the action.

"So, back to your Vegas trip. Did you go up to the desk with Ray-Ray when you checked in at The Flamingo?"

"No, I hit the casino right away. It's a real nice place, but next time, I want to stay at The Venetian. That was so beautiful. It was just like you were in Venice. Me and Franchon might even move out there after the baby's born."

"You ever think you might get out of the business when you have this baby?"

"Sure, all the time. I just don't know what I'd do for money."

"There are programs, grants. You could go to school, get a legitimate job."

"I don't know how to do all that."

"Go talk to a Hennepin County social worker. They can steer you in the right direction."

Her face fell into a contemplative look.

"Has Ray ever mentioned Michael or Paul Hawkinson?"

"Who?"

"Michael Hawkinson. You know . . . the man whose stolen credit card Ray used when you were on your vaycay in Vegas."

"Oh, that."

"Did you meet Michael or hear his name mentioned?"

"No, but at the bar when we bought our drinks, they said, 'Thank you Mr. Hawkinson.'"

She should have been arrested too.

I called Tamika's cell phone and asked her to bring down the other woman. Their footsteps were heavy and slow as they descended the wood stairs. Franchon shuffled in wearing frayed jeans shorts cut up to her buttocks and a short tank top with no bra. I know this because the outline of her nipple rings showed through her shirt. She had blond, straggly hair, dark at the roots. She was a skinny, heavily tattooed woman with more body piercings than anyone I'd laid eyes on: nipples, belly button, several up both ears, nose, several in her cheek, eyebrows, and I'm guessing there's one or more below her Mason-Dixon line. Tamika escorted Roseanna out of the kitchen, and I asked Franchon to take her place at the table.

"That lady says you work in Birch County. Where that?"

"Do you know where Brainerd is?" I asked.

She shook her head.

"It's northwest of here. When did you move to Minnesota?"

"I was born here."

Okay then. Did she know what I meant by northwest?

Her face was prematurely wrinkled and spotted with scars and sores most likely due to heavy meth use. She had tattoos of roses up her forearms, a face of a young child inked on one upper arm, CiCi scripted underneath.

I pointed to it. "Who's CiCi?"

"My baby girl. She died when she was two cuz her daddy shake her to death."

"I'm sorry to hear that."

"Thank you. That was terrible hard. He in prison for it."

"As he should be." I showed her a picture of Nevada Wynn. "Do you know this man?"

"Sure."

"What's his name?"

"Nevada Wynn, but he go by Snake. Yeah. He moved in a couple months ago."

"Where does he work?"

"North Cross Shipping. He drives a big truck for them. He asked me if I wanted to ride with him next time."

"What do you know about his trip up north a couple weeks ago?"

She made a face and said, "Nothing."

"Wynn's connected to a kidnapping/murder in Birch County."

Her head jerked back. "Murder? I don't know nothin' 'bout a murder!"

She told me she and Snake exchanged sex for drugs for a while before he moved in. Now they all got their goodies for free.

"Does he deal drugs at present?"

"He doesn't tell me nothin' about his business, and I don't ask."

"Has he ever mentioned Michael or Paul Hawkinson?"

"Who?"

I repeated the names. She shook her head. I asked her a few more questions, then asked the Minneapolis police officers to keep an eye on the women while we searched the house for evidence in our case. All we took was a 2014 Mac Book Pro Franchon said was Wynn's, hoping it'd give us something.

We then stopped by North Cross Shipping to talk to Haldis Moore about Nevada Wynn's employment. She used to be the personnel director; now her desk plate said DIRECTOR OF HUMAN RESOURCES. She was a stocky woman, with curly, gray hair and a big rump. She stood and shook my hand. I told her I had questions about Nevada Wynn.

"I remember you," she said. "You spoke with him last year."

It had been two years, but I didn't correct her.

"So, now he's driving truck? Is that a promotion?"

"Yes, the move was recommended by management to send him to driving school. I was told to sign off on it, so I did."

"Who in management recommended him?"

"I'm not sure, exactly, but we have a commitment to hire ex-cons to give them a chance to become good community members."

"I'm not sure it's working for Wynn. He's a person of interest in connection with a burglary and the disappearance of Michael Hawkinson in Birch County."

"Oh, my."

"May I speak with his current boss?"

"Certainly, that would be Zeke La Plante. Follow me."

We were shown to a small office just down the hall. An overweight guy looked up at us between his caterpillar eyebrows and his eyeglasses. His tie lay diagonally across his bloated belly. The buttons of his shirt were stressed and ready for takeoff.

"Can I help you?" he asked.

"Maybe." I introduced Tamika and myself then told him I was looking for Wynn.

He tapped keys on his computer then said, "Chicago."

"Returning?"

"Tomorrow."

I told him of the arrest.

"Well, there must be some mistake. Nevada has been an excellent employee."

"No mistake. So what makes him so excellent?"

"He's does what's asked of him. Always on time."

"How many deliveries did he have on May 12?"

He set to work on his computer again and said, "Just one to your area. Estelle's Candies."

"No other stops?"

"Not that I can see."

"So once he's made his delivery, is he required to come right back to Minneapolis?"

"Depends on the run. If it's an eight hour turn around the drivers need to get the trucks back and loaded for the next day."

"What kind of business does North Cross service?"

"Manufacturing companies."

"What type of goods?"

He lifted his head, opened his mouth and made a weird buzz in his throat. "Varies. Mainly parts for industrial use and home medical equipment."

"So North Cross delivers these warehoused items to other businesses like stores or other manufacturing companies?"

"Exactly."

"Is there a list of these companies I could see?"

He cocked his head. "Of the companies who warehouse with us?"

"And the companies you ship to."

"Well, I don't have a list . . . just files."

Tamika piped up. "For cryin' out loud, doesn't your company have a distribution list for Christmas cards?"

Zeke's face went blank. "I guess someone does."

I said, "That's a very good idea, Deputy Frank. Then Zeke here doesn't have to spend all afternoon generating it for us. I'd also like a copy of Nevada Wynn's delivery schedule for May."

His brows furrowed. "It's going to take me some time for all that."

Tamika put her hands on her hips, gave him an attitudinal face and said, "We'll wait."

"Let me see what I can do," Zeke said through clenched teeth.

He made some calls and soon had printed off two distribution lists. There were only six companies who used North Cross, but there were twenty-five pages of companies who bought the goods they stored.

At Tamika's insistence, before we headed back to Prairie Falls, we stopped for lunch at a Thai restaurant on Washington Avenue. I looked for Roseanna and Franchon on our way out, but it was way too early for them.

We were back in the office by mid-afternoon. Crosby had left a note on my desk.

Cal, the Hawkinson's cell phone company just sent a list of phone calls received, sent, and missed. In the first few days your friend Hawk was missing, he had several missed messages from his mother, wife, brother, company, and you. Nothing after May 18. I'm still working on them.

I checked in Wynn's computer as evidence, then Samantha Polansky would check it out to see what she could find that might be of use to us. I spent the rest of the day doing the paperwork on my interviews. When we left the office, I told Tamika that on Monday we would research the companies that warehouse with North Cross and the ones they ship to.

BULLET MET ME AT THE DOOR. I loved him up as he wiggled in next to me, then walked him outdoors. I left him to his sniffing and went inside and called for Clara. I found a note she'd left on the counter: *Shannon picked up the twins for the family party. I'm home. Call if you need me. Otherwise, I'll be back tomorrow afternoon. There's tuna salad in the refrigerator. Clara*

Canned tuna *anything* was not going to cut it. However, I was hungry for a Minnesota Fare walleye dinner. All showered, shaved, and dressed in a light blue Polo shirt and khaki slacks, I stood in the lobby of the restaurant in Birch County Park South asking for a table for one.

A new hostess said, "So sorry, sir, we're booked."

Should have figured. I told her it was okay and turned to exit when I heard my name called. It was Madison Mitchell. She lived in a spectacular log home next door to Adriana on Lake Emmaline—before Adriana's house was torched and the lot was repurposed as a park. Maddie made and sold jewelry and stained glass art online.

"How are you?" I asked, giving her a hug. She was short and cute, reminding me of Renee Zellweger.

"I'm great," she said. "Hey, we saw you come in. Aren't you staying?"

"No, I was turned away—no reservation."

"Well, perfect. You can join us."

I looked around to see who "us" was. Of course, it was Adriana.

Pushing down the pinpricks of apprehension I agreed and followed Maddie to the booth. I slid in beside Maddie, so I wouldn't have to sit next to Adriana.

Adriana, looking beautiful in a white shirt with tiny black buttons, tipped her wine glass, half-filled with red, at me. Her chestnut-brown hair was down, slightly curled. I'd always liked it like that.

The waiter brought over another wine glass and asked if I wanted the Stag's Leap Cabernet sitting on the table or if I wanted something else.

"He wants this, Kirk," Adriana said.

I nodded my agreement.

After Kirk poured my wine and left, I asked her, "Did Troy testify today?"

"Yes, I expect it will be Tuesday before it's my turn."

Maddie asked, "How did it go?"

"Victoria's attorney, a woman by the name of Elizabeth McCall, made Spanky and I look like a couple of horny dogs."

Adriana gave one of her airy laughs. "I heard Beth the Barracuda was on the case."

I raised my eyebrows. "Beth the Barracuda? Yeah, well, our sex lives are now part of the court documents. She stopped short of asking how you liked it."

"Darn," Adriana said, snapping her fingers.

Maddie laughed.

"All the attorneys Adam uses are the best in the business, smart and ruthless. I spoke to Oliver, and he thought you and Austin did fine considering."

"So, how are you doing?" I asked.

"Fine."

"Good."

I couldn't think of anything else to say, so I asked about her boy, which precipitated a fifteen minute show and tell, complete with cell phone photos.

"Marcus looks like you."

"You think?"

"Definitely," Maddie said.

"Cal, did you know Troy moved out?"

"Oh?"

"I asked him to. Marcus loves his daddy, but it isn't good for him to hear us fight all the time."

"You did the right thing, Adriana," Maddie said.

"He found an apartment in Maple Grove."

I lowered my brows attempting to squelch my smile.

"Are you still living with your mother?" I asked.

"Yes, she was so excited to have Marcus all to herself for a few days, but insisted I take Tino."

Tino was Adriana's harlequin Great Dane.

"And I love him, so it's a win-win. I'm thinking of buying one," Maddie said.

"They're great dogs," I said.

"How's Bullet?" Adriana asked.

"Good."

"And your children?"

"Great." I pulled out my camera and showed her the few photos I had. Shannon was the one who snapped pictures.

Thinking Maddie must be bored with the kiddie talk, I asked how her on-line jewelry business was doing. Every single time I glanced at Adriana, she was looking at me, not Maddie.

The dinner conversation was somewhat awkward—forced, and to make matters worse, when the check came Adriana snatched it up before I could.

"No, sir, this one is definitely on me," she said with the look I knew to mean *don't argue.*

When we were in the parking lot about to head to our cars, Adriana leaned into me for a hug she held longer than comfortable. After she finally released me, I gave Maddie a hug I purposefully held for a few seconds longer than I normally would just to even it out. The women got into a light blue BMW, Adriana's replacement for the red convertible Victoria destroyed with silver paint. I waited and watched them drive away. When I turned around, there was Troy getting out of a white SUV. I gave him a half smile and said, "Hey there."

"What're you doing?"

"Just on my way home, but I could go out for a drink if you'd like."

"Stay away from Adriana. We're still trying to work things out," he said way too loudly. A couple walking across the lot slowed to watch us.

"Look, I have no intentions of getting back with her. Okay?"

"Right." He leaned against the SUV and crossed his legs and arms as if to settle in for a long talk.

"I'm leaving," I said. I wasn't going to put up with the asshole's bullshit. I didn't look back until I was pulling out of the park. There was no white SUV following me, so I drove home.

An hour later, I was sitting on my deck hoping Iris Kellogg would walk over, when a car pulled into my driveway—a light blue BMW. Adriana got out and walked up to me with a shopping bag in each hand.

"I need to talk to you," she said.

"Didn't we just talk at the restaurant?"

"I have wine and dessert," she said as she lifted the bags.

"Have a seat," I said against my better judgment.

I went inside for wine glasses and a corkscrew. When I returned, Adriana grabbed the corkscrew from me and deftly opened the bottle, filled them, then handed one to me.

"So did your testimony *really* go so badly?"

"Yes."

She chuckled. "Phillip said Oliver has a solid case and if the jury acquits, they've been tampered with."

"Man, I wouldn't doubt it."

"And if she's found guilty, you know she'll appeal. This could go on for years and years."

"At least she'd be in prison for a while."

As she crossed her long legs and smiled at me, I wondered why she was really here.

"You didn't see anyone follow you, did you?"

"You mean Troy?"

"Yes, of course I mean Troy. After you left Minnesota Fare, he showed up and threatened me to stay away from you because you were still working on things. But here you are."

"I've made it very clear we were over. Should I let Troy control me?"

"No, I'm just saying he won't like it."

"Too bad. We're just talking."

"So talk."

She patted my hand. "Okay, I want your opinion because I value your judgment. You have a great deal of common sense."

My common sense was telling me her being here was a bad idea.

She lifted her hands, palms up. "Should I marry Troy because he's Marcus's father?"

"Do you love him?"

"No."

"Then no. He deserves to have a woman who loves him."

"Oh, wow. Okay, *not* getting married is in *his* best interest too."

We both took sips of our wine.

"See, you always know what to say."

"Want further advice?" I asked.

"Sure."

"I think you should avoid relationships with men for a few years—concentrate on Marcus. That's what I'm going to do. Focus on Henry and Lucy."

She smirked. "Oh, really? What about your great *physical* needs?"

"I'm suppressing my sex drive with work and exercise."

"Ah." She waited a few seconds then asked, "Is it working?"

"Nope."

She laughed. "I have a proposal for you."

Here it comes. "Which is?"

"Let me refill our glasses first."

As I watched the ruby-red liquid fall into the glass, I considered my reasons for not reconciling. Our relationship failed. We were both on the rebound. We wanted to live in different locations. But she was Adriana—beautiful, sexy Adriana.

I took a gulp of wine.

She cocked her head back, gave me one of her half-smiles, and said, "My proposal is no-strings-attached-periodic-sex."

"With?"

She laughed. "Each other, of course. And I agree, with your thoughts about avoiding a committed relationship at this time, but I could use a little manly action every so often—with someone I like and trust. We could meet somewhere in between, say at a B & B in St. Cloud, enjoy each other's company without anyone knowing. It ends when one of us wants it to."

"Can you do that? Because I'm not sure I can."

"What bothers you about it?"

"I don't like having to be secretive, and I'm not sure we can be that cool."

"That's part of the deal—to stay detached and cool. Just think about it."

"What if I wanted to ask out one of your friends?"

"I thought you said you were going to avoid relationships."

"Well, serious relationships. Everyone needs companionship."

Her eyes had narrowed. "And who are you thinking about as this *companion*?"

"See how you jumped on that?"

"No, I just want to know who you would be interested in? Maddie Mitchell?"

"I'm being hypothetical here."

"Maddie's sweet, but I don't think she's right for you."

"Because you're good friends?"

"Okay, if you'd want to see Maddie Mitchell we'd call off our deal."

I laughed. "How the hell could this ever work?"

She got up, sat in my lap, and kissed me. It was a quick, sweet kiss. But then we moved in for another, our mouths opened and our tongues softly explored as they once had. The scent of her seemed to erase the years away, and I felt myself responding in an-oh-so familiar way.

"We should go inside, so my neighbors won't break out their binoculars."

She got up and took my hand. Just inside the door, we kissed again and before long we were in the main floor guest room, clothes off, and having hot, sweaty sex. She'd picked up a few moves I didn't want to know how she learned. We fell asleep and when I felt her touching me again in the middle of the night, we replayed the lovemaking only more slowly and tenderly. She always did like sleepy sex. Why would I have a problem with this?

18

May 31
Nineteen days missing.

I SENSED THE WARM BODY next to me. Without opening my eyes, in my sleepy haze, I put my arm around Shannon. Then I caught a whiff of perfume and my eyes popped open. Dark hair splayed across the pillow. *Adriana!*

Awash in dread, I gingerly removed my arm and rolled out of bed. I tugged at my pants Bullet was laying on. He gave me a pitiful look and slowly rose. I grabbed the rest of my clothing that lay scattered across the floor and numbly walked across the hall to the bathroom. As I looked in the mirror I whispered to my image, "You dumb shit."

After I took out Bullet and fed him, I made coffee and looked in the refrigerator to see what I could make her for breakfast. I had to feed her, right? Eggs. I heard the bathroom door close and then a few minutes later, Adriana entered the kitchen fully dressed.

She gave me a coy smile and said, "I should go."

"Want something to eat first?"

"No, I have to be on my way. I promised Maddie I would golf with her this morning."

She gave me a quick peck, gathered her purse, and left. And then I was alone, confused and weary. Man, I did not need this shit.

I PICKED UP THE WINE GLASSES, washed and dried them, then put them away. I looked in the bag on the counter. It contained a white box. I flipped the lid. Chocolate cake. I put the box on top of the fridge, then wiped down the granite counter and went to put the wine bottle in the recycling basket we kept in the closet. Seeing it was full, I took it out to the garage where we kept the large blue bin. The contents clanked as glass hit metal. When I turned around, a fist flew

163

straight at my nose. I was knocked back against my truck. Troy Kern stood there all red-faced and mean looking. I pushed myself off the truck and touched my nose, which hurt like hell. When he pulled back his arm to land another strike, I power thrust my fist right at his face. He flinched, so I caught him on the jaw. *Ow. Hand hurts.* He lunged and tackled me to the garage floor.

As he rolled me out onto the blacktop, I slammed my fists into his back again and again. Ooof! He caught me a good one in the kidney. We landed hard punches over and over. I vaguely heard dogs barking, shouts and more barks, then sirens. The metallic taste of blood filled my mouth.

LEGS IN BLACK UNIFORM pants surrounded us. Strong hands and arms pried us apart. I looked up to see Spanky and Greg Woods. Greg stopped Troy from popping me again. Blood and spit dribbled from Troy's mouth.

"What the hell you are you two doing?" Greg asked.

Troy shrugged off Greg's grip, rolled to his feet and brushed off his clothing. His nose was bleeding; his face and arms were skinned up. I must look similar. Not only did my nose kill, but my cheekbone, and elbows too. After I touched the cool wetness on my face, I looked at my hand. It was covered in blood.

As Troy walked away he yelled, "Stay the fuck away from her, or I'll destroy you."

Greg said, "Hey, Troy, wait a minute?"

He just kept walking.

That's when I noticed the people gathered at the end of my driveway. Two squad cars, with their flashers and sirens attracted attention.

My neighbor, Doug Nelson, yelled from his deck, "Cal, we saw the whole thing. We were having our morning coffee out on the deck here, when we saw that guy come up from behind and punch you. I called 911."

"You did the right thing, sir," Spanky said.

Doug waved. "You bet."

"Thanks, Doug." I returned the wave and smiled which caused a sharp pain to shoot through my nose and up my forehead.

Spanky said, "What got into Troy?"

"Hard telling."

It wouldn't have been too difficult for Troy to figure out Adriana and I had a sleepover with her BMW in my driveway all night.

"Want to press charges?" Spanky said.

"No," I said, shaking my head.

"I've got good news and bad news."

"Yeah, what?"

"Your nose is swelling pretty bad, and you're bleeding pretty good," Spanky said.

"What? You're a comedian now?"

"I think it's funny," Greg Woods said. "We better call paramedics."

"No, don't. I'm fine." *More explanations, more paperwork.* "I'll ice it.

"No need to write this up," I said to the guys.

Greg's eyebrows shot up, and he caught Spanky's eye. I knew they'd need to write something after a 911 call. Spanky told Greg he'd stay and take care of it, and I was glad. Greg was a veteran and too professional not to illicit the whole story, which I no way wanted to tell. But Troy could spread the word about the sleepover if he chose to. That wouldn't be good. I couldn't feel so high and mighty around Shannon anymore.

AFTER SPANKY TURNED OFF his squad lights and Greg left, he pulled out a leather folder off of his front seat.

I said, "Let's take this party inside."

Bullet was at the back door, barking his head off, as I'm sure he'd been during the entire fight. Poor boy had to watch his master get pummeled. I wondered if he'd been outside with me if he would have bit Troy. A guy could fantasize, couldn't he?

Once in the house, I reached down to pet Bullet to calm him. His tongue landed a swipe on my skinned hand. I put him out, and he ran lickety-split down the steps to check out the battle scene where blood stains dotted the blacktop.

"Why don't you get cleaned up while I start the report," Spanky said.

I went upstairs to the master bath. I stood before the mirror. My nose was a swollen blob; blood was dripping down my face. I had abrasions on my elbows, the likes of which I hadn't experienced since I wiped out on my bike when I was thirteen. My new pants were ripped at the knees. Shit.

I grabbed a clean washcloth and began to clean my face. I winced as I dabbed near my nose. I put the biggest bandage I could find on my elbows.

SPANKY'S FACE CONTORTED when he saw me, "Yeah, maybe you should get that nose looked at. You hurt anywhere else—like in your mid-section? You boys were landing some pretty serious punches."

"If I have pain in my back and abdomen, I'll go in. Okay?"

"Okay. So, what the heck set him off?"

"It's been a long time coming. You know."

"Yeah . . . I'm thinking Adriana is the center of this . . . or because he thinks you nixed him getting his old job back."

"Who told you that?"

"Greg. He talked to him last night at Buzzo's."

"I had nothing to do with it. I didn't know he asked Patrice to come back until she told me she'd turned him down."

"When I saw him at the courthouse yesterday afternoon, he told me he applied for detective with Hennepin County and thinks he should get it, so I don't know what he's thinking asking for his job back in Prairie Falls. Why would he move back with his kid in Minneapolis?"

"Don't know."

While Spanky and I had coffee and talked about how to write up the call, I iced my nose with a bag of frozen peas.

"How about I write it up as a concerned neighbor misunderstood a disagreement between friends. Sound good? Or do you want to press charges? You have a witness."

"Nooo, I don't want to press charges."

After Spanky left, I thought about the mess I'd created by sleeping with Adriana again. Troy had been waiting to pounce, and I justified his paranoia—Shannon's too. Maybe they were both right, and Adriana and I never did get over each other, but acting on it was really stupid. I took a long slow breath. If Adriana contacted me, I was going to have to tell her I wasn't interested in her plan of casual sex. I also decided I was going to lie low all weekend, spend today with Henry and Lucy while I iced the sausage my nose had become.

I quickly stripped the linens from the guest bedroom and threw them in the wash. I had just finished remaking the bed when Clara arrived. She took one look at me and said, "What on earth?"

"Long story."

"I have time," she said.

I didn't know why I was so open with Clara, but I spilled the beans like she was my best friend in the world. Only she wasn't. My best friend was missing. He was dead because his loser brother owed ten thousand big ones to a drug dealer.

CLARA AGREED TO BE BACK from the market by the time Shannon arrived with the twins, so she wouldn't see my battered face. But today she decided to show up two hours early. Her eyes narrowed as she handed me Henry, who didn't seem to notice his daddy's nose was twice its normal size and he was starting to resemble a raccoon.

Henry cuddled into me. I loved that he favored me, especially now with the imminent divorce.

"I'm almost afraid to ask," she said.

"Then don't."

When she returned with Lucy, my baby girl's little brow furrowed when she took her first look at me.

"Daddy has an owie, Lucy girl," I said and kissed her forehead, taking in her little girl scent.

As Shannon followed me inside, she said, "Something tells me it wasn't work related, but personal, and I know Mac wasn't involved, so it must be . . . hmm . . . let me guess . . . Troy?"

Henry was reaching down for Bullet, who was at my feet, so I set him down. My nose throbbed as I bent over.

Bullet licked Henry's face, and he giggled.

"How was the party?" I asked.

"You're not going to tell me what happened?"

"No."

She placed Lucy down beside her brother, and Bullet licked her face too. They followed him off toward the dog's toy box.

"The party was great. The twins were the hit. We're lucky they have such good dispositions."

"They inherited it from me," I said.

"Right. Always so controlled until . . . what?"

"Someone threatens my family."

"Who?"

I pointed to my face. "This was different. It was dark. I walked into a door."

"Right. How does other guy look?"

"The door? Well, I imagine it has a big dent."

"Oh, Sheehan. What am I going to do with you?"

"You don't have to do anything with me anymore, now do you?"

Shannon scowled and let out a sigh to let me know how exasperating I was.

"Shannon, do you have a few minutes? I have a couple things I'd like to talk to you about."

"I guess."

The twins were annoying Bullet by trying to ride him, so I put him out then turned on the television like the good parent I was. As an afterthought I grabbed a basket of educational toys to place in front of them.

Meanwhile, Shannon had brewed us each a cup of Keurig coffee. She set them on the counter and took a sip. And for a few moments we behaved as if all was well. We sat at the counter together, sipped coffee, and watched the Twinks, who were mesmerized by a squeaky-voiced nitwit in a bee getup on television.

She turned to face me. "Well? Are you going to tell me something, or did you just want to share a Starbucks moment?"

"Okay. Two things: I found out from someone else you saw Mac while he was still married."

Her cheeks flushed a bright pink. "Tamika?"

"She thought I knew."

"She was the only person who did know. It was a long time ago. It lasted less than a month. And now? You and I were struggling before the accident, then after, well, we never dug out of the hole. And to be honest, I was never quite sure it was me you really wanted."

I took a breath refusing to react to the same old conversation. "I just wish you'd been honest with me about Mac. I would have been more cautious about our marriage in the first place."

That touched a nerve because she looked down, then away. "I met with Brett yesterday . . . at his request. He recommended we hold off on the divorce for a year and put a hold on other relationships."

"For what purpose?"

"To continue healing before any big life change."

"What did you say?"

"I said I'd think about it."

"Did you tell Mac?"

"Not yet."

"Because you haven't decided."

She nodded. "You said two things. What's the other?"

"Why aren't you telling the truth about who was texting just before the accident?"

"What do you mean?"

"Emerson's attorney claims he has proof you were texting while driving."

"Cal, I didn't."

"I know because it was Luke. Wasn't it?"

She nodded. "He was playing a game, but then he must have seen your incoming text."

"Why? What did he say?"

Her eyes were filled with tears. "He told me you'd written you wanted a divorce, that we were done."

"No. I asked if *you* really wanted a divorce, he answered *yes*. Then I said I was going to fight for us, for our family. He answered, *fuck you*."

"Oh, my God."

"You didn't know this?"

"No, because they took my cell phone, remember? Why didn't you bring this up a year ago?"

"Because we had lost our Colby and I was heartbroken, and when I saw you and Luke in the hospital beds, battered and bruised, none of it mattered anymore. We seemed so close for a while."

"Yes, I guess we were. Until we had to deal with reality and the legal matters."

"Do you blame me for the accident?"

"Why would I? I was the one driving. I was the one who didn't see the Estelle's Candy truck coming."

"You had the green light."

"Yes, Cal, I had the green light, but I should have been aware."

"We have to tell Phillip what Luke did."

"Why?"

"It proves you weren't texting at the time of the accident."

"I don't want to subject Luke to the witness stand."

"The case will never make it to trial. Estelle's will settle."

"I don't want the money. I want Colby."

"Me too, babe. I'll always be there if you need me."

She let out a sob.

I put my arm around her, and we shed some silent tears together.

"I'll call Phillip," she said.

"Thank you. I think Luke feels responsible for his brother's death. You got upset and weren't concentrating on driving because he lied to you about my texts."

She swallowed. "Yes, I suppose he does. I'll talk to him."

Shannon kissed the Twinks good-bye, then said to me, "You know I love you. That was never the issue."

"And I you. Whatever you decide, I want us to have an amicable relationship for the kids' sake. And you don't have to hide things from me."

"Like what happened to your face?"

"I'm embarrassed, okay?"

"You and Troy had a fight."

I nodded.

Just before she opened the back door to leave she said, "Well, I hope he looks as bad as you do."

"Golly, thanks."

As I watched her pull out of the driveway, I asked myself what the hell had just happened. Did she say she was willing to try again? Should I even allow myself to feel hopeful? I hate this wishy-washy crap. Either you love me or you don't, and you want to stay or you don't. How could I live with the wait-a-year limbo bullshit? I sat down at the computer to compose an email telling her just that. After I changed the text a hundred times, I decided to delete it entirely. She'd end up with Mac anyway.

19

June 1
Twenty days missing

I WOKE WHEN SOMETHING soft and wet brushed my face. I opened my eyes. Bullet, who never came on my bed, was straddling me licking the wounds on my face. I yelled, "No, Bullet! Down!" He gave me another good lick, then jumped off the bed. I grabbed a tissue to wipe the slobber off, then thought it best to run hot soapy water over the cuts so they wouldn't get infected. You know what else dogs liked to lick.

At noon on Sunday, I dropped the Twinks at Shannon's. I loved them dearly, but part of me was relieved when I could hand them off. Shannon greeted me with a shit-eating grin. I hadn't seen her smile for a very long time.

"Are you happy to see me, or are you just pleased I resemble a raccoon?"

"Oh, come on, Rocky, let me have a little fun."

"The Twinks ate a good breakfast. I took them to the Sportsman. Tony gave them each a mini-cinnamon roll after they ate their scrambled eggs and sausage."

"Did you buy a bag, and do you have extras?"

"No, sorry. I ate only one at the restaurant."

"Eleanor still coming over bearing treats?"

"She is."

"Has she ever hit on you? Be honest."

"Of course not."

"Now the word has spread I moved out, I imagine you have women banging on the door."

"Yes, as I matter of fact I have mobs of female raccoons at my door."

She smiled again. "Are you going to have to testify again this week wearing the raccoon mask?"

"Oh, I hope not."

I wondered what Troy looked like. He had to testify again tomorrow. People would put two and two together.

171

ALTHOUGH IT WAS TECHNICALLY not a workday for me, I went in to do more research on the six manufacturers North Cross did business with, and to plot the areas where Nevada Wynn made deliveries.

The six companies were located across the Twin Cities metro area: Minneapolis, St. Paul, Brooklyn Park, Inger Grove Heights, Plymouth, and Roseville. They manufactured a variety of products that were shipped all over the country: industrial pumps, valves, motors, medical equipment, kitchen utensils, and office furniture.

In the last month, Wynn made deliveries to companies located in Minnesota, Iowa, Wisconsin, Missouri, and Illinois. He could easily be using the North Cross trucks to deliver drugs. On Monday, May 12, just like his boss said, Wynn made one delivery to Estelle Candies in Prairie Falls—on the very day Hawk disappeared. The next day, he was back in the metro making deliveries to several locations. So, it was true, Wynn would have had to get the truck back to the warehouse on Monday afternoon to load for Tuesday. I compiled a list of all the companies he delivered to for the past two months, including their phone numbers and addresses.

I'd have to wait to talk to someone at Estelle's until Monday morning because although the plant operated twenty-four/seven, their business office hours were eight to five, Monday through Friday.

I wrapped up what I could do, then stopped to get Chinese takeout for dinner. The young man (I believe he was the owner's son) who took my order acted as if he didn't notice my face had been a punching bag. When he handed me the warm, fragrant bag, he said, "What happened to you?"

"When I took out the recycling, a deer attacked me."

"Oh . . . did you shoot him?"

"Wish I could have."

He nodded and said, "See you next time."

None of the employees ever smiled or laughed in Chin's Gardens.

While I ate, I surfed the television channels until I found a Jesse Stone movie, but I found it hard to concentrate. My mind was on Shannon and the kids, Adriana, Paul Hawkinson's problems and, of course, Hawk. Wynn had to be the mastermind behind his kidnapping. He was in town because he had a delivery in the area, and while here, he thought he'd push on Paul for his money. Hawk shows up at Paul's driving a fancy car. Wynn decides to kidnap Hawk. But how would kidnapping Hawk get Wynn his money back?

20

June 2
Twenty-one days missing

FIRST THING MONDAY MORNING after signing in, I drove to the Estelle's plant located just northwest of town. Downwind from the facility, I could smell the sugar in the air, reminiscent of cotton candy at the county fair.

I walked into the front door and over to the counter where a young woman was sitting behind the desk. She looked up and smiled. Then her eyebrows lifted as she noticed my bruised and swollen face. I could tell she wanted to ask about it, but said politely, "May I help you?"

"I'd like to speak to someone regarding a delivery that was made in early May—whoever could help me confirm the time."

"That'd be Jim in purchasing."

Within a couple minutes, Jim stood before me. His face was scarred pink and shiny—he must have been badly burned. He didn't react to my bruises like others had. He placed his hands on his hips and listened to me ask for information about a delivery from North Cross shipping. He took me to a small office down the hall where he pointed to a plastic chair in the corner of the room.

Jim began typing on his keyboard, and I pulled the chair over. It was dusty, so I wiped it off with my hand as best I could. I had black pants on and didn't want to walk around with a dusty butt. Jim didn't seem to notice or care.

"North Cross, you say?"

"Yes."

As he deftly clicked the keys with two fingers, he said, "Why would one of our deliveries be of concern to the sheriff?"

"I'm actually tracking the driver, Nevada Wynn."

"Okay, well, North Cross delivered a positive displacement pump on May the twelfth."

173

"Who was the manufacturer?"

"Ahh, let me look." He tapped on his keys. "Okay, it was ALP."

"Ames Lyman?"

"Yes. You know pumps?"

"I've heard of the company. Do you know Michael Hawkinson?"

"Sure, he's the ALP salesman."

"When was the last time you saw him?"

"Not for a while. I talked to him on the phone a month ago. Told him we needed a new pump ASAP. He said he'd have it by the fourteenth. It arrived early, on Monday."

"Did you accept the delivery?"

"No, that's be Darrin Bjorklund in receiving."

"Then I need to speak to him."

I PARKED IN THE LOT in the back of the plant, walked behind the three trucks waiting their turn to unload at the open double doors, and rang the bell next to a steel door marked RECEIVING. A few minutes later, a man wearing a white uniform with Estelle's Candies embroidered in blue on a pocket opened the door.

"You must be Deputy Sheehan. Whoa. What happened to your face?"

"I tripped over my dog in the dark."

"That happened to me once. Screwed up my elbows." He pulled up his arms to show me an invisible injury. "Well, come on up to the office."

I followed him up a set of concrete stairs to a row of small offices. His was the second one in.

Darrin looked to be in his early forties, medium height and build, had sandy-brown hair and a massive amount of freckles.

"So, how can I help you?"

"Do you have a record of what time North Cross Shipping delivered a pump to you on May 12?"

"I sure should."

He walked to one of three four-drawer metal file cabinets, opened the top drawer and fingered the files. He pulled one out and set it on his desk. On top of the paperwork was a requisition form, stamped and initialed.

"Looks like the shipment for the positive displacement pump was accepted on May 12 at eight oh three."

"Do you remember anything about the driver?"

"Yeah, I remember the cobra tattoo on his neck. I was expecting Hal, but this guy was new. His name was Vegas or something like that."

"Nevada Wynn?"

He pointed at me. "Yeah, that's it. I thought to myself I wouldn't want to meet him in a dark alley. But we get all kinds of drivers, most of 'em, nice as pie."

"Did you happen to know if you were his only delivery in the area?"

"I thought for sure we would be, the pump's big, filled the trailer, but I saw a few cartons lined up in the back."

"What size were they?'

"Maybe twelve by eighteen."

North Cross had listed only this one delivery. Snake could have been moving drugs in those boxes, possibly to Woody Nash.

AS I WAS WALKING ACROSS the lot to my department Explorer, my cell phone rang. It was Patrice.

"Cal, the sheriff of Crow Wing County just called me. They have a body on a farm south of Brainerd—a male, no ID. That's all he knows. I think we should drive over to take a look."

WHEN SHE SAW ME, Patrice frowned then tried not to laugh—unsuccessfully, I might add.

"I'm not even going to ask," she said, putting up a hand.

"Thank you, because I'm not talking about it."

She insisted on driving. I suspected she thought I'd be too upset to operate a motor vehicle after I identified the body of my friend. She hadn't said a word for several blocks, so I filled the uncomfortable silence by updating her on what I'd found out from Darrin Bjorklund at Estelle's.

"So this Wynn character delivers for the company your friend works for? Seems too much of a coincidence."

"My thoughts exactly."

"And you believe he was transporting illegal substances in the boxes."

"Yeah."

We drove on Highway 10 another several minutes without either of us speaking. When we passed through Motley, Patrice turned on country western music and drummed her fingers on the steering wheel in time to the beat. Never thought of her as a country music kind of gal.

"Cal, do you think your friend could be involved in drug trafficking?"

"No, not at all. I'm wondering if he figured out Wynn was and Paul was involved."

She nodded. "That very well could be."

"I originally thought they killed him because of the money Paul owed Wynn, but what sense would it make for them to kill Hawk—if they thought he was good for the money?"

"Whoever said criminals had good sense?"

ONCE IN BRAINERD, we turned south on 45 and until we got to 100th Street and turned east.

"Oh, look. The media vans are lined up," Patrice said.

"It's a party no one wants to miss."

She tossed me a frown.

Patrice passed the vans parked along the south side of the gravel road, and drove up to a deputy stationed at the end of the driveway. He checked us in, and we continued onto the farm site. Yellow crime scene tape was strung around the exterior of the farmyard. We parked among the several vehicles from Crow Wing County and the BCA (Bureau of Criminal Apprehension).

Crow Wing County Sheriff Tim Hudson and his investigator, Lee Sabin, met us at our vehicle. Hudson's tan uniform was slightly small for his husky but muscular frame.

I hoped Patrice took note that Sabin was allowed to wear street clothes, like our investigators used to under former sheriffs.

We shook hands, and Hudson pointed to my face and said, "What's the story?"

Patrice put her index finger to her lips. "Shh. He's not talking about it."

Hudson grinned as he told us Leslie Rouch was in the house. Leslie was an excellent investigator with the BCA I'd worked with before. As we approached the old, two-story farmhouse painted white with black trim, nothing looked awry. Leslie greeted us at the screen door.

"My gosh, what happened to you?" she said.

"It's a long story."

She gave me a pitying look, nodded once, and said, "Okay, I've been waiting for you to arrive before we removed our victim from the basement. Come take a look."

We walked through a small porch into a small entryway. The kitchen was to the immediate left where an investigator was dabbing a swab on a drinking glass to get a DNA sample.

The basement was set a few feet straight in from the entry. I caught a whiff of its musty smell as we tramped down the wood stairs. The gray paint was worn off in the center from years of use. They were open backed like the kind my grandparents had at the lake house. When I was a little kid, it was my job to go down the stairs to the basement at night to get the ice cream out of the freezer. I'd descend in slow motion, worried the boogeyman was waiting to grab my legs through the open slats. When I'd get to the bottom I'd hurry around the corner, grab the pail from the freezer, and run back up as fast as I could. This basement had a real boogeyman who had come and gone.

As we approached the basement level, the musty smell gave way to the foul odor of urine and feces. One of Leslie's co-workers was swabbing for DNA samples on the wood railing. He stepped down and away so we could pass by.

Approximately ten feet from the stairway, near the washer and dryer, a man lay on his back on the cement floor. He was bald, except for a few wisps of hair. His arms were bent upward at the elbows as if he had his hands up before being shot in the chest. His light eyes were open and still clear. There was a small laceration and contusion above one eye. His gray shirt was stained dark red surrounding the wound, his blue jeans were wet in the crotch. This man wasn't Hawk.

I looked to Leslie. "Who is this?"

"Norman Kramer, the farmer who lives here."

"We were told a body had been found, and we assumed it was Michael Hawkinson," Patrice said.

"What do you know about this man?" I asked.

"He's a fifty-year-old bachelor. No current romantic interest. His sister said he had cancer and had just finished chemo. She found him at nine o'clock this morning."

"Best guess for a time of death?"

"Rigor mortis is just setting in his jaw and head, so five or six hours ago. " She looked at her watch. "It's nearly eleven o'clock so somewhere between five or six o'clock this morning."

"No firearm near the body, not suicide," I said.

"No," Leslie said. "My initial guess from the size of the room and the visual of the wound he was shot from a range of about twelve feet. We'll have our blood-spatter expert do his digital work with virtual strings for the trajectory."

"Twelve feet?" I backed up and almost stepped on a grubby floral lawn chair cushion. A gold woolen blanket, and a decorative pillow were beside it.

One end of yellow polypropylene rope was tossed across the mat, the other looped around the bottom step. A bike lock lay open on the floor next to used pieces of duct tape. The edges were uneven like having been torn. The putrid odor was not coming so much from the corpse, as the contents of the plastic ice cream pail placed a reach away from the foam pad—it had been someone's toilet.

"Was the farmer tied up down here?" Patrice asked.

"I don't think so. He has no ligature marks on his wrists or ankles. But the bucket samples will tell us for sure who was."

"You think Michael Hawkinson was held captive here?"

Leslie nodded and said, "It's a possibility, isn't it? DNA testing will tell us for sure."

"Why would this sick farmer hold him captive?" Patrice asked. "And where is Hawkinson now?"

"Good questions and unfortunately Mr. Kramer can't give us the answers," Leslie said.

"With words anyway," I said.

Leslie nodded. "He may have been forced to," she added. "We called a cadaver dog in, and we may find something upstairs that can tell the tale. One more thing." She pointed to the wall. "See the bullet hole? The bullet must have ricocheted off and landed across the room where that marker is." She pointed to the other side of the room.

"Didn't pass through the body?"

"Not that one, we have the slug that did. You should also know we found a shoebox filled with marijuana on a top shelf of a bedroom closet. His sister said he smoked it when he was a teenager, and she believes he smoked it now to help the nausea from chemo."

I glanced around the room to see if I could spot anything out of the ordinary. "Jesus, what's that purple shit growing on the cement wall?" I asked.

"It's some kind of some kind of mold I've never seen before. See that opening above it? There's a cistern behind the wall," Leslie said.

"Perhaps you should be wearing masks. Could be carcinogenic," Patrice said.

"Anything in the cistern beside water?" I asked.

"No, we checked with a camera."

I made my way past the furnace sitting just beyond the stairs to the room on the opposite side of the basement. It was partially filled with boxes of junk and stacks of old furniture, warped and musty from the damp conditions. Multiple spider webs draped from the small window set high on the wall to the back corner of the room and the junk piles.

Leslie had followed me in. "This area looks undisturbed."

"Hey! We have another body in a field!" someone yelled down the stairs.

None of us wasted any time climbing the basement stairs. The fresh air was a welcome relief from the stench.

We all silently followed the deputy across the yard, past the buildings, and through a path cut in the grove. We stepped over underbrush and over fallen limps, snapping twigs with each step. Crows cawed in the distance. Once we came out of the grove the scene was visible. Several yards into the field, three deputies waved away several persistent crows from a body that lay facedown across rows of young corn plants. The canine and his handler were standing off to the side.

When I was close enough to see the body build of the victim, I knew it was Hawk. He'd been shot twice, once square in the back, and once in the back of the head. I fought back tears, as I stared at the wounds apparently pecked by the crows. My stomach turned, my throat constricted. I fought the urge to wretch.

"We found a Remington shotgun over there," a deputy said as he pointed to the yellow numbered evidence marker.

Patrice and I shared glances.

"We have a cabin burglary with a missing Remington," she said.

Patrice said, "We can stay as long as you want."

I nodded, and we stepped back away from the scene and toward the tree line to watch the crime lab investigators photograph the body from every angle and make molds of shoe prints in the soil. Leslie pulled a wallet from the back pocket of the victim and looked at the identification, then at me. She replaced the card and threw the wallet in a brown evidence bag. When they rolled the body over to transfer him to the body bag, I moved in closer to see the face, although now unrecognizable because of the exit wound. But I did recognize the goatee.

"Whose name was on the ID?" I asked.

"Paul Hawkinson," Leslie said.

"Not Michael?" Patrice asked.

"No."

She put her hand on my arm and tilted her head. "I don't know what to say."

"Nothing to say."

Sadness crept in through its familiar channel beginning in my stomach, traveling quickly through my chest and into my throat.

Paul? This was bad—very bad. The Hawkinsons could very well have lost both their sons.

21

SHERIFF HUDSON WANTED to notify the Hawkinson family—it was his county after all. Patrice mentioned I was a friend of the family, so we were invited to join him. Several vehicles were parked along the street near the Hawkinson residence. Sheriff Hudson pulled up behind Cat's Lexus sedan parked in the driveway, and Patrice parked behind a black BMW 7 series next to it.

I led the way to the door. Sydney Dirkson, Hawk's private-eye cousin, answered the bell. She took one look at me and raised a brow. "Jealous husband?"

I shook my head and said, "Raccoon. Never try to get one out of your garage."

She smiled and said, "Raccoons must have a heck of a good left-hook."

"Yep."

She touched my arm. "Since you all are here, I'm assuming whatever's going on at the farm south of town concerns Mike."

I gave her a shrug, then introduced the sheriffs.

"Please come in," she said, stepping aside.

The living room was packed with people: Tom and Barb, Cat and her parents, and others I didn't recognize.

The only sound was a heartbreaking moan coming from Barb as she anticipated what she was about to hear. Cat met me just inside the room and clutched my arms, her face full of despair.

I whispered, "It wasn't him."

Her eyes narrowed, and she cocked her head. "Not him?" she whimpered. A hand flew to her mouth. "Oh, thank God."

I made quick introductions then the sheriff asked Tom and Barb if they wished to speak in private. They declined. So in front of the family and friends who had gathered in their living room, the sheriff announced that it was Paul who had been found shot to death.

A collective gasp filled the room. Every face reflected pure shock and horror. Irving Ames broke the silence to ask, "Are you sure?"

I nodded. What a question. "Yes, I'm sure."

As Cat had begun to sob, Cat's parents rushed to her side. Irving held his daughter as she whimpered, "He's still missing, Daddy. He's still missing."

The Hawkinsons remained motionless on the couch. I went to Barb and knelt on one knee. I took one of her hands. "I'm so sorry. Let me know if there's anything I can do."

She looked up at me and said, "Can you tell Tulia? She should be told."

The look on her face broke my heart. "Sure."

"Are *you* okay?" she asked, touching my cheek. "What happened to your face?"

"I tripped. We'll get out of your way."

Tom walked us to the door. "I want to see Paul," he said.

"I'm not sure it's a good idea," I said.

"Why?"

Hudson said, "I tend to agree with Cal. He was shot in the back of the head and the bullets do terrible damage coming out."

Tom gave his head a shake. "It's something I gotta do."

The sheriff said he'd get back to him on when and where.

PATRICE DROVE ME directly over to Tulia's house.

When we pulled up she said, "Want me to go in with you?"

"Up to you."

"I've had enough for one day, thank you."

As I approached the front door, Tulia was at the picture window in her front room. She met me at the door.

"Hi, may I come in?"

"What happened to you?"

"Nothing, really."

"*Something* happened."

"Doesn't have anything to do with Hawk or Paul."

"Are you looking for Paul? Because he ain't here and he didn't *bother* to come home last night."

"Are you gonna let me in?"

She pushed open the screen door, then stood just inside with her arms crossed tightly across her mid-section.

"Let's have a seat somewhere," I said.

She walked to her kitchen and plunked herself down with a thud in a chair. I walked around and sat opposite her. She picked up her Marlboro Lights pack and pulled out a cigarette and lit it with a pink lighter, took a deep drag, then blew the smoke out the open window. She stared out and said, "Who's with you?"

"My boss."

"I'm not trying to be rude, but what do you want?" She took another pull of her cigarette.

"When was the last time you saw Paul?"

She exhaled the smoke, this time not trying for the window. "Last night at the bar. He left about nine o'clock, said had to take care of something, and he'd see me later. But he didn't come home. The rat bastard's probably with another women."

"Tulia, Paul was found dead this morning on a farm south of town."

"A farm? What was he doing there?"

Her eyes went round and quickly began to glisten with tears. She slowly lifted her hands and covered her face bringing the cigarette precariously close to her hair. I reached across and pulled it from her hand and stubbed it out. Then I walked around the table, bent down and put my arm around her shoulders. Her body shuddered as she sobbed.

"How did he die?" she asked, pushing through her tears.

I returned to my seat. "He was shot."

Tulia looked at me, her face contorted with the agony of grief. "It was those creepy shit birds who killed him, wasn't it?"

"Which shit birds?"

"The ones you showed me pictures of—the ones who were talking to Paul the day Mike disappeared."

I returned to my chair. "We don't know anything yet."

The only shit bird out of that crew of dirtbags who wasn't incarcerated at the moment was Nevada Wynn. I'd mention his name and Woody's to Tim Hudson. If Paul told Woody what he told me. That'd do it.

"Did Paul know Norman Kramer?"

She hunched her shoulders. "Norm? Sure."

"That's where it happened—at Norm's. Norm's dead too. Were they friends?"

She looked confused. "Not really. Norm came into The Dive once in a while. You know how Paul talks to everybody."

"Did he ever tell you what they talked about?"

"I'm sure it was bullshitting: sports, weather, that kind of thing."

"There's a group gathered at Hawkinsons. You might want to join them."

"I don't think so." She lit another cigarette. The smoke curled up from her fingers as she held it in her hand. "Tom and Barb will blame me, you know."

"How would they?"

"Because of our former drug use."

"Former? Because I'm pretty sure Paul was taking something."

"All he's had in months was Valium. He's been clean lately."

"Valium, or oxycontin?"

"Whatever."

"Valium, oxy, beer, and pot? You consider that clean?"

"Well, pot and beer don't really count."

"Of course they do. And he's associated with bad people because of it."

She flicked the ash of her cigarette, but she hadn't taken another drag.

"What do you know about Woody?"

She sent me a puzzled look. "Not much. I introduce Paul to him at The Dive. Paul needed a job and Woody had an opening."

"Who was Woody to you?"

"A customer?"

"Were you his as well?"

She crinkled up her nose as if she didn't understand.

"Did Woody ever give or sell you or Paul drugs?"

"Oh . . . um . . . yeah . . . sometimes."

Paul had been a pothead since he was thirteen and easily hooked into the drugs Tulia had introduced him to. There was a reason marijuana was called the gateway drug, just like oxycontin was a quick slide to heroin.

"And you thought Woody would be a good person for Paul to work for?" I said.

"Why are you on *my* ass, for chrissake? My boyfriend was just killed!"

"You should know the kind of scrutiny you're going to be under now. And you better give straight answers, so they can find Paul's killer."

A look of fear crossed her face. "Am I in danger?"

"You shouldn't be alone. Is there someone I can call?" I asked.

"My sister?"

"Where does she live?"

"In Wadena."

"You might be better off staying with her, because not only Crow Wing County but the media is going to be at your doorstep any minute. I'll let the sheriff know where you'll be."

"Shit."

"Give me your sister's number. I'll call her while you pack a bag."

On the way back to Prairie Falls, Patrice said, "What do you make of all this?"

"I know there are two individuals who have motive: Paul's boss Woody and Nevada Wynn, who, by the way, I can't believe was allowed to make bail. I want to know who bailed him out."

"You won't get an argument from me."

"The task force and Tim Hudson should be filled in on what we know."

"Tim and I talked back at the farm. He said they found nothing at Woody's shop or residence. They used a canine unit."

"He may not keep drugs at his house or he's had the time to get rid of the evidence."

"Well, I, for one, am glad the murders happened in Crow Wing."

It may be Crow Wing's case, but there was no way in hell I was going to stay out of it.

22

Twenty-three days missing

ON TUESDAY, MINNESOTA'S media coverage had switched from Victoria's trial in Prairie Falls to the double homicide in Crow Wing County. The national stations soon picked it up.

For the last twenty-four hours my mind was on nothing else but Paul and Norman Kramer's deaths and how they were connected to Hawk's disappearance. One thing bothered me: I hadn't seen Paul's car at the farm. As soon as I got to the office, I called Investigator Lee Sabin., but I had to leave a message. I suggested they check The Dive's parking lot.

Tamika arrived. She grimaced when she saw me. "Oh, Lord have mercy. I thought Troy looked bad."

"I look worse than he does?"

She scrunched her face. "A teeny bit."

"Great."

Spanky entered the room, took a look at me and winced.

"I suppose everyone knows about the tussle?" I asked.

Tamika jerked back. "Tussle? You call that face the result of a tussle?"

Spanky sat at his desk and leaned back in his chair. "I didn't tell anyone. People knew before I got back to the department."

"Is Troy still in town?"

Tamika said, "No, he was on his way home last night when I saw him."

"What exactly did he tell you?"

"That you slept with Adriana, so he kicked the shit out of you. His exact words."

"Gaw . . . that's just great."

Spanky swiped a hand through the air. "People know you got your punches in too by just looking at him."

"I tried. This has been a long time coming."

186

Tamika threw her hands on her hips. "So, it's true? You did sleep with Adriana?"

"Whose business is it?"

"Uh-huh, that means you did. She's testifying today you know."

"Good, then she can head on back to Minneapolis." And to redirect the conversation, I asked how their testimonies went.

Tamika puffed up her chest and said, "Oliver said I was a rock star. But then, I didn't sleep with any of the witnesses."

I shot her a dirty look. "And you, Spanky?"

"Not so good. I think I may have lost the case for Oliver."

"Couldn't have done any more damage than I did," I said.

"Hey, what do you know about your friend's brother's murder out at that farm?" Tamika asked. "That's like crazy stuff."

"All this shit leads back to Nevada Wynn." I told them what I knew.

"Someone either silenced Paul Hawkinson, or it was a revenge killing," Spanky said.

"Could be both," I said.

Five minutes later, Investigator Lee Sabin called. "Sheriff Hudson said I should meet with you to pick your brain."

"Slim pickings," I said.

He laughed. "How about we meet at the Peppermint Café in Dexter Lake?"

"It'll take me a half hour."

Crosby walked in and said he'd planned on working on phone records all day.

I PACKED UP MY CASE FILES and my laptop, upon which I had downloaded Paul's interview, and headed over to Dexter Lake, our eastern most city in the county. The Peppermint Café was downtown and although a popular spot with the locals for breakfast, it was fairly empty this morning.

As I entered the café, every eye followed me to a booth in the back corner. The waitress, who looked twelve, arrived with a menu and a glass of water. She'd stared at me with her overly made up eyes like she wanted to ask about my face. "This is what my wife did to me when I ate the last of the ice cream."

She squinted her eyes at me. "You shouldn't have eaten her ice cream."

"Now you tell me. There'll be one more. Could I please have a cup of coffee while I wait?"

She left and never came back. Ten minutes late, Sabin walked through the door, and all the heads swiveled toward him as he made his way to the booth. He had a strange gait—he was pigeon-toed. Sabin was around my age, a bit shorter. We shook hands. He set his briefcase on the seat next to him.

"Sorry I'm late. Did you order yet?"

"I was waiting for you and apparently the waitress was too because here she comes with a big smile and coffee."

She looked at Lee and practically crooned, "Coffee?"

"Sure," he said.

She filled his cup, then stared and smiled at him and asked if he was ready to order. I guess women like his blond surfer looks.

I pushed my cup toward her. "Coffee for me too, thanks."

She filled the cup but didn't smile at me like she had him. I'm losing it. Then again, it could be my beat-to-shit fighter face.

She waited while Lee looked at the menu. We both ordered scrambled eggs, hash browns, bacon, and toast, and the waitress strutted off.

"So, what did happen?" Lee asked as he pointed to my face.

"I was sucker punched."

"By someone you arrested?"

"No, my former girlfriend's ex-boyfriend."

He gave me a crooked grin. "Oh. So, are you married?"

"Separated."

He nodded but didn't press any further. I didn't really know him, but I liked him. I might have told him the truth.

I tapped my file folders. "So, how should we do this? Do you have questions or do you want me to give you what I have?"

"Give me what you have."

He pulled a yellow legal pad out of his briefcase, found a pen. "I'm ready."

I told him everything I knew about the players, and before I could show him Paul's interview, our food arrived. After we finished eating, he asked if I would send the interview via email and he'd watch it later, then asked what I needed from him.

"Did you find Paul Hawkinson's car?"

"No, and it wasn't at The Dive." He made a note.

"Also, are the DNA tests taken at the farm back yet?"

"They should be in within twenty-four hours. Your sheriff thinks Michael Hawkinson was never on Kramer's farm. She thinks he was killed earlier this month."

"Does she?"

"What's she like?"

"Generally supportive, thorough. Makes investigators wear uniforms."

"That's a bummer."

"It is."

WHEN I GOT BACK to the office, I called North Cross and asked for Zeke La Plante, Wynn's boss. He was out of the office for the day.

"Where is he?" I asked the receptionist.

"I'm not allowed to give out that information, sir."

"Please connect me to Haldis Moore."

Haldis said Zeke called in sick.

"Can you locate Nevada Wynn for me?"

"I will try."

"Thank you."

"Is he in trouble again?"

"He was arrested in connection to a burglary and kidnapping."

"Jeepers. I don't get why we keep him on. I have your card in my desk. I'll get back to you."

"Did anyone at your company post bail for him?"

"Not that I'm aware of."

Someone bailed him out, and he was kept on the payroll because he served a purpose. Knowing who bailed him out might get me closer to finding answers. I paid Dale Shepherd at Absolute Bail Bonds in Prairie Falls a visit. Dale was a round, hairy guy who wore a Packer's sweatshirt everyday, and played classical music in his shop. He checked his paperwork for me.

"I remember that case. A Minneapolis attorney name of George Ball co-signed for the bond. Dressed like a chump, but I was told by my Minneapolis colleagues, he always delivers his clients to court."

I called George Ball's office and was told he was unavailable. I left my number. I sincerely doubted I would hear from him.

I DIDN'T WANT TO DRIVE down to the Cities yet again, but I had to find Wynn because I was convinced he knew what happened to Paul and Hawk. I called Patrice to share my plans to go to Minneapolis tomorrow. I decided to be a team player and ask Lee Sabin if he wanted to ride along.

23

June 4
Twenty-four days missing.

BRIGHT AND EARLY Wednesday morning, I picked Lee Sabin up at the Crow Wing County Sheriff's Office on Laurel Street in Brainerd. He wore black slacks and a light yellow shirt without a tie. I could have worn street clothes but chose to wear my uniform when dealing with Wynn and North Cross.

As I drove out of the lot, he said, "Thanks for asking me to go along." Then a few seconds later, "How long have you been in investigations?"

"Going on three years. You?"

"About the same. Tell me what you know about Michael Hawkinson," he said.

"I'm not sure you're aware, but he's been a close friend of mine since we were kids."

"Really? Jeez, man, I'm sorry."

"I don't want the media to know, or they'll make something of it. Anyway, he made a lunch date with me and never showed. I didn't think much of it until his mom called me to tell me she hadn't been able to reach him for three days. His wife was out of town, and it wasn't like him not to answer his phone."

"And now his brother is dead. Must be terrible for his parents. What was Paul like?"

"He was a nice kid, but weak and associated with the wrong people, his boss included."

"Woody Nash. He sure acted fidgety when we searched his shop and residence. Started breathing rapidly. I was afraid he was going to have a heart attack."

"He's a candidate. I probably set Paul's murder in motion by hauling him in for questioning. Are you looking at Woody for Paul's murder?"

"Yes, and you can't blame yourself in these deals. We have to do our jobs."

191

As we headed down 371 to 10, we decided on a plan. We would start at North Cross Shipping then make our way to Wynn's residence. Lee might enjoy talking to the hookers.

WHEN WE GOT TO MINNEAPOLIS, we checked in with Haldis Moore, who sent us over to see Owen Jedowsky, the warehouse manager. The warehouse was just next door and about the size of a supermarket. The loading dock door was open, so we walked up the cement steps located to the left side and walked around a forklift parked just inside. No one was around, so we walked in and looked down the rows of shelving for Jedowsky. The space smelled of cardboard and motor oil. It was strangely quiet.

"Can I help you?" a voice bellowed.

I spun around to see a man's silhouette against the sunlight streaming in from outdoors.

"We're looking for Owen Jedowsky. Haldis Moore sent us over."

We walked toward the man and showed him our badges. He was an odd-looking fellow with widely spaced eyes and super-sized nose and jaw. He pulled a walkie-talkie from a pocket of his olive green coverall.

"Owen, some cops are here to see you."

"Send them up," a voice answered.

The old guy pointed to the set of cement stairs located along the inside wall. As we ascended, a man appeared at the top and leaned on the metal railing. Save for his olive coverall, he looked like a member of a biker gang with his long, dark curly hair and untrimmed beard. His narrow black glasses were too small for his large face.

I introduced Lee and myself, then told him we were investigating homicides in Crow Wing County.

"Jedowsky," he said, shaking our hands.

He showed us past two small offices and into a lunchroom where there was a scuffed wood table with four chairs. He gathered the *Star Tribune* and *City Pages* strewn across the table and threw them on the counter by the refrigerator. He wiped food crumbs off the table and onto the floor with his hand.

"Have a seat," he said.

Once settled at the table, Jedowsky said, "Haldis said you were trying to track down Nevada Wynn. He's on the road. Won't be back until tomorrow."

"Where's he been lately?"

"Des Moines, Chicago, and Olathe, Kansas."

"When I spoke to Zeke, he said Wynn had a single delivery on Monday, May 12, to Estelle's Candies in Prairie Falls."

"That's right. That woulda been a pump."

"Is there any reason he would have had more boxes in the trailer?"

"He didn't. I helped load that pump myself."

"When did he return the truck on that run?"

"The truck was back here by six o'clock when we closed up."

"You have quite the memory. Remembering a detail like that three weeks later?"

He pointed to his forehead. "I remember everything."

"May I see the records?" I asked.

"Not without a warrant."

I nodded. "You've kept him busy since he was bailed out of Birch County."

"Had to make up for lost time."

"I guess so. Who put up his bail?"

"I wouldn't know." He sat back, his lips set in a tight line, indicating he was done answering questions. I was fairly certain he did know how Wynn made bail, and I also thought he needed Wynn on the road for a reason.

As we got up to leave, he pointed to my face. "Get in a bar fight?"

"You got it, pal."

On the way to Wynn's house, I made a call to Hennepin County and alerted them as to Jedowsky and North Cross Shipping's possible criminal activity.

FRANCHON OPENED THE DOOR and yawned.

"Remember me?" I asked.

"Oh, you that deputy cop guy from up northwest?'

"Yes, Detectives Sheehan and Sabin."

"Oh, I never seen you," she said to Lee, as she flopped her hand out like he should kiss it. He gave it a tentative shake. She kept her eyes on Lee as she answered my questions.

"Where's Snake?"

"I haven't seen him for a week. I don't know what he's up to."

"And Roseanna?"

"On her way to St. Cloud to see Ray-Ray. He back in now. Wasn't s'posed to leave the state. He don't think ahead, like Snake do."

I showed her the search warrant. "Mind if I check?" I asked.

"You go right 'head. He ain't here, and I got nothing to hide."

I had Lee stay with Franchon while I searched the house and then went back to the garage. He wasn't there, just like she said. When I walked back into the house, Lee was sitting in a straight chair across the room from Franchon. His cheeks were bright red, and then I saw the reason why. Franchon was sitting with her knees spread wide, and she wasn't wearing underwear. She was messing with him.

"Close up shop," I said to her.

She gave me a pouty look. Lee stood and headed out the door.

"You still have my card?" I asked.

She gave me a wide smile and said, "Yes, sir."

"Call me if you see Snake."

"Your pretty face got a little messed up, huh?"

"Yep."

LEE WAS WAITING outside near the Explorer. Once we were inside and buckled in, he said, "She's somethin'."

I laughed. "She liked you. What did she do beside give you a view of the wares?"

"Right before you walked in she licked her finger and put it inside . . . right there in front of me."

I laughed.

"She seemed cooperative though. Do you think she's telling the truth about not seeing Wynn for a week?" he asked.

"I'm not sure. There doesn't seem to be the loyalty you usually see with real couples. These four seem more like symbiotic roommates."

"Something is going on at the warehouse, and that Jedowsky character seems shaky to me."

"I agree. They could be running a drug operation or laundering money out of there—or both."

"And you said your buddy was a salesman for one of the companies that uses that warehouse."

"I have a sneaking suspicion he found out something he wasn't supposed to."

We made cop talk all the way to Brainerd, and when I dropped Lee off, he said, "Hey, you golf?"

"I do."

"Maybe we can play a round together sometime?"

"I'd like that."

I SAT ON MY DECK and watched the sky turn from pink to purple to indigo. When the day fell into night, Iris's interior lights came on. I watched her move throughout her house. I'd have to tell her the counselor recommended to Shannon that we postpone the divorce. Did Brett think he could save our marriage? Or was he trying to stop her from remarrying too soon? I took a deep breath of the fresh night air, trying to clear my head of everything negative.

The pool lights cast shimmering waves on the surface of the water. Its hypnotic appeal enticed me to sit on the edge and put my feet in. The pool wouldn't get much use this summer, unless I used it myself. I went into the house, put on my suit, dove in, and after getting over the initial shock of the unheated water, I swam several laps working out the tightness in my shoulders. I swam to the ladder on the deep end and was about to climb out, when I saw headlights reflect off my kitchen windows.

An old burgundy Mazda pulled in my driveway. Who the hell was that, and what were they doing in my yard?

Bullet, who'd been poised on the pool edge waiting for me, gave out three barks, then trotted over to the car. He barked a couple more times while wagging his tail. I climbed out of the pool just as a man came out of the passenger side. I was acutely aware of my current vulnerability. I had a friendly lab as a guard dog and no firearm stuck in my swim trunks. The man slowly approached me with his hands in his pocket.

"Stop right where you are!" I thrust my arm out in defense—like my hand could stop a bullet.

His made one step as his hands came out of his pockets. I stopped breathing, bracing for the gunshot.

"Cal, it's me. Hawk."

24

ESUS CHRIST, HAWK, I thought you were dead. Where have you been?"
He looked back to the old Mazda in my driveway.

"Who is that?" I asked.

"Can you loan me fifty bucks?"

"What?"

"My ride. I promise the kid I'd give him fifty bucks for a lift."

"Not on me. Hold on."

I went inside, found my wallet where I'd placed it, upstairs on my dresser, and pulled out all the bills. I had three twenties and two ones. I took the three twenties and went downstairs and handed it over to Hawk. He walked to the driver's side and handed over the cash. The car pulled out and he faced me.

"Thanks, I'll pay you back."

"Sure. Man, I really thought you were dead. I'm so happy to see you. I'd give you a hug, but you really stink, man. Those are the same clothes you were wearing the day you disappeared."

"How do you know?"

"Caught you on camera at Frank's Plaza."

"Didn't do you much good, did it?"

"No."

He followed me inside. "What happened to your face?"

"Long story."

Bullet was sniffing Hawk's feet and legs, then moved up to his crotch. I pulled him away.

"Can I have a glass of water? I'm really thirsty."

"You bet."

I poured him a glass of ice water. He gulped it down. I refilled it and he finished that one as well. He was dirty, smelly, had a three-weeks beard growth, but he looked in surprisingly good shape. But still—I didn't know what he'd been through.

"I should take you to the hospital," I said.

He threw both arms up. "NO! I'm fine. You look like you could have used one recently. So tell me what happened to your face?"

"Troy Kern and I had a little disagreement."

"The jerk you work with?"

"Not any more. The fight was over Adriana. I'll tell you about it later. Right now, I'm gonna go up and put some dry clothes on. I'll be right back."

When I came down, he was looking at the photos on the fireplace mantel. What I should have done right then was call Patrice—but not yet—I had too many questions.

"Are you hungry?"

"Yeah, very." His eyes darted around the room. "Where's Shannon?"

"We're separated."

"Nooo. What happened?"

"Colby's death did us in. It's been a tough year."

"Sorry, I haven't been there for you."

"Hawk, I have some bad news. Paul's dead."

He nodded. "I know." He tried to blink away tears, but they rolled down his cheeks.

"How do you know?"

"The guy who gave me a ride told me about the murders in Crow Wing."

"I'm sorry. Your folks took it pretty hard."

He wiped his eyes and sniffed. "I'm sure. It doesn't surprise me—shit he was into. Man, I wanted to get him out of it."

"Look, we need to talk, but first I want to snap photos with my iPad to document what you looked like when you showed up at my door."

"Photograph this." Hawk pulled up a cuffs to reveal the open sores on his wrists. He lifted up his pant legs to reveal his ankles also rubbed raw. Then he showed me the reddened skin of the sides of his neck.

"This is from the bike lock around my neck."

"Jesus."

I took several photos then said, "Okay let's get you into a shower, so I can stand being around you. I'll go get you a set of clothes, a toothbrush and razor—some gauze for your wrists and ankles. While you clean up, I'll make you something to eat."

"Could you order a pizza? I've been dreaming of pepperoni pizza and beer."

"Sure." Hawk had taken all my cash, but I could order online and pay for it with my credit card.

I gave him a garbage bag to throw his clothes into, then I ordered the pizza.

BY THE TIME HAWK was cleaned up and had a beer, the pizza arrived. I was hungry too as I hadn't eaten since a late McDonald's lunch Sabin and I had. We each devoured four big slices in silence. Then he pushed away from the counter and burped. I burped in response. We laughed like we were twelve again.

I slapped his back. "I have so much to ask you."

"Can I have another beer first?"

"Sure." I pulled two out and handed him one. "Okay, talk. I'm going to record this on my iPad."

We moved to the couch, and I propped the iPad on the table in front of him. I pulled up the camera, slid it to video—then the phone rang. I looked at the display.

"It's Shannon," I said. "I have to take it. It could be one of the kids is sick or something."

"Of course."

I moved to the back of the house and looked out at the pool. "Hi."

"Did you sleep with Adriana? Is that why Troy came after you?"

"Not now, Shannon."

"I just want to hear it from you!"

"Look, I can't get into this right now."

"Why? Is she there?"

"No, of course not. I'll explain tomorrow."

"Goddamn it, Sheehan."

"Two words, sweetie: Mac Wallace."

She hung up. I turned around and found Hawk frowning.

I said, "It's okay. Where were we?"

He sat up, blinked a few times, and said, "I'm not sure where to begin."

"Let's start with the Monday we were supposed to have lunch. But first, I have to give my identifying information. I pressed the red record circle then gave the date, time, case number, and who was present.

"Okay, Mr. Hawkinson. Please tell me what occurred after you left your parents' home on Monday, May 12."

"Okay . . . well, first I stopped by my brother Paul's to talk to him. On Sunday morning he'd asked if he could borrow ten thousand dollars. I'd just given him three grand six months ago, so I went to tell him no, that enough was enough. When I got there, he had a houseful of thugs he'd gotten involved with. He took me outside and told me they were there to collect for some pills stolen out of his garage he was storing for Woody Nash, that's why he needed the ten grand."

"Did you know the thugs?"

"I knew one guy from North Cross Shipping, the warehouse where we store our pumps, which is another story."

"Tell me about it now."

"Okay, so this guy worked on the loading dock, now's he's driving a delivery truck. But I suspect he's using North Cross trucks to transport drugs. Once when I stopped by to check on our inventory, I overheard him talking about meeting up with his Texas hombre in Kansas City, then he's up in Brainerd sitting in my brother's living room? Doesn't take a genius to figure out he's connected to Woody's pills stolen out of Paul's garage."

"What's his name?"

"They called him Snake. Has a tattoo of a cobra on his face, and it wraps around his neck."

"His name is Nevada Wynn. He's an ex-felon now out on bail."

"Not one bit surprised. The other guy they called Ray-Ray."

"Raybern Ginty. So pills? What kind?"

"Paul said they were prescription drugs from Mexico, like oxycodone. Street value was upwards of twenty-five grand. Man, my brother was sucked into some dangerous shit. That's what I was coming to talk to you about. I wanted to see if you could find a way to help him."

"How did you think I could help?"

"It was only a matter of time before he got caught. I thought maybe he could turn himself in or be a confidential informant or something—get these guys off his back and off the street. I wanted your advise on the best way to handle it."

"Did you say anything to Wynn at that point—at Paul's?"

"Not then, no. I could tell Paul wanted me out of there, so I left to meet up with you. Anyway, I had time to stop for gas in Prairie Falls and who should pull up at the pump behind me, but the pricks from Paul's. They asked me if we could go somewhere and talk. I said I didn't have time. The big dude was pushing it, Glenn somebody, so I only pumped a quarter tank and pulled away. I was headed straight for the sheriff's department."

"Then what happened?"

"They followed me and rear-ended me at a stoplight. That's where I made my mistake. I got pissed and got out of my car to walk back to their van. Before I could say a word, the big dude decked me. The next thing I knew I was being shoved into the back of the van."

"Funny no one saw that happen."

"No one was around. They held a gun on me, and I thought for sure I was gonna die right there. I figured I was Paul's example."

"Where did you go? What happened to your Mercedes?"

"Glenn drove it out to some cabin in the woods. We followed him in the van. He said it was a family cabin, but he had to break into it. They tied me up in a chair and told me they would kill Paul if I didn't pay them the ten grand."

"What did you do?"

"I told them I didn't have that kind of money sitting in my bank account. I'd have to make some calls, and it would take days. I told them to take the Mercedes. It was worth way more."

"And did they?"

"Yeah."

"They abandoned it not far from the cabin."

"Really? I thought they'd chop it."

"Maybe they were going to go back for it later, or they were worried about it being spotted en route. How long were you at this cabin?"

"Overnight."

"They used your debit card shortly after they abducted you. Did you give them your pin?"

"Yeah, I told them to take my cards, go to Vegas, get some cash, just let me go."

"So it was your idea to give them your cards and pin number?"

"They were threatening to *kill* Paul, my parents, my wife, if I didn't give them the money, so yeah, I handed everything over!" He was shouting. His face had turned crimson.

"Calm down, Hawk. I'm not judging you, I'm just getting the information."

He sat back and blew air out his nose. He took a pull of beer. I didn't tell him, but he'd have to do this all over again officially—at Crow Wing County.

"So they took your wallet and left?"

"Glenn stayed. He kept a loaded shotgun on me."

"What brand?"

"I don't even know. I didn't notice, okay?" he said, raising his voice in agitation.

"Okay. Then what?"

"Then Ginty came back that night, and Glenn was worried about his uncle coming around the next morning, so they moved me. They covered my head with a smelly T-shirt and drove me to where I later learned was a farm south of Brainerd, but at the time I had no idea where I was."

"What happened at the farm?"

"They tied me up in a basement, handed the farmer the shotgun they stole from the cabin, and told him to guard me. They said to shoot me if I was any trouble."

"You've been gone a little over three weeks. Where you at the farm the entire time?"

"Shit. I thought it was longer than that. Yeah, that's where I've been."

"So, tell me about your time there?"

"I was tied up in the smelly basement, and at first, the farmer only came down to give me water and food and empty my piss bucket. He said very little to me. About the fifth day, it started getting to me, so I started hollering at him to let me go. He took it for a full day before he came down with the shotgun and fired one off above my head. Scared the livin' shit out of me. I couldn't hear very well for a day. So I took a different tact. When he came down to feed me, I tried to engage him in conversation and pretty soon he'd stay on a little longer to talk. I think he was lonely, and after a while, he'd stay and talk for a long while."

"Why were they holding you captive?"

"Because they were making me cash an annuity for the ten grand Paul lost. I tried to delay it as much as I could by lying. I told them I had to have the paperwork sent to my home address knowing that process would take five to seven days. I also said I had to get the form online, so they brought me down an old shitty laptop and watched as I did the transaction. Luckily, no one caught when I checked the box to send the form rather than complete it online. I was hoping one of the neighbors would see one of those bastards stealing my mail and call the cops. How well would Ginty or Wynn fit in my neighborhood?"

"Not very."

"Must have been a week before they brought the envelope back up to me to fill out. Then we had wait for the check to come, so I could endorse it."

"Were they going to have you cash it?"

"I'm pretty sure they were going to have Paul do it. Then they were going to kill both of us."

"So had the check come?"

"Not yet. I convinced the farmer into letting me go before it did. I told him Wynn would kill both of us once I signed the check."

"Did you see Paul during this time?"

"No. He may have known about the annuity, but I don't know that for a fact. If he knew they were going to kill me after they got their money, he'd never have gone along with it."

I wasn't so sure.

"So you withdrew ten thousand?"

"More. When I was online and had signed in, Wynn saw my total—I had around $53,000 in that account. He said he'd take forty and leave me thirteen. Nice of him, don't you think?"

"This extortion scheme was much more elaborate than I thought. Do you have any idea why the farmer went along with it?"

"He was scared . . . we never knew when Ray-Ray and Snake would pop in unannounced."

"Did Glenn Hayes ever drop in?"

"A few times."

"So who was the brains of the bunch?"

"Definitely Snake. He gave the orders. I was to be fed finger food in an unbreakable dish. No utensils. So I ate out of a metal dog dish." He smiled. "After a week or so, the farmer offered me some weed."

"You and the farmer smoked weed together?"

He lifted a hand and smiled. "I was trying to be his buddy, one he might save . . . and he did."

"Paul must have known where you were."

"Why?"

"He was killed there."

"Maybe he came to save me."

"His car wasn't on site."

"It wasn't?"

"No. When did you leave the Kramer farm?"

"Early this morning. When the farmer came down, he said I needed to get out now or never. He cut me loose and told me Brainerd was a five-mile walk. I didn't think about it; I just started walking. Not moving much for three weeks, I tired easily. I stopped at the nearest farm house, I banged on the door, but no one answered. I looked like hell, so who would answer?"

"Did you think to tell them to call 911?"

"No, I should have, but I just moved on. I'd just made it to the yard of the next farm when I saw a black Buick driving by. It looked like Snake driving it.

"No one answered there either. The house was all locked up tight. I thought about breaking in, but thought the neighbors could have called them, and I'd get shot if I tried to get in. They had an old friendly collie who followed me around, wagged his tail and never barked. Then I noticed there was absolutely no activity around that house, no animals or anything to take care of but the dog, and he had two big bowls by the back door. Food dish was pretty full, so I figured they might be gone, so I felt safe there for a while."

"How long did you stay there?"

"I intended to wait only until I saw Snake's car leave. I crawled in the backseat of an old Plymouth parked out behind a shed where I could see the road. After a while I heard the dog panting outside the window, so I opened the front passenger door and he hopped in, curled up, and went to sleep. I eventually fell asleep too, I don't know how long. But when I woke, I took off walking west thinking I'd run into 371 and could hitchhike into town. I put up my thumb, but nobody would stop, but I wouldn't have picked me up either. Finally the kid stopped. I told him I'd been car camping, and my car wouldn't start."

"Why didn't you tell him the truth, or at least have him drive you directly to the police?"

"Because I . . . well, obviously I wasn't thinking clearly. Anyway, the kid said he was from Prairie Falls, so I told him to drop me off at your place. He also told me he knew the two guys who had been murdered."

"He knew Paul? How?"

"From The Dive. He knows Tulia too."

"Jesus Christ. So he also knew Norman Kramer?"

"Who?"

"The farmer's name was Norman Kramer."

"Oh. It fits him, I guess."

"Did anyone ever come by? Neighbors? Relatives?"

"His sister brought him over some chicken soup and chocolate cupcakes once. When she left, he shared it with me. That day he let me use a spoon. She lives in Cross Lake and has three teenage kids. He showed me their pictures."

"So he fed you pretty well?"

"The first week he just gave me sandwiches. Later, he fed me meals he made for himself."

"He saved your life, Hawk."

"I know." He bent forward and began to weep.

I kept the video rolling while I let him cry it out. Then said, "Why don't we put you to bed and finish this in the morning?"

After I showed him to the guest room on the main floor, I got a pillow and blanket and took the couch. I wanted to be close in case he needed something. I stared up at the ceiling and thought about everything I'd been told. *Man, I'm going to be in trouble for not calling Patrice.*

25

June 5

I DOZED ON AND OFF for a few hours. Around 3:00 a.m., my eyes popped open. I tossed and turned, punched the pillow a few times, and finally gave up. I looked in on Hawk. He was sleeping soundly. Poor guy must have slept poorly on a thin pad in the stinky basement.

When I went back to the great room, I picked up yesterday's *Minneapolis Star Tribune* I hadn't taken the time to read. WITNESS IN THE HEIRESS TRIAL REFUTES DEPUTIES' TESTIMONIES. The article stated that Brock Snyder, a war veteran and flight instructor in Minneapolis, testified Ms. Valero was with him at the time the fire occurred at the Valero residence. He had given her a flight lesson out of Flying Cloud Airport in Eden Prairie.

Brock Snyder was Victoria's flight instructor? She was going for her pilot's license? My God, was it those two buzzing over my house in a bi-plane? What was she planning? She could drop anything from a plane on anyone's house.

I skimmed the rest: Snyder testified that after the lesson they went to lunch and back to the Lewis compound in Orono. That afternoon they went on a boat ride on Lake Minnetonka and later had dinner in at Gianni's Steakhouse in Wayzata. Sounded like a lovely afternoon for an heiress.

Brock. What kind of a name was Brock? It was the name of a guy who'd be willing to be bought by Victoria's father, that's who. Damn it. We had overwhelming evidence Victoria was guilty on all counts, then the lying son of a bitch says he was with her in Minneapolis. I wonder how much *Brock* was paid.

I turned on the TV and tuned into CNN. It took only a few minutes before an aerial video of the Kramer farm was shown.

The reporter said, "Authorities in Minnesota are investigating a bizarre set of circumstances surrounding the death of two Crow Wing county residents on a farm near the resort community of Brainerd. Norman Kramer was found shot to death in his basement, and yet another victim, Paul Hawkinson of

Brainerd was found in a nearby field." They also showed film of two ambulances exiting the Kramer farm without lights or sirens.

The screen changed to a photo of Victoria wearing her business attire: a black suit and white blouse.

"Meanwhile, in nearby Birch County, the heiress to the Lewis fortune is being tried on several charges, among them arson. County Attorney Oliver Bakken says he has all the evidence he needs to convict. He disputes Brock Snyder's claims that Ms. Lewis was with him in Minneapolis on the day in question. The case hinges on his testimony and that of deputies who allege Victoria Lewis was masquerading as her roommate Sadie Jones and was in the area at the time of the crime. The prosecution contends Ms. Lewis vandalized and later set fire to the home of her former stepmother, Adriana Valero. But defense witness, Brock Snyder, testified the defendant was with him the day in question."

Then they moved to a story of yet another athlete caught on camera punching his wife in the face. I turned the TV off and closed my eyes.

I woke when Bullet licked my hand. I glanced up at the clock. It was 6:30. I texted Patrice and told her to call me ASAP, and within seconds she did.

"You're never going to guess who's at my house?"

"Who?"

"Michael Hawkinson?"

"What? Seriously? Is he okay?"

"Says he is. He's still sleeping."

"Still sleeping? He was there all night?"

"Since about ten o'clock last night."

"And *why* wasn't I notified *last night?*"

"He was exhausted. I thought he should get a good night's sleep before we put him through the interview process."

"Not protocol. I'll be right there."

I MADE PATRICE a mug of coffee, then we sat at my counter while I showed her the film of Hawk's interview. When it was over, she said, "I'm not happy you didn't notify me last night, and there are no excuses. And he should have been taken directly to the hospital."

"He seemed okay. How about I take him to the hospital now, then if he's up to it, to the department to have someone else question him."

"That goes without saying. Wake him up. It starts now, and I'm taking over. We will not notify the media until after he's questioned and has a chance to see his family. Where and when will be determined by me later. Clear?"

"Clear."

"Just so you know, I'm furious with you."

"I surmised that."

"But, I would have done the same thing."

I nodded. "Thank you."

"Don't thank me. I still may write you up."

I nodded again, and then went to wake Hawk. She agreed to let me make us all a breakfast of bacon and eggs before we left for the hospital.

After her first bite, she said, "I must say, Michael, except for the marks on your wrists and ankles, and the faded bruise on you forehead, you don't look like you're in bad shape. Cal looks worse than you."

"Ha-ha," I said.

"Were you fed well?"

"Yes, after a week or so, Norman brought me real meals instead of peanut butter sandwiches. He was a good guy. They forced him to keep me captive."

"You do know he could have called 911 at any time," Patrice said.

"I told him that . . . over and over. I tried to convince him to call Cal, that he would help us. But he was too scared they'd kill his dog, Willie."

"You saw the dog?"

"Yeah, he was a border collie/golden retriever mix. About five days in Wynn took him and told him if he didn't do exactly what he was told, he'd shoot Willie. The farmer broke down after he left. I felt bad for him."

"You're going to be questioned fully down at the station, but I want to know one thing. Did you ever see your brother at the farm?" she asked.

"No, I don't think he knew I was there." Hawk looked to me. "He would have told you, Cal."

I didn't believe that for a minute. Paul was about Paul.

Patrice sighed deeply. "Okay, I'm going to take Michael to the hospital. You can drive over to notify his family." Then to Hawk, "We'll arrange a place where you can meet them privately, Michael."

"Thank you," he said.

After I cleaned up the kitchen, I drove over to Brainerd to notify Tom and Barb Hawkinson their son was alive. A Subaru Outback was parked in the driveway. Tom answered the door.

"Oh, Cal, we were just talking about you."

"Oh?"

"We want to know if you'll be a pallbearer for Paul's funeral?"

"Sure, when is it?"

"Next Wednesday. We can't show him, you know. His face was . . ." Tom broke into shuddering sobs, and I pulled him in for a hug for a few seconds.

"Where's Barb?"

"In the kitchen with Sydney. She's coming with us when we go to the mortuary, then to see Pastor John."

Barb and Sydney were sitting at the kitchen counter, a laptop before them, an opened bible next to it. WCCO was playing on the old green radio they had twenty years ago when I hung around their home.

"Cal's here," Tom announced, then went to turn off the radio.

They looked up, dread filling their faces.

"No, no. It's good news. Mike's alive."

There was a second's delay before anyone said anything. Barb stood, her hands frozen midair. "What?"

Sydney shoulders dropped inches, her face went slack. "Oh, my God, I never thought we'd hear those words."

"Thank the Lord," Barb said. Tom and Barb gravitated toward each other and embraced, and began to weep.

"Where is he now?" Sydney asked.

"He's being checked out at the hospital; if he's physically able, we'll question him at the department, then arrange a place for you all to meet."

"Can't he just come home here?" Barb said.

"I'm going to be honest with you. It may not be safe. He's seen the faces of the men who kidnapped him and feels he knows who killed Paul and Norman Kramer."

Barb lifted her hand to her mouth and said, "Dear God."

"How did you find him?" Sydney said.

"I didn't. He showed up at my door. Norman Kramer let him go. We figured that's why he was killed."

"And Paul?"

"We're not sure why he was killed."

"He was probably there trying to help Mike escape," Barb said.

"Possibly."

"Once the men who kidnapped him are in custody, he should be safe. Right, Cal?" Barb asked.

"We need to know who all the players are before I'd feel comfortable."

"Did he say why they took him?" Sydney asked.

"Evidently Paul owed them ten grand for drugs stolen out of his garage, and they were extorting him for the replacement cost. Mike can tell you about it later."

"Oh, my God," Barb said.

"What was he doing with drugs in his garage?" Tom asked.

"He was storing them for Woody."

Tom shook his head. "I knew Woody was a crook."

"Did you tell Cat yet?" Barb asked.

"No, where is she?"

"They're staying at a place on Dexter Lake until after Paul's funeral."

"Give me the address. I'll run over."

"I don't know it. You'll have to call her for it."

"I have her number. Unfortunately, you need to keep this good news to yourselves until we get Mike to a safe place. Don't talk to anyone, especially the media."

When I left Hawk's family, they were standing huddled together in the middle of their kitchen. At least one of their boys was safe.

26

I TURNED ON THE GPS and entered the address where Cat and her family were staying. Dexter Lake sat two miles north of the city by the same name. It had a population of 1,800 and was one of the communities in the county that managed to keep a small police force and a volunteer fire department operating. At the one stoplight in town, I was prompted to turn left (north) onto County 81, then drive another two miles before I was told to turn left in one-quarter mile. The map indicated a single access road circled the small lake.

The voice on the GPS system said, "Uncharted territory," then shortly thereafter said, "Destination ahead." But there were no houses visible. I drove until I spotted a T-intersection with two mailboxes, and took a chance and turned left. As I drove beyond the stand of pines screening the property, an immense modern-style house came into view. A silver Lexus, a black BMW 7 series, and a black Tahoe were parked in the circle drive. I knew I was in the right place when I saw Cat standing at the front window.

Before I had a chance to ring the bell, the front door burst open. Cat bounded out onto the stoop. Her eyes were red and puffy, and her face was contorted in agony.

Her face changed as she took in my raccoon look. "What happened to you?"

"Nothing serious. Cat, I apologize. I should have told you on the phone that it's good news."

Her brows furrowed. "Really?"

"Michael's alive."

She squealed and lunged at me, giving me a tight hug. "Oh, my God. Oh, my God. Well, come on. Let's go tell everybody."

I stepped inside to an expansive open space. The décor and furnishings were ultra modern—all metal and glass with cream marble flooring throughout. To my left was a library, and toward the right was a large seating area with two sets of stone-colored leather couches facing a fieldstone fireplace. The kitchen/dining area was in the far right corner.

"Wow," I said, as I caught sight of the spectacular curved steel staircase. The walls of which were three-foot-high glass panels inset with vibrant geometric stained-glass designs. The front of the house had a cathedral ceiling, while the rear was two-stories, thus the need for the staircase.

"This is quite a shack," I said. "That staircase is magnificent," I said.

"Yes, but stop yapping about the frickin' house and tell me about Michael. Where is he?"

"We're having him checked out medically . . ."

"What's going on?" a voice boomed.

Cat's father came out from a hallway off the kitchen. He was followed by a man who looked to be right out of a mobster movie. He was dressed in a black suit and shirt, had a short haircut, square jaw, and angular face. His dark, deep-set eyes gave him an angry tough-guy appearance. I had the feeling he had skills—like Bobby Lopez.

"Daddy, Michael's alive!"

Ames brought his hands up. "That's wonderful news. Where is he?"

"We think he could be in jeopardy, so we don't want the media to know he's been found. We're having a physician examine Michael before we question him."

Concern rose in Cat's eyes. "Is he okay? Was he hurt?"

"He seems to be in good condition—considering."

"Cal Sheehan, right?" Irving Ames asked me. "You look like a damn raccoon."

"Yes, I know."

We shook hands. Then I looked to the mobster.

Ames said, "This is Cheney, my personal assistant."

"Is Cheney your last name?" I asked.

"No, first," he said. "My last name's Martin."

"Where's Michael been all this time?"

"He was held against his will at the Kramer farm. Kramer cut him loose. He hitched a ride and came to me."

Cat knitted her brows. "Why did this happen?"

"Evidently his brother owed some money to the wrong people. They were trying to extort Michael for it."

"Did they get it?" Ames asked.

"Some by way of his debit and credit cards. It wasn't Michael using your company credit cards in Vegas. Have you been watching your accounts lately, Cat?"

"I have someone on it," Ames said.

"You should have your mail stopped, Cat. They forced Michael to withdraw funds from an annuity, and it should be coming by mail any day. You can go online to do it."

Irving pointed at Cheney. "Go help Cat with it."

Mrs. Ames came into the room, her beaded flip-flops snapping on tile flooring. She was wearing a short robe that landed a few inches above her knees. *Nice legs.* She must have been a beauty in her prime because she was still attractive.

"What's going on?" she asked, hands on her hips.

Cat told her the news, and Mrs. Ames put both hands on her chest and said with a sigh, "Oh, thank God."

After a brief discussion, the Ames family decided Hawk would stay at the Donavan house, and Irving would hire a security team.

He offered me a cocktail. It was ten thirty in the morning.

"Ah, no thanks. I'm working, and I best be on my way. Michael will be in touch soon."

Cat hurried to my side and grabbed my arm. "Thank you," she said. "I'll never forget everything you've done."

"He's my best friend," I said.

She nodded. "I know, he's mine too."

As soon as I got back to the department, I went to check in with Patrice on Hawk's status. Georgia, her secretary, said Patrice was with Hawk in Interview Room Number Three.

I entered the observation room to see Crosby Green was operating the camera. He lifted his head by way of a greeting.

"Hi. How's it going?"

"Okay, I guess. I think your friend's lucky he got out of the Kramer place alive."

"I would agree. I'm rather surprised you're the only one in here."

"Sheriff wants to keep it on the down low."

I took a seat and watched. Hawk was seated, Patrice stood above him as she fired questions.

"Has she been hammering at him the whole time?"

"Yep, and in the hour they've been going at it she's gone over everything multiple times."

"Has he changed his story?"

"Not at all."

She asked him how long he had been at the cabin, who was there, and what transpired. Then she went on to rehash all those days at the Kramer farm and his escape. I began to pace the small room.

I pointed at the observation window. "She's trying to trip him up. Doesn't she believe his story?"

"Not sure, but I believe him."

She stabbed a finger at the photos of Ginty, Wynn, and Hayes. "When did you really meet these men for the first time?"

"I told you I knew Wynn from the warehouse. I saw the other two at Paul's the day they abducted me."

"Is it typical for a salesman to know the truck drivers?"

"I didn't *know* him. He was just there once when I dropped by the warehouse."

"What do you know about Wynn's drug deals?"

"Not a blasted thing."

I said, "She can't think he was part of the drug operation?"

Crosby looked at me and hiked his brows. "She has to question him about it. Cal, you know you're not in there because he's your best friend."

"Did you just say that? Is that what you all think? That I'm not able to be objective?"

He shrugged.

"Maybe you're right, because I get the sense I need to save him."

I continued to pace as I watched and listened to her work him over for another half hour. Finally, she said, "Well, Michael, I'm sure you're anxious to see your family."

He nodded. She led him out in the hall, and I joined them. I hadn't expected to see Hawk look quite so pale. His face was damp as were the front and underarms of the dress shirt I'd loaned him. He looked pitiful. I fought my urge to reach out and hug him in front of my boss. I was going to appear objective, you see.

He gave me a weak smile and asked to use the restroom. After the door closed behind him, Patrice said, "I need you to stick around until after I make some calls. You keep him out of sight. Take him to your office."

"Okay."

She walked off, her high heels clicking on the terrazzo floor.

When he exited the restroom a few minutes later, I asked, "Are you okay?"

"Yeah, but do I need an attorney?"

"You're the victim, so I wouldn't think so, but if you'd feel better, you're entitled."

I took him up the elevator to my office on the third floor and somehow managed to avoid running into anyone. He sat in Tamika's chair and asked, "Got any booze in here? I could use a drink."

"I totally understand, but no. I can get you some soda or water."

"Water. Thanks."

When I came back from the squad room he was standing at my desk reading something.

"What are you looking at?"

"Why do you have a list of all of Ames's companies?"

"Ames's Companies? What do you mean?"

"This." He held up my list of the companies who warehoused with North Cross Shipping.

"They're all Ames's companies?"

"Yes."

"What do you know about them?"

"Not much. I'm only involved with Lyman Pumps."

"Are all them legitimate companies?"

He screwed up his nose. "Yeah, of course."

"Including North Cross Shipping?"

"Sure."

"Is there a parent corporation managing all of them?"

"IAE," he said.

"Acronym for?"

"Irving Ames Enterprises."

"Did you happen to mention your concerns about Wynn and the drugs to your father-in-law or anyone in IAE?"

"Cheney."

"Cheney was at the house where your family is staying."

"Not surprised. He's Irv's executive assistant. They have to keep the business running."

"He looks like an assassin."

Hawk raised his head and snuffed out a laugh. "He runs on the serious side, but he's a good man."

"Why not mention your suspicions directly to Irving?"

"Because he doesn't deal with the small stuff."

"Cheney does."

"Yes."

"Hawk, watch out for Cheney. If you feel threatened, call me, or better yet, call 911."

"It's Wynn I have to worry about, not Cheney. How close are you to finding him?"

"We're trying."

"When can I see my wife?"

"After we meet again with my boss. You did tell the whole truth, right?"

He scowled. "Of course."

"I spoke with your neighbors, the Cavaras."

"We don't get along with them."

"No kidding. Your co-workers love you though."

He nodded. "Good to hear."

"Do you like your work any better?"

"Nope."

His terse answers were telling me I'd offended him when I asked him if he was telling the truth.

Patrice appeared at my door.

"Michael, do you want to meet with your wife alone somewhere, or are you okay with seeing her at the home in Dexter Lake? By the way, they're staying at Sonja Donavan's vacation house. She's a friend of mine—and coincidently a friend of your father-in-law. She told me she offered Irving her home when she found out you were missing in my county."

"I remember her from the wedding. Tall, classy-lookin' older lady?" Hawk said.

"Yes, you may have heard of her, Cal. She has a radio show."

"Doesn't ring a bell." I turned to Hawk, "So, the sheriff asked you what you wanted to do."

"I want to be with Cat's family."

"Cal, you give him a ride over. Michael, until we pick up Wynn, I've arranged for a deputy to be stationed around the clock while you're in Birch County."

"Do I need to stay up here for some reason?" Hawk asked.

"Crow Wing County also needs to question you. They're willing to wait until tomorrow morning at nine o'clock."

"Then I can go home?" he asked.

"The media will hound you if you do," I said.

Patrice crossed her arms and said, "After the interview, you're free to go when you wish, but I suggest you stay out of sight. Sonya's home is as safe as any. We have an APB out on Wynn, and, hopefully, we'll have him in custody by the joint press conference tomorrow afternoon at one o'clock—which you can choose to be a part of."

Hawk leaned forward. "Sheriff Clinton, when you were questioning me, you acted like you didn't believe me." His face flushed beet red. He pointed a quivering finger at her. "I was *abducted* at gun point and treated worse than an animal."

Patrice nodded. "I do believe you, Michael," she said. "I know you've been through a lot, but I needed to make sure. You've given us what we need to arrest Nevada Wynn and his freak-show."

"Paul's boss is a part of it too, you know."

"That's Crow Wing's deal," she said. "I will pass along the information."

27

WHEN HAWK CLIMBED IN the front seat of the department Explorer, I said, "I'm sorry if I offended you when I questioned your truthfulness. It's just that some people leave out details."

"It's okay. I'm just kind of an emotional mess right now. I miss my wife so much. I . . . I can't wait to see her."

"I could go a hundred with lights and sirens."

"No." He smiled.

I let a few seconds pass before I said, "You did good in there, Hawk. Sorry my boss was rough on you."

"It's okay." He wiped tears from his eyes, and said, "Baugh. I'm a crybaby."

"I can't imagine how frightening your experience was."

"I didn't know if I was going to live to see Cat again." He gave out a big sigh. "Norm was pretty cool . . . I wasn't too worried about him, but every time one of those other dickheads came by, I thought that was it. Thank God for red tape with the annuity, or I'd been shot as soon as the check came."

"You played it smart."

"I can't believe they didn't take my Mercedes."

"Nice car. You're doing well, Hawk."

"So are you . . . you know, considering everything that's happened."

"It's been a tough year, but, yeah, things are slowly getting better."

"Do you believe in karma?" he asked.

"I'm beginning to. You?"

"Yeah. What goes around comes around, you know? They'll all get theirs in the end."

"They will."

"You know I've always envied you?"

"Why?"

"Because you've always been your own man. I don't like being beholding to my in-laws."

"I wouldn't have my house if I hadn't inherited life insurance money when my birthmother died."

217

"Glad you got something from those deadbeats."

"Part of me didn't want to take the money."

"That's your stubborn nature, my friend."

"Stubborn? Me?"

He laughed. "Yeah, you."

"Maybe the divorce is my fault."

"Takes two. I thought you would make it, buddy. You looked so happy at the wedding. Well, at least you have kids. You're lucky there. Oh . . . I'm sorry. I'm an idiot. What a heartbreaker to have lost Shannon's son. Cat and I felt terrible. How have things been? Well, not good . . . if you're divorcing. Is it for sure?"

"I'm afraid so."

"Life sucks sometimes. Cat and I fought about having kids before she left on her trip. I'd give anything if she'd change her mind."

"She might be so happy to see your ass, she'll do just that."

There was a pause in the conversation, then Hawk said, "I'm sorry I wasn't there for you this past year. You were going through a tough time, and I dropped the ball. I kept thinking I'd call you, but I'd get busy with work, and Cat keeps our social calendar overbooked. I'm sorry, man."

"It's okay, Hawk. Life gets in the way of living."

It was a good lesson for me—to reach out to people who are grieving. Grief doesn't end the day of the funeral. It occurs in waves. But at first it's like trying to crawl out of a deep, dark hole and just when you are at the top, this crush of sadness knocks you back down. Everyone handles grief differently; as I threw myself into my work, Shannon and Luke withdrew.

WHEN WE PULLED into the drive at the Donavan home, Cat ran out the door. When Hawk stepped out of the vehicle, she jumped on him. She wrapped her legs around his waist, and he held her in his arms. After he set her down, she got on her tiptoes and kissed him all over his face. I stood ten feet away watching, wishing Shannon and I had the same emotional connection and passion. It was ironic. I thought Shannon and I were the ideal couple, and Hawk was a chump for marrying a superficial bitch.

Monica and Irving Ames came out of the house. Monica was wearing a dark-pink-and-white sundress. She moved in to give Hawk a long hug, followed by

Irving who'd changed into khaki shorts and a flowered Hawaiian shirt. If Cat and her family were faking joy and relief to see Hawk, they all deserved an Academy Award.

Cheney slunk out of the house like a cat and went to Hawk. The two men shook hands and gave each other a single nod. Cheney was short on words.

Irving Ames said, "Well, let's not stand out here. Come on inside."

"Mind if I stick around until the first deputy on watch arrives?" I asked.

"Of course not," Monica Ames said. "Can I get you a beer?"

Although I enjoyed beer, I resented she pegged me as a beer drinker.

"No thanks. I'm still on duty."

I stood behind the seating area where the family had assembled and observed the scene. Hawk was being pummeled with questions. He held up his hand and said, "First, can I have that beer you offered Cal, Monica?"

"Oh, of course." She hustled off to the kitchen and returned with a large glass of dark beer.

Cheney Martin leaned against the fireplace, his arms crossed, his expression sober as he quietly observed the reunion. Normally the more Hawk told a story, the bigger it got. This time he stuck to the same details.

A half hour later, Deputy Jenny Deitz sent me a text saying she was in position.

When I excused myself, Cheney said he was also leaving. Before I got to the door, Cat sprinted over to hug me. "Cal, thank you for bringing Michael back to me."

"Happy to," I said.

Hawk came up behind Cat to give me a hug. "Thanks, buddy."

"You bet."

"Cal, any chance you can go with me tomorrow when I'm questioned by Crow Wing County?"

"If you like. I'll pick you up at eight thirty."

I gave him a quick hug, and then Cheney and I stepped outdoors.

"Mr. Martin," I said.

"Yes?"

"Do you have a business card?"

He removed his wallet from his back pocket, pulled out a card, and handed it to me, and I did the same.

"Just in case you think of something that could help us."

He nodded.

"Are you a Johnny Cash fan?"

Remaining expressionless, he said, "No, why?"

"Your outfit could be out of his closet."

His mouth twitched.

"By the way, your window tint is darker than permitted by Minnesota law."

He gave me a minuscule nod. He waited a couple seconds, then said, "You gonna write me up?"

I smiled. "No, I'll wait and get you for a more serious offense."

For a brief moment, one side of his mouth lifted. His sunglasses hid his eyes, so I wasn't sure if he'd attempted a smile.

Without a goodbye or a nice meeting you, Cheney started his truck and drove off. I followed him down the driveway. He rolled past Jenny parked at the end of the road.

Jenny checked him out as he pulled out onto the road. I pulled up behind her squad and walked up to the driver's side.

Her window was open. "Who was that?" she asked.

"An employee of Hawk's father-in-law. Why?"

"He was totally hot."

"Was he? Pulling overtime?" I asked.

She was normally on dogwatch 7:00 p.m. to 7:00 a.m.

"Yep, we're saving for a house and need the extra money."

"Good for you. You should drive up past the T and to the left. It'll draw less attention."

"Good idea, then I can pee in the woods."

I flinched. Not an image I wanted.

"Oh, come on, Cal. It isn't much of a problem for you guys to be on guard duty for twelve hours without a bathroom like it is for us squatters. The trees will come in handy." She chuckled.

"Okay then. Watch out for the poison ivy and keep one hand on your firearm." I patted the top of her car and walked back to mine.

"Thanks for that, Sheehan."

BEFORE I WENT BACK to Prairie Falls, I stopped by Woody's Custom Builds. The doors were locked, no lights were on, which was weird for the middle of a business day. Thinking Woody split, I called Lee Sabin to tell him he might want to check on Woody's whereabouts.

"I was about to call you, Cal. Jerry Ketka, one of Woody Nash's employees, said Woody didn't show on Monday. He'd complained he hadn't been feeling well, so Jerry thought he stayed home to rest. Then this morning he finally went over to his house and found the back door open. Woody was sitting in his recliner, bullet through his forehead. Ketka called 911 and Brainerd's chief called me right away, figuring it might be connected to our homicides."

"Not self-inflicted?"

"Nope. His TV was on, three empty Millers were sitting on the table next to him, one in his hand, one left attached to the plastic rings in the cooler at his feet, so there was one missing can. Shooter probably took it."

"Killing makes you thirsty, I guess."

"I guess."

"Maybe he was having a friendly beer with his killer. Sounds like he was taken off-guard."

"That's the way it looks. Anyway, thought you'd appreciate knowing."

"Yes, thanks. Only the one shot?"

"Yes, from about five feet. We recovered a nine millimeter bullet lodged in the wood frame of the chair."

"Man, I was convinced Woody killed your other two victims."

"You had me thinking the same thing. Murder count is up to three now."

"BCA on it?"

"They're here now if you want to stop by. They said it looks like he's been gone three, four days."

"Oh, I think I'll stay out of this one. Are you looking at Nevada Wynn for it?"

"You bet."

"Okay, keep in touch."

I found Patrice and filled her in on the news of Woody Nash's demise.

"Do you think Wynn killed him as well?" she said.

"Could be. But there's a new player in the mix. Guy by the name of Cheney Martin."

"Cool name. Who is he?"

"Irving Ames's executive assistant. Hawk mentioned his suspicions about Wynn to him."

"And you think Martin is part of a drug operation running out of the warehouse?"

"I have no proof."

"Do you think Ames knows?"

"I have no idea. Hawk says their companies are all legit, but if he only works with the one, he may not even know what all's going down."

"Well, perhaps someone should start asking Mr. Ames some questions."

"I'd be delighted to."

WHEN I ENTERED THE OFFICE, Crosby was sitting at Spanky's desk.

"Hey, Cal, I finished with Hawkinsons' phone records."

"Let's hear it."

"During her vacation, Catherine Hawkinson exchanged texts with only one number, her mother's. I saw no other phone calls except the ones to and from her father, and you."

"What about the three amigos?"

"They call each other all the time. Wynn had a few to North Cross, which would make sense since he works for them. Right? But Paul Hawkinson also called Wynn on May 8 and again on May 12. Here's something else: Wynn called Norman Kramer on May 8, and Kramer called Ginty on May 12 and May 13."

"Interesting."

Crosby handed me a yellow message slip. "Oh, and Rex Balcer called. The bi-plane that's been flying over town belongs to Brock Snyder. You know, the pilot who testified he was with Victoria on the day of the arson."

"I know who he is."

"I also did some research on him for you. He's employed by Gopher Aviation based in Eden Prairie, and is Adam Lewis's private pilot. Flies his Lear jet for him."

"Holy shit."

"But here's the best part: Gopher Aviation is also one of Lewis's companies."

"Does Oliver know this?"

"I don't know."

I immediately dialed Oliver Bakken and shared what Crosby had discovered.

"I appreciate your late effort, but the jury's out, Sheehan, there's not much left to do."

"If you could prove to the judge Brock Snyder had been paid off to commit perjury, well then, you'd have it all tied up in a pretty pink bow."

"I had a witness at Flying Cloud Airport testify Snyder hadn't listed Victoria on his lesson roster. No employee saw her—that's good enough. And, by the way, it was your job to investigate the case. Why didn't you bring me this information weeks ago? Even yesterday before the goddamn jury went out? So, if anyone is to blame, it's you."

"Wait a minute. I wasn't told about Snyder."

"Join the club. I thought he was going to be a character witness. Her attorneys pulled a fast one."

"Couldn't you have objected?"

"I did! Jesus, how incompetent do you think I am?"

"I don't think that at all, but Victoria needs to be sent away for a very long time."

"She will be. Have anything more for me on the Hawkinson case?"

"I have another individual to question, guy by the name of Cheney Martin. He's Michael Hawkinson's father-in-law's badass executive assistant."

"Why him?"

"I don't like his looks."

"Oh, now there's something I can use. Any word on the APB for Nevada Wynn?"

"Not that I know of."

"Well, somebody shot Woody Nash. Who else would have motive? The badass Martin Cheney?"

"Cheney Martin."

"Whatever. Gotta keep my line open in case the jury comes back." Click.

THERE WERE PARALLELS between Adam Lewis and Irving Ames. Both were powerful businessmen owning multiple companies and knew how to manipulate the system. Adam Lewis was perfectly willing to do anything to shelter his wacko daughter from the law. Was Ames involved in any or all of the abduction business because Hawk stumbled onto something he wasn't supposed to?

I Googled Cheney Martin and got a few hits. Linked-in profile: He graduated with a master's degree from St. Thomas University in 1998. Employed at IAEI for three years. He didn't have a Facebook account, but neither do I.

No prison record. One speeding ticket in the last three years. He had a conceal/carry permit. Big surprise there.

Through Cat Hawkinson, I contacted Irving Ames. I asked him and Cheney Martin to come to the department for interviews. I asked they bring in any firearms they had with them. Both said they didn't bring them with, which was bullshit.

WHEN THE TWO MEN ARRIVED together an hour later, I had them placed into separate rooms. I interviewed Ames first. When I entered the interview room, he was sitting with a straight back, arms crossed in front of him, chin up, defiant expression. He exuded the confidence of a rich man who believed he was in charge. Not in my interview room.

I went through the ritual of giving all the required information.

"Mr. Ames, I was told you weren't thrilled about your daughter marrying Michael Hawkinson."

"You have kids?" he asked.

"I'm asking the questions today, Mr. Ames."

He narrowed his eyes and gave me a *How dare you, you little shit* stare. He took the time to take a deep breath and lean forward as he stared deliberately into my eyes.

"Well . . . if you have a daughter, no one will ever be good enough for her. That's just the way it is, so at first, no, I wasn't thrilled. But the more I got to know him, the more I appreciated him."

"And when did you offer him a position in Ames Lyman Pumps?"

"A few months after they were married. Why?"

"And has Michael met your expectations in his job performance?"

Ames lifted a hand and glowered. "What the *hell* does this have to do with anything?"

"Has he?"

"Yes, as it turns out, he's an excellent salesman."

"Does he treat your daughter well?"

"Yes, she seems happy."

"And what role does Cheney Martin play in your operation?"

"He's my right-hand man. Why?"

"What made you hire him?"

"I liked his style, and he was a Navy man like me, a seal. Did three tours of duty. Did you?"

"So he's skilled in combat—but what about his business training?"

"He has a business degree from my alma mater, St. Thomas. Why is this pertinent?"

"From your alma mater? No wonder you promoted him to your assistant."

Mr. Ames shot me a dirty look. I could have gone too far, but I couldn't seem to stop myself from continuing. "I should think it's a bit unusual for a recent graduate to rise to his level."

"It was my choice, wasn't it? And if he hadn't done well, I would have fired him."

"Tell me. Does he make decisions on his own, or does he run things by you?"

"Everything is passed by me ... the important things anyway. Not the day-to-day piddling bullshit."

"Would suspicion that there may be illegal substances stored in your warehouse and transported in your trucks be piddling bullshit?"

"What the hell are you talking about?"

"North Cross Shipping is your warehouse, right?"

"It is."

"Michael mentioned to Cheney that he suspected Wynn was transporting imported illegal drugs through North Cross. If I were the boss, I would certainly want to be told that kind of information."

His lips jutted forward. "If that's true, I'm sure Cheney checked it out and found the complaint without merit, but I will discuss this with him."

"When I questioned Estelle's Candies in Prairie Falls about a delivery Wynn had made to them, the plant manager noticed additional boxes behind the pump in the truck. Zeke La Plante at North Cross said Wynn had no other official shipments. We know Wynn and his minions are drug dealers and are responsible for Michael's kidnapping and were extorting money from him. They *killed* his brother and they would have killed him if Kramer hadn't let him go—and because he did—Kramer was also shot."

"First of all, I don't know this Wynn personally. Cheney told me he was in our Second Chance Project where we hire former convicts to give them a new start in the community. I suppose there's always failures in any program like this."

"The recidivism rate is higher than we like."

"So, you believe Wynn is responsible for the two deaths in Crow Wing County?"

"Three—Woody Nash, Paul's brother's boss, was also killed. We're pretty sure Woody and Wynn were working together to transport drugs up to this area. We believe Wynn transported boxes containing illegal substances, which he later dropped off at Woody's shop the day Michael was taken. They were to replace what had been stolen from Paul Hawkinson's garage a few days earlier. Wynn was making Paul come up with the money to replace the drugs. That's why they were extorting money from Michael. So either Wynn killed the three, or someone connected to him did."

"To silence them?"

"Leave no witnesses behind. Michael isn't safe until we have Wynn in custody. You do understand if your son-in-law is in danger, so is your daughter."

Ames took a deep breath as he contemplated what I said. "So what do you what me to do?"

"Keep Michael and Cat in a safe place. Hire security, although Cheney sounds like he's bodyguard material. How long can you stay in the Donovan house?"

"Sonya said as long as I want."

"Right now, no one knows where he is. After tomorrow's news conference you will be followed by the press. I know a guy who may be able to help. I'd have to ask him if he's interested." *Lord help me, I was thinking of Bobby Lopez.*

"All right. We'll do whatever you say." He pulled his wallet out and picked out a card. "Here's my card with my private number. You call me when you have that bastard."

I nodded. "Sir, I meant you no disrespect, when I questioned you. I apologize for the remarks I made about hiring Cheney. You have every right to hire whomever you like."

"Are we through here? This room smells like sweat and piss."

I smiled. "Yes, well most people sweat in this room and a few have pissed their pants."

I WATCHED CHENEY MARTIN through the observation window before I entered. He appeared calm, cool, and collected, more so than any person I'd ever seen awaiting interrogation. His body was still, and he stared straight ahead while his jaw worked a wad of gum. He gave his nails a look and picked at one, then resumed his dead-ahead stare. When I entered he glanced up at me. Up close he still didn't appear particularly nervous. I shook his hand. It was dry. He was cool and collected. He was a trained Navy Seal.

"Is this the first time you've been questioned in a police or sheriff's department?"

"Yes, sir."

"Ever been in legal trouble?"

"No, sir."

"You are a Navy seal?"

"Yes, sir."

"Where did you serve?"

"Mostly the Middle East."

"Do you remember the day Michael notified you of his concerns about the North Cross warehouse?"

He looked at me then off to the left. "He mentioned he thought his stock at the warehouse was on the light side. He asked why, and I told him the factories store product as well, or we can build to order, like the large pumps."

"Not what I meant. Did he tell you he thought there was something weird going on with one of the truck drivers at North Cross—Nevada Wynn?"

"I checked into it. I couldn't find any proof."

"Did you share this information with your boss at the time?"

"No."

"Why not?"

"Because it's more of a personnel issue. Plus, Mr. Ames doesn't want to know about something until it's proven. I had nothing to tell him."

"Do you still believe that's the case?"

"Obviously not. I have since apologized to Mr. Ames for not bringing Michael's concerns to him."

Bing! A discrepancy: Ames said he hadn't known Hawk told Cheney about Wynn. Who was lying? And why? If I put Bobby Lopez in the mix, he could be my eyes and ears while he watched out for Hawk.

28

M Y MOTHER WAS GIDDY with excitement when she accepted my dinner invitation. On my way home, I'd picked up some steaks and asparagus; mom was bringing the salad and dessert. I cracked a Stella beer and sat on my deck waiting for them to arrive. The moment my mother accepted the invitation, I regretted even considering involving Bobby. And now I was stuck with them for dinner.

I looked up and noticed Iris Kellogg, my neighbor and divorce attorney, walking around my pool fence and up onto my deck.

"Thought I should come check to see if you're crying in your beer," she said.

"Why would I be crying in my beer?"

"Because of the hung jury in the Lewis trial?"

"What? No."

"See what money buys?"

"Perjury?"

"That's what Phillip said. I'm sorry, Cal. I know how much you wanted the guilty verdict. When we heard the news, Phillip had me call Adriana. Needless to say, she was very upset and was worried about you. Seems like you two still harbor feelings for one another."

"Would you like a beer? Watch me cry into mine? Or better yet, a glass of wine?"

"Sure. I'd love a beer—any kind. Not going to answer my question about Adriana, are you?"

"Nope."

I'd placed myself in an awkward situation. If my mom arrived on time, which was rare, I'd feel compelled to invite Iris to dinner as well, and maybe her presence would make it easier to tolerate my mom and Bobby.

When I returned with a Stella and a dish of Gold Fish crackers, I said, "This was all I could find to snack on."

"They're good. I heard Michael Hawkinson turned up at your place."

"Where did you hear that?"

"Phillip told me. Said it was hush-hush until tomorrow."

"How did Phillip find out?"

"Oliver told him. They gossip like two old women. Anyway, I'm so glad he's alive and well. I'm curious to hear his story, but that's not why I came over."

I tossed her a sexy smile. "Yeah? So why did you?"

She smiled back. We both took long pulls of our beer.

"I came over to ask if you were putting the divorce on hold."

"Oh."

"I don't mean to push, I'm just wondering whether I should proceed or halt."

"No, I understand. I'll let you know ASAP."

"Seriously, Cal, there's no rush. I'll stop until I hear from you."

"Perfect. I think I'm going to have a party Saturday night. Want to come?"

"Sure."

"A let's-cry-in-our-beer party."

"Sounds fun." She rolled her eyes, and we laughed together. "Can I bring a friend?"

"Um, sure. The more the merrier. Boyfriend?"

She laughed. "No."

"Good."

When my mom and Bobby Lopez pulled up in his Cadillac Escalade thirty minutes late, we were into our second Stellas, and I had already invited Iris to join us for dinner. My mother moved on from my romantic relationships with the speed of a comet, so she took one look at Iris and grinned. She didn't waste time feeling sad with her own romantic losses either, except for Patrick. I believe she still harbors contempt for my father—but he really shit on her. Now grief was a different story for Mom. She wears her grief for my brother Hank, who drowned when he was six; her father, who died when I was sixteen; and my Colby, whom she loved instantly, like a badge of honor.

Mom took Iris's hand and held it. "Sooo, how do you two know each other?"

"We actually met while jogging. We found out we're neighbors. I live right across the alley." Iris pointed to her house.

"Isn't that convenient?" Mom said.

I liked how Iris handled that, not mentioning she was my divorce lawyer.

I HAD A BETTER TIME at dinner than I anticipated. Bobby, as it turned out, had quite the sense of humor and made us all laugh, especially the women. When we were finished eating, he pulled me aside to say: "So your missing friend just showed up at your door?"

"How the hell did you find out?"

He lifted his scared eyebrow. "I have my sources." Then he broke into a laugh. "His mother called Hope this afternoon to tell her you were a hero."

I grimaced and said, "Hardly. Look, I want to ask you something. Until we catch Nevada Wynn, I'd like to have someone keep an eye on Hawk. I'm not sure about some of the people he's close to and . . ."

"You want me to be his body-guard?"

"Well . . . if you do that kind of thing. You'd be paid."

"You couldn't afford me. But . . . I'd do it for you . . . for free."

"Why?"

"Because something screwy's going on there."

"What do you know about it? Jesus, *how* do you know?"

"Uh-uh . . . remember? You don't want to know. So just tell me what you want me to do."

"Okay, pick me up at home here at eight o'clock tomorrow morning, and we'll discuss it with him."

He grinned. "Okay, but are you sure you wouldn't rather have me find Nevada Wynn?"

"What? You could do that?"

"Sure. Probably. Maybe."

"Okay, let's just stick with the bodyguard deal for now."

"You got it. Eight o'clock sharp." He slapped me on the back. "It meant a great deal to your mother you invited us for dinner. I won't tell her it was because you wanted to hire me."

Now I was the jerk.

Iris stuck around until after Bobby and Mom left.

"Your mom and her boyfriend are interesting people. I love how they reconnected after meeting in California when they were young."

"Humph."

"What do you think about him moving in with her while they find a house she likes?"

"They're going to live together?"

"That's what she said."

"I didn't hear her say that. Shit. This is so typical of my mother—she doesn't think through things before she jumps right in headfirst. Why would you move in with someone you've only known a couple weeks? Do you know how many men she's had in her life?"

"How many?"

"I've lost count."

She let out a giggle. "Well, I like her. She's a free spirit."

"Oh, she's a free spirit all right."

"Hey, let me help with your party. What do you need me to do?"

"I don't know. I'd never thrown a party by myself. Maybe bring an appetizer?"

"Sure. Want me to grocery shop for you? I have time. Let's make a list of what you'll need."

Before she left, we also made a guest list and created an invitation, then I sent it off by email. Within minutes, I had several acceptances.

"We're having a party," I said.

She gave me a high-five. I really liked this woman—and I think she liked me.

When she left, I added Clara and Shannon to the list. I emailed Shannon and told her she could bring a guest.

Later that night as I lay in bed, the two beers and four glasses of wine having lost their effect, I realized what I'd gone and done. "What the hell are you thinking? Having a party? Inviting Shannon and a guest? And asking Bobby Lopez to guard Hawk?" I've started talking to myself.

29

June 6

FRIDAY MORNING, Bobby Lopez was ten minutes early. He wore a gray two-toned Charlie Harper shirt, a pair of jeans, and gray athletic shoes. As we rolled out of my drive I said, "You going bowling? Because I expected you'd wear a black spook suit—white shirt, black tie, and sunglasses."

"Funny man. I'm always incognito, unlike you wearing your uniform."

"You carrying? I supposed that's a silly question."

"I have my favorite little .22 in an ankle holster, a Beretta nine mill in the glove box, and a Barrett 98B Centerfire rifle in the back . . . if we should need it."

"Jesus."

"Isn't that what you're paying me *absolutely nothing* for?"

"You want to be paid, you'll be paid."

"I told you the deal. I'm doing this for you."

"Not sure why."

"Your mother is why. I care about her, and she cares about you and your friend . . . and don't ask why I care so much about your mom so early in our relationship because I don't know, I just do. I need coffee. We have time?"

"Sure. Northwoods has a drive-through."

"And homemade peach scones."

"Somehow you don't seem like a scone guy."

"There are many things about me that may come as a surprise to you."

"That I believe."

THE YOUNG CLERK who handed us over our coffee and bags of scones stared at Bobby with raised brows like he was Jack Nicholson in *The Shining*. When he handed her a ten-dollar tip, she gave him a toothy smile and thanked him, but her eyebrows were still raised which gave her a comical expression.

As he drove off, he chuckled. "I love doing that."

"What? Scaring young women? You ever gonna get your new eyeball?"

"I have it. I don't particularly like wearing it."

"And you look scarier without it."

"That too. Hey, kid, last night your mom was going to tell you we were moving in together, but she chickened out."

"She thought it safer to tell Iris, who told me after you left."

"Good then." He glanced over. "We like your new gal. Your mom said she'd be a good one for you."

I let out an audible sigh and shook my head. "She's *not* my *gal*. We're just friends."

Bobby had a smirk on his face.

"You okay with your mom and me moving in together?"

"No. You haven't been together very long, and I don't know w*ho* you are . . . or *what* you are, besides secretive."

"It's not me you need to fear."

"Oh, okay. Who then?"

"A man who's desperate to conceal his actions."

"How is that not you?"

"I'm not desperate."

That shut me up for a spell.

As we sipped our coffee and ate our scones, I listened to Bobby list all the things he liked about my mother: her hippie ways, her choice of music, her carefree attitude, her style, her joy with the simple things in life, her lack of materialism, her easy laughter, blah, blah, blah.

And some of the things he liked about her drove me absolutely nuts, especially when I was in high school—her hippie persona, for example. Strands of beads in doorways were not only embarrassing, but annoying as hell to walk through; her insistence of driving an old rusty van plastered with political bumper stickers—when she could have afforded a new one; the way she'd put on her sixties music and want my friends to dance with her. Of course *they* liked it—they were horny teenagers thinking she was Mrs. Robinson. Who knows, maybe she was.

I had to admit, I'd never seen my mother happier. However, I would be stupid not to be concerned about who Lopez was and what he did for a living. Part of me thought he was just yanking my chain. But if he and my mother were together, I needed to get to know him better.

He pulled a toothpick from his shirt pocket and put it in his mouth. "She's told me about your dad and the secrets she'd kept, how guilty she feels about it."

"She should. It was wrong."

"She thinks you haven't forgiven her."

"I've forgiven her, but I won't ever forget she lied to me my whole life, and this subject is close."

"Sure, but just one comment, if I may." He didn't wait for me to object. "She was terrified you'd be taken from her by your biological father and mother."

"So she said. So, you gonna marry her or just shack up with her?"

"Now, now. What a negative spin you just put on our relationship."

"My grandmother is shacking up and soon my mother will be. Never thought I'd see the day."

"It's a changing world." He looked at me reflectively. "I think change may be difficult for you, Cal Sheehan."

"You don't know me and, therefore, are not qualified to have opinions about me, Cisco."

He gave me a smug look and nodded. "Fair enough, and ditto."

WHEN HE PULLED into the Donovan house, he whistled. "Now this is the kind of property I'm talking about. Who owns it?" Bobby said.

"Sonya Donovan, some radio personality. Must be worth well over a million."

"I wonder if she'd sell it."

"What? You have that kind of dough?"

He glanced at me and raised the scarred brow above the eye patch. "No, I'd want her to hand it over to me for free. Of course I have the dough. I sold a house in California and need to reinvest this year so I don't get socked with capital gains . . . if you must know the details."

"Huh, I thought maybe you just got paid for a hit."

"That too." He laughed.

"You have fun with me, don't you?"

He pulled the toothpick from his mouth and put it in his pocket. "I do."

As Bobby made a visual appraisal of the Donovan house from the great room, I told the Ames family about him being willing to guard Hawk until Wynn was apprehended.

"Oh . . . well . . . that's . . . good," Monica Ames said. She looked to Irving, and he shrugged.

Irving moved his head from side to side as if contemplating the offer. "I've hired a couple security guards to keep watch on the place twenty-four/seven."

"Do they have surveillance equipment?" Bobby said.

My eyes narrowed. We hadn't spoken about equipment. Probably necessary.

"Hey, there he is!" shouted Hawk from the top of the stairs. He bounded down the stairs dressed in khaki slacks and a light-blue Polo shirt. Cat followed him, but took the steps slower. He was grinning like he didn't have a care in the world. Had he taken a mood elevator?

"This okay to wear? Cat went out and bought me some new clothes at . . . what's the name of that store, honey?"

"Herbergers! Would you believe they had Polo?" Cat said. "Anyway, I told Michael even if we picked up his car, he had nothing suitable to wear. When can we get his Mercedes anyway?"

"You can pick it up after the news conference today. We should head out, Hawk," I said.

No one said a word about my using my nickname for him. I was through pretending he was Michael.

Hawk leaned over to kiss his wife. She looked up at him and said, "Are you sure I shouldn't come along?"

"Absolutely positive, sweetheart," he said, and kissed her again.

Irving came to give him a hug. "Good luck, son. I know it's hard for you to talk about all this again and again, but you're strong."

Monica also hugged him. "This will be all over soon, and you can go home and get back to normal."

The thing is—nothing would be normal again. Victims of this kind of trauma often suffered the psychological affect for years.

Hawk sat in the rear passenger seat behind Bobby. His cool persona had changed once in the car. He was twitchy: unconsciously bouncing his legs, touching his face, licking his lips.

He said, "Will they drill me like your sheriff did?"

Bobby looked at him in the rearview mirror.

"Just tell the truth and you won't have anything to worry about," I said.

"Can you come in with me?"

"I'm not sure. Relax, Hawk. You'll be fine."

He gave me a faint smile. "I just hate talking about it. Makes me relive all of it."

"Understandable."

LEE SABIN MET US in the lobby. I asked if I could accompany Hawk while he was being questioned.

"No, sorry."

So Bobby and I waited in the lobby.

"He's nervous," Bobby said.

"I realize that."

"He needs yoga."

"Yoga?"

"To ground him."

"You do yoga?"

"I do a lot of things."

"I'll bet."

"Yoga enhances your sex life."

"No sex talk. Let's go get a cup of coffee."

We found a cafe downtown and bought a cup of coffee. Bobby ordered peach pie.

He held up a forkful of pie and said, "Has your mother always been so politically liberal?"

"Yes. Have you met Dee and George yet?"

"No, but your mom said her mother is her polar opposite, but they get along."

"All true. Grandma Dee is a Lutheran church lady and a republican. She wouldn't set foot in Mom's old van because it still had a Gore/Lieberman bumper sticker on it, among others."

"I think she misses running that gift shop with your grandmother. She said you two lived with your grandparents since your dad left, and Dee and George gamble too much."

"That's it in a nutshell."

"She's very proud of you, you know. She brags about how you were an A student, and a star athlete. So why did you pick law enforcement?"

"Because I like to help people."

He laughed. "Yeah, me too."

We finished our coffee, and because we didn't know how long they would keep Hawk, we went back to the police department to wait. Bobby had a way of pulling information out of people. I finally told him I preferred we sit quietly while we waited. He gave me that grin again.

ABOUT A HALF HOUR LATER, Lee Sabin came out to say they were taking Hawk out to the scene, and I could ride along. He said to meet them in the parking lot.

As Bobby and I walked outdoors, he said, "I find that curious."

"I guess they want to get a better picture of what occurred."

"Hmm. Call me when you want to be picked up."

The sheriff and Deputy Sue Anderson, who was along to record what transpired, rode in the sheriff's squad car, while Hawk and I rode with Lee Sabin. Hawk took the backseat.

"Hey, Lee, did you ever find Paul's car?"

"Oh, yeah. I meant to call you. It was in Kramer's garage where he keeps his restored cars. The officer who first checked it thought Paul's was part of his collection."

"How many did he have?"

"Three. All restored by Woody Nash. We found three boxes of pills in Paul's trunk packaged in gallon size plastic bags. Tested positive for oxycontin."

Hawk shook his head. "Shit."

Sabin looked in the rear-view mirror at Hawk. "The steering wheel and door handles were wiped down. Strange, huh?"

I said, "Very. If it'd been Wynn, he'd probably have taken the oxy."

"See, I think someone moved the car, so Wynn wouldn't know Paul was there."

"Hey, Hawk, why didn't you take one of Kramer's cars?" I said.

He looked out the window. "I don't know. My mind was pure shit."

"PTSD," Sabin said.

A WARM GUST OF WIND swept across the gravel farmyard creating a dust devil. The yellow crime scene tape still surrounding the property fluttered in the breeze. A crow flew into the oak tree beside the house. Others cawed from a distance, causing a sudden cacophony in the grove of trees north and west of the buildings. An image of the crows pecking at Paul flashed in my mind. Nausea flooded through me. I took out my phone and looked at a photo of the Twinks.

Once we were all crammed inside the back porch, Sue Anderson began filming with a hand-held video camera as Lee began his questioning.

"Mr. Hawkinson, you stated earlier that once you arrived at the Kramer farm in Ginty's van, you were taken directly down to the basement at gunpoint by Glenn Hays and Raybern Ginty."

"Yes. Hayes had a shotgun and Ginty had a pistol."

"Were you restrained in anyway?"

Hawk rubbed his wrists. "My hands were tied behind my back with zip lock ties."

"Where was Mr. Kramer?"

"Standing just inside kitchen. They told him I was going to be his houseguest for a while, then took me down the stairs to the basement."

"Okay, let's go down," Sabin said.

When Hawk got to the bottom step he pointed to the bloodstain on the cement floor.

"Is that his blood?"

"It is," Sabin said.

"I wonder why he was down here if Hawk was already gone," I thought aloud.

"I told him to make it look like I escaped, to rip the tape."

"What time did he let you go?" Sabin asked.

"Early in the morning. He said I should get out before Wynn showed up. He asked me to hit him on the head to make it look like I knocked him out."

"Back to your first day. You mentioned they used a bike lock around your neck to secure you."

Hawk took a deep breath and said, "It was Ginty's idea. He said he saw one used that way in a *Breaking Bad* episode. I sat on the cement floor with my back to that post, bike lock around my neck, so I couldn't really bend over to get the tape off my legs."

Sabin pointed to the floor beside the stairway. "There was a lounge chair pad down here."

"On about the third day, I asked Norman for a blanket and pillow, and he brought the pad too. At night, he moved the bike lock lower so I could lay down and sleep."

"Did you consider trying to overpower Kramer when he was changing the lock position?" I asked.

"What?" he snapped. "He'd move my hands behind my back first. He had a system."

"You said all three of the men took turns to check on you?"

"Yes, and it wasn't predictable as to who or the times or days. But Wynn was the one who showed up to handle the annuity paperwork. They'd throw a few threats around like they'd kill his dog. Wynn described my house to me. He'd been there. He knew *exactly* where I lived. And if I didn't do as they wanted, he said they'd rape and kill my wife."

"So, why do you think Mr. Kramer let you go?"

"I think I got finally through to him." Hawk looked at the bloodstain and blinked back tears. "Can we get out of here?"

The sheriff said, "Let's go upstairs. I have a map. I want you to show us your route to Deputy Sheehan's."

Sheriff Hudson spread a map out on Kramer's kitchen table. He showed Hawk where we were.

Hawk said, "I was afraid Snake or Ginty would see me if I walked along the road, so I cut through the grove and walked to the first farm, that way."

"West? Through the cornfield?"

"Yes, newly planted"

"Let's go on out to where you cut across," the sheriff said.

As we walked out, the crows flew from tree to tree, cawing as if upset about our intrusion. If I was alone and had a rifle, I would have shot them all.

As we approached the wide area marked off with crime scene tape, Hawk pointed to it and said, "Is that where Paul was found?"

I nodded. He turned and faced the grove, and after a few seconds, he turned and pointed in the distance. That's the first farm I went to."

Lee Sabin said, "How long do you estimate you were at the second farm?"

"Hours, because I slept."

"Did you hear any shots?" the sheriff asked. "That farm is pretty close."

"I may have been sleeping."

"Shots fired inside would have cut the sound," Lee said.

"Not the ones fired right here," I said without thinking.

Hawk winced. Those shots killed his brother.

Lee said, "When you hit the highway, how long before you got a ride?"

"Awhile. I looked pretty bad and people weren't stopping. Truthfully, I wouldn't have picked me up either. But then after a time, the kid stopped."

"Did you get his name?" I asked.

"Jesse something. He said he knew you, Cal."

I thought a moment. "The only Jesse I know of is Jesse Emerson."

"Yeah, that's it."

The son of the man who killed my kid?

"Well, that should wrap things up, unless Deputy Sheehan has any questions," the sheriff said.

"Just one thing. Why didn't you or Kramer call 911 from the farmhouse?"

"I wondered that too," the sheriff asked.

"In hindsight, I know I should have, but all I could think of was getting out of there before Wynn arrived, and then my next thought was to get to Cal . . . so we could warn Paul."

We took that in and were quiet for a few seconds until the sheriff said, "Okay, Lee will run Mr. Hawkinson by the two farms, take some film, but I have a press conference to get ready for. Are you going to join me, Deputy Sheehan, or is Sheriff Clinton?"

"Sheriff Clinton will handle it."

"I'll drop you off at your car."

"After we're through, I'll take Michael wherever he wants to go," Lee Sabin said.

"Back to your lot is fine," Hawk said. "My wife can pick me up. Thanks, Cal."

ONCE ON THE ROAD, my thoughts centered on how Hawk handled his escape. If he didn't think to use one of Kramer's cars or call 911—or me for that matter, why didn't he tell the people at the first farm to call 911 and tell them who he was and that he'd been held captive? My only conclusion was that someone under those extreme circumstances would operate differently, even irrationally.

"Sheriff Hudson, does the evidence jive?"

"Pretty much. There is one thing I found interesting. Michael says Norman was a nice guy, but his sister said she didn't like him much because he had a mean streak. But then again that could be sibling rivalry from way back. A lot of families don't get along."

"What's her name?" I asked.

"Polly Jacobs. She lives in Cross Lake. She said the only thing Norman loved as much as himself was this dog."

"Wonder if they killed him too."

"My guess is yes."

"Have you spoken with Jesse Emerson?"

"Not yet. Michael didn't know his last name until you supplied it, but I expect his story will check out. Now, we need to find Mr. Wynn pronto. Is he as bad as everyone says?"

"He is. Any prints or DNA on the shotgun?"

"Wiped clean. The rope and bike lock had Ginty's, Kramer's, and Michael's DNA, but the ice cream bucket contents contained only Mr. Hawkinson's DNA."

ONCE IN THE CROW WING Sheriff Department parking lot, I thanked the sheriff, then headed over to Bobby's Escalade. As I hopped in, I said, "We can go. They're visiting the farm sites. Hawk's wife will pick him up."

"How'd he do?"

"Sheriff Hudson thought he did all right. I think it was difficult for him to be back in his prison of three weeks."

"Learn anything?"

"Paul's car was hidden in plain sight, in Kramer's garage, bags of oxy in the trunk. I question if Kramer was somehow involved."

"Dead men don't speak."

"Kramer's sister didn't like him."

"Oh?"

"Hawk said he was a good guy. Why wouldn't his sister like him?"

"Look at your own family. You don't like your father, even though Hope says he's basically a good man."

"She said that? In my opinion, a good man doesn't abandon his children."

"I'll give you that one. Hey, while I was waiting for you, I got a call from Irving Ames. He said he wouldn't need my services. His men have installed outside cameras to catch anyone trying to come on the property. It's all good," Bobby said.

"That makes me think Ames didn't want you hearing his conversations, especially if he was involved in Hawk's abduction? He could know the drugs were being routed through his businesses. Hell, maybe it's *his* major business, and the others are fronts. Hawk was getting close to the truth, so he ordered a hit."

"If he ordered a hit, why's Hawk still alive?"

"Because Ames saw how miserable his daughter was without her husband?"

Bobby rubbed his chin with his hand. "No, I don't think so."

"Well, I doubt he would keep him alive to extort a few thousand out of him. I think that was Nevada Wynn's brilliant plan."

"By the way, I spoke to him on the phone."

"Who?"

"Wynn."

"Are you kidding me?"

"I tracked his cell phone down while you were doing your thing."

"And you're just telling me now?"

"I was getting to it."

"How were you able to find his number?"

"I know some people in communications. Anyway, when I told him you needed to talk to him, he said he needed to talk to you too, because he didn't murder anyone."

"And you believe that?"

"I don't know the man."

"Where is he?"

"I told him to meet us at my place. He may be there now."

"Your place? That's nuts."

"Where would you suggest we meet? It can't be a public place. He's more likely to think he can come in safely to a residence out in the country."

"What about your family? Are *they* safe with that lunatic at your place?"

"I sent them to Hope's. Wynn was in Minneapolis when we talked. It'll take him a while to get here."

"And now my mother is involved."

30

BOBBY HAD A SURVEILLANCE room in one of the bedrooms. He had a large portable table covered with monitors, covering all sides of his property, plus the entrance to the driveway.

"A little paranoid, are we?"

"I could set you up with a nice system."

"No thanks. I have windows."

"I have trees blocking my view."

Bobby made coffee and sandwiches. I accepted the coffee and watched birds and squirrels on the cameras. He stood in the doorway watching me watch the cameras.

"You're acting a bit nonchalant under the circumstances," I said.

"The kid is an amateur."

"An amateur killer. I'm comforted."

"He said he didn't do it."

"Yeah, and that means he didn't."

After that, we didn't talk much. I ate an egg salad sandwich, drank another cup of coffee, and watched two squirrels going at it.

About an hour later, I was taken aback when a black Buick Enclave showed up on the driveway screen. Bobby picked up a remote and zoomed in.

"It's Wynn."

As we both made a beeline to the front door, Bobby's cell phone rang. On the way he grabbed his Barrett rifle leaning against the wall. I pulled my Smith and Wesson M&P nine millimeter.

Bobby spoke into the phone. "Get out of your car. Walk to the door with hands on your head. You move one hand toward your body and you're dead."

"I'm surprised you don't have a sound system."

"I do. I'm just not using it."

I watched Wynn through the window as he walked toward the house. "I want to cuff him. Have him lie on the ground."

"Stop where you are and lie on the ground. Hands on your head."

Wynn complied. I moved the six feet he was from the door, and cuffed his hands behind his back, then frisked him for weapons. He was clean. Then the thought occurred to me that this whole thing could have been a set-up. That I could have been the one they wanted to take out—and I had played right into it.

I abruptly stood and looked for Bobby. He was right behind me with his rifle trained on Wynn. I let out the breath I hadn't realized I was holding. With one hand, I lifted Wynn to a standing position by his waistband and escorted him inside the house. Bobby pushed him into a stuffed chair.

Wynn looked up at me and said, "I didn't kill anybody like the TV said I did."

"Who did?"

"I need a deal in place before I tell anybody anything."

"What makes you so sure you'll get one."

"Because I have information?" He wiggled away from the back of the chair. "Will you take these cuffs off?"

"We can put them to the front," Bobby said, and nodded at me like he was in charge.

"He's fine," I said to Bobby. Then to Wynn, "So, why should I believe you?"

He closed his eyes. "Look, I did some things wrong. I'll take the hit for whatever I did."

"Like?"

"Like forcing Mike to pay Paul's debt. But after I got the money, I was going to let him go. I told Mike that. I'm a man of my word. Ask anybody. Snake does what he says, they'll tell you."

"Where did you hold Michael Hawkinson?"

"At Norman's."

"Why there?"

"No one around."

"Here's the deal. My cases are only those that happened here in Birch County: the abduction of Michael Hawkinson and the burglary of the Brooks cabin—add in the breaking and entering. We have you for those. Believe that. Now the three murders that occurred in Crow Wing County are not mine to investigate. But unless you give names, Crow Wing won't bargain."

"All I know is everybody was alive when I left town. And there were only so many people who knew Mike was at Kramer's."

"Who?"

"I won't say anymore until I get a deal."

I shrugged. "Tell me what you did with Willie," I said.

"Willie? Norm's dog?"

"Yes."

"I dropped him off at the animal shelter in Brainerd."

My eyes narrowed and my head tilted toward Wynn. Hard to believe Snake would do something honorable.

"Why?"

"Norm asked me to because he was sick and thought he was going to die. The place was called HART. It's on Dellwood Drive. Call and ask them."

"Easily enough checked. Now get up," I said. "I'm delivering you to Crow Wing County."

As Bobby put Wynn in the front passenger seat of the Escalade, I called to tell Patrice what was happening, but she wasn't answering. Then I remembered she was already in Crow Wing at the press conference. I left a message.

I aimed my firearm at the back of Wynn's head all the way to Prairie Falls. Bobby guarded him as I signed in and checked out a vehicle, then we transferred him to the backseat.

"Who's he going to give up?" Bobby asked with a whisper.

"Maybe Cheney or Ames."

"Keep an open mind when you hear what he has to say."

"What do you think he's going to say?"

"I'm not a mind reader. How are you getting home?"

"I can walk, and thanks for whatever you did today."

"You owe me big time."

I screwed up my face.

"I'm kidding. Catch you later."

I BROUGHT WYNN DIRECTLY to the Crow Wing County Jail on Laurel, where they placed him in a holding cell. I then walked over to the courthouse to find Patrice. The press was packing up, and obviously, I'd missed the news conference. Cat's Lexus passed right in front of me. Hawk was sitting in the front passenger seat. He waved at me, but they didn't stop, which I found odd.

"Cal!" I turned and spotted Patrice by her squad car.

She walked toward me.

"How did it go?" I asked.

"Fine. Did you hear that goddamn jury in the Lewis case couldn't reach a verdict? I mean really?"

"In all fairness, they had conflicting testimony."

"Oliver's going to retry her."

"Maybe it's a good thing. If he can uncover Brock Snyder's close ties with Adam Lewis and can prove there was a payoff, he cinches a conviction."

"He said you told him about Snyder's employer after the fact."

"It's my fault?"

"No, it's Oliver's. Anyway, I got your message about bringing Wynn in. You're a rock star, you know that?"

"Not exactly. I had help from Bobby Lopez."

"The guy who brought Victoria into the courtroom?"

"The same. He's banging my mother."

A smile slowly materialized. "Good for her."

"Really?"

"Anyway."

"Anyway, Wynn claims he didn't kill anyone."

"I wish I had a dollar for every time I heard someone tell me they were innocent. Sheriff Hudson told me you questioned why Michael didn't call 911 from Kramers. Were you just trying to prove your objectivity?"

"No, it struck me as odd." *And yes, maybe I was.*

"Hudson said he was running scared."

"Maybe so."

"Well, let's go find Tim and talk about the lying Snake in the grass."

"You punster."

"I thought it was clever."

"It was."

PATRICE AND I MET BRIEFLY with Sheriff Tim Hudson and Lee Sabin before they questioned Nevada Wynn. Lee was to call me afterward. Then we drove our separate vehicles back to Prairie Falls. After checking in, Patrice said, "You look exhausted. You should go home, get some rest before your big party tomorrow night."

"Are you coming?"

"I plan to. If I hear anything, I'll call you."

WHEN I GOT HOME, Clara was in my kitchen cooking.

"Aren't you at Shannon's today?" I asked.

"They're at her parents. So, I thought we'd get started on the party food."

"We?"

An attractive woman rounded the corner, followed by a black-and-white dog, and Bullet at his heels. She had the most amazing aquamarine eyes. When she smiled, deep dimples appeared in her cheeks.

I said hi to her—clever devil that I was.

"Cal, you haven't met my daughter Dallas. She's volunteered to help me with the party food."

"It's very nice to meet you, Dallas, and thanks for helping."

"It's nice to meet you too. I've certainly heard all about you."

"Oh-oh."

"All glowing, believe me."

"Whew, that's good because your mom sees me at my worst. So you have two other children, right, Clara?"

"Yes, Jamie lives in Minneapolis, and Scott lives in Chicago."

I knelt down to pet the dog. "And who's this?"

"*This* is my new rescue dog, Willie," she said. "He's a real sweetie."

Bullet moved in, jealous I was giving another dog some attention. I petted them both.

"Willie? Did you get him at the shelter in Brainerd?"

"Yes, how did you know?"

"I bet he's Norman Kramer's dog."

"He is. When I called about him, they said his owner was ill, but then when I picked him up I was told he belonged to one of the men who'd been killed."

At least Wynn was telling the truth about the dog, or at least gave the same story to the shelter and me.

"You look like you could use a beer," Clara said. "Sit down and Dallas will get you one."

Clara nodded toward the fridge. Dallas gave her a look.

"No, I'll get it," I said. "Anyone else want one?"

Dallas picked up a large knife. "Not while I'm handling these."

I pulled a Stella from the fridge and sat at the counter to watch the two women slice and dice. Dallas resembled her mother, except for the color of her eyes and hair, but I suspect Clara might get her red hair out of a bottle; Dallas had light-brown hair cut short. They were both approximately five feet six inches, and had the same body build, although Dallas was slimmer.

"Thanks for doing this. I didn't think this thing through. You're coming, right, Dallas?"

She smiled. "I think I can make it."

"Good."

"Dallas works at Prairie Veterinary Clinic."

"Are you a vet?"

"I am. Maybe I'll be able to see Bullet sometime."

Both dogs were flanking Dallas as she worked at the counter. Bullet was looking up at her adoringly.

"I think he'd like that. Be sure to let me know what I owe you for the food and extra time."

"Food's on the debit and the time I consider part of my salary. I'm making a pork roast tomorrow for pulled pork sandwiches."

Dallas said, "Your neighbor, Iris, dropped by. She seemed surprised to see us here."

"Oh?"

"She dropped off a bag of groceries, mostly chips and nuts. She said if you needed anything else you should call her."

Clara said, "Are you seeing her?"

"No, she's just a friend."

My cheeks tingled, and Clara and Dallas exchanged those raised eyebrow looks women give each other whenever they think they're being lied to.

31

June 7

JUST BECAUSE I DIDN'T GO in to work on Saturday, didn't mean I wasn't working. What Nevada Wynn told Crow Wing was on my mind all day as I helped Clara clean the house and complete the errands on her list, and when I mowed and edged the lawn. By three o'clock I finished all my chores and couldn't stand it any longer. I called Lee Sabin and asked the burning questions.

"I was just going to call you, Cal. Okay, Wynn claims Woody killed Kramer and Paul, and he thinks one of Woody's employees killed him because he's such a dick to work for."

"Come on."

"I know, right. According to the BCA, Woody died before Kramer and Paul. And Wynn's DNA showed up on Kramer's refrigerator handle and a water glass."

"So he was there recently."

"He was definitely there. We're going to charge him because he had motive and opportunity. His only alibi is his prostitute girlfriend Franchon Smith, but she says she wasn't home and doesn't know where he was. You're right about the loyalty not being there."

"Did he say who his drug boss is? That's who we should be looking at."

"He says he picks up the product from a guy in Kansas City, sometimes Des Moines. I passed that info along to the task force."

"And you don't think anyone connected with Irving Ames Enterprises is responsible? The warehouse employees, Cheney Martin?"

"At this point we have no evidence to support Martin's involvement."

"I expect not." With Cheney's skills, there would be none.

"Well, thanks for the information. Good luck wrapping it up."

"It's been good working with you."

"You too."

I almost invited him to my party, but thought better of it. But I did give Hawk a call via Cat's phone.

"He has a new phone number, but here he is," she said, obviously handing the phone over.

"Hey, buddy," he said.

"I'm having an impromptu party tonight and if you're not busy, I thought you and Cat might want to come."

"Man, that is just what I need. What time?"

"Six o'clock."

AT FIVE THIRTY, I was showered, shaved, and ready for the party dressed in khaki shorts and a black T-shirt, when my doorbell rang. I was stunned to see Clifford and Jesse Emerson standing on my stoop.

"Hello. What can I do for you two?" I asked, wishing I was wearing my firearm.

"We came to give you your money back. Jesse took sixty dollars for delivering your friend to your house. He was the one who was missing. Right?"

"Right."

Jesse pulled three rumpled bills out of his pocket and handed them to me, barely making eye contact.

"I shouldn't have taken the money. I didn't know who he was at the time, but still I shouldn't have taken it."

"That's it," Clifford said, and the two turned and walked off toward Jesse's Mazda.

"Thanks."

Clifford raised a hand but didn't look back.

I stood in my door, completely stupefied, and watched the two of them drive off. I had demonized Clifford, and maybe he deserved most of it for driving while still under the influence, but just maybe he was a man with integrity who used alcohol to dull his pain. Wow. People never cease to surprise me.

WITHIN MINUTES, Dallas and Clara arrived bearing plates of food.

"You're the best, Clara."

"Dallas helped with all of it."

"You're the best too, Dallas." She was wearing a sundress that matched her aquamarine eyes. "Pretty dress, it suits you."

She gave me a face like she wasn't buying it. "Where do you want these, Mom?"

"On the counter."

"And, Clara, you're looking lovely tonight as well."

Clara wore a pair of white crop pants with a yellow and white floral shirt. She was wearing make-up and had her hair styled.

"Boy, you're full of it tonight," Clara said.

"You two need to accept my compliments. I mean what I say."

Clara fluffed her hair with her hand and smiled. "We went to the spa. Dallas treated me to the works: cut, color, a manicure and pedicure."

"She'd never do it for herself," Dallas said.

I made a mental note to give Clara a gift card to a spa salon for Christmas.

"How's Willie?" I asked.

"He's great. He'd been well taken care of."

"Always good to hear. Thanks for all you've done, ladies. I appreciate this."

"I'm happy to do it because this house needed a party . . . we *all* need a party with the year we've had," Clara said.

I hadn't considered how much our family troubles had affected everyone around us.

PATRICE ARRIVED FIVE MINUTES early—alone.

"I was hoping you'd bring your husband," I said. He'd managed to avoid all department social affairs.

"He sends his regrets. He had other plans."

And it wasn't to hang around with deputies.

"I just got off the phone with Tim Hudson. They're charging Nevada Wynn with murder one."

"I can guarantee you he will plead not-guilty, and there'll be a trial."

"Fine by me. You know Michael is extremely lucky. He very well could have been victim number four."

"He knows. I've invited him to the party. I thought he could use a little celebrating."

"We all can, can't we? What a year!"

Her too?

Others arrived: Eleanor Kohler, Tamika and Anton Frank, Spanky and Sadie, Crosby, my mother and Bobby, Hawk and Cat, then more deputies—for one, Matt Hauser, the widower who I thought Eleanor might like—but still no Shannon.

Iris walked through the backyard with her friend. Wait. Was that Erica, the new EMT everyone was gossiping about? She's tall, slender, athletic and tough looking with the scowl she usually had on her face. Her short black hair was sheared to a buzz cut. Tonight as she strode across the lawn in a light-green sleeveless top and white shorts, she looked softer—sexy—appealing.

Iris took me by surprise when she leaned up and kissed me square on the lips. She then took my arm and introduced Erica. With Iris still attached, I turned to see Shannon standing alongside the house watching the whole thing. I disengaged my arm from Iris's grip, mumbled to Erica it was a pleasure, then hurried to Shannon, who held me at bay with both hands jutted out in front of her.

I put my hands in my pocket. "Glad you came."

"Right. Things never change, do they?" she said.

I took a deep breath. She was jealous of Iris. *No, things don't change.* I gave her a smile. "I bought Bud Light and Clamato Cheledas just for you."

"Do you think I'm blind? This was a mistake, I'm leaving."

Just then Cat ran up and hugged Shannon telling her she was so happy to see her. They walked off arm in arm and into the house, suddenly bosom buddies. Women were weird. They were friends with people they don't even like. I walked over to Eleanor Kohler, who was sitting with Matt Hauser. Things were looking up.

"Beautiful evening," Eleanor said. "I hope the rain holds off."

"Me too."

"Matt, how are you?"

"Getting better all the time." He smiled at Eleanor.

I then moseyed over to Dallas and Clara, who were fiddling with dishes on the food table.

"Oh-oh. I'd say Shannon saw the kiss Iris planted on you," Dallas said.

"Obviously you did too."

A loud burst of laughter came from the group surrounding Hawk: Spanky and Saddie, Patrice, Tamika, and Anton.

"Excuse me," I said. "I've always felt the need to monitor what Hawk tells my friends about me."

Spanky put his arm around my shoulder. "Hawk was just telling how in seventh grade you got caught stealing pumpkins from the police chief's garden."

"Oh, see, Hawk was part of it. It was *Hawk's* idea, and he neglected to mention to me it was the chief's garden, and Sparky and I were the ones who got caught, because Hawk ran off."

Hawk shrugged and burst into laughter. "His wife was a kindergarten teacher, so he wrote a ticket saying their fine was to carve pumpkins for his wife's class."

"It was kind of fun."

"Then there was the time at St. Cloud when he went to freshman English class still drunk from our first kegger. He fell asleep during class. The professor threw an eraser at him, and he didn't even wake up," Hawk said, howling with laughter and in the process stumbling backward.

That was when I understood he was absolutely blitzed.

"The professor said to ignore the bonehead, and he passed back our essays all the while telling us what horrid writers we were. He put Cal's on top on his head and read his score aloud to the class. He said Cal got a C+ which was the highest score in the class, which didn't say much for the rest of us."

"And here I thought you were Mr. Perfect," Tamika said.

"Let's hear about your young and dumb days," I said, stopping to cast a glance at everyone individually.

Tamika's husband, Anton, said, "Yeah, honeybuns. Let's hear your stories."

"Now that ain't gonna happen, and I need a refill," Tamika said.

"Let me get it."

When I entered the great room, Shannon and Cat were huddled together on the couch. They saw me and stopped talking. They were obviously commiserating on what an asshole Shannon was married to.

"Ladies, are you enjoying yourselves?"

"Not exactly," Cat said. "I'm leaving. I can't stand to be around Michael when he's drunk."

"Why did you let him drink that much, Cal?" Shannon said.

It's my fault? "I wasn't monitoring his drinks and normally he can handle his liquor."

"Well, look what he's been through," Cat said.

"He can't drive. I'll help you get him in the car." I said.

"I'm not taking him. I don't want my parents to see him like this."

"He can stay in your guest room, Cal," Shannon said.

"That's fine," I said.

Cat and Shannon grabbed their purses and left out the front door without saying goodbye to anyone. Not that I blamed Cat for being angry, but if she'd been outside, maybe Hawk wouldn't have gotten sloshed.

I went back. Tamika looked at me and said, "Where's my wine?"

"Oh, sorry. Was it white or red?"

"Red," she said.

Before I refilled her glass, I took the opportunity to use the main floor restroom. I opened the door, which was slightly ajar, and saw Iris and Erica kissing full on the mouth, with their hands up each other's shirts.

"Whoops. Sorry."

For a few seconds they stared me and I at them. I yanked the door shut and stood stunned, my back plastered to the wall. I could hear giggles from the bathroom. After I regained my wits, I left to go upstairs to use my own bathroom.

"Holy shit," I said to my reflection in the mirror as I washed my hands.

When I came back down the two women were in the kitchen nonchalantly refilling their glasses of wine.

"Sorry about the intrusion," I said, as I filled a glass of red wine for Tamika.

Iris smiled. "We should have locked the door."

Or waited until you got back to your place?

"It's a great party," Erica said. "We'll have the next one. Right, hon?"

"Right."

"Sounds . . . like a plan," I said.

They walked out as if nothing had occurred. I shook my head as I recalled all the flirting I'd done, the fantasizing, and the kiss when she arrived. I had no fricking clue she was a lesbian, even though her friend, Erica, was rumored to be one. And, damn it, Iris led me on.

I was shaken out of my musing by a crash on the deck. I sprinted out. Hawk was on his butt next to an overturned table, plates and drinks scattered across the deck out onto the lawn. Hawk jumped up and said, "I'm okay."

I handed the glass of wine off to Tamika, told Hawk to sit down, then with everyone's help cleaned up the mess.

"Woo, he's wasted," Dallas whispered.

It wasn't too long before Hawk was snoring in the lounge chair.

"Poor guy," Patrice said. "He's self-medicating."

"Is that was he's doing?" I asked.

"And I need to run."

Clara came to tell Dallas she could stay later because Patrice was giving her a ride home."

"Thanks for coming, you two."

The remaining guests carried on, ignoring Hawk, just like they had me in my freshman English class. By eleven o'clock, only Spanky, Saddie, and Dallas remained. After the four of us cleaned up, I asked Spanky to help me get Hawk to the guest bedroom on the first floor. We tried fruitlessly to get him to walk. We ended up grabbing shoulders and feet, carrying him in. After throwing him on the bed, Spanky left the room. I had taken off one of Hawk's shoes when he murmured, "Fucking, Paul. That fucking Paul. He made me kill him."

"What do you mean, he made you kill him? Who?"

He answered me with a snort.

I shook him, asking him the same questions over and over. I stared at Hawk awhile not knowing what to do. He was out cold. It'd have to wait until morning. I closed the door and walked out.

Sadie and Spanky were standing at the back door. He said, "Good party, man. Just thankful I could stay for the duration." He was on call for the weekend, so he'd remained sober.

I thanked them for coming and helping with the cleanup, then gave them hugs goodbye.

Only Dallas remained. "They are such a cute couple. I fully expect those two to have an announcement soon."

When she picked up her purse, I found myself not wanting her to leave.

"Would you like one last drink?"

"Sure. I could use a beer."

I grabbed us each a Stella, and we went back out. In the distance lightning danced across the sky illuminating the billowing clouds. Ten seconds later the thunder rumbled indicating the storm was only two miles away.

Dallas held out her hand. "I just felt a drop."

"We should get inside," I said.

"How about we sit on that wonderful front porch of yours and watch the storm?"

"Great idea."

We walked through the house and out onto the porch, each taking an Adirondack chair. We sat in silence as we listened to the light rain hitting the roof in an uneven cadence. The leaves rippled from the swollen drops. A sudden brisk breeze blew in bending even the largest branches of the trees.

"And here it is," Dallas said. "I love storms. Lucky the party was over before it hit."

"And lucky for Hawk I had second thoughts about throwing a blanket on him and leaving him out on the deck."

"I don't usually have sympathy for drunks, but I can't believe his wife just left him here after everything he's been through."

"She didn't want her folks to see him in that condition."

"I fully understand. My ex was a drunk. I hid it because I never wanted anyone to know how stupid I was to have married him."

"How long were you married?"

"Three years."

"Was he a drunk before you got married?"

"Yes, but our crowd was all about alcohol. That's all we did—drink with friends. Then, one day I decided it was time to grow up, but he didn't. In fact, he became so livid when I suggested he had a drinking problem, that he smacked me across the face. That night I locked myself in the guest room, and the next day when he went to work I called my boss and asked for a leave. I told him my Dad was sick, which was true. I moved home with mom, and I was able to help her with his care. When Dad died, I was ready to go back to work and find a place in the western suburbs, when Dr. Foster with Prairie Vet called. So, I made the decision to stay. I practically have the house to myself because Mom is either at your place or Shannon's most of the time."

"Seems like it works out well for both of you."

"And here I don't have to worry abut running into Vince every time I go out."

"Are you afraid of him?"

"I haven't seen or talked to him since he hit me, but our mutual friends say he's drinking more than ever."

"It's good you're out of it. Can I ask you something?"

"Sure."

"Do you wear colored contacts?"

She chuckled. "No, I get that all the time."

"You have amazing eyes, Dallas Bradley."

"Well, thank you. Cal, I have something I need to say to you."

"What?"

"That I'm here for you as a friend. I know you've been through hell and back this past year, and I feel you need someone to talk to who isn't trying to hit on you when you're vulnerable—like Iris."

"Oh, I don't think we need to be worried about Iris. I caught her and Erica feeling each other up in the bathroom."

"Oh, my God. Seriously?" She let out a giggle.

"Yep."

"Wait until I tell Mom. We thought Iris had a thing for you." She began to giggle, and it turned into one of those times when you can't stop laughing. We'd both get control, then one of us would burst out with a laugh, and we'd carry on for another minute while wiping tears from our eyes.

When we finally got hold of ourselves, I asked, "Why were you named Dallas? Did your dad want a boy?"

"No, his favorite team was the Dallas Cowboys. He and Mom played blackjack before I was born to see who got to name me. Dad won. True story."

"What did your mom want to name you?"

"Grace."

"Huh. That was my mother's name."

"Really? Anyway, so, I'm Dallas Grace."

I smiled.

"Dallas Grace, let me ask you something. What if you knew something about someone you loved that would send them to jail?"

She squeezed her eyes to slits. "Are you asking me if I'd turn him or her in?"

"I guess so."

"Depends on who it was and what they did."

"I think it's bad, but I don't know for sure."

"Did you just find this out tonight?"

"Yes."

"I'd sleep on it to get clarity. You want to talk about it?"

"No. Sorry I brought it up."

We took pulls of our beer.

"Mom says Shannon's a jealous one."

"I've never gave her a reason to be."

"Some people are insecure. My ex was. If I'd even looked at someone longer than he thought I should, he accused me of having an affair."

"Have you ever cheated?"

"No, that's not how I roll."

"I cheated on Shannon recently."

"Is it cheating if you've been separated for months?"

"I don't know, but we hadn't had sex since the accident a year ago. She wouldn't let me touch her, but she's been with Mac Wallace."

"I know. I saw them together at a restaurant—Minnesota Fare. I think it's understandable for a man in those circumstances."

"I had no intentions of sleeping with this person. I had a weak moment. And I don't know why I just told you this."

"Don't worry. I'm closed-mouthed." She patted my hand. "You're a good man."

"Dallas, I like you and I like being around you, but I can't really see anyone until my divorce is final. No reason other than I wouldn't feel right about it."

"We could pal around once in a while—with other friends."

"I'd like that."

We talked for a long while, and when the rain let up, she glanced at her watch and stood. "It's getting late. I should be on my way."

I wanted to kiss her, but didn't. And as I watched her taillights disappear, I hoped I'd see her again soon. I faced the front door and remembered what Hawk said to me in his drunken stupor. I vomited over the porch railing.

32

June 8

SUNDAY MORNING, I picked the newspaper up off of the bottom step. As I walked back into the great room, I yawned. I'd slept horribly. I made myself a cup of coffee, then glanced at *The Star Tribune*'s headline: LEWIS HEIRESS THOUGHT TO BE ABOARD MISSING LEWIS COMPANY JET.

"What the?"

I read on. *A family spokesman said the Lewis jet departed from MSP airport late Saturday afternoon with a scheduled stop in Quebec to pick up another passenger before heading on to Paris for a family member's birthday party. Victoria Lewis, Minneapolis, MN, was the only passenger aboard at the time the plane went off the radar in Canadian airspace. The crew aboard were pilot Brock Snyder, co-pilot Emily Strom, and flight attendant, Gretta Holmgren. Adam Lewis, Victoria's father, was unavailable for comment.*

"Holy shit."

I flipped the television on and tuned in to CNN. They had more information. Somewhere over Ontario west of Ottawa, the plane had simply vanished. Weather may have been a factor. They showed photos of Victoria, spoke of her recent legal troubles and the hung jury case in Birch County. They aired a clip of her giving a statement after the trial. She said the fraud case was all a misunderstanding. She had used her roommate's ID with permission when she'd lost hers—it was no big deal. They then showed a film of her dressed in a red gown, obviously attending some gala—she looked beautiful. Yes, her sociopathic soul had a beautiful wrapper.

But was this for real? Brock Snyder flew a stunt plane; he could have pulled off flying under the radar, changing planes in some small airport. Until they found a crash scene, I'd doubt its validity. This could be Lewis's way of handling his daughter's legal problems. She could be anywhere in Europe by now. Then again, maybe Adam Lewis sabotaged the plane to get rid of Brock Snyder—a witness he paid off—and Victoria hadn't even been onboard.

259

HAWK WAS STILL SLEEPING when Clara arrived at eleven. Shannon would bring the twins here at noon. She set her purse on the counter and said, "Did you see the news about Victoria Lewis's missing plane?"

"Yes."

"A fitting end for an evil one. Boy, oh, boy, your friend, Hawk, was three sheets to the wind last night."

"He's still sleeping."

"Have you checked on him? When Scott was in college, he almost died of alcoholic poisoning at a fraternity party. His fraternity brothers let him lie in his vomit in the bathroom. One of the pledges finally called 911."

I went to the guest room, opened the door to listen for Hawk's breathing. I moved in closer until I saw his chest rise and fall. I closed the door behind me.

Clara said, "Well?"

"He's alive."

"Good. That boy isn't going to feel well when he wakes up." She took a bottle of Advil out of the cabinet and set in on the counter. "Dallas had a wonderful time last night."

"Did you?"

"Yes, I very much enjoyed talking to your sheriff."

"Your sheriff, too."

"She's one smart cookie. I hope she's reelected next year."

"Hmm."

AFTER THE TWINKS were down for their naps and Clara left for the grocery store, Hawk strolled into the great room.

"What time is it?" he asked.

"One o'clock."

"Really? I never sleep this late. Do you have any aspirin?"

"Advil okay?" I said.

"Sure."

I handed him the bottle and a glass of water, and he shook out four pills.

His eyeballs looked like a road map, and he smelled as if he'd fermented in a barrel of beer overnight.

He set the empty glass on the counter with a clunk and said, "Wow. I didn't know where I was when I woke up. I had one shoe on and one off." He touched his temple. "Man, I tied one on. I apologize."

"It's okay."

"No, no, it's not. I hope I didn't embarrass myself or Cat."

"She left early because you were drunk."

"Oooh. I'm in trouble. Damn. I don't remember much of the evening. I suppose she took the car. Can you give me a lift to Donovan's?"

"You don't remember anything?"

"I remember coming to the party."

"You don't remember telling me you killed *him*."

His eyes flashed to mine. "What did you say?"

"You told me all about how you killed him."

He put his hand to his mouth. "Anyone else hear?"

"Just me. Now I want to hear your sober version."

He slapped his cheeks with both hands, let them slide down the side of his face stretching his skin. He looked at the floor. "Fuck me."

Then his face changed, hardened. He made fists and jabbed one toward me. "He knew I was tied up in Kramer's basement. Fucking Paul. He was part of the whole goddamn thing. And by the way, Kramer was a real prick. We weren't buddies—we didn't smoke pot together. He threw my food at me like I was a dog—less than a dog. He showed me pictures of Woody with a bullet through his forehead. Said he killed him. Told me I was next, if the check didn't come. He said he would send Wynn to rape my wife and kill her."

"Who did you shoot first?"

"Kramer. The first chance I had to put that monster down, I took it—like you suggested. And by the way, you were being a prick the day we went out to the farm—asking me why I didn't call 911 or drive off in one Kramer's cars. What was that about? I thought you were my friend."

"I know. Tell me how it went down."

"He started getting careless. I was waiting for him to make a mistake, then the night before I escaped, he forgot he'd given me a fork. I spent the night tearing the duct tape off the back of my wrists and ankles, so it looked like they were still bound. That morning he set the shotgun down close to the stairs, then this one time he took the bike lock off before he moved my hands. He didn't know what hit him. I whacked him in the head with my food dish—a nice *heavy* metal dog food bowl—he stumbled backwards, and I grabbed the shotgun. He looked pretty stunned when I cocked it. Bastard begged me not to shoot him. It felt damn good to pull that trigger. I heard footsteps come down the stairs, expected it to be Ginty or Wynn, but it was Paul. He took one look at Kramer, and the fucker took off like a goddamn baby-ass coward. I followed him and yeah, I chased him down and shot him too. My fucking brother betrayed me, Cal!"

Clara flung open the door. She took one look at us and froze. I took the groceries from her and set them on the counter.

"Is everything okay?" she asked.

"Yeah, why don't you go up with the kids? We can deal with the groceries later."

She didn't hesitate. She scurried out of the room.

When she was gone, I asked, "Was Wynn expected that day?"

"I don't know."

"Why didn't you call 911 or take a car and drive out of there?"

"I started to drive Paul's car out, but then I started to think about what the hell I was going to tell the cops. I panicked. I didn't plan on killing anyone. It just happened. So I thought a dramatic escape would make sense. I drove Paul's car into Kramer's garage next to his other cars, made sure I wiped my fingerprints off it and the shotgun before I dropped it in the field, then I hoofed it over to the farms for help. Only I didn't get any. That's when I came to my senses and realized I needed a believable story. I hid in the old car and thought things through. And I did fall asleep, like I said."

"If only you'd called 911 after you shot Kramer, you'd be guiltless."

"If only . . . if only. Like I don't ask myself that a hundred times a day."

"Oh, Hawk."

"The thing is—this can be our secret. The Crow Wing sheriff bought my story. Don't you think those assholes deserved what they got for what they did to me? Stealing my money, keeping me tied up in a smelly basement, making me shit in a bucket? Christ, after being tied up for a month, I had a hard time catching up with Paul."

And for a split second, I considered what he was saying. They probably did deserve what they got. But then he just had to add, "You're my friend. You have to cover for me. I've *always* been there for you, man."

I wanted to deck him. I stood and calmly said, "No, you haven't really, have you? For the things that really matter? And for your whole life, you've gotten away with so much shit. But not this time, not for murder. I can't let that one go."

"You fucking rule follower."

"You're right. It's what I am. It's what I do for a living."

"I should have known you'd choose your career over your friend."

"Fuck you. And you stink like alcohol. You need to shave and shower before I drive you to Brainerd. And don't try anything stupid."

"I'm too hung over to try anything."

As soon as I heard the shower on, I hurried out to the garage and pulled down the plastic bag of clothing he had worn when he arrived at my door. I'd saved it just in case anyone asked for it. Now, it could be tested for traces of blood and gunpowder residue.

HE CAME OUT of the bathroom wearing the same clothes he wore last night, and although he looked rumpled, he smelled slightly better. I handed him a Sprite, then called 911 and asked for a squad to be delivered to my house, so I could transport a suspect to Crow Wing County Sheriff's Department.

As we waited, Hawk said, "If you'd been in my place, you would have done the same damn thing."

"Maybe so. Crow Wing will sort it out. But they have a man in custody for the killings you committed. I don't like Nevada Wynn, but he had the balls to turn himself in, and he didn't kill anybody."

His eyes closed, then slowly opened. "Will you let me call Cat?"

"Go for it."

He pulled out his phone and blubbered to his wife about his situation, then stopped abruptly, looked incredulously at his phone, then redialed. He let it ring for a long while before he shut it off. Evidently she wasn't being sympathetic either.

WITHIN A FEW MINUTES, two department Explorers pulled up on the street in front of the house. Shannon exited the first vehicle, and Crosby the second. I opened the front door for them so the doorbell wouldn't wake the Twinks. Hawk was in the living room, sitting in a chair, his elbows on his knees, his hands covering his face.

"I checked out your vehicle for you, Cal," Crosby said, eyeing Hawk.

"Thanks."

Shannon glanced at Hawk then at me. "What's going on? Are the kids okay?"

"Yes. They're napping. Clara's upstairs with them. Can I have a set of cuffs?"

She took them off her belt and handed them over.

Hawk groaned. "Is that necessary?"

"It's procedure. I'm a rule follower, remember?" I said.

He rolled his eyes then looked away while I secured his hands in front. I walked him out and put him in the backseat of the second Explorer. He didn't say another word.

Crosby and Shannon had followed us out.

"Are you going to tell me what's going on?" she said. "As soon as I heard our address on the radio, I freaked."

"Hawk shot Kramer and Paul."

She gasped. "Was he even held captive?"

"Yes. He can probably plead self-defense on Kramer, but not with Paul. He chased him down and shot him. I'll tell you more about it later."

"That's horrible. Maybe he can plead temporary insanity."

"Maybe."

I was so pissed at him, I didn't care what the hell happened to him.

AFTER CONTACTING BOTH PATRICE and Lee Sabin, I drove Hawk to Brainerd. Neither of us spoke at all, until we were approaching the jail garage.

"I needed time to consider my options before you forced me to come here."

"And just so we're straight, you had a choice—you could have held the gun on Kramer while you phoned 911 from his landline. You could have let the deputies handle Paul. That's what the county attorney's going to say."

He looked out the window.

"Hawk, ask for an attorney after your rights are read. Don't give a statement until after you've consulted with him or her. I'm telling them you're turning yourself in."

Hawk nodded.

Lee was waiting for us when we pulled in.

"Michael's coming in voluntarily."

He nodded, then said, "The DEA is here waiting to speak to Wynn. They've already arrested North Cross employees Zeke La Plante and Owen Jedowsky."

"Well, hot damn."

"You had a big part of that. You have good instincts, Cal."

"Kramer was part of the drug ring—maybe even center figure for this area. Maybe he was holding Paul's car as collateral until the annuity had been cashed." I pointed to Hawk. "This one was a tough one for me."

"I can imagine."

This morning, a lifelong friendship had died.

I DROVE DIRECTLY to Hawkinsons' house. My stomach ached with the thought of telling Barb and Tom the truth, but they had a right to know. I sat in the quiet of their kitchen. With a lump in my throat, I told them everything. They listened thoughtfully until I got it all out, then Barb said, "Well, we'll see what Mike has to say about this. When can we see him?"

"Not for a while. You should call an attorney and see if you can get him out on bail. You'll have to wait until tomorrow morning."

"Why did you do this to him, Cal?" Barb said.

Her question shouldn't have caught me off guard, but it did. "Me?"

"You should have brought him to us, so we could discuss how to proceed. I don't know much about the law, but I do know we should have hired an attorney to get his advice."

"I tend to agree with Barb on this one," Tom said.

"He confessed to murdering Paul. Don't you get that?"

"None of us know all the circumstances," Barb said.

"You should get an attorney for him right now. If you like, I'll ask Adriana for names of the best of the best."

Barb's expression turned hard. "No, we'll handle it. Now I think you should go." She stood and crossed her arms.

Typical Barb Hawkinson reaction: Her darling boy couldn't possibly be guilty of anything. It just pissed me off.

I pushed away from the table and said, "This time Mike has to face the consequence like a man, and there's nothing you can do to protect him."

THE TWINS WERE AWAKE when I got home, so I suggested to Clara we take them to the park. I needed to clear my head, and playing with the twins was the best way I knew. Clara must have sensed I didn't want to talk about Hawk because she didn't mention him. Both kids loved the baby swings, so we spent an hour pushing them. Listening to toddler giggles cleared my mind of negativity.

WHILE CLARA PREPARED the meal, I took the kids outside and brought out the beach balls. Teddy and Alicia Kohler busted on over to play with the twins, so I took the lounge chair Hawk had fallen asleep in and listened to the sweet sound of children's voices and laughter. As hard as I tried to keep Barb's words out of my mind, they broke through: *I don't know much about the law, but I do know we should have hired an attorney to get his advice.*

AFTER HER SHIFT, Shannon stopped by. The Kohler kids were still playing with the twins. Teddy ran up and hugged Shannon—it made her cry because Teddy and Colby had been so close.

She sat in the chair next to me and said in a soft tone, "Cat called me this afternoon. She's beside herself. She wants to know what really happened, but I don't have the whole story."

"Hawk completely changed his story. He says Kramer was a real prick. He showed him a picture on his phone proving he killed Woody. Anyway, Hawk escaped because he was able to remove the duct tape with a fork. He hit Kramer with a dog food dish, then grabbed the gun and shot him. Paul was upstairs, came down to have a look. When he saw what happened, he took off like a scared rabbit. Hawk chased him down and shot him too."

"Kramer's shooting sounds like self-defense."

"But he wouldn't have had to take Paul down."

"If Paul betrayed his brother, he probably deserved it."

"Why are you defending Hawk? He executed his brother. Shot him in the back and again in the back of the head."

"I'm not defending him. Forget it. You did what you had to do."

She touched my arm, then reached across for half a hug. "I know this wasn't easy for you."

"No, it wasn't."

She pulled away and smiled at me. I'd had it with the yoyo vibrations I was getting from her. "Shannon, what do you want to do? I'm not willing to live in limbo for a year. You either move back home and we work on our marriage, or we file for divorce."

She blinked a few times, then teardrops slid down her face. I took a deep breath, and my eyes pooled with tears. I touched her hand.

"Luke's refusing to go to any more counseling sessions with you, and he won't move back here."

"You wouldn't give him a choice."

"I can't do that to him."

I took a deep breath and took back my hand. She was choosing her son. "Okay, I get it. I'll call Iris tomorrow and tell her to proceed."

"I'm sure she'll be happy to get that news."

"Iris is a lesbian. She and Erica are a couple." I didn't mention how I knew.

Shannon's eyes grew wide. "No kidding? Oh, my God. Tamika was right. I pictured you two walking back and forth in the middle of the night."

"Your imagination is your biggest enemy," I said.

Her mouth took a hard line. "I was right about a few things, Cal, and you know it."

"Can we agree to be civil through the process?"

She hesitated then nodded. "Yes."

Clara stuck her head out the door and said, "Are you staying for dinner, Shannon?"

"No, I promised Luke we'd go out for pizza. I better pick him up from Mom's." Before she left she touched my arm and said, "I love you, and I'm so sorry."

"Yeah, me too."

And my real best friend walked off.

That evening, Tom Hawkinson called and said they were withdrawing the request for me to be a pallbearer at Paul's funeral, and it would be uncomfortable if I attended.

33

June 9

ONDAY AFTERNOON, Sydney Dirkson called me.

"I thought you'd want to know Mike was charged with second-degree murder for shooting Paul and was released on bail. He's staying with Tom and Barb."

"Okay, how's everyone handling it?"

"Not well. Cat's filing for divorce."

"Big surprise there."

"Cal, Pete and I know you did what you had to do."

"Thanks. I've been down about it—it feels like I betrayed a friend."

"But Mike betrayed all of us. Barb told me you were asked not to attend Paul's funeral."

"Yes."

"It would be weird for you, anyway. Listen, it was a pleasure meeting and doing business with you. If you ever need my services, just give me a jingle."

"Thanks. Tell Hawk I wish him well, because I do."

"I will."

MONDAY'S NEWS LED with: "A BIZARRE TWIST TO THE CROW WING COUNTY MURDERS."

Crow Wing County hadn't released the details, but the media had a presence at his bond hearing and heard enough to portray Michael Hawkinson as a survivor escaping captivity by shooting his drug dealer captors. He was a hero, now being charged with murder—the television reporter said so.

Hawk called me that night. His speech was sloppy from booze as he told me his attorney said they weren't going to accept a plea agreement because they could convince a jury he felt he was in mortal danger when he shot both Kramer and Paul.

"Good luck, Hawk. I mean that."

"I don't hold what you did against you, Cal buddy. See ya."

"Right."

He was smoothing the waters because I'd have to testify against him. His attorney probably told him to reach out. I doubt I'd see him before the trial. It was quite possible he could be acquitted, and if so, it was highly unlikely he would kill again because no one would ever do to him what Paul had. Maybe Hawk was right, and I'd have done the same thing.

AT THE END OF JUNE, I accidentally on purpose ran into Norman Kramer's sister, Polly Jacobs, at her place of employment, the bookstore in Baxter. I introduced myself to her as I paid for Dennis LaHane's latest book. She recognized my name from the newspaper.

"Since Norm was diagnosed with bone cancer a few years ago, he was so nasty I only saw him a few times a year, not that he was ever easy to get along with. But because of the pain, he got hooked on pain killers, and that's how he met those criminals."

"Was he dying?"

"Last time I spoke to him, he said he was in remission, but the autopsy said the cancer had moved up to his brain. The tumor was small but evidently big enough to mess with his mind."

"He showed Michael Hawkinson pictures of your kids."

"I don't have any kids. They must have been of his girlfriend's children. She was a nice lady, but she battled depression. She took her own life five years ago."

"Oh, wow. Your brother was a walking tragedy. Well, I'm sorry for your loss."

"I lost him years ago. The man who shot him was your friend?"

"*Was* is the operative word there."

"Well, who can blame him for shooting Norman? I don't get with all the money Norm had, why he would be part of holding Paul Hawkinson's brother captive to get ten thousand dollars for drugs Paul stole. It makes no sense."

"Paul stole them?"

"The sheriff figured he had the drugs in his trunk because he was going to give them back to Norm if his brother didn't come through with the money."

"He had a lot of money?"

"Oh yes. I'm not sure you know I sold the farm a month ago, and when I was cleaning out the house last week, I found a false wall in the closet of my old bedroom. I knew it was way bigger than that, so I pushed on it. It not only held drugs but cardboard boxes of money. I called the sheriff and the DEA confiscated all of it. They told me he was selling drugs. Mom and Dad would roll in their graves if they knew."

I left that afternoon with way more information than I had expected. Perhaps Hawk's defense can capitalize on Norman's criminal activity.

ON JUNE 17, THEY found the Lewis plane wreckage in Ontario, and a month later, Victoria was officially identified as one of the victims. That same day, Shannon and I accepted a five million dollar settlement from Estelle Candies, and put three million in equal trusts for the three kids. The remaining two million, we split. Mine's invested.

34

September 25

I PARKED MY TRUCK, grabbed my chair out of the back, and made my way to the soccer field. The late afternoon sun shone on the trees surrounding the soccer fields making the brilliant golds and reds even more spectacular. I was *allowed* to attend Luke's soccer game for the first time tonight. He promised his mother he wouldn't storm off the field and refuse to play because I was there. When I placed my chair next to Shannon's on the sidelines, she patted my hand. Luke was doing warm-ups with the team, and he glanced over our way. Shannon waved at him, but he ignored her. Dick and Donna arrived shortly after and set their chairs next to mine, rather than Shannon's. I stood and Donna came to give me a hug.

"Don't be a stranger," she said.

Dick shook my hand. "Glad you could make it."

When I took my seat, Shannon said, "Did you get the papers in the mail today?"

"I did. I had no idea the process of divorce was so speedy. It's only been three months since we filed."

Iris had been a great mediator, and Shannon and I agreed on the settlement. We each retained our own residence, and we split custody of the twins. I agreed to Shannon's full custody of Luke, although I contribute equally to his child support. We both deposit money into a joint bank account to be used only for the kids' expenses.

Because Clifford Emerson joined AA and had been sober for one hundred twenty days, Shannon and I agreed to drop our civil suit against him. I talked Eleanor Kohler into training him as a baker—she said he's a good worker. His son, Jessie, plans on going to community college next fall.

So Shannon and I are almost best friends again. Maybe it's because she and Mac Wallace ended their relationship, although I had nothing to do with that. Mac was caught having sex with a potential buyer in the seller's master bedroom.

271

Love is in the air: Last week Spanky and Saddie announced their engagement and are planning a May wedding. Eleanor Kohler and Matt Hauser are dating. My mom and Bobby are on a European cruise and seem obnoxiously happy for an old hippie and a mysterious stranger.

And me? I keep myself busy with the Twinks and sports. I play golf in the men's league, and basketball two nights a week in the high school gym with a group of deputies, firefighters, and teachers. I also have Dallas Grace Bradley for a friend. She's taught me the value of canoeing, kayaking, and hiking. It's a platonic relationship . . . at least that's what we tell everyone. Oh, and Bullet and Willie have become best friends.

After pleading guilty to multiple charges, Ginty, Hayes, and Wynn are spending some quality time with the Minnesota Department of Corrections.

As for my former best friend, Michael Hawkinson, I haven't spoken to him since the night he called to tell me he didn't hold it against me for turning him in. Lee Sabin, who I've golfed with on a couple of occasions, says Hawk's unemployed and still living at home until his trial scheduled for December. As far as I'm concerned, I believe Barb and Tom deserve having their adult son dependent on them once again.

Cheers from those around me brought me back to the present and the soccer game. Shannon and her parents stood, their arms rising high in the air. Luke had just scored a goal. I'd missed seeing it. When he searched the crowd, he looked at me first, and I gave him a thumbs-up. He tried not to, but he smiled. It made my day.

I was invited to go out for ice cream with the family after the game. He didn't object. When the pressure is off, maybe the gloves come off too.

Acknowledgements

There are many people to thank: my husband and family for the continuing support and encouragement; my friends, old and new, who faithfully buy and read my books and tell me kind things about my work; and my friend Darrell Maloney, who accepted the daunting task of proofreading *Crow Wing Dead* for me.

I also wish to thank the Hennepin County Sheriff's Department and personnel who participated in 2015 spring Citizen's Academy class, and especially to CSI Deputy Sarah Buck for the ride-along. The experiences and information learned are invaluable.

Thanks to the Twin Cities Sisters in Crime and Women of Words, for their wonderful support and friendship.

And of course, thanks to Corinne, Anne, and Curtis at North Star for taking on another Cal Sheehan book.